VAGABONDS

BOOK 1
OF
THE SCOTTSTOWN HEROES SERIES

A. A. Woods

AMONOUX

This book is a work of fiction. Names, characters, places, and events are either the products of the author's imagination or are used fictitiously. Any resemblance to actual events or persons, living or dead, is purely coincidental.

ISBN: 978-1-951803-03-2

Cover Design by Rebecacovers

Books by the Author

The Scottstown Heroes Series
Vagabonds (Book 1)
Renegades (Book 2)
Runaways (Book 2.5)

Other Books
Hooded (Hooded Book 1)
Project Recollection (The Affinity Book 1)
The Star Siren
The Face of the Universe: A Short Story
Collection

CHAPTER ONE
Life at Meru

If there's a hell, I bet Meru Academy could give it a run for its money, Eliza thought as she made her way across campus, shouldering her backpack and glaring at the intricate Latin that decorated the arch of the Liberal Arts building. She rolled her eyes at the pretentiousness of it.

A Liberal Arts building for a high school? Please.

But after the fourth time Eliza had gotten into a fight at school, her parents had made up their minds. There had been no discussion, no bargaining, just a sit-down at their mahogany dinner table and a stern command.

You're going to boarding school, Elizabeth Mason, and that's final.

Now, with a frustrated sigh, Eliza waited on the steps beneath the inscribed Latin as she watched the other students milling through the double doors, all on their way to homeroom or gym or advisor meetings or the parking lot behind the athletic facility where they could get high while cutting class.

No one so much as looked at her.

Guess that's what I get when the most popular girl in school hates my guts.

"Howdy," came a familiar voice from behind her.

Eliza's brooding scowl cracked down the middle as one side of her mouth twitched up.

"Joe, you can't say *howdy* and not expect to have your head shoved in a toilet."

"Aw, come on, that's old-school stuff. No one does that anymore." Joe leapt up the final stair. "Besides, who would hit a kid with glasses?"

Eliza couldn't help but chuckle as her best friend in the world—well, her only friend really—stood beside her, those very same glasses winking in the morning sun. Joe Fagan was cursed with an endlessly entertaining last name, coke-bottle glasses, and skin so pale that it looked almost translucent, except for the spattering of freckles. It didn't matter that he was tall and handsome in a rangy sort of way. He was a nerd who read books older than their headmaster and watched more Marvel movies than was good for him. If it weren't for the fact that his parents ran the most successful news outlet in the United States—Hermes News Network, HNN for short—he would have spent his days shoved in lockers and picking his lunch off the cafeteria floor.

Which meant that he and Eliza basically *had* to be friends.

Eliza opened her mouth to greet him when a burly hockey player knocked into Joe from behind.

"Watch where you're walking, queer."

Joe grabbed Eliza's shoulder with one arm as she made to lunge after the jock, ready to tackle him from behind.

"Let me go," Eliza snarled, but Joe just adjusted his glasses with his free hand.

"That dumb Neanderthal didn't even get it right," Joe said with a half-smile. "My last name is similar to *faggot*," he shouted into the swinging doors. "At least insult me correctly."

Eliza took a deep breath, glaring into the bustling entrance hall.

"Why do you always have to be such a pacifist?" she said, shrugging off his hand.

"What can I say, the sight of blood makes me queasy. Come on, Rambo, let's get to homeroom."

Eliza followed Joe inside. She was already seething and it was only eight o'clock. And the heady atmosphere of a school on Friday was only making it worse. Everyone was talking about the *parties* and *dances* they were going to that weekend, some driving as far as Boston to spend their parent's money and make bad choices. But of course, Eliza and Joe would be here. Him because he had no interest in being a proper teenager. And her because her parents had cut her off, taking the car and the credit card away to 'ensure good behavior'.

"I'm not, you know."

Eliza started, pulled from her thoughts as Joe bumped into her shoulder.

"What?"

"Gay. Not that I have anything against the idea," he said, the words tumbling out of him. "I'm sure it would be awesome to be gay. Then at least I could respond to them with an enthusiastic *hell yeah*." Eliza laughed as Joe continued. "But I'm not."

"Joe, I've seen your collection of Taylor Swift posters."

He ducked his head, pale cheeks flushing with color.

"Too many?"

She shoved him gently.

"Come on, you weirdo, we're late."

Eliza and Joe were the last to enter homeroom, which of course made things more awkward than usual. Mrs. Henderson immediately launched into her disapproving lecture about *timeliness* and *work ethic*, but Eliza wasn't listening. She could feel the eyes on her, hot with malice and cunning. The female student population at Meru seemed to think that Eliza was a barely tamed zoo animal, still reeking of the wild. She guessed that the stories about her last school—where she'd been suspended twice for bloodying a bully's nose—had circulated enough to give her what her mother would call a *reputation*. But not enough to make them back off. If anything, it was like they were poking her. Looking for a weakness, a button, a trigger. Wanting to be around to watch the show.

And it didn't help that deep down, Eliza wanted to give them one.

Finally released from the *early bird gets the worm* sermon, Eliza followed Joe to the back of the classroom, hunching her shoulders to avoid the haughty stares. Worst of all was Tori Bent, as beautiful and cruel as a winter storm.

And unfortunately, Eliza's roommate.

"Did you get lost on the way to class?" Tori hissed as Eliza slid into her seat, Joe taking the one behind her.

Eliza made a coughing sound shaped suspiciously like the word *harpy*.

"Look, I know we aren't exactly friends—" Eliza snorted "—but I want to make it up to you. The girls and I are having a bit of a, shall we say, *affair* in the woods tonight. By the Fitzgerald Base fence. You know, that clearing off Exit Two."

Suspicion prickled along Eliza's arms. Disgruntled by the sudden appearance of a roommate in what had been a private room the year before, Tori had taken on the mission to exclude or humiliate Eliza as if it were her holy calling. So Eliza knew there must be something more to the *affair* than Tori was letting on. Especially since Joe was kicking her seat from behind in silent warning.

"I think I'll pass," Eliza said, swallowing the urge, the *need* even as it welled inside her.

"Come on, are you *scared*?"

It was as if Tori knew the passcode to Eliza's brain. She fought it, tried to breathe through it, but the instinct to prove herself ran marrow deep. Ever since Katie's death, Eliza hadn't been able to resist a call to action. A way to stand out.

A dare.

And this was just that.

"Fine," Eliza said, ignoring Joe's foot now hammering on the underside of her molded plastic chair. "What time should I be there?"

CHAPTER TWO

Dare

"This is a terrible idea."

"Shut up, Joe."

"Come on, Eliza, you know this is dumb."

But she ignored him, slamming the door of his truck closed as if that ended the discussion.

The whole drive from Meru to the woods outside Scottstown, Joe had voiced his complaints. And his warnings. And his threats. He'd said he would turn the car around, that he would tell the dormmaster, that he'd tie her to a desk chair. But Eliza had ignored him, instead watching her reflection in the side-view mirror as the small, sweet city had faded into evergreens and bushes. Even she had to admit that Scottstown was idyllic. It was safe, small, and just the right amount of friendly. Eliza could imagine being forty and smiling at the kids biking down suburban roads or playing tag in the park. Maybe, if she was a different kind of sixteen-year-old, she could have enjoyed it now. Found peace in boutique shopping and coffee shops and gossip.

But she wasn't that person.

Not anymore.

She ground her teeth together as Joe joined her by the tree line.

Eliza didn't care that this was some kind of trick. For months, her friendship with Joe had been a balm on her frayed nerves, a way to postpone the inevitable. She'd appreciated his calming presence in the way a surfer must appreciate a break between waves. But something about this Friday had made Eliza ready to explode.

Maybe Tori had known it.

Now, with the moonlight playing off her dark skin and threading silver through her tightly curled cloud of her hair, Eliza led the way into the forest.

"Eliza, this is giving me the creeps."

"Shhh."

"You know I'll be the first to die, right? The funny handsome one always dies."

"Joe, shut up."

Eliza could hear something, the low murmur of female voices, as soft as the babbling of a brook. She scanned the dark trees, picking apart the shadows.

There.

A figure moved. Blonde hair shimmered in the silvery moonlight.

"I was worried you wouldn't come."

Tori stepped forward, arms extended in mocking welcome. They fell as her bright blue eyes snagged on Joe.

"I didn't say you could bring company."

"Think of him as my insurance policy," Eliza said, folding her arms. "What are you doing out here?"

"I told you," Tori said with the gleam of teeth. "We're having a little get-together. Come join us."

Eliza and Joe exchanged a wide-eyed look before following Tori into the clearing.

Five other teenagers were already there. Eliza immediately picked them out as the most popular kids in school. Greta Smith, the shoe-in for homecoming queen next month. Yuri and Marta, two style icons that shaped the fashions of the year. Fabia, whose wealthy Italian father had taken her sky-diving last spring. And Hector, the burly German-born boy who had infamously refused the summons to join the football team.

"Howdy," Joe said, his voice cracking.

"So you're the freak-show from Atlanta?" Greta asked, kicking her heels as she sat on a fallen tree, swigging out of an embossed metal flask.

"Careful, Greta," Eliza said with a grin, plopping down in the grass. "You wouldn't want anyone to think you're racist."

Greta's lips puckered. Eliza smirked as Joe folded himself down next to her, his gangly frame bending awkwardly in the narrow opening between two trees.

"So what's the plan?" Eliza asked, a bit more aggressively than intended. "Are we here as your charity project? Or is there something else going on?"

Even in the darkness, Eliza could see Tori roll her eyes.

"We just wanted to be nice."

"People are never just nice," Eliza said, the bite to her words unmistakable. Joe tensed beside her.

Tori offered her the flask and Eliza eyed it as if it might bite her.

"Just last week I overheard your parents telling you to make friends," Tori said.

"And what does it take, to be your friend?" Eliza asked.

Tori grinned, her teeth glittering white in the woven shadows of the trees.

"If you want to be one of us," she said. "You have to go *in there*."

She cocked her blonde head toward the chain-link fence that they could all glimpse through the trees. The security lights and roving high beams of the huge army-issue trucks going in and out of Fitzgerald Base were barely visible, but everyone knew they were there. It was the most secure place in Scottstown, crawling with soldiers and secretive enough to inspire the most ludicrous speculation. In the few short months since Eliza had arrived, she'd heard more than her share of rumors about the kinds of things that went down within the confines of that fence. *Medical experiments.*

Spy training. Assassination planning. UFO research. Who knew what was true and what was urban myth, but one thing was certain.

Breaking in there would be trouble.

And trouble drew Eliza like a moth to the flame.

"You want me to climb a fence?" Eliza said, raising her eyebrows.

"We want you to touch the wall of their lab building."

Eliza snorted.

"That's the stupidest dare I've ever heard," she said, even though the urge to go was like an itch beneath her skin.

Tori shrugged.

"Eliza, come on," Joe said beside her. "You don't need this."

"That's right, *Eliza*," Tori cut in mockingly. "Be a good little girl and run on home."

Eliza burst to her feet.

"If I touch that stupid building, none of you will ever call either of us names again," Eliza snarled.

Tori sneered. "You touch that building and we'll call you the Queen of England if you want."

Eliza knew that this was all kinds of bad ideas rolled into one. She could be arrested. Interrogated. Maybe even shot.

But she couldn't help the trilling adrenaline as it called for her to *move*.

She straightened, swallowed, glared at the distant fence.

"I'll be right back," Eliza said and strode off into the darkness, leaving Joe's hissed warnings in her wake.

CHAPTER THREE

Over the Fence

The chain-link fence looked like a cage as it drew closer, looming larger with every step. Eliza's heart was beating in her ears, a war-drum of fear and excitement pounding through her whole body.

This is a bad idea. This is a bad idea. This is a bad idea.

The words were circling her mind in Joe's voice, her mother's voice, her father's voice.

She ignored them all.

Eliza didn't stop when she reached the fence, instead using a protruding stone to launch herself halfway up. She climbed like a squirrel, her body strong and graceful after almost twelve years of gymnastics. Before everything had fallen apart, the gymnastics center had been a place she excelled, a thing she'd been *good* at, besides giving her parents headaches of course. But when Katie died, her joy on the uneven bars soured. Her parents stopped cheering at meets. Her coach's eyes had gone from hard and proud to soft and sympathetic. And worst of all, the other girls had begun to fall silent when she joined them, tense and awkward and just like every other goddamn person who'd heard the sob-story of the Mason family.

That was until Eliza had provoked one of them into a fight, of course.

Being kicked off the gymnastics team hadn't been quite as satisfying as she'd hoped it would be.

Arcing her body like a dancer, Eliza threw her leg over the fence and dropped cat-like to the other side. She landed in the grass and tensed, waiting for the lights to swoop down on her or an alarm to wail in the night. But the only sound was the hum of blood through her veins.

She grinned.

Straightening, Eliza began to jog toward the squat shape of the lab building in the distance. She could see the shadows of guards as they marched around the perimeter, but it was almost midnight. Everyone knew that the bulk of the Fitzgerald soldiers went to Howl on Friday nights to dance and drink and blow off steam. It had been a club that Eliza had only *barely* resisted visiting, knowing that going there would be like lighting a match in a gas station.

But here she was, doing something even worse on a dare from someone she didn't even like.

No time to think about that now, Eliza thought as she pressed her slender, muscled body against the wall of an equipment shed, waiting for the two blurry shadows to pass under the spotlights.

Fitzgerald Base was laid out in a series of rings around a central point. Barracks and mess halls and gear barns orbited the lab building like planets around a sun, all of them drawn in by the huge, square building in the middle. And Eliza could see why. Where the other parts of the encampment were casual, open, maybe even relaxed, the behemoth in the middle was a fortress. No windows. No decorations. Lights coating every surface. Probably pressure sensors and infrared scanners too. Eliza could only imagine the kind of security it would have inside.

What the hell are they doing in there, she wondered, glaring at the flat concrete side of the building.

But she'd seen enough movies to know that it was probably better she didn't find out.

Touching her phone in her pocket for comfort, Eliza took a deep breath. Bounced her knees. She waited for the guards to come around again, listening to their soft voices as they drifted through the darkness like wraiths. And then, the moment they'd moved past her, she was off. Sprinting through the grass, sneakers slapping the ground, Eliza flew towards that dull cement wall. She felt exposed and dangerous and vulnerable and *free* as she ran, arms pumping, breathing heavy. The wall loomed high, shadowing her like a giant monster.

She slammed into it and pressed her hand against the hard cement.

Eliza wasn't sure if Tori was watching, but it didn't matter.

I wish you were here, Katie, Eliza said, leaning against the wall, feeling calm for the first time since arriving at Meru three months ago.

Suddenly, the quiet night was broken by a shout.

"Stop him!"

Eliza shoved off the wall, panic crawling over her skin like insects. She crouched, but she may as well have been in broad daylight the way the side of the lab was illuminated. So she threw herself forward, not caring where she was going so long as it was dark.

Gulping air, Eliza managed to duck into the shadow of a long, low building, clutching the wall as she scanned the grass. Her fingers brushed a teetering pile of empty cans—a recycling pile? The hollow aluminum hummed and creaked, threatening to expose her, and she yanked her hand back as if it had touched something hot.

More voices were rising, sharp with urgency.

"Hey!"

"What are you doing, man?"

"Restrain him!"

Terror seeped into Eliza's bones. Had they seen her? Were they coming to arrest her?

But no, the shouts were on the other side of the building.

Swallowing her fear, Eliza allowed the tug of curiosity to lure her to the edge of the wall. Blood pounding, Eliza tilted her face around the edge of the building to peer into the training field.

It was in chaos.

Soldiers poured out of a nearby barrack like bees from a hive, joining some kind of melee in the middle of the green. Eliza squinted, trying to see what was going on. She could barely make out flailing

15

limbs, hear a snarling voice. Through the shift and churn of bodies, she glimpsed a face twisted into a kind of demonic snarl.

Instinct was a live wire inside her, screaming for her to *run*. But she didn't, which is why she saw the soldiers go flying.

"What the—"

Eliza gasped, throwing herself back as the bodies of fully-grown, thickly-built men went sailing through the air like paper airplanes. One landed in the grass and skidded, leaving a long earthy smear. Another slammed into a nearby wall, crumpling to the ground in a broken heap. Eliza's mouth fell open as she watched the man in the middle of it all release a guttural howl, eyes wild as he grabbed an advancing officer by her wrist and swung her around like a child.

"Contain him!"

The command broke the night like a stroke of lightning. Eliza's gaze snapped to its source. A short, slight woman was standing with her hands behind her back, eyes cold, black hair perfectly combed so that it traced the sharp line of her chin. Something about the woman made Eliza's blood freeze, but she couldn't put her finger on why.

The only thing she knew was that it was time for her to get out of there.

Eliza took a step back as the soldiers surrounded the man, her mind churning with *whys*. Why was the man so strong? Why were they trying to contain him? Why were his eyes so twisted with rage?

But her questions were cut short as one sneaker slipped on dewy grass. Her hand flew out, scrabbling for something, anything to hold as she fell.

Her fingers hit the pile of cans.

For a moment everything froze. Eliza's brain locked.

Oh shit.

And then the cans toppled, a waterfall of appallingly loud aluminum rolling away from Eliza… and into the training field.

The black-haired woman's eyes snapped to the side, scanning the building.

Eliza could feel the exact moment that those eyes fell on her.

"There has been a breech in security," the woman said, her voice carrying despite the snarls of the super-strong man. "Contain it."

Those two words settled on Eliza and she knew with the deep instinct of a hunted animal what it meant. She'd seen something dangerous. Something secret. And the woman's icepick eyes made it clear that she wasn't about to let this secret escape.

Eliza scrambled to her feet and swung around the wall. She could hear the thundering of boots behind her, shouts for her to *Stop. Halt. Freeze.* But she didn't. Sliding on the wet grass, Eliza raced toward the fence, yanking up the hood of her Meru sweater as she went. She could hear engines revving, headlights slicing through the inky night.

Suddenly, a jeep swung in front of her.

Eliza screamed and veered to the right, sprinting without any knowledge of where she was going. The night had become a blur, trees and buildings streaking by. She could hear the Jeeps bumping along behind her, hear footsteps in the grass surrounding her, closing in.

"Freeze!"

She didn't. Couldn't. Something deep in the well of her subconscious told her that if she obeyed, she wouldn't see the next sunrise. So she ran, but the fence in front of her was taller. Spiked. There was no way she had time to climb it without giving the soldiers ample time to shoot her down. She crashed into the chain-link, the warbling noise amplifying her fear. Panic clawing up her throat, she spun. Squinted into the headlights.

And saw something else.

There was another shape behind the advancing soldiers, someone just as tall and muscled as the men around her. But bigger,

17

wider, with a strange, sloped darkness protruding from strong shoulders, sweeping out like a painter's brushstrokes.

Were those... wings?

A commotion rose as the other soldiers noticed the shape. Eliza saw one of them disappear into the shadows, another slammed into a stopped Jeep. She took the opportunity to throw herself at the fence and scramble to the top, toppling over to the other side. She cried out as her arm hit the ground, eyes filling with tears as pain radiated up a bruised elbow. But there was no time. She ripped into the grass with her fingernails as she clambered to her feet and scurried into the forest. The noise of the base seemed to follow her, tangling with the frantic rasping of her own breath. But she kept running, panting, unable to get the images out of her mind.

What the hell is going on in this town?

Finally, as gunfire and rumbling engines faded into a woven tapestry of forest sounds, Eliza slowed. She grabbed a tree to hold herself upright, sucking in air as she wondered where she was. How far had she run? Had they seen her face? Were they still coming after her? Her head was spinning and her thoughts were a jumble and no matter how much she tried to calm herself she couldn't stop her stomach from knotting and twisting.

A twig broke behind her.

Eliza spun, heart leaping into overdrive.

"Jumpy, aren't you?"

Someone was standing there, tall and thin, shadowed face glinting as if his eyes were made of mirrors. Eliza stumbled backwards, holding out her hands.

"D-don't come any closer—"

But her plea was cut off as she bumped into something. At first, she thought it was a tree, scaly and rough against her hand. And then she realized it was warm.

And it was *moving*.

"Watch it, Daisy."

"I told you this was a mistake, man."

"We couldn't just *leave*. She might have been hurt."

Eliza spun in a slow circle. Her eyes traveled up the figure behind her, taking in the strange, mottled skin covered in… thorns? Spikes? Her vision seemed to narrow as it reached the creature's head, met wide, brown eyes that were all the more dizzying for their humanity.

The world tilted.

"Careful, dude!"

But Eliza was only vaguely aware of the arms that surged forward to catch her. They missed. Her head hit something hard. Pain exploded in a starburst of white that enveloped the world like a camera flash, and then dragged her softly, inexorably into darkness.

Eliza's last thought was that the shadow standing over her looked *shiny*.

And then she was gone.

CHAPTER FOUR

A Shape in the Window

She woke to the deep bass ticking of a grandfather clock.

"Urg," Eliza groaned as she fought to open her eyes, a knot of pain tightening at the base of her skull. She reached for her head to make sure it was still in one piece.

"I'm glad you're awake, my dear. You gave me quite a fright."

Eliza's eyes flew open at the unfamiliar voice. She threw herself upright only to groan as the world spun, tilting on its axis like a cheap carnival ride.

"Careful, careful, take it easy. That bruise is not nothing, you know."

Forcing herself to squint through the brewing storm of a vicious headache, Eliza glared at the man sitting in front of her. He was old, with tufted gray hair and kind eyes, wearing a padded red dressing gown over elegant pajamas.

"Where am I?" she croaked, peering around the room. It was as opulent as the man's robe, plush and welcoming despite the subtle aura of wealth. It was still night, the huge windows dark and reflective. The man leaned away from her as she straightened.

"Why, you're in my home, dear. I was ever so worried when you tumbled off my roof, but I'm glad you seem to be alright."

"What?" Eliza mumbled, clutching her head and leaning over her knees as she struggled to remember what had happened.

Had she... climbed a roof?

"Well, don't you worry. I won't be pressing charges. As the young people say, no harm no foul."

The man's chuckle was warm, but there was something beneath it that made Eliza prickle with unease. She closed her eyes, focusing on her body. The agony in her head sought to drown everything out, but as she breathed through it, she realized that there was another pain.

Her elbow.

The fence.

"Now, I've called one of those Ubers to take you home. You can get some rest and we can pretend this little mishap never—"

"Fitzgerald Base," Eliza said, opening her eyes.

"Excuse me?"

"I wasn't climbing your roof," she said, almost to herself. "I was sneaking into Fitzgerald Base."

She tilted her head to see his expression, just in time to catch the ghost of a frown. He covered it with a wheezy laugh.

"Well, dear, that wasn't a very wise thing to do."

Eliza wasn't listening. She was staring at her hands, at the fingers scraped from the chain-link barbs. Green with grass stains.

"I was rescued there..."

"My, my, aren't you a fanciful—?"

"By a boy with wings."

The man went silent. Eliza chanced another look at him, but his expression had gone completely blank, his kind smile gone.

And with his face set into that serious glare, she recognized him.

Ian Eckelson, Scottstown's reclusive millionaire who lived in a huge gated estate outside the city center. She'd seen his likeness in Meru's main hall, walked by his portrait almost every day.

Eliza frowned back at him.

"Mr. Eckelson why am I here?" she asked, careful to keep her voice neutral.

"You should go home, dear. I think your injury needs tending."

"I know what I saw—"

"Clearly that's not true," he said with what might have passed for a grandfatherly smile, if not for the frozen warning behind it. "And if you keep on with these… inventions, I'm afraid I'll have to tell the police the real story."

"And what's that?"

"That you attempted to break into my house and rob me."

Eliza pursed her lips, but there was no leeway in his steely gray eyes. He had her and he knew it. Eliza came with a record. A history of breaking rules.

And if she got kicked out of Meru, she'd never find out what really happened last night.

"I think I'll go home then," Eliza said.

Mr. Eckelson's face melted back into that friendly smile and he pushed to his feet, saying something about asking Mrs. Fields for a car.

Eliza followed the old man to the entrance, letting him ramble on about head injuries and missing housekeepers as she took in the enormous central staircase, portraits, thick carpet that squished like moss beneath her feet. The mansion was beautiful, yes, but there was also a worn comfort to it. As if people actually lived here. Scratches on the bannister, the folded edge of a carpet.

A comic book barely visible on a side table beside the kitchen doors.

Eliza paused, staring at the comic book, but Mr. Eckelson grabbed her elbow and steered her toward the front door.

"Come along, don't want to keep the kind Uber-man waiting."

As much as Mr. Eckelson put on a show of shuffling age, he was surprisingly strong as he shoved her outside.

"Now, remember what I said. No harm, no foul, right Miss Elizabeth Mason?"

Eliza froze at the use of her full name. She turned back and found those steely eyes, holding her there like a challenge. She met them, unblinking.

"No harm, no foul," she repeated.

Mr. Eckelson nodded, stepped back, and slammed the door in her face.

Eliza stared at the closed door for a long moment, thinking about that comic book.

Do housekeepers for wealthy hermits read comic books? she wondered as she trudged down the marble steps toward the white Honda waiting for her in the circular driveway. The memories of the night before were tugging at her mind like impatient children. The soldier with insane strength. The headlights of the jeeps.

The voices in the forest.

Eliza reached the car and yanked open the door, burning with frustration. She turned to glare back at the mansion, wishing she could march inside and demand answers from the old man.

But something caught her eye.

There, in the top window, backlit like a ghost, was the blurry shape of a person. A boy, with broad shoulders tapering to a narrow waist, one arm holding back a thick curtain.

And behind him, barely visible from this distance, were the sloping mountain-peak edges of his shadow.

Wings.

Eliza clutched the door, unblinking. She willed her eyes to be stronger. Maybe she was wrong. Maybe it was the shadow of a dresser, or a strangely shaped lamp.

But that didn't explain why there was a boy in Ian Eckelson's mansion, or why he was hiding on the top floor.

As if sensing her eyes on him, the boy dropped the curtain. It rustled shut. Eliza frowned at the black glass for a moment longer. The only sign that anyone had been there was the gentle fluttering of the curtain's edge.

"Hey lady, are you gonna get in or what?"

"Yeah, sorry," Eliza said, ignoring the driver's hot glare as she slid into her seat. The man huffed, asking for her address, and she gave it with numb instinct, her mind miles away.

CHAPTER FIVE
Unsolved

"Jesus, Eliza, you scared the crap out of me!"

Joe had been waiting on the dorm's front steps, pacing back and forth and muttering to himself. When she'd stepped out of the Uber, he'd rushed over, grabbing her shoulders and checking for wounds in the illumination of the campus security lights.

"Come on, Joe, for the millionth time I'm *fine*."

His eyes were huge and panicky, filled with the fear of a boy who'd never received so much as a parking violation. "There were *sirens*, Eliza. It was like the apocalypse in there. We all watched you sprint away from the lab. I wanted to come and help, but Tori told us all to run for it and in the chaos I didn't see where you went and I spent hours searching the woods, but you weren't there—"

"*Joe!*"

Eliza pressed her hands to either side of his face, stopping the tirade.

"I'm fine," she said, careful to keep her words even. Because she was fine, wasn't she? She was in one piece. She hadn't been shot by military grunts or died from a head injury.

So why did everything feel so *not* fine?

Eliza sighed, letting her hands drop.

"Look, I jumped the fence. And I...." She swallowed. "I accidentally ended up in Ian Eckelson's mansion."

Joe's eyes, impossibly, grew even wider.

"*What?*"

Eliza shrugged, peering into the distance where she could just make out the spired rooftop of the estate. She wondered what was going on in there, in the wake of her exit. What Ian Eckelson was thinking now.

"I can't explain it," she said, frustration twisting into her voice. "I just kind of... woke up there."

Eliza knew she was treading dangerous waters. Could she tell Joe about what she'd seen? About the boy with wings and the super-strong soldier? Or would that be dragging him into her mess, putting his life at risk for her curiosity?

Swallowing the conflicted tangle of her emotions, she tried to smile at her best friend.

"Hey, it was an adventure, right?"

Joe's breath exploded out of him.

"I think that's enough adventure for one school year, don't you think?"

This time, Eliza didn't have to fake her smile.

"Oh, you're not getting the quiet life that easy."

"Lord help me," Joe said, but he was grinning with relief, ruffling his auburn hair. He threw one arm around Eliza's shoulders and pulled her tight against his side. "Come on, you lunatic, I'll walk you to your door."

"At least they won't be calling you names anymore," Eliza said, letting Joe steer her inside.

"We'll see. I don't trust the honesty of drunk people."

Eliza paused in the entrance to her hallway, emblazoned with a big sign that read **No Boys Beyond This Point**. Questions fizzed like Pop Rocks on her tongue, desperate to be released. To be validated. She met Joe's eyes. This was the person who had invited her to sit with him on that first awful day at Meru, who had stood by her despite the tender spots on her soul that sometimes made her act without thinking. She wanted to tell him so badly it ached.

But she couldn't. She'd seen that woman's expression, and worse, seen the destruction of the rogue soldier.

Eliza wouldn't forgive herself if Joe got hurt because of her.

So, rocking onto her tiptoes, Eliza pressed a light kiss to Joe's cheek, pretending to ignore the way his flush climbed all the way to his coppery eyebrows.

"What was that for?"

Eliza grinned.

"For tolerating me."

Joe straightened, his face cracking into a wide grin.

"Well, life would be pretty boring without you."

If only you knew, Eliza thought.

"Get some sleep," she said instead, shoving open the hallway door.

Tori was waiting for her, still fully clothed and scrolling through Instagram on her phone. She barely glanced up as Eliza entered but her thumb froze over the touchscreen.

"So you're alive then?"

Eliza smirked as she hung up her hoodie. She imagined Tori had been sitting here, wide awake for all the hours Eliza was gone, wondering if her roommate been arrested, if Eliza would rat on the one who'd sent her into the base.

Or maybe, just maybe, the blonde monster had been *worried*.

"I touched the lab," Eliza said as she plopped onto her narrow twin bed, covered in a floral comforter her mother had insisted on sending along, despite her protests.

Tori rolled oversized blue eyes, letting her phone fall onto her chest as she leveled a cold glare at Eliza.

"Look, let's just pretend it never happened, ok? It was stupid. I didn't think you'd actually do it."

"Well I did," Eliza said, folding her arms.

"Fine. I'll leave you and your boyfriend alone. But let's just drop it, alright?"

"Why? Worried the teachers might realize that their favorite student spends her weekends drinking in the woods?" Eliza said in a mocking voice.

They glared at one another, both refusing to blink. But Eliza had bigger things to worry about than Tori's reputation.

Like a boy with wings who'd saved her life.

"Whatever," Eliza said, rolling onto her side so that her back was turned. After a long, stretched moment, Tori huffed and turned off the light.

Eliza lay there in the darkness for a long time, thinking about super-soldiers and mansions and millionaires. But her mind kept circling the image of that boy in the window, watching her. Who was he? Why did he save her? And who were the other shadows who had loomed over her in the dark? The questions tumbled through her mind like gymnasts, but after hours and hours of puzzling Eliza came to only one conclusion.

She wasn't going to rest easy until she figured out what was going on.

CHAPTER SIX
The Chase

Eliza poked at her cereal, watching the patterns the Corn Flakes made as they got soggier and soggier.

"You know, I don't think you can absorb nutrition through your eyes."

She didn't answer Joe, her mind still tangled in the thoughts that had kept her up half the night.

"I'd say a penny for your thoughts, but it looks like I'd need a lot of pennies."

She sighed, letting her spoon fall into the slop and sitting back in her chair.

"Sorry, I'm just... distracted."

"No problem," he said with a cheerful shrug, swirling his orange juice. "I can't blame you, we all had quite the ordeal."

"Yeah," Eliza said, her gaze drifting to the table by the window where Tori and her entourage sat.

"On the bright side, no one's called me names today. But then, no one's really spoken to me yet, so it's too early to tell."

Eliza forced herself to smile, trying to drag herself back to the present.

Joe cocked his head. "Do you wanna go see that new movie this afternoon?"

"New movie?"

"Yeah, the one about aliens."

Eliza chuckled, but her brain latched onto that word.

Were those shadows aliens?

"I mean, we don't have to if you don't want to..."

"I think I'm going to bike by the base," Eliza said suddenly, snapping to a decision. She couldn't just keep wondering and hoping that some answer might magically appear. She had to do *something* or she was going to lose her mind.

Joe's smile fell.

"I don't think that's a good idea. What if they recognize you?"

"They won't."

"Look, I know you're not exactly into sitting things out, but that was nuts last night. Can't you find a better way to blow off steam than poking the freaking *army*?"

"I'm not poking anyone. I just want to check something out."

"Eliza..."

"You don't have to come with me," Eliza said, folding her arms.

"Maybe I won't. Unlike you, I like my weekends to be *relaxing*. Have you heard of the word? It's quite a novel concept, I—hey wait, you're leaving *now*?"

Eliza had shoved to her feet, pushing the bowl of cereal away and ignoring the way Tori's eyes flicked to her before returning to her own posse.

"I'll only be gone an hour."

"Now hold on—"

"Get tickets for that movie, I'll be back by noon."

Ignoring Joe's open-mouthed shock, Eliza snatched her messenger bag and hurried out of the dining hall before she could lose her nerve.

Her bike was parked in front of the dorm, rarely used on the entirely walkable campus but invaluable when it came to getting away. The center of town was a good mile and a half from Meru and, in order to keep Eliza from going totally stir-crazy in the quiet little Western Massachusetts town, her parents had relented and bought her a blue cruiser bike with tall handlebars and a wide, plushy seat. Perfect for popping into the city for some groceries or a quick trip to the mall. Terrible for long distances.

Her parents knew her well.

Eliza popped off the U-lock and swung her leg over to settle on the wide seat, cursing the mandatory skirts of Meru's uniform. What she wouldn't give for a few pairs of jeans, but their headmaster insisted that Meru students needed to look polished and professional *at all times*, even on weekends.

It was a warm, sunny Saturday morning, so naturally the bike lane that followed the highway into the woods was full of mothers and strollers and dogs. Eliza had to move slowly to keep from hitting anyone, which only made her anxiety sharper, her doubts thicker. Was Joe right? Was this a mistake? Maybe she should go back....

But no matter how much the uncertainty settled into the pit of her stomach, she couldn't bring herself to turn around.

Katie, I hope you're keeping an eye on me, Eliza thought as she drew closer to the military base and the sprawling hills of Ian Eckelson's endless estate.

Eliza had been the bold one. The one to drag Katie into lakes and through fields, making up wild stories so they could pretend to be magical spies or poison testers. But, despite being six years older, Katie had always gone along with Eliza. Together they'd climbed trees and built forts and chased after terrified squirrels. Katie had moderated the wilderness in Eliza's soul, kept her safe without making her tame. No one else had accepted the natural restlessness that seemed as much a part of Eliza as her skeleton. But Katie had.

If she were still alive, Katie would be right here, biking beside her, trying to talk her into a more rational course of action without talking her out of it entirely.

Damn, I miss you, Eliza thought as she passed a pair of gossiping moms fast-walking back to Scottstown.

She could see the fence now. The pedestrians had thinned so that Eliza was almost alone. Cars sailed past as she stopped and leaned to the side so she could peer into the metal cage of Fitzgerald Base. A few soldiers were outside drilling and the line of jeeps stood suspiciously silent and undisturbed. It looked just as it had every time Eliza had seen it—orderly, quiet.

Normal.

Eliza rolled into the driveway that twisted into the heart of the base.

Did she dare get closer?

Suddenly, Eliza felt something approaching. Predatory. *Dangerous*. Her senses hummed for her to run. She twisted on her bike seat just in time to see a black, unmarked car crest the hill and slow.

She felt as if the car's headlights were eyes, looking right at her.

And then, with an impatient roar, the car began to accelerate, veering into the bike lane.

Right at her.

"Shit!"

Eliza kicked herself into motion, pedaling frantically. There was no way it was aiming for her, no way it was *trying* to hit her. That would be insane. But as she cast a terrified look over one shoulder, she couldn't deny that the car was driving way too far right.

Taking a chance, Eliza swung into the empty left lane.

The car followed.

"Shit, shit, shit," Eliza muttered, throwing her whole body into pedaling.

She'd almost reached the exit where they'd met Tori the night before, but that was a car lane. The crazy person on her tail might follow her. Eliza threw another look behind her and saw only black metal, close enough that she could feel the heat radiating off its surface.

The trees whistled past.

No one was around to see what was happening. There were no witnesses.

She had to act fast or she was going to die.

31

"Damn it," Eliza growled and yanked her handlebars to the side, throwing herself off the road.

It was like someone had put the world into a blender. Her messenger bag went flying. Her body was launched over the front wheel and into the underbrush. Thorns and sharp branches scratched her face. Her hair caught on the underbrush hard enough to make her cry out in pain. In some distant, detached world she heard the squeal of tires, the harmonizing of engines, the roar of oncoming traffic.

And then, as abruptly as it had started, everything stopped.

Eliza lay in the crunchy October leaves, gasping for air. If she had ached before, she felt *brutal* now. Her whole body was a constellation of bruises and cuts and abused muscles.

But she was alive.

Wincing with every movement, Eliza pushed to her knees. Her eyes scanned through the bars of the trees, glared back at the road. A minivan whooshed past and a Subaru sped by in the other direction. But no black car.

Using a nearby sapling to pull herself to her feet, Eliza frowned at the underbrush, wondering if she'd imagined the whole thing, if the knock on her head really had destabilized her enough that she was seeing things, inventing fantasies as she'd once done with Katie.

But when her gaze found the empty pavement of the road, her jaw clenched. Because there, dark and swerving, were unmistakable skid marks, still smoking and reeking of burnt rubber.

"The hell...?" Eliza breathed, her heart beginning to slow.

The forest didn't answer, so she had no choice but to get moving.

Fighting through the pain, Eliza began to gather her scattered things which had gone flying in the crash. Her bag, her books, her cellphone. Thankfully, the screen remained unbroken.

Her bike wasn't so lucky.

The front was bent at a jagged angle, the metal wheel bed twisted into a reaching claw.

"Damn," she said aloud as she untangled a cluster of leaves from the loose chain. She'd have to bring her bike to the shop, maybe even get a new one. The thought made her feel claustrophobic. She'd be totally dependent on Joe for rides, and she already knew he wasn't interested in the mystery of what was going on in Fitzgerald Base.

Hauling the mess of metal out of the bushes, Eliza managed to crawl her way back into the bike lane. She peered around, waiting for that black car to show up again. But the stretch of road between Scottstown and the outlying district was quiet. She squinted up the highway to where she knew the giant gilded gates protected Ian Eckelson and his secrets.

An engine rumbled behind her and she spun, heart hammering.

Joe's pick-up truck crested the hill, squealing to a stop beside her. Eliza exhaled in relief, trying to get her pulse under control.

"Oh my God, Eliza, what happened to you?" Joe said, leaping out of the rumbling truck and running over to her.

"Had a bit of a tumble," she said, ducking her head.

"You look like you got in an accident!"

"It's nothing, I just fell." She took a deep breath, squinting at her friend. "What are you doing here?"

"My spidey senses were tingling. But really, did the trees gang up on you or what?"

"I told you, it's nothing. Come on, Joe, I need a bath."

"Alright, whatever you say. Although for the record, I think the trees won."

Eliza punched him in the arm and they both released nervous half-laughs. Joe knew she was hiding something. She could see it in his expression, in the way he curved toward her like a question mark.

So she gave him the sheepish grin of a person who had just done something clumsy.

"Will you help me with this thing or what?"

"Always in need of the big strong man, aren't you?" Joe said, nodding sagely.

It took both of them to wrestle the heavy, twisted bike out of the bushes and into the high bed of his truck. By the time they were done, both Eliza and Joe were panting and dirty and covered in bike grease.

"You know, I can think of better ways to spend a Saturday," Joe muttered, pressing his handkerchief to the bloody gash Eliza hadn't noticed on her forehead.

"Really? I can't," she said, pushing his hand away. "You're gonna stain your fancy tissue."

"It's fine, that's what they're for," he said, tossing her the bloody linen. "Here, you do it then. If you come back to Meru looking like that, people are going to think you're part of a fight club."

"Maybe I am."

Joe sighed, turning off his hazards and shifting the truck into first gear.

"You know, I wouldn't be surprised."

Under the guise of checking on her bike, Eliza turned and glared down the road. She could see the base's iron fence glimmering through the trees, shining in the sun as if it had nothing to hide.

"I hope you'll take this as a sign," Joe was saying. "I think this is the universe's way of telling you to behave yourself."

Eliza frowned.

Screw the universe, she thought, pinching her eyebrows together. *I'm just getting started.*

CHAPTER SEVEN
Impulses

By the time Monday rolled around, Eliza had almost fully healed from her ordeal. Physically, at least. Joe had forced her to go to the movie—a thoughtful and somewhat boring flick about the sociopolitical consequences of an alien invasion—and dragged her to the library to study for their history exam that week. Things were threatening to settle back into normal, the universe bending itself back into shape as if the weekend had been nothing more than an uncomfortable blip on the radar.

Which was exactly what Eliza was afraid of.

Her mind drifted as she followed Joe into the main hall, exhausted from going over the same questions over and over and over again. She felt like she'd worn a rut in the gray matter of her brain, a groove that wasn't doing anything but making her antsy and irritable.

"Do you think Mr. Veran will ask about King Henry's five wives, because that seems like a fairly obvious question?"

"Huh?" Eliza asked as Joe opened the door for her. He rolled his eyes.

"Good to know you're listening."

Eliza smiled.

"Sorry. Just tired, you know."

"I don't know *why*. I mean you only almost died twice this weekend. You should be bright eyed and bushy tailed, as my granddad would say."

"Well, at least I have you to take care of me."

Joe's cheeks turned dark red and Eliza slid past him, grinning to herself. Poor Joe tried so hard, but he couldn't quite master the graceful confidence of his parents. Eliza had watched them once on the HNN, at some gala for top-rated news shows. They'd been crisp and witty and smooth. Alluring in their self-possessed, fascinating way. It was impressive, really. No wonder their only child felt like he had a lot to live up to.

But Eliza's thoughts were dragged back to reality as she stepped through the door. Something in homeroom was wrong. There was an energy to the gathered students that felt toxic, unwelcoming. Eliza slowed as she shuffled between desks, trying to find the cause.

"Slut."

Eliza spun at the word, meeting Fabia's cold brown eyes with a hard expression of her own.

Eliza took a step toward the other girl's desk.

"What did you call me?"

Fabia didn't answer, just sat back in her seat with a cat-like smirk.

"Come now, everyone, sit down," Mrs. Henderson called, sweeping in with a rustle of her heavy skirt. "I know it's Monday, but that's no reason to dilly dally."

Shaken by the vitriol swirling around her, Eliza slid into her seat as Joe settled in behind her. He hadn't heard the slur or else he would have stood up for her, but she wondered if Joe felt the wrongness just as much as she did.

Turning to face Mrs. Henderson, Eliza tried to focus on the morning. But a tap on her shoulder interrupted the failed attempt. Joe's long fingers passed her a jagged piece of paper ripped from his notebook.

I'll investigate, it said.

Thanks, Eliza scribbled back, letting Mrs. Henderson's announcements drone on, the dull Monday monotony sharpening the jagged edges of her temper.

~~~

"So?"

Joe winced as Eliza cornered him in the cafeteria, dragging him to a table in the back.

36

"You're not gonna like it," Joe said, not meeting her eyes.

"Tell me."

Joe ducked his head as Tori swept past, followed by a sneering Fabia and the twins. None of them so much as looked at Eliza.

Her morning had been worse than bad. Whispers had followed her like persistent mosquitos, most of them faceless and gone before she could turn. Only Fabia had been bold enough to meet Eliza's eyes as she hissed that foul word, but the sentiment had clearly spread far and wide. On Friday, Eliza had been nothing more than a weird newcomer, barely worth a glance.

Today, she was notorious.

"Joe, I'm dying here. It's been a hell of a morning. Please tell me."

He looked ready to squirm out of his seat, but Eliza didn't let up. She leaned toward him, putting her hand on the metallic cover of his applesauce.

"Please?"

Joe lifted his eyes, peering at her from beneath thick auburn lashes.

"Tori's spreading a rumor about you. That you slept with a soldier this weekend."

"*What?*"

"She said you've got a... boyfriend on Fitzgerald Base. That you snuck in to see him over the weekend and when the officers busted into his bunk you had to run naked through the forest." Joe blushed. "She said that's why you're so covered with cuts and bruises."

Eliza's mouth hung open. A part of her had known that Tori wasn't the kind of girl to leave things to chance, that her roommate would do something to cover up what had happened.

But *this*?

"And people *believe* her?" Eliza hissed, glaring at the table of rich princesses.

Joe shrugged.

"I mean, it's high school. People like gossip, no matter how dumb it is."

Eliza's eyes scanned the cafeteria, fast enough to catch the stares before people averted their eyes.

She curled her fingers into fists on the table.

"Assholes."

"Look, ignore them," Joe said soothingly. "It'll pass. Last year someone spread a rumor that Beth was pregnant and it was all anyone could talk about for two weeks, but of course even these idiots had to drop it when it became obvious she wasn't. I mean, she did quit the drama club and went home for the third quarter to mentally recover from the bullying, but she's back this year."

Eliza was glaring into her soup. A week ago she would have marched up to Tori and challenged her in front of everyone, pushed it into the open in the brazen way that had landed her in trouble so many times she'd lost count. Insults would have been exchanged, perhaps a few blows, and both girls would have ended up crumpled and sheepish in the headmaster's office. Tori would have gotten a stern reprimand.

Eliza would have been sent home.

So she forced herself to remain in her seat, her knuckles white as the whispers fluttered around her with their sharp, treacherous wings.

"Eliza?"

She sighed, glancing up at Joe.

"What?"

Joe reached out and wrapped his pianist fingers around one of her fists, squeezing in comfort.

"You know I don't care if you're into military grunts or nerds. Although I strongly hope for the latter."

She couldn't help the laugh that burst out of her, bright and surprising in the unfriendly cafeteria.

"Glad to hear it, Joe."

But he didn't let go of her hand. His eyes were intense, drilling into her with something she didn't want to deal with, not in her current state.

"I'm going to talk to her tonight." Eliza said, pulling back and glaring at the far table. "Privately. In our room."

Joe grimaced to conceal the flinch from when Eliza had withdrawn.

"That seems like a *great* idea."

"Look, she can't be all evil. I've heard her humming to herself in the shower."

"Yeah, because plotting monsters don't *hum*. Only nice, warm, kind-hearted people are allowed to make musical noises."

Eliza smiled, dipping her spoon into her soup without really intending to eat. Her thoughts were far away, wandering down the road to a place where more interesting things were happening than rumors about illicit boyfriends.

"Don't worry about me, Joe. I can deal with her."

"Your funeral," Joe muttered, knowing better than to try and stop her.

CHAPTER EIGHT
Wrong-Headed

That evening, as dusk began to bleed into night, Eliza was the one waiting for Tori in their tiny box of a dorm room. Her limbs were locked together, legs crossed, arms folded, every muscle taut and shaking with rage. She fought to control it. Lashing out blindly, tempting as that might be, wasn't a good solution.

Eliza should know.

There must be an explanation.

Finally, she heard the scrape of a key in the lock. Eliza popped to her feet.

"What?" Tori snapped as Eliza glared at her.

The door clicked shut, closing them in.

"I think you know," Eliza said.

Tori tossed her hair, filling the room with the cloying scent of coconut. It would have been a pleasant smell, had it not been ruined by association.

Unshouldering her backpack, Tori waved a dismissive hand. "God, it's like you just won't leave me alone—"

"You're a walking stereotype, you know that?" Eliza spat. "Why did you do it? Why did you spread those lies about me?

Tori met Eliza's eyes with an expression of controlled indifference, shielded and armored and all kinds of cold.

"The school deserved to know who the *real* Eliza Mason is."

For a moment, Eliza's mouth hung open. Tori brushed past her, settling on her bed as she flipped her phone over and connected it to her Bluetooth speaker with a cheerful *beep*.

"Tori," Eliza said, half in shock that anyone could be so utterly inhuman. "I wasn't going to tell anyone. Honestly, I didn't even want to deal with it. I don't *care* what you do with your time."

Tori ignored her. Kanye West began to drone from the speaker, filling the silence with an angry, hypnotic beat. Eliza's eyes prickled as if poked with tiny needles.

"Will you at least talk to me? Treat me like a real person?" The sleepless nights were strangling Eliza's voice, making her feel dizzy with rage and impotence and so many unanswered questions. She didn't ask for this this. She didn't ask for any of it. That familiar itch was swelling, the urge to shout, to break something, to push past the societally established boundaries of conduct until she felt powerful again.

Her fingers ached from clenching them so hard.

"Look, I don't know what your problem is," Eliza said, betrayed by her own voice cracking. "But I don't even want to be here. I miss Atlanta. I miss the heat and the storms and my parents and my goddamn *sister*. But what do you care about that? What would you know about family?"

Tori, of course, didn't even look up.

Furious tears were making Eliza's vision blur. She grabbed her hoodie, spinning away. She had to get out of there. The memories were bubbling up, slicing her open like so many razors, inescapable and unforgiving as they threatened to drag her back into the sea of grief that she'd only just begun to haul herself out of.

And then, as if by divine providence, Eliza's eyes fell on Tori's bike key.

She stared at it for a moment, weighing her options. Thinking through the outcome as Joe was always pleading for her to do. *This* would be poking the dragon. It would make things infinitely worse. Tori would be enraged; her friends would lash back with a vengeance. Eliza's life at Meru would become a living hell, for real this time. And that was only if she managed to keep herself from getting kicked out for breaking curfew. On every single level, it was a bad idea.

Her favorite kind.

Screw it.

With a lightning-quick movement, she snatched the keys.

"Hey!" Tori shouted, but Eliza was already out the door and down the hall. She leapt, clearing the front stairs of their dorm building, hitting the ground at a run. Sprinting for the line of bikes, she felt a pang of sadness when she didn't see her own bulky cruiser there among them.

But there was no time to think about those crumpled metallic remains, now rusting in the back of Joe's truck.

She hurried down the looping metal of the rack.

The door crashed open behind her.

"Get back here!" Tori shrieked, but Eliza had already found the fancy road bike that Tori had rolled in the third week of school. It was glossy and spindly, freshly painted a sleek silver with blue trim. Stylishly old-fashioned and retro, perfect for Instagram and terrible for actually *going* anywhere.

Eliza had it unlocked in seconds.

"Bitch!" Tori howled after her.

Chased by Tori's high-pitched shouts, Eliza wheeled through the puddles of illumination the streetlights threw and onto the shadowy bike path. It was reckless to be out at night, stupid to be riding off on a stolen bike, foolish to have made a true enemy of the most popular girl in school. Eliza could feel the consequences of her reckless choices circling, closing in like vultures. Soon enough, one of them was going to get her. Tear her apart. Force her to reckon with the consequences.

She didn't care.

Peddling like a madwoman, she careened down the dark road like an unleashed demon. The air whistled by her head, autumn-crisp, welcoming her to be rash. Because she was *doing* something. She was going to get answers. Perhaps those answers could chase away the ghost of her sister, give her some modicum of relief from the constant aching pain of *loss*. And even if they didn't, at least they'd be a welcome distraction.

Eliza snarled into the darkness, knowing exactly where she was going.

Because the Eckelson mansion was only a few miles away, and the journey was well worth whatever mysteries it might solve.

CHAPTER NINE
Vindicated

Standing before the gates of the Eckelson mansion, it was easy to convince herself that she was losing her mind. The night was silent, broken only by the ragged sound of Eliza's breathing after the long trek here. Tori's bike lay discarded in the grass. Eliza pressed her forehead to the gilded gates, willing something strange to happen.

But the mansion just stared back at her, smug and elegant and still.

"Come on," Eliza whispered, wrapping her fingers around the bars. "Come *on*."

Her eyes were fixed on the upper window where she'd seen the shape of that boy. But her mind was elsewhere. In another time, another place, when Eliza had pressed her face against the iron bars of a different institution shut down for the evening.

Sunset Hospice Center, where the old and decrepit went to die.

The last place on Earth a nineteen-year-old girl should have ended up.

Eliza slammed her fist against the metal, snapping the quiet night with a warbling metallic sound.

"I know you're in there," she hissed, scrubbing away furious tears. "Show yourself."

But she didn't know anything. Her therapist had told her to be careful of delusions. Had she made the whole thing up to escape her pain? The thought made her lean into the metal slats like a tree bending in heavy wind.

She glared at the mansion, heart sinking.

She would have to go back to the dorm. Apologize to Tori. Tomorrow, Joe would be waiting for her on the steps. They'd get breakfast, go to homeroom, deal with the endless taunts and jabs and whispers and sneers. She'd take her history exam and probably pass because of Joe's help.

And everything would go back to normal.

Eliza sighed, her mother's words echoing back to her from another day, another mistake.

One of these days, Elizabeth, you're going to have to grow up.

Shoving off the metal bars, Eliza trudged over to the stolen bicycle. She picked it up, prepared herself for the long, lonely ride back to campus. Pausing, she threw one last look over her shoulder.

That's when she saw the shadows on the roof.

She froze, her eyes straining to make out the two figures darting between spires. For a moment they were nothing more than blurry smudges in the night, visible only because of their movement in the stillness. But then, as a cloud rolled away and the moon's light made the gilded trim shimmer, they were thrown into relief. One gangly and narrow with glinting eyes.

The other burly, muscled, and unmistakably *winged.*

"Holy shit," Eliza breathed, dropping the bike and darting back to the fence. She fought the urge to blink as the figures made their way to the corner of the vast roof, teetering over a gutter bed. Masculine whispers floated toward her on the breeze, accompanied by the burst of a tenor laugh. The winged boy put his hands on his hips. The other threw out his arms. Eliza could just barely hear two cajoling words.

"Come on..."

And then, as if bursting out of her very dreams, the boy's wings unfurled.

Eliza couldn't help it.

She gasped.

They were *huge*, almost double the boy's height, thickly feathered and iridescent even at this distance. He beat them once and she could feel the distinct *whomp* of shifting air. The skinny one let out an excited cackle and leapt. Eliza pressed herself closer, heart pounding.

But there was no need to fear, because the winged boy swooped off the roof, twisted in midair like the most graceful gymnast Eliza had ever seen, and hit the shape of the falling body. There was another *whomp*, another beat of those glorious wings, and then their misshapen shadow was rising into the night, illuminated by the moon like a creature of myth.

For a moment, Eliza could only watch, a triumphant grin unfurling on her face. She'd been right. Damnit, she'd been *right*. Screw Tori and Mr. Eckelson and all the councilors who told her to get her head out of the clouds.

She'd give a million dollars to show them what she'd just seen.

With a jolt, Eliza realized that the boys were gliding over her, growing more and more distant.

Heading into town.

"Wait, wait, wait."

Eliza lunged for Tori's bike, leaping onto it before it was even straight. It wobbled precariously, threatening to tip her into the bushes for another tumble in the trees, but she managed to find the pedals and propel herself forward.

It was probably the most dangerous ride of Eliza's life as she chased after the gliding shadows, barely glancing at the road in front of her. Twice she had to veer precariously to avoid a car swinging around the bend, and once her back wheel jerked as it slid off the pavement, but she managed to follow the flying shapes all the way into central Scottstown. Even from this distance, she could hear the steady thumping of air, almost *feel* the power of those wings. Her whole body felt electric and giddy and wildly alive as she ignored the questions and pumped her legs as fast as she could. They were fast, but she was beneath them, chasing them, zigzagging into town.

Someone honked behind her, forcing her to look away. She moved to the side of the road, throwing out one leg to prevent herself from toppling over. Swearing under her breath, Eliza righted the stolen bike, kicked off the curb, looked up.

And froze.

The sky was black, the silver clouds shifting in dizzying, unpredictable patterns, none of them the one she was looking for.

She'd lost them.

"No you don't…" Eliza breathed, tightening her grip, shifting back into motion.

This night wasn't over yet.

CHAPTER TEN
Flying and Falling

"Stupid streetlights," Eliza growled as she squinted at the blurry sky, trying to see through the haze of the city's illumination. But it was no use. She weaved her way through the middle of town, growing more and more impatient with every block. Everything was quiet, almost creepy in contrast with its usually bustling daytime cheer.

But in the distance, a loud crush of bodies spilled out of Mr. Tim's 24-hour Pizza.

Eliza pedaled over, senses humming.

Everyone at Meru knew to stay away from Mr. Tim's after ten. It was where the trainee soldiers hung out when they were kicked out of Howl, most of them drunk and irritable after a day of being pushed beyond their limits. Tori liked to sneer that she couldn't go near the place without a chorus of catcalls, but even she didn't dare test the theory.

Eliza took a deep breath.

She wouldn't forgive herself if she didn't investigate.

Carefully, frayed nerves jacked up to eleven, Eliza wheeled forward. Her eyes scanned the crowd, passing over chiseled jaws and buzz cuts and tattoos without any real interest. Maybe in another life, in another burst of rebelliousness, Eliza would have shoved into this crowd and tossed her hair, asking for trouble.

But tonight she was after a different sort of mischief.

"Where are you?" Eliza whispered, glaring at the crowd, the sky, the moon. Why would the boys have come into town at this hour if not to get a snack? They might be wildly strange, but they were still boys. And boys had to eat.

Right?

Eliza shook her head. Maybe she'd finally lost it, thinking that the alien shadows might want *pizza*....

But she waited. Glared.

There!

A figure appeared between two clusters of heavily muscled privates, standing out like a greyhound among bulldogs. His brown hair was jagged, his sweater and jeans hanging off a frame so narrow he looked like he'd been stretched. But it was the way he *moved* that attracted Eliza's attention, so fast that Eliza wondered if there was a strobe light on him. He didn't seem to pass through air so much as *jump* through it, his hand disappearing in one part of the world and reappearing in another.

The boy turned, holding a pair of pizza boxes aloft with a wide grin.

He was wearing goggles.

Eliza squinted. That was strange, even for Mr. Tim's at eleven o'clock. And they weren't just the regular goggles that students wore during chemistry lab. They were opaque, huge, taking up most of the boy's face. They shimmered orange despite the hazy white of the streetlights.

Remembering that night outside the base, Eliza held her breath.

As if his eyes were made of mirrors...

Was he the one who had found her in the forest?

The boy was skipping away from the cluster of soldiers, toward the bridge that ran over the Scott River. Moving slowly, careful not to take her eyes off him, Eliza leaned Tori's bike against a tree and followed. She scurried through the park, avoiding the treacherous circles that the streetlights made. But as the road narrowed into the bridge, it grew harder to keep herself hidden. The boy seemed to twitch so much that Eliza was terrified he'd turn and see her. Realize he was being followed.

And then what?

49

Only one way to find out.

Eliza waited behind a thick sycamore, taking deep, steadying breaths. Gathering the tattered edges of her courage, she clenched her fists. Straightened into her tallest, most intimidating posture.

And leapt out from behind the tree.

The boy was gone.

Eliza ran to the bridge, scanning the night. But there was no sign of the tall, twitchy creature and his pair of pizza boxes. She spun around, raking her gaze through the clouds and the dark river and the lights of Scottstown.

Nothing.

"Urg," Eliza sighed, letting her head fall back. She slapped her hands to her face, raking them down her cheeks, frustration bubbling up from her stomach like acid.

She'd failed.

Again.

How could she go back to Meru now?

"What's a girl like you doing out at a time like this?"

Every hair on Eliza's body prickled at the slurring voice, accompanied by heavy footsteps. Slowly, Eliza turned, pulse beating against her eardrums.

Three privates were wobbling toward her, two supporting each other. The other, the strongest looking of the bunch, was looking at her the way a cat looks at a mouse.

Like prey.

Eliza backed away, her knees hitting the low barrier of the bridge.

"I love being so close to the prep school," the strong one said to his drunk companions. "Something about girls in uniform just revs all my engines."

"You see girls in uniform every day," mumbled one of the pair, leaning against his friend.

"You know what I mean, Ted. Nothing compares to a checkered skirt."

"Leave me alone," Eliza said, wishing she hadn't left the bike in the park. Wishing she'd watched her surroundings or been smart enough to bring a weapon.

"Aw, come on love. We're just having a bit of fun."

The largest of them was stepping toward her, his hands held out in friendly supplication, revealing an enormous dragon tattoo curled around his wrist and forearm.

"Leave. Me. Alone."

Her voice was a snarl, but still he drew closer. The river whispered below them, a ten-foot drop behind Eliza with unknown depths.

"Hey dude, maybe we should—"

As the man closest to her glanced behind him, Eliza made a run for it. Exploding off the railing, she lunged for the space between the burly one and his two drunk friends. She moved fast.

But he was faster.

Wrapping a forearm around her waist, the strong one swung Eliza's body into his. Eliza opened her mouth to scream but a hand clapped over it, muffling her. Her body was electric with fear.

"You're a fighter," the man whispered in her ear, making her skin crawl. "I like that."

Then you'll love this, Eliza thought before biting down on his fingers. Hard.

His scream split the night. Eliza tasted blood. He stumbled back and Eliza peeled away, but the man wasn't done. He grabbed her elbow, spinning her around. She heard the crack before she felt the slap. A blinding pain radiated along her jaw, down her whiplashed neck.

"I'll teach you some fucking respect!"

One of the drunk soldiers had grabbed his friend and was trying to hold him back. But Eliza wasn't about to stick around to see if he could. Backing away from the soldier, Eliza lifted one foot and stepped onto the railing. Throwing a glance over one shoulder, Eliza peered down at the dark water, hoping, praying it was deep enough.

Suspecting that it wasn't.

"Dude, calm the fuck dow—"

The soldier broke free.

Eliza jumped.

The air whistled by her head, terrifyingly fast. She took a deep breath, wondering if her cellphone would survive the plunge, realizing that she probably had bigger things to worry about.

Picturing broken legs and knees smashed on shallow rocks, Eliza tensed her body for impact.

And then a strong shoulder slammed into her stomach, lifting her away.

CHAPTER ELEVEN
Bird's Eye View

Eliza's scream was cut off as strong arms clenched around her middle. Her body jerked to the side. She watched with breathless shock as the inky water, the bridge lights, the warbling shadows all vanished, moving away from her like she was falling up. By the time Eliza registered the soldiers' surprised shouts, they were already gone, swallowed by the angry whistling of air and a heavy, sonorous beating that surrounded her in a cocoon of noise. It was as if the night itself was absorbing her.

She twisted around, eyes scanning the darkness.

"You know, you're one hell of a person to keep safe."

Eliza let out a strangled cry of surprised. But it faded as her eyes adjusted to the moonlight and she began to make out her rescuer's face. Strong nose, sharp jaw, thick hair whipping in the wind. *Handsome.* But Eliza's gaze kept sliding from his face to those huge, shimmering, feathered, inconceivable *wings*.

"What... what... I..."

A deep chuckle reverberated through Eliza's back as the boy laughed.

"Yeah, I know."

He was circling, tilting their bodies downward, towards the forest. Eliza twisted back to see her own feet dangling high, high, high above the ground. It was enough to make her head spin even more than it already was.

"Who are you?" Eliza gasped, the words ripped away by the frosty October wind.

For a moment, there was no response. Just the steady *thump* of air and a strong heart beating against her spine.

"Someone you never should have seen."

Eliza took a deep breath. "Well I've seen you now."

"Unfortunately."

"So you should answer the question."

Another chuckle, rumbling like thunder over her ribcage.

"Something tells me you've given your parents more than their fair share of migraines."

Eliza opened her mouth to respond, but at that moment the boy folded his wings, aiming them between tree branches like an expert diver. They began to fall. Eliza fumbled for the boy's arm, hard and solid around her waist. Another panicked shriek burst from her throat as the forest floor rushed up to meet them.

Just when she was sure they were about to break both their legs, the boy's wings unfurled. He swept them once, twice, hovering over the grass for an endless second.

And then they touched down.

The moment his grip slackened, Eliza spun away, knees bent, fists up.

He smiled, folding his arms and making his T-shirt wrinkle down the middle.

"You going to fight me for rescuing you?"

Eliza didn't smile back, keeping a good distance between them.

"Why should I trust you? I don't know who you are."

"Because I saved you? Twice?"

That made Eliza pause. She swept her gaze up and across his body, taking in the sandy brown of his hair. The iridescent blue of his feathers.

The sad curl of his smile.

She straightened.

"It *was* you, wasn't it?" she said, dropping her hands. "In Fitzgerald Base. You stopped the soldiers from…"

From what? Killing her? That seemed like a melodramatic thing to say aloud.

I'm looking at a boy who literally has bird wings sprouting out of his back. I think we've gone past drama.

"Thank you," the boy said, cutting through the chaotic tumble of Eliza's thoughts.

"For what?"

"For saying *who*," he said, feathers rustling. "Not *what*."

Eliza opened her mouth with no idea what she was about to say. Luckily, she was spared having to form coherent words as another figure crashed into the clearing. Eliza scrambled out of the way as the boy from Mr. Tim's burst through the trees, wind-milling his long arms to stop himself from falling.

Everyone froze as the boy's goggles glinted, fixed on Eliza.

"Ooooooh shit," he said with a low whistle, breaking the silence. "Aquila you are *so* dead."

The one with wings—Aquila—shrugged, his expression strangely adorable as he ducked his head.

"I couldn't do *nothing*," he said in defense.

"Ian's going to *kill* you, man! You broke rule *numero uno*. I can't believe it, our fearless leader, the first to expose us to the world."

But the boy didn't seem the least bit upset by the idea. He was grinning, his fingers twitching with barely subdued excitement. He circled Eliza, yellow-tinted goggles sparkling like gems in the moonlight.

"You're going to put us on *YouTube*, aren't you? Going to make us *famous*?" He cackled, as if there was nothing more he wanted out of life.

"No," Eliza said. Aquila straightened, eyes brightening. "I'm not going to tell anyone. I just wanna know what's going on." The winged boy looked at her as if he could hardly believe what she was saying. She folded her own arms, mimicking his posture. "You going to tell me who you are or what?"

Aquila's expression wavered, the ghost of a smile threatening to shine through his nervousness. But it was the other one who jumped in front of her, appearing as if by magic.

"Musca at your service, pretty lady." He held out one bony hand. "But you can call me Moose. I'm the prettiest of the Vagabonds, but don't let that fool you. I'm the brains too."

Eliza couldn't help but laugh as he took her hand and jerked it up and down so fast that her wrist ached.

"Ooookay," she said. "Who are the Vagabonds?"

The boy—Moose—winced, glancing over his shoulder.

"Oops..."

Aquila sighed.

"Don't mind my brother. He's... excitable."

"I can see that," she said with a grin. "I'm Eliza."

"Well, as you heard, I'm Aquila. The oldest."

Eliza took a step forward, glancing between the two of them.

"So... there are others?" Eliza said with a conspiratorial smile.

Aquila flinched and Moose fell quiet, his goggles turning first to Eliza and then his brother. She could feel the two of them withdrawing like a tide, curling away from her as if she was something dangerous. And she could see why. Just the fact that she'd laid eyes on Aquila meant that she had the kind of power over them that people were killed for. But they weren't going to kill her. They were just teenage boys who lived in a stranger world than Eliza had ever known.

And she wanted a part of it.

Eliza held out her hands, trying to look as harmless as possible.

"Come on, I swear I won't tell anyone. Honest."

Neither of the brothers relented. Eliza's lips curved in a shy smile.

"Look, I'm new in Scottstown and I kind of hate it. It would be really nice to make some friends here."

Moose's face jerked up at the word *friend*. He glanced at Aquila, shoulders popping up into a rapid shrug.

"I mean, she's not running away screaming, bro," he said, vibrating as if the very act of standing still was making him boil over with energy.

"And I don't plan to," Eliza inserted in a calm voice.

Aquila met her eyes and it felt like looking at the sun. Eliza felt the urge to run from the strange brewing *something* that was making her stomach squirm and her limbs feel like jelly. But she didn't. She met his gaze, keeping her face as open as possible.

"Please," Eliza said as Aquila stared at her, his expression inscrutable.

One hand unfurled from his bicep, lowering until his palm was open between them.

"Give me your cellphone."

"Yes!" Moose said, pumping the air.

Eliza flipped her phone out of her skirt pocket and handed it to him without hesitation. She could almost hear her mother's groan as Eliza offered two perfect strangers her one link to the world, effectively putting herself at their mercy. But she didn't care. And she wasn't afraid. Aquila radiated with a subtle, comforting strength that made her feel safe just being close to him.

He took her phone and slid it into the pocket of his jeans, offering her a half-terrified smile.

"So... you wanna meet the rest?"

"Absolutely," Eliza said with complete conviction.

CHAPTER TWELVE
New Friends

"I *knew* I saw you in the window," Eliza hissed as Aquila landed on the roof of the Eckelson mansion, their feet touching down on the coppery ridge line of the tallest wing. It was magically surreal, to be this high up, standing on her own two feet and feeling like she could touch the sky. And really, hadn't she just been doing that. She'd just been *flying*, soaring through the night like a dream. But this wasn't a dream. This was real and exciting and oh so wonderful.

Eliza felt like a helium balloon was inflating in her chest.

"Careful," Aquila said, releasing Moose but keeping one arm around Eliza's waist.

"I was a gymnast for twelve years," Eliza said. "I think I can keep myself from toppling off."

But she didn't push his hand away.

In front of them, Moose was fumbling with one of the huge windows.

"We have to be careful," Aquila said into the silence as they waited, his deep voice making Eliza feel heady and raw. "Ian can't see you."

"You mean Mr. Eckelson?"

"Yeah, he's kind of our... dad." Again, Aquila's cupid's bow lips curled in that bashful smile. Eliza's cheeks went red-hot and she averted her gaze.

"Lucky you," she said, hoping he couldn't see the flush in the moonlight. Averting her eyes, she watched Moose's wild hair dance in the breeze, scanned the delicate filigree that hung like icicles where gutters should be. "I can't imagine living in a place like this."

"You wouldn't like it so much if you weren't allowed to leave."

"You left tonight."

"Yeah, under cover of darkness and without permission."

There was a note of bitterness in Aquila's voice. But before Eliza could think of a joke to lighten the mood, the window popped open.

"Welcome," Moose said with a gesture too fast to be seen. "To our humble abode."

Glancing back at Aquila, Eliza stepped past Moose and onto the window ledge. Inside, she found herself looking at a dusty attic filled with covered furniture and cobwebs. There were old-fashioned trunks and shimmering surfaces that might have been tarnished silver; wooden boxes labeled with tidy writing; a whole wall of bookshelves. It was, in Eliza's mind, the organized detritus of a sophisticated life. She set her feet carefully on creaking planks, part of her waiting for a ghost to appear, scanning the shadows for more surprises. In the nearest corner was a stack of paintings, the one on top of an elegant woman with graying hair and the kindest smile Eliza had ever seen. She stared at it as she moved aside so that the other two could climb in after her, Aquila ducking low to leave room for his massive wings. Little clouds of dust rose around their feet, tickling Eliza's nose.

"Not exactly five-star," Eliza said with a smirk as Moose darted to the far door.

"What were you expecting for us creatures of the night?" Aquila said, but Moose was already beckoning through another doorway and into a completely different world.

Eliza fought the urge to gasp.

Walking through the Eckelson Mansion was like walking back in time. The walls were cream-colored and plastered with art. Portraits. Landscapes. Fruit. Wrought iron sconces flickered in even intervals. Gilded trim made everything seem at once soft and bright. It was all the kinds of things that she'd seen in museums but never in someone's house. Eliza drifted through all the splendor like a sleepwalker, wondering when she was going to wake up.

"This is…"

"Boring, right?" Moose said, appearing at her shoulder as if he'd been there the whole time. "The real fun is downstairs. Come on, we'll take the elevator. I'll bet Ian's having his midnight cookie in the kitchen."

"You have an *elevator?*"

Neither brother answered, Moose because he was already bounding forward, Aquila because he looked too embarrassed.

"This is insane," Eliza said as she took in the beautiful fresco on the hallway ceiling, swirling like a real Italian sky.

"Do you mean us? Or the house?"

Eliza exhaled a laugh.

"Will it offend you if I say both?"

"I'd be worried if you didn't."

"You guys are so *slow*," Moose complained from in front of them, standing in the frame of an old-fashioned elevator.

"So are we going down to your secret lair or something?" Eliza asked, half-joking. But Aquila only smiled.

"Something like that," he said, stepping aside to let her enter first. She did, drinking in the detail of the clanking door and the velvet carpet of the elevator walls. Aquila had to curl his wings in tight to fit into the cramped space.

The ride was awkward. Moose was bouncing beside her like a kid before Christmas, but Eliza could feel Aquila's tension. And Eliza didn't have the wherewithal to soothe him. Because the whole night had veered so dramatically off the tracks that she had no idea what to expect. The only thing she could do was keep putting one foot in front of the other. Because she didn't want to go home. She felt like she'd just fallen into Wonderland. The Vagabonds, whatever they might be, were the most exciting thing that had happened to Eliza in a long time and she wasn't about to walk away from the ludicrous, wonderful *strangeness* of it all.

So she tightened her shoulders, tried to catch Aquila's eye. But he wasn't looking at her. He was staring at the tips of his boots, strangely timid for his huge size.

Eliza vowed that whatever happened, she wasn't going to let him down.

"Here!" Moose said, leaping around his brother to get the door.

She heard the squeak of ancient hinges. Felt cold air rush in to fill the elevator. But she couldn't see beyond Aquila's bulk. He was avoiding her gaze, frozen in the middle of the elevator, wincing as the machinery clacked and sputtered to a stop.

Finally, as if feeling her eyes on him, he looked up.

"Ready for the freak-show?" he said in a would-be joking voice.

Eliza smiled, summoning all the confidence she could muster. "You bet."

And then she stepped around him, more than ready for whatever came next.

CHAPTER THIRTEEN
Where's the Pizza?

Eliza stepped into a cavern, vaulted and enormous and cluttered with so many things that her head started to spin as she took it all in. One corner was sloped and polished with a few discarded skateboards piled in the middle. Next to it was a cluster of gym equipment, dumbbells and heavily laden bars, ropes climbing the smooth stone walls like ivy and stretching toward the shadowed ceiling. Eliza's eyes scanned over the fitness area and into the carpeted half of the room, hemmed in by bookshelves and decorated with scattered TV's and monitors.

Moose scurried past her, toward two figures playing Mario Kart on an enormous screen, hunched over their controls and tilting back and forth as their characters spun out on the animated road.

"Guys! Hey guys! Hey, guess what!"

"No, no, no, no," muttered a voice even deeper and more sonorous than Aquila's.

Eliza glanced back, but Aquila wasn't looking at her. He was glaring at the ground again, ruffling his feathers uneasily. Eliza had the sinking feeling that he'd just realized what a bad idea this was and was debating how to get her out of there.

In a would-be casual step forward, Eliza slid out of his reach, squinting at the two figures. Her eyes were adjusting to the bright lights and she could feel her brain locking as it tried to make sense of the skin that didn't look like skin…

But something else caught her eye.

A head was tilting out from around a bookshelf with a complexion as dark as her own. It was another boy, hair buzzed, eyebrows pulled together. Eliza lifted an awkward hand to wave in greeting.

Then she realized that the boy's pupils were a milky, ghostly white.

"A-A-Aquila, what do I s-smell?"

Before Aquila could answer, Moose whistled, making everyone flinch.

"*Guys*, you're being rude to our guest."

"G-guest?" the black boy said, emerging from behind the bookshelf and revealing another set of magnificent wings sprouting from thinner, more bony shoulders. Eliza's mouth fell open as her eyes drank them in—leathery rather than feathered, seeped in shadow like something out of a fairy tale.

She jerked back involuntarily as Moose grabbed one of the gamers' heads, forcing it to turn. Her wide eyes shifted from the featherless wings to the face now looking at her. It belonged to a bald, textured body covered in spines, bristles curling over a hairless skull and into the neckline of a shirt like pale tattoos. Soft brown eyes found Eliza's.

The eyes from the clearing...

The other one spoke, back still turned as he drove his cartoon avatar off a cliff.

"Moose, where's the fucking pizza? We send you out with one order and—"

"Girl!"

The spiny boy's voice was strangled, rusty, as if he didn't use it much. But his shout froze in the air, made everything solidify. Moose rocked on his heels, wearing a huge grin beneath his goggles as the final brother turned to face Eliza.

Shimmery, opalescent skin, narrow eyes, dense muscles, and a shock of white hair almost as chaotic as Moose's.

"What... the fuck..."

Eliza fought the urge to scream or run or collapse into a ball and protect her neck.

I've always wanted the world to be stranger than it is, she told herself sternly as all of them stared at her like *she* was weird one.

"Creatures of the underworld," Moose said with an excited flourish, "meet Eliza."

"Aquila, what the *shit*?" said the one with glistening skin.

"I-is that an *o-outsider*?"

The boy with spines stood stock-still, mouth open, hovering in the background. He was the only one whose curiosity didn't draw him closer.

"Hi guys," Eliza said, the words so incredibly inadequate that she flinched in embarrassment.

The blind kid gasped at the sound of her voice, clutching an enormous book in his arms as if it might shield him from the dangerous intruder.

"A-Aquila, what h-have you d-done?"

"Oh, come on you ninny," Moose said with a dismissive wave. "This is way better than *pizza*."

"If I-Ian finds o-out—"

"Eliza, meet Tero." Moose appeared beside the other winged boy as if he'd teleported there, vibrating with excitement. "Short for Pteropus, but that's a mouthful so might as well forget it. He's basically our resident Batman."

"D-don't c-call me t-that."

But Moose had already moved on, leaping over to the short, burly one with shimmering skin.

"This brainless hothead is Otto—" Moose darted away from Otto's fists as they swung toward him, "—whose real name is even worse. *Gymnotiformes*." Moose made a face. "I know he looks like *such* a huggable teddy bear, but I don't recommend giving him a snuggle. That gross slime is toxic."

"You fucking *mosquito*—"

Moose evaded Otto's angry grab with ease, dancing backwards toward the fifth and final brother, hiding behind the rest with his head low and his spines half-raised.

"Finally, we have our resident pincushion and armored tank, Dasypus. But call him Daisy, because he won't hear you anyway."

Moose brought his hands together beside Daisy's head, clapping loudly, but the boy didn't respond. His soulful eyes remained fixed on Eliza as if her appearance spelled the end of times.

Suddenly, Moose was back in front of her, arms thrown wide.

"And you know me, the most important of the Vagabonds. Don't be fooled by their size, the others are more like sidekicks, but I—"

A strong arm appeared, throwing Moose to the side. Otto's wide eyes replaced the goggles, leaning so close to Eliza's face that she could see the way the slime on his skin shone like mother-of-pearl.

"You're a *girl*."

Eliza forced herself to smile, to shove aside her mind's disbelieving protests.

"Well observed," she said.

"B-but h-how did you f-find u-us?" said the blind one. Tero.

"Call me persistent."

"We saved her," Aquila said, appearing at Eliza's shoulder like a guardian angel. "Again."

He smiled down at her, but she couldn't return the expression. Fear was brewing on their faces. Otto, Tero, Daisy; all three of them were looking at her as if she had come here to hunt them. And, in a clear flash of understanding that broke through her haze of shock like light through clouds, she understood. They were scared of *her*. Of what she could do now that she'd seen them.

She couldn't have that.

So Eliza pulled her mouth into the warmest grin she could, meeting each of their eyes.

"Pleasure to meet you all."

Otto snorted.

"Yeah right, like you're not here to throw some peanuts at the fucking circus show?"

"I'm not," Eliza said, taking a deep breath and stepping into the circle. "You saved me at Fitzgerald Base. I thought it would be appropriate to thank you in person."

Silence fell. The cheerful Mario Kart music still played the background, making the whole scene feel even more surreal than it already was.

"Y-you're not a-afraid of us?"

Eliza grinned.

"Why would I be? You seem like good guys to me."

Moose's smile grew until it spread across half his face.

"Yeah, we're heroes. No big deal, you know, rescuing damsels is pretty much our daily routine."

Eliza went to punch his arm, but her fist found only air.

"I'm not a damsel," she said as Moose reappeared behind Tero, peering at her from around the leathery black wings.

"Careful, boys, this one hits back."

But the tension was lifting, dissipated by Eliza's laugh.

With a bold stride, she moved out of the circle, spinning around to take in the enormous cavern.

"This place is amazing," she said, throwing her arms wide. "Wow, is that an original Pac-Man?"

Ignoring the animal instinct to keep her eyes on them, Eliza trotted over to the huge, old-fashioned arcade game.

"I used to love these as a kid."

She could feel them staring, drawing closer, but she kept the determined smile plastered to her face as she jostled the game's joystick.

"Dad got it for Moose," Aquila said, shifting into her line of vision. "It shut him up... for a while, at least."

"Hey!"

Eliza laughed, spun, and settled her hips against the edge of the console. The five boys were clumped around her, so close that her heart hammered in warning. But she grinned at them, exploding with a wild excitement she could barely contain.

"Alright, boys, here's the real question." She cocked her head. "Who's going to play me in Mario Kart?"

CHAPTER FOURTEEN
Something Better

Aquila almost had to wrestle Moose to the ground to keep him from joining them as he took Eliza home.

"I can't carry both of you!" Aquila had exclaimed.

"You did last time!"

"Because I had to! And besides, it was dark out!"

"So?"

Eliza stepped in and patted Moose's arm, grinning at the way the quick-moving boy froze under her touch.

"Don't worry, I'll be back. You're not getting rid of me that easy."

But now, with Aquila setting her down in the shadows outside Meru's central green, she felt a moment of doubt.

"So," Eliza said, tilting her head up to face him as he stepped away, folding his massive wings tight against his body. They looked lustrous in the morning light, shimmering in every shade of blue. "*Will* I be back? Or did I just lie to your brothers?"

Aquila's eyes were pools, deep and swirling with conflicting emotions. She could see the fear, the curiosity, the *hope*. But running beneath it all like a relentless undertow was something Eliza knew all too well.

A bone-deep need to protect his family.

"Eliza, I—"

"I meant what I said before. I won't tell anyone about this. Ever."

Aquila's strong shoulders lifted once and dropped quickly.

"I know you say that now. But what about next week? Or next year? Or what if you meet someone and they ask you about—"

"Aquila," Eliza said, savoring his name, letting it linger in the air. "I never betray my friends."

At that, his face seemed to crack open. She could see past the strong, older-brother facade and into a person just as lost and fumbling and terrified as her.

On impulse, she reached out and curled her fingers around the broad plane of his hand.

"Trust me," she said, squeezing gently. "I'm on your side."

His lips twitched up in a strained attempt at a smile.

"Ian's the only... normal person whose ever been on our side."

"Well he's in good company now." Eliza released his hand, stepped back so she could peer up at him. "Although I don't think Otto likes me much."

Aquila's laugh was as warm and thick as honey.

"Don't worry, he doesn't really like anyone."

"And Daisy? Do you think he'll ever talk to me?"

Aquila's smile faded.

"Maybe. But it's hard for him, you know? He can't hear, so he keeps to himself a lot."

There was more to it than that. Eliza watched a shadow pass over Aquila's face. But she didn't want to spoil the night by asking.

In fact, she didn't want the night to end at all.

"So he's deaf and Tero's blind?" Eliza asked instead. "That's unlucky."

"Ian thinks it's the cost of our, um, modifications." Aquila shrugged again, his feathers rustling in harmony with the autumn leaves. "We each lost a sense."

Eliza cocked her head. "Really?"

"Otto can't feel."

"That sucks."

"Not really," Aquila said with a chuckle. "It makes him really hard to beat in a fight."

"Oh."

"And Moose can't smell…"

Eliza waited, knowing what was coming. Aquila tilted his head back to watch the sun spear through the clouds on the horizon, streaking the darkness with light.

"I… can't taste."

Eliza's mouth fell open. "No. Way. That's awful! You can't taste ice cream? Or Oreos? Or *pizza*?"

Aquila sighed, looking back down at her.

"It's a small price to pay, considering the alternative."

"Says *you*." Eliza shook her head. "Food is awesome."

"I guess I wouldn't know."

"Poor thing."

"Hey," Aquila said, "at least I can fly."

"Touché."

Eliza glared at the roof of her dorm building, now orange in the dawn. She had to go in there. Soon enough, Meru would start waking up. Students would mill around campus and the morning joggers would puff by and the cars would rumble to life and the world would continue as if nothing had changed. But *everything* had changed. Eliza felt like the universe had opened up and let her in on a grand secret and she was already dying to go back to that huge, cavernous basement and laugh with Moose and read books with Tero and watch Otto work out and try to get Daisy to talk to her.

But she had to go back to the real world.

For now.

"Promise me," Eliza said, perhaps a little more forcefully than she'd meant to. "Promise me this isn't goodbye."

Aquila grinned.

"You're not getting rid of us that easy."

"That's my line," Eliza said, shoving his arm and finding him entirely immobile. "I guess you should go, before someone sees you and runs screaming."

"I'm pretty terrifying, you know."

70

"Straight out of a horror movie."

Watching Aquila unfurl his wings and lift into the air, throwing one last smile over his shoulder, Eliza knew then and there that she would do anything to keep his secret.

Her body felt supercharged as she trotted toward her dorm. Light and electric and maybe even... peaceful? For once, she didn't want to start a fight or draw attention or ignite chaos. Her writhing demons were satiated, curled up and quiet for the first time in ages. All she wanted to do was get through the day without trouble so that she might see Aquila and his brothers again. Return to that separate, shining world beneath the Eckelson mansion. How was it possible for so much to change in just twenty-four hours?

She wasn't sure, but she never wanted to let it go.

She was strutting, hips swinging, practically dancing...

And then she saw the headmaster standing in front of her dorm, staring at her with an expression that told her that it didn't matter if she had no desire to find trouble right now.

Trouble had found her.

"Elizabeth Mason," the headmaster growled. "You have some explaining to do."

CHAPTER FIFTEEN
Secrets

Eliza sat in the most aggressively unhelpful position she could fathom, arms wrapped around her torso, legs splayed, eyes fixed on the plaque that read *Headmaster*. She looked every bit the surly teenager brought in for disciplinary action. But what they couldn't, what she wouldn't *let* them see, was the fear arcing through her like solar flares and the instinct making the back of her neck prickle.

They know.

"I'll ask you again, Ms. Mason, where were you last night?" said the woman from the army base, those dark eyes glittering.

When the headmaster had shown Eliza into his office, she'd expected her homeroom teacher or dorm mother, maybe even the cops. But instead, to Eliza's horror, she'd walked in to find a short woman with a sharp haircut sitting behind the headmaster's mahogany desk, two men in uniform looming behind her. The woman had introduced herself as Amile Robillard, head of science and operations at Fitzgerald Labs.

And then the questions had begun.

"Ms. Mason, we know you were not in your dorm this morning. Your roommate says you left last night with her bike and didn't return."

"She's lying," Eliza said through clenched teeth.

"I'm afraid we have more reason to trust Victoria Bent than we have to trust you, don't we Private?"

One of the soldiers saluted, fingers snapping to his forehead. Eliza glared at him, taking in the blonde hair, blue eyes, thin lips.

It couldn't be...

"Private Bent here vouches for his sister's honesty. Who will vouch for yours?"

Eliza dropped her gaze, struggling to hide her surprise.

Tori has a brother in the army?

How had she never known that?

The woman leaned forward on thin elbows, glowering at Eliza.

"Ms. Mason, it's a simple enough question. Tell us where you were between the hours of eleven and six."

Eliza bit the inside of her cheek, thinking of bashful Tero who had finally allowed Eliza to run her hands along the velvety skin of his wings, of excitable Moose who had practically tumbled over himself to show her his collection of vintage N64 games. If they traced her to Ian Eckelson's estate, if they found out about the Vagabonds...

An idea came to her, as unappealing as it was brilliant.

Might as well make Tori's rumors useful.

"Haven't you heard?" Eliza said with a smirk. "I have a boyfriend off-campus. I was with him."

Amile's smile was sharp enough to flay skin from bone.

"Very well. Would you provide us with a name and address?"

"I will not," Eliza said.

"Now Eliza—" the headmaster piped in, but Amile cut him off.

"You're making a most unwise decision, Ms. Mason. Do you know who we are?"

"Yeah. Grunts in uniforms."

"We are the *army*, Ms. Mason. Do you really want to make an enemy of the United States government?"

"Sounds exciting."

"That's not the word I'd choose."

Eliza met the woman's eyes with her own stubborn ferocity, unblinking, unshifting, her body twisted into a knot of total resistance.

For a long, brittle moment neither of them moved.

Finally, Amile sighed.

"Very well, Mrs. Mason, if that's your decision."

"It is."

The headmaster appeared in the corner of her vision, twisting his hands.

"I'm so sorry, Ms. Robillard, our students are not usually so difficult. But this one came with a file as thick as my laptop, so I'm afraid it's not exactly surprising that she'd be off getting into trouble."

Amile pushed to her feet, not a single strand of black hair out of place as she nodded to the two privates.

"We'll be in touch. Just make sure she doesn't go anywhere."

"Of course not, absolutely. Please, let us know if there's anything we can do to help with your, er, investigation."

Eliza glared at the toes of her sneakers, seething with fury at the obsequious headmaster, the woman, her bodyguards.

But mostly, Eliza was terrified as Amile answered, the words as slimy as Otto's skin.

"I'm afraid its top secret, headmaster. But the army appreciates your concern."

~~~

"What was *that* about?"

Joe was waiting for Eliza on the front steps as usual, his expression one of apprehensive concern.

"Nothing," Eliza said, glancing over her shoulder and chilled to find Amile watching her from the driveway. A car pulled up behind the woman, black and unmarked.

Eliza spun away, fear pulling tight around her spine.

"Is this about Friday night?"

"Joe, drop it."

"Eliza, we're friends."

"Joe…"

"You can tell me anything."

Eliza stopped in front of homeroom, shoulders tight, adrenaline pounding so hard she felt like her body was on fire. *I can't, can I?* Telling Joe would mean dragging him into this mess. And it was a mess, she could see that now. The night at the Eckelson mansion had been a magical bubble. But she'd crashed back to the real world, a world that wouldn't welcome the five strange boys the way she did but seemed just as interested in finding them.

Eliza took a deep breath, facing her best friend.

"Trust me. You don't want to know."

She made to turn away, but Joe's voice stopped her.

"Is that... is it true? That you have a boyfriend? I mean, that would be fine, you know, if you did..."

Joe's eyes were earnest enough to break Eliza's heart. She put a hand over his, squeezing his fingers, thinking of all the things she wished she could tell him.

"No, Joe. It's not a guy."

At least, it's not just one *guy.*

Joe's lips twitched up in a sad smile.

"I know I'm always saying that I don't want to be a part of your adventures, Eliza. But I think you need me. As a voice of reason and all that."

A laugh surprised its way out of Eliza, bright and calming. She bumped her elbow into Joe's side, as grateful as ever for his stalwart presence.

"I'll keep that in mind," she said, and meant it.

CHAPTER SIXTEEN
Reckless

It took everything Eliza had to make it to dinner without punching someone. The scandalized whispers had morphed into slurs, taunts, questions. People weren't bothering to keep their snide voyeurism quiet anymore, now wearing their curiosity as openly as their disgust. Even the teachers looked at her with expressions of worried aversion, as if she'd developed a bad smell.

Only Joe stayed by her side, plopping down at her cafeteria table with his steak and fries.

"I wonder if there's a vaccination against gossip," he said, a frown wrinkling the freckles on his nose. "It sure seems like a virus to me."

Eliza sighed.

"You okay?" he asked.

"What do you think?" Eliza said, her head in her hands. She stared forlornly at her salmon fillet, unable to eat as fury and fear gnawed on the empty lining of her stomach.

When would the army be back for her? What was Amile doing right now? Were the Vagabonds safe? Was Aquila staying out of sight? When would the students of Meru move on?

How was she going to keep this up?

"I think boarding school is like a pressure cooker." Joe lifted a fry and bit down thoughtfully. "Like, if we could all go home and cool off and be reminded that there are more interesting things to life than high school, don't you think they'd be a bit less..." He gestured with his fry as if he could envelop the whole day with a fried piece of potato.

Eliza chuckled halfheartedly.

"Maybe. But I've watched *Mean Girls*. I don't think it gets any better."

"Oh come on, that movie's clearly exaggerated for comedic effect."

Eliza tilted her face up, eyebrows rising.

"I think you need to get out more often."

Joe threw a fry at her. "For your information, I happened to go through a human psychology phase when I was thirteen. I wanted to understand why people don't make any sense, so I read a bunch about interpersonal dynamics. It was quite fascinating."

"I don't think you can learn about people from books, Joe."

"I'd argue that's the only place you can learn about them," he said with a sniff. "Besides, I'd rather deal with fictional characters and theories than with *them*." He gestured with another fry to where Tori and her entourage were sitting, heads together like some kind of sports group.

Eliza scowled.

"Can't argue there."

But even as she glared, Tori was peeling away from the cluster, tossing her hair in a shimmer of gold as she stalked between tables. Toward the back of the cafeteria.

Toward them.

Eliza straightened. Joe's eyes widened.

"Tori," Eliza said in greeting.

Tori looked around. Tossed her hair again.

And then slid into the seat beside Eliza.

"Look," Tori said in a low voice as the whispers swirled around them, fed by the strange sight of the girl everyone wanted to be sitting beside the girl no one wanted to get close to. "I know you saw... something. In that office."

Eliza sat back, folding her arms.

"Yeah, I saw some*one* very interesting."

Tori's lips pursed but she continued.

77

"It's not worth talking about. I don't think anyone needs to know about... him."

Eliza frowned, meeting Tori's clear blue eyes. They were such a different shade than Aquila's.

"I disagree, Tori. I think he's just as interesting as boyfriends on army bases. Don't you?"

"Come on, Eliza, don't be a bitch."

"Oh, I don't think *I'm* the bitch."

"Um, ladies, I'm not sure—"

But Tori rolled right over Joe, leaning in so that her whisper filled the crackling air between them.

"I don't want things to get ugly."

"Maybe I do."

"You think I can't make things worse?"

"Oh, I know you can."

"Eliza, I don't give a shit about your stupid tragic past or whatever. If you don't keep this between us—"

Eliza shoved to her feet, rage clawing up her throat. Her fingers tightened into fists. If she didn't get out of here soon...

"Tori, this has been a *lovely* chat, but my illicit boyfriend is waiting. Can't disappoint my fans."

Forcing herself to smile, Eliza pushed her salmon away and stalked out of the cafeteria, leaving behind a shocked Joe and a red-faced Tori.

She felt like a thunderstorm as she rolled back to her dorm. How could Tori *say* that? Eliza would give everything she owned to have her sibling back, and here was Tori trying to *hide hers*? The gall of that girl, the god damned *nerve*...

Kicking her door open, Eliza crashed into her bedroom, ready to plug herself in and listen to angry rock music and try not to cry. But before she could take another step, a figure emerged from the shadows.

"*Aquila?*"

Eliza rushed inside, easing the door shut behind her, not daring to believe. But there he was, filling her room like a giant, surrounded by a constellation of shoes and discarded clothing.

"What are you doing here?" Eliza hissed.

"I saw them pull you aside this morning. What happened? Did you tell them anything?"

"Of course not. How did you find my room?"

Aquila shrugged.

"Tero's pretty good with computers."

"Ok, I will save being creeped out for later, but you should go. Really, I have a roommate and she's awful and she could be back at any minute."

Eliza made to shove Aquila toward the open window, throwing wild glances over her shoulder. But Aquila stopped her, fingers curling around her wrist. He ducked his head to look her in the eye.

"Hey, are you okay?"

Eliza froze. Sighed.

"You're lucky you don't have to deal with high school," she said before realizing how *stupid* she sounded.

She shook her head.

"Sorry, that was insensitive."

Aquila chuckled.

"I have four brothers. That's the most sensitive thing I've heard all week."

Eliza lifted her face only to find Aquila's right there, shockingly close. His lips were slightly parted, perfectly sculpted, inches from her own. In the dim light of her bedroom, he looked mythical and huge, his wings taking up more space than seemed allowed. But his eyes were soft, radiating the kind of warmth she had spent so many years chasing since Katie's death and had never found.

"Eliza, I—"

But at that moment, they both heard the ominous click of a key entering a lock.

"Go, go!"

Aquila didn't need to be told twice. As Tori's key turned the handle, Aquila leapt onto the window frame. He shifted, ducked, stepped out onto the ledge to make way for his enormous wings.

Eliza's breath caught in her throat as Tori burst into the room.

"Look, Eliza, maybe we can..."

But Tori's words trailed off. Her mouth fell open. Wide eyes rimmed in make-up slid off Eliza and onto the feathered wing still visible through the window. Eliza tried to step in, block Tori's view of Aquila. It was too late. She heard a *whoosh*, felt the rushing shift of air. Aquila was gone.

But the damage had been done.

Eliza forced herself to smile, held her hands out as Tori's lips hung open in a perfect, almost comical O.

"I can explain everything."

CHAPTER SEVENTEEN
Oops

"Tori, talk to me," Eliza pleaded.

But just like the night before, Tori refused to meet Eliza's gaze, moving around their tiny dorm room as if nothing had changed. As if it was any old morning.

As if she hadn't seen a giant blue-green wing slipping out of their window.

Eliza watched helplessly as Tori pulled her hair into a ponytail and began to paint on her mascara.

"It's not what you think. It's—"

Tori grabbed her bag and made to leave the room. Desperate, Eliza lunged forward, grabbing the other girl's arm.

"Okay, fine, we both have secrets here. But if you don't tell anyone about last night, I won't tell anyone about your brother."

Tori curled her lip in that imperious smirk that made her at once beautiful and ugly.

"I don't know what you're talking about," Tori said, yanking her arm out of Eliza's grip and stalking into the hallway. "And don't threaten me."

Eliza followed.

"This is a two-way street, Tori," she whispered, swinging her own bag over her shoulder and ignoring the scandalized looks from the other students at her untamed hair, untucked shirt, mismatched knee-high socks. It didn't matter, the school would be talking about her anyway. She had more important things to worry about.

Tori shoved open the front door and Eliza squinted in the sudden light.

"I don't know why you don't want people to know about him," Eliza said, making Tori freeze. There were people around. Popular boys and girls hungry for new gossip. If they heard Eliza, if they put the puzzle pieces together…

"Leave me alone," Tori hissed. "You're a freak and your boyfriend is a freak and I don't want anything to do with it."

"Then swear to me you won't say anything."

Tori opened her mouth, but at that moment three shadows fell over them. Eliza blinked, eyes still adjusting.

It was Amile, flanked by two new privates. Tori's brother was nowhere to be seen.

"Ms. Mason, if we could have a word?"

Eliza froze.

When she was five, her parents had taken them to a ski resort in Maine. There had been a pond outside their cabin, frozen and sparkling and so *alluring* to Eliza that she'd dragged Katie out for an impromptu midnight ice-skating session while Mom and Dad slept. But when they'd reached the middle, Eliza had heard a reverberating *crack*. She'd watched, petrified, as the spidery, sinister threads of broken ice whipped toward them under the dusting of snow. Eliza had been so scared she couldn't move, but Katie—always the one with more sense—had grabbed her arm and dragged her to shore, sprinting even as the surface of the pond started to fracture beneath them. They barely made it to the shallows when the surface finally failed, but luckily emerged with only wet feet and the chilling knowledge that the night could have ended very differently.

Now, in the bright October sunshine eleven years later, Eliza felt that same cracking. That same feeling of dread rushing toward her beneath the deceptive cover of the real world.

"Not now, I have to get to class," Eliza said, trying to push past. But from the corner of her eye, she caught Tori's lips curling into an ominous smirk. The girl's blonde head tilted up, offering her most innocent smile to the two soldiers.

"I'm sure Eliza's just exhausted," Tori said, voice dripping with malice. "After all, she had such a *strange* guy over last night."

Time slowed. Eliza spun to Tori, met her eyes.

"You vindictive—"

"Detain her."

Those two words, spoken with such cold calm, cleaved through Eliza's shock.

She ran.

The men made to grab her, but Eliza twisted out of their grasp. She leapt onto the railing, propelled herself off it and into the garden. Greenery crumpled beneath her sneakers. Shocked gasps rose like mushroom clouds behind her. She barely noticed. Her arms pumped as she sprinted around the corner of the dorm, followed by the heavy thuds of booted feet. She didn't dare look back, didn't dare check how close the soldiers were behind her.

One thought pulsed above all others.

She had to warn Aquila.

Tori didn't seem at all motivated to keep what she'd seen to herself. And now Eliza *had* to reach him, tell him to stay hidden. It wasn't safe for the brothers to be out, not now, not with Amile and her soldiers circling like vultures.

Eliza needed to reach Ian Eckelson's estate and *soon*.

But Tori's bike was still in town, probably stolen by now, and her own...

Joe's truck!

Veering sharply and vaulting another railing, Eliza crashed through a cluster of outraged students, sprinting for the front doors.

Please be there, please be there.

But she needn't have worried. Joe was as reliable as Meru's ability to spread gossip, standing on the steps as he had every morning for the past month and a half. He grinned automatically when he saw her, but his smile faded as he took in her flushed cheeks, pumping arms, the way her sneakers dug into the grass and sent it flying.

"Eliza, what the—"

"Where... are your truck... keys?" Her voice was ragged, barely audible over her rasping breath.

"What?"

"Your truck, Joe! I need you to drive me somewhere!"

Joe stepped back.

"But it's homeroom, and we have an exam..."

Eliza chanced a look over her shoulder and was horrified to see the two soldiers emerging from around the dorm, crashing toward her. She spun back, panting as she leaned in toward her best friend, guilt and fear pulling tight around her lungs.

"Listen to me, Joe, you were right. Something is going on and it's weirder than you can imagine. I'll tell you everything, I promise, but right now we need to get in your truck and *leave*, okay? Trust me on this."

Joe's eyes flickered between Eliza and the two men shouldering their way through the morning rush of students. Eliza held her breath, not sure how far Joe's loyalty could be stretched. He was a good friend, but was he willing to break the law for her? Ignore army orders? Go against the government's will?

"Come on," Joe said, grabbing her hand and yanking her through the doors.

CHAPTER EIGHTEEN
P.E.

He led the way, shoving through the bodies cluttered in the entrance hall. Indignant cries filled the air, but they moved like cannonballs through the main building. Behind them, deep voices barked orders, but the words were lost in the chaos that the corridor had become. Eliza ducked her head, pulling Joe down another hall.

"This way," she gasped.

They were scrambling past chemistry labs and dissection rooms. Eliza found herself thinking about the five brothers, the Vagabonds. What would happen if the army found them? Would they end up on some table somewhere, being peeled apart like anesthetized frogs?

Eliza would never let that happen.

They reached an emergency exit, emblazoned with a big red sign that read **Alarm Will Sound.**

"I've always wanted to see if that sign was lying," Joe panted as Eliza planted one hand on the metal bar and pushed.

A wailing shriek split the air.

Eliza grinned, thinking of all the homerooms spilling out into that central hallway.

That should hold those bastards up, she thought as the two of them tumbled out of the dark building and back into the sun.

"My truck's... over... there," Joe said, struggling to breathe. Eliza snatched his hand and they were off again, ducking through cars and sprinting across hot pavement.

"Come on, come on," Eliza chanted as Joe ripped open his messenger bag, fumbling for his keys, tripping over his own feet and almost crashing to the concrete before Eliza grabbed his arm and hauled him upright.

"Got em!" he shouted, ripping out a jingling keychain.

"Open it!"

Eliza swung herself around the bed of the old-fashioned pick-up, bouncing her knees as she waited for Joe to leap into the high cabin and lean over to unlock her door.

"Go, go, go!" she shouted before she'd even sat down.

The truck started with a cough. It had always been a paradox with Joe, that his parents were as rich as gods but he drove a car that was held together with duct tape and prayers. He said he liked it old-school, but in the third week of the semester Eliza had discovered that Joe paid for the truck himself. For six sunburnt summers he'd worked as a lifeguard to save enough to buy himself a car. Bashfully, he'd admitted that his parents paid the insurance on it. But Eliza had seen the pride in his face when he'd told her about walking into the dealership all by himself and picking out Old Betty.

Right then Eliza found herself wishing that Joe had accepted his parents' offer for a fancy sports car.

Old Betty growled to life, trundling out of the parking lot as fast as Joe could accelerate her. Eliza twisted, glancing over her shoulder through the dirty sliding window.

The two soldiers burst out of the main building. Their cold eyes found the rusty old truck as it pulled onto the road.

Without a word, they spun back, caught the closing door, and disappeared.

"The clearing," Eliza panted, trying to ignore the roaring in her ears. "Go to the clearing we went to on Friday."

"But there's nothing there," Joe said, his eyes frantic as he clutched the wheel.

"They won't be able to see us from the road. We'll lay low for a bit and wait for them to stop looking."

Joe took a shaky breath. Another. His knuckles were white, his eyes fixed dead ahead.

Eliza had never been embarrassed of the things she did. Punching bullies, accepting dares, leaping off cliffs into churning oceans. It had always been just her. Her against the world, her taking risks, her dealing with people who deserved it. Despite what her mother said, Eliza had a code.

And she'd broken it.

"Are you... are you okay?" Eliza asked, shame squirming in her belly.

"Oh yeah," Joe said, his voice strangely high-pitched. "I'm *fine*. You know, I've never skipped class. Maybe it's something I needed to do before graduating."

"Joe..."

"I mean, the running from the army part wasn't exactly in the plan. And I'd rather not have missed our exam. But maybe it's fate and all that."

"Joe, I'm so sorry," Eliza said.

"So when are you going to tell me what's going on?" Joe glanced at her, eyes enormous. "Before or after they start shooting?"

Eliza sighed as the truck swerved onto the highway, Old Betty whining in protest.

"So that night... on the army base..." Eliza inhaled. "I did see something." Joe's knuckles grew whiter and Eliza stared at them, unable to look at his face. "Something I wasn't supposed to see."

"Of course you did," Joe said in that *I-should-have-known* voice that her mother sometimes used.

Eliza flinched but forced herself to continue.

"I think they're doing experiments there. There was something... wrong with one of the soldiers. He was strong, but like... insanely strong, throwing people around like they didn't weigh anything."

"Maybe you hit your head falling off the fence."

"*I know what I saw*," Eliza snapped before catching herself. She clenched her fists in her lap. "Sorry, it's just... I ran. And they chased me. And then..."

Eliza trailed off. How could she make Joe understand? How could she tell him about Aquila? About the Vagabonds? About the wonderful, strange world she'd tumbled into beneath Eckelson's mansion?

Joe swerved the truck off the highway and down the dirt road of Exit Two. He drove all the way into the woods, turning off the truck only when they were both sure they couldn't be seen from the road. In the silence of the deep forest, broken only by the cheerful birds and muttering wind, Joe just stared at the trees, every muscle in his body taut enough to snap.

"And then what, Eliza?"

She winced. Half of her had been hoping he'd lost track of the conversation.

"And then... I met someone."

"You *met* someone? What on Earth does that mean? Like, *someone* someone?"

She inhaled, long and slow.

"Five someones, actually. They're the reason those men are after me. The army wants to find them too."

Joe seemed to deflate, slumping in his seat.

"I'm losing my mind."

"I know how you feel," she said with a wan smile.

"So what now? Where do we go now that we're *fugitives*?"

The last word came out strangled, filled with all the fear and frustration that Joe was not taking out on her. In that moment, Eliza could have kissed him. He'd done everything she asked, gone along with her mad scheme even though it was so out of character that Joe might as well have followed her into a night club. Like a true friend, Joe had trusted her despite all the reasons not to.

It was time to return the favor.

Eliza curled one hand around his shoulder, ignoring the way he flinched at her touch.

"Now I have some friends I'd like you to meet."

CHAPTER NINETEEN
Unlocked Doors

As Joe's eyes jumped between the gold-tipped spires and the gilded front door of the Eckelson mansion, Eliza couldn't help but wonder if this was a bad idea. Maybe they should run back to the pickup they'd pulled off into the manicured forest inside the fence, come back another way, try something else. But what? She had no way of contacting Aquila. No way of climbing onto the roof and sneaking in the way Moose showed her. And they had to get inside before someone drove by and saw them standing there.

The only thing she could think of was the front door.

Unfortunately.

"Um, Eliza, are you sure about this?" Joe lingered at the bottom of the steps, scratching at a bug bite on his forearm. "I mean, maybe we're already fugitives or whatever, but trespassing is still a crime."

"I told you, I've been here before."

"Oookay," Joe said, and Eliza could see the effort it took to keep the apprehension out of his voice. The spot on his arm was growing redder and redder against cream-pale skin.

She stepped up to him, wrapping her dark fingers around his hand and squeezing, pulling it away from the bite.

"Do you trust me?"

"Of course."

She smiled.

"Then let's go inside."

Tugging Joe behind her and praying that she wasn't about to get everyone into even *bigger* trouble, she stepped up to the front door. With a quick glance over one shoulder to make sure there wasn't any black car—or black-haired woman—watching through the fence, Eliza knocked.

There was no answer.

"Maybe he's not home?" Joe said with a shrug. "Or taking a nap. Don't old people do that a lot?"

"He wasn't that old," Eliza said, knocking again.

Still no response.

"Oh darn, looks like we'll have to come back another—*what are you doing?*"

But Eliza wasn't listening. She was wrapping her hand around the bronze door handle, pursing her lips.

The thing about being surrounded by rich private school students was that Eliza knew all too well how wealthy people behaved. When money wasn't an issue, who cared about a little thing like theft? Phones could be replaced. Police reports could be filed. And security footage could be checked for the really valuable things. There were probably cameras coating every inch of this mansion, sensors monitoring the lawn and walls, and because of that she suspected that someone like Ian Eckelson wouldn't be too worried about anyone coming through his front door.

She turned the handle.

Just as she thought, it was open.

"*Eliza.*"

But she ignored Joe, moving inside on cautious, cat-like feet.

The main room was silent, pristine, almost eerily neat. Last time Eliza had stood here, she'd seen the comic book on the side table. The folded-over carpet. Those things were gone, leaving the room strangely lifeless.

A thought occurred to her.

Oh no.

Terror bubbled in Eliza's stomach, pulsing nauseatingly in her veins. Was she too late? Had that woman already found them? Had the army somehow traced her steps, raided the mansion in the time between the chase and their arrival?

Or did the Vagabonds leave, knowing it wasn't safe for them in Scottstown anymore?

"Eliza, are you crazy?" Joe was hissing behind her, leaning through the doorframe without actually setting foot inside. "This is breaking and entering! You're going to—"

She didn't stick around to hear what she was going to do.

Instead, she lunged up the stairs.

No, no, no.

The word beat in tandem with her heart, brimming with dread. They had to be safe. They had to be. If they got into trouble because of her, if they *left*...

She crashed onto the top floor, hitting the opposite wall and rattling a painting that probably cost more than her tuition. She paused, panting, attention flashing over gilded frames and hardwood doors.

Where was that stupid elevator?

"What's gotten into you?!" Joe gasped, trailing her onto the landing. "First you run from the *government*, now this? Did they slip you something in the headmaster's office?"

"Joe, help me find an elevator."

"*What?*"

"An elevator!"

She began to run down the hall, glancing down side-corridors and feeling the weight of the mansion settling on her shoulders. It was so huge. Sprawling and vast and endless and *not helping*. How was she ever going to find the—

There!

It appeared down a long hallway, the bronze cage almost gold in the warm light of the sconces. Eliza veered, barreling toward the old-fashioned grate.

"That thing... looks... like a death trap," Joe panted.

92

"Get in," she said, yanking open the grate and swinging herself inside.

Thankfully Joe did, although his eyes were swarming with misgivings. He leaned against the other side of the elevator, looking at Eliza as if she'd finally cracked.

"Am I allowed to ask questions now?" Joe asked in a tone that might have been joking if not for the tremor in his hands.

She ignored him, unable to think beyond her throbbing fear, glaring at the rocky shaft as it slid past beyond the door.

Please let them be safe, please let them be safe, please let them be safe, Eliza chanted in her mind. But it wasn't just that. Selfishly, pathetically, she was almost more terrified that they'd gone away and left her behind, ended her whole adventure before it could even begin. Eliza couldn't go back, not now, not knowing that there was more to the world than Meru and Tori and Scottstown.

So she prayed to the tune of the elevator trundling into the basement and squealing to a halt.

"Eliza, please," Joe whispered as she went to open the door. "You gotta give me something."

She froze in the act of yanking open the creaky grate. Guilt knotted her intestines. She'd put him through so much today, asked him for more than she had any right to expect. But what could she say? *There might be some people beyond these doors that are like no one you've ever met. They're the reason the military is after us. But they might be gone or captured or somewhere else and I have no idea where.*

Eliza forced herself to smile, contorting her features into an expression she could only hope was comforting.

"You'll see," she said, opening the door. "Just... you'll see."

She tried to have no expectations, but she still held her breath as her eyes adjusted to the shadowed cavern.

CHAPTER TWENTY
Gone

The cavernous basement of the Eckelson mansion was in chaos.

"What the—?"

Eliza let the door slam shut behind them as she and Joe stepped into the huge chamber, both of them gaping at the scene. Ian Eckelson was hovering behind Tero, who was bent over a keyboard, Moose flitting about nervously behind them. Aquila and Otto were shouting, standing on opposite sides of the skate park.

"Why can't you *think* about what you're saying for once?"

"Well why does he have to be such a fucking wuss!"

"Why do you have to be such an asshole?"

"Fuck you!"

Daisy was nowhere to be seen.

Eliza made to move forward, to help, and then remembered Joe. If things looked strange to *her*, she couldn't even begin to imagine how he was taking it. She touched his arm, tried to snag his huge, round eyes.

"It's okay. They're the guys I told you about. They're friends."

Joe's mouth still hung open, but he managed to meet her gaze. She reached up, tapping the bottom of his jaw to close it.

"Just… follow my lead," she whispered.

"Eliza!"

Aquila's voice filled the cavern and she swung around to meet him, shielding Joe with her body and holding her hands wide.

"Look, I can explain—"

"Have you seen Daisy?"

Eliza balked. "No, what happened?"

His eyes were wild, frantic, as if Eliza's fear from moments ago had been injected into him instead.

Aquila ran his fingers through his hair, making it stand on end.

"He ran off earlier today and we have no idea where he went."

A new voice rolled over her response, rumbling with disapproval.

"Aquila, what is the meaning of this?"

Aquila winced and Eliza fought the urge to reach up and wipe away the crease between his eyebrows. He hunched his shoulders, shifting aside as Ian Eckelson marched up to them, radiating with much more power than she remembered from the tottering old man.

"You again," Eckelson said, eyes sweeping up and down Eliza's strong frame.

"Dad, she's—"

"A mistake," Eckelson interrupted, folding his arms.

"Please sir, I promise," Eliza cut in. "I'm only here to help."

"And your friend?"

"He's...." Eliza glanced back, grimacing at the shell-shocked expression on Joe's face. "Safe."

"I doubt that. You should have taken my advice, child."

Eliza straightened at the word, clenching her fists at her sides as she struggled to keep her response civil.

"Look, the military knows about them. They were questioning me today at school."

"So you led them here?" Eckelson said, gaze flinty and terrifying.

"I came to *warn* you," Eliza snarled. "Your... sons are in danger."

"They're always in danger."

"Not like this."

Eckelson's eyes narrowed.

"What would you know about *this*? You come here once and suddenly think you understand everything? You have no idea the situation you seem so determined to nose into."

Eliza glared at him, unblinking.

"And you have no idea what I'm capable of."

"I have an inkling."

It didn't sound like a compliment.

Aquila stepped between them, fingers splayed wide.

"Look, can we deal with this later? We need to find Daisy. If what Eliza's saying is true, then we don't have much time."

"Especially with that idiot looking like a fucking tree trunk," Otto muttered.

"Will you *shut up*," Aquila spat, rounding on his brother.

"Moose," Eckelson said, his deep voice cutting through the air. "You and Aquila go find him. We'll try and track his phone."

"Of course, yes, yeah, we'll do that," Moose said, moving so fast he seemed to shimmer.

"H-his c-cell is still o-off, but I-I think I-I can turn it on r-remotely," Tero said, fingers flying over the Braille keyboard, a single headphone dangling from one ear.

"We can help," Eliza said, side-stepping Aquila's bulk and facing Eckelson. "Listen, I know you have no reason to trust me. And maybe I never should have climbed that fence."

"Among other things…"

"But," Eliza said, talking over him. "I'm here now. Joe has a truck. We can scout on the ground while your sons look from the sky, see what we can find. He can't have gone far, right?"

She looked to Aquila, suddenly struck by the ludicrous thought that maybe Daisy *could* have gone far. Maybe he had some crazy speed or teleporting ability that she didn't know about.

"No, he's got to be close," Aquila said, nodding. "With your help, we can cover twice the ground."

96

"And maybe he's in town. We can search there, try to find him before someone else does."

"I think people might notice his fucking *spines*," muttered Otto.

"*You* will stay here," Aquila snapped. "I'll take Moose."

"At your service," said Moose, appearing at Aquila's elbow. His usually bright face was marred with worry, but he vibrated with the same frenetic energy Eliza remembered from before. "Hi, Eliza. Who's the guy? Did he follow you here? Do you need me to deal with him?"

Eliza winced.

She'd almost forgotten about poor Joe, thrust into an adventure he hadn't asked for and, unlike her, probably didn't want. Turning, she found him frozen and wearing a silent scream of an expression. She reached out, squeezed his hand, and felt a smidgen of relief when he snapped his mouth shut.

"This is Joe. He's a friend. No need to, er, deal with him."

"Hi," Joe wheezed, eyes fixed on Otto's glistening skin.

"We'll do introductions later," Aquila said, eyes dropping to Eliza's hand on Joe's and then snapping back to her face. "Right now, we've got someone to find."

"Be careful," Eckelson said, but he wasn't looking at his sons. He was staring at Eliza, his expression etched with all the concern of a worried parent.

And Eliza had the distinct impression that she was the very thing he was worried about.

CHAPTER TWENTY-ONE
The Funny One

"Are you okay?"

Joe didn't answer. His eyes were fixed on the Scottstown streets as Old Betty looped between houses and through the downtown, round as dinner plates. Eliza's attention kept flickering to the city that had long ago gone dark, hunting for the telltale spines and armored skin and soulful brown eyes.

Nothing.

They'd been driving all afternoon in silence, hunting for the missing Vagabond. And now, with their continual failure pulling her temper tighter, spreading her patience thinner, Eliza couldn't keep herself from glancing at Joe, desperate to know what was going on behind his wide-eyed shock.

"Joe?"

He blinked. Eliza leaned in, playing with the frayed edge of her sleeve.

"Look, I'm sorry. I know this is a lot, but I can explain."

"No, it's fine," he said, strangled voice, strangely high-pitched again. "I should have known, really. I mean, it makes sense, right, that you'd have some kind of secret like this. Things were too good to be true."

"What do you mean?"

A red flush bloomed on Joe's neck, creeping up the pale edge of his jaw.

"Nothing."

"Listen to me, this *just* happened. The night I climbed the fence into Fitzgerald base, I ended up getting…" She swallowed. "Saved. Those guys, they took me back to Ian Eckelson's mansion. That's how I ended up there."

Joe's eyes didn't stray from the pavement as the streetlights bloomed to life above them. The silence was dense and frustrating. What could she do? She couldn't force him to speak, couldn't make him talk to her or be magically OK with the sheer weirdness of everything that had happened. And besides, her mind was too full of her own worry to try and placate his. Eliza twisted to look behind Old Betty, wondering when the military was going to track them down, knowing she wouldn't stop searching until they got word that Daisy had been recovered, Amile Robillard be damned.

Finally, Joe spoke.

"Who's *they*?"

"What?"

"When you say *they* took you to the mansion... who do you mean?"

Eliza winced but forced herself to answer.

"Moose. The fast one. And... Aquila."

A muscle was twitching in Joe's jaw, his teeth clenched so hard it was a wonder they didn't break.

"The guy with wings?"

"The feathered ones, not the black ones," Eliza said with another wince, resisting the urge to check the skies and see if Aquila was flying over them now. "He's kind of like their leader, I think. The other one with wings is Tero. And Otto has the shimmery skin."

Joe grunted noncommittally. Eliza shifted in her seat so she could scan the alley behind Mr. Tim's pizza, trying to ignore the shrill voice in her brain reminding her how the words coming out of her mouth must sound to Joe, who hadn't been there, hadn't seen what she had.

"Look," she went on, "they're really great. Just give them a chance, I know they look... unusual." She pretended not to hear the disbelieving snort. "But they're nice guys."

"Right. Of course." Joe swallowed, as if to gather his courage. "Eliza, have you even stopped to think about how *dangerous* all this is?"

She swung back to face him, gaze sharp and blazing.

"They're not dangerous."

Joe chuckled, but it was a mirthless, drawn-out sound, filled with the stress of the day.

"Clearly, you haven't seen enough Marvel movies. Eliza, we're the *normal* people. If things go down, we'll be the first to die. I mean, you probably won't since Aquila likes you..."

"It's not like that."

"... but I'm gonna die for sure. I failed gym class. My mom had to bribe the soccer coach to let me on the team. There's a *reason* I like to stay home and read books!"

"Joe," Eliza snapped, cutting through his rising panic. "It's going to be okay."

"Easy for you to say, you're with them."

"What's that supposed to mean?"

"It means they save you. No one's going to save me."

Her mouth fell open, but she couldn't help but think about the night on the bridge, the woods outside the base. Aquila *had* saved her. Twice.

Damnit.

But now wasn't the time to worry about feminism.

She curled her fingers around Joe's forearm, his muscle stiff from clutching the wheel. At this rate his hands were going to freeze into claws.

"Nothing's gonna hurt you. I'll make sure of it."

Joe's smile, when it finally came, was wry and pale. But it was a start.

"Always so eager to take on the world."

She smiled back.

"Only when the world starts it."

"Oh dear." Joe sighed. "It seems so weird now, how quiet my life was last year. What did I even *do* with all my time? I'd like to think that I—"

"*Joe, stop!*"

Eliza slapped both palms against the dashboard. Old Betty jerked to a halt with a wheezing, squealing skid as Joe slammed on the breaks. They both looked up, half-panting, at the cluttered parking lot in front of them and the squat, busy building on the other side.

"Oh no," Joe groaned. "Not *Howl*."

But it was unmistakable. Against the throbbing, pulsing backdrop of the town's only real nightclub, already thrumming with life as the sun dipped below the horizon, a single figure stood backlit by the open warehouse doors. Hood pulled up, shoulders hunched, fists clenched.

Eliza leaned in close to the windshield, squinting, willing herself to see despite the inky darkness.

"Is that…" Joe started to ask, but cut off as the figure moved, shifted from foot to foot.

When the boy finally glanced over one shoulder, his face was unmistakably mottled with spines.

CHAPTER TWENTY-TWO
Spotlights

"There he is!"

"And here I was hoping they wouldn't need us," Joe said as Eliza whipped out her phone and dialed Aquila.

"We found him, we found him.... Yeah, he's in front of Howl. I'll go and—"

But before she could finish, Daisy stepped forward, vanishing into the churning crowd.

"Oh shit," Joe said.

"He went inside. Damnit, we'll have to go in after him. Yeah, ok." Eliza hung up. "They're coming down."

"Wait, wait, wait, don't you think someone will notice the guy with *wings*?"

"Aquila will stay outside."

Kicking open her door, she leapt out of the truck and began scanning the sky.

"Why the hell would he even want to go in there?" Joe asked, coming around to stand beside her.

Eliza lifted her eyebrows. "Besides the obvious?" She shrugged. "He's deaf. Maybe he's drawn to the lights."

"Or maybe he wants a bit of bumping and grinding." Eliza rolled her eyes as Joe let out a strained laugh. "What? Isn't that what the kids do these days."

"You don't."

"Obviously. But hey, if you've been cooped up your whole life in a weird old dude's mansion..."

Eliza chuckled, tapping her fist against Joe's arm in a show of comfort. She could feel the immense effort it was taking for him to avoid freaking out. It touched her how hard he was trying.

Aquila settled down beside the truck with a *whomp* of shifting air. His face contorted with worry as Moose exploded out of his arms, darting from them to the front of the truck and back again.

"He went in *there*?" Moose said, words coming so fast Eliza almost didn't understand them. "Is he crazy? He's not *me*, if anyone sees him there will be like riot-level pandemonium, like a zombie movie but with just one zombie who doesn't like brains or fighting back or talking much. He's dreaming if he thinks—"

"We'll go in with you," Eliza said, putting a hand on Moose's vibrating shoulder to stop him. "Maybe together we can lure him out." She turned to Aquila. "Don't worry, it'll be fine."

Aquila hunched his shoulders and the pain in his eyes made Eliza's heart tighten.

"It's my fault. I always assumed he'd just..." He shrugged. "I should have been paying more attention."

"Brothers, amirite?" Joe said.

Everyone ignored him.

Eliza reached up and cupped Aquila's jaw with the hand not holding Moose steady.

"We'll bring him back," she said, weighting each word with her conviction. "Nothing is going to happen. You'll go home and talk to him there and we'll find a way to keep everyone safe."

"Careful making promises you can't keep," Aquila said with a miserable flinch of a smile.

"Try me." Releasing Aquila, Eliza glanced between a quivering Moose and a grim-looking Joe. "Let's go."

Even on a Wednesday night, Howl radiated life and noise and the raw pulse of reckless youth. As the three of them drifted into the open warehouse, walking right past the disinterested bouncers, Eliza was shocked to see how many familiar faces she saw in the crowd. There was Yuri and Marta in glittering minidresses, jumping up and down with Hector. A group of jocks that she'd often seen throwing peas at each other in the cafeteria knocked into one another in a churning circle, scattered wide on the thinly populated dance floor. Two blonde girls from homeroom teetered in impossibly high heels as they sipped from unmarked Solo cups.

And, everywhere Eliza looked, buzzed army recruits with deep voices and sharp eyes.

How long until someone sees Daisy?

She prickled with unease, surrounded by the laughing, shouting men and women from Fitzgerald base. These people might be perfectly nice, normal even, but they followed orders. Orders given by that horrible black-haired woman. And they were trained to keep the peace.

If anyone saw one of the Vagabonds here, it would be anything but *peaceful*.

Swallowing her fear, Eliza plunged deeper into the melee, Joe and Moose trailing behind her like an entourage. The closer they got to the dance floor, the brighter and more insistent the lights became. They flashed over everything, making the world inside the warehouse technicolor and strange. A DJ pumped his fist in one corner, turning the music up so high it was almost painful.

"Eliza!"

Joe swung her around just in time to see Moose drifting off in the opposite direction, moving almost... slow.

"Shit!"

Eliza lunged after him, grabbing Moose by the arm.

"This way," she said, tugging him back. But Moose didn't turn away from a huge spotlight roving over the crowd, blinding them as it passed. "Moose, come *on*."

"It's so pretty," he murmured, tilting his head.

"What's going on?" Joe shouted over the bone-deep hum of the bass.

"I don't know," Eliza said, casting about frantically. She couldn't lose Moose *and* Daisy; Aquila would have a heart attack. Thinking about him hovering by Old Betty, unable to come inside, she leaned hard on Moose, shoving him away from the light. "Help me!"

Between them, Eliza and Joe were able to wrestle Moose away and guide him to the other side of the dance floor. When they were finally in the corner, shadowed by a pillar, Moose shook his head.

"Woo boy, that was a head rush. Did you guys see that? It was like looking at the stars, but all kalidescopy and weird. I can see why people like these places so much. Maybe I can come back when Daisy's home, would you guys come with me?"

Joe's eyes were huge, filled with unspoken things, but she wasn't looking. She was glaring at a hunched shape in the alcove next to theirs, staring out at the dance floor with longing, soulful brown eyes.

"Daisy!"

She made to surge out after him, but hesitated when Moose didn't follow. A girl was teetering toward them on stiletto heels, grinning at the tall kid in goggles.

"Those are pretty rad. Can I try?"

Eliza's breath caught in her throat as the girl reached up, as if to stroke the skinny boy's face. Moose grinned, shrugging off Eliza's grip, straightening his shirt.

"Hi there hey there, nice to see a—"

But Moose, who hadn't grown up with girls tugging his hair and stealing his lunchbox, didn't realize until too late what she was doing. Drunk, flirtatious, her hormonal curiosity mingling poorly with the alcohol, the girl was making a move. Under the guise of curling her fingers around the back of Moose's head, she slipped them under the dark green band corralling his wild brown hair.

"No!" Eliza screamed.

The goggles whipped off. For a moment, everything was as still as the woods outside Scottstown. The girl's grin froze on her face. The spotlight roved over them.

And Eliza saw, for the first time, what made Moose a Vagabond.

Beneath the orange-tinted goggles, Moose's eyes were baseball huge, lidless, and glittering, infinitely faceted like the world's most complex diamonds. They were the same iridescent blue as Aquila's wings, but horrifyingly alien embedded in the oversized eye sockets.

Of course.

Numb with shock, Eliza thought about his quick movements, his frenetic energy, his hypnotic draw to the bright spotlight.

And understood.

Housefly.

Moose, predictably, was the first to move. His hand flashed out, snatching the goggles as they arced through the air. But the damage had been done. The girl's lips opened once, twice, like a fish flopping on land. Eliza made to grab her, clap a hand over her mouth. Too late. Drunk feet stumbled away, the clicking heels barely audible over the pumping dance music.

But everyone heard her scream.

Chapter Twenty-Three
A Shot in the Dark

"Come on!"

Eliza grabbed Moose's hand and plunged into the crowd, knocking aside the screaming girl and barreling toward Daisy.

"I'll get him!" Joe shouted.

"No, don't!"

But Joe didn't hear Moose's warning. His hand came down on Daisy's shoulder, hard.

"AHHH!"

Blood spurted. Eliza shrieked. Moose darted around her, leaping in front of Daisy.

"Come on, bro," he said, aloud, his hands fluttering through frantic sign-language. Joe was clenching his wrist, dripping blood on the ground, staring at Daisy as if he was something diseased. But Eliza had no time to comfort him. The girl was still screaming incoherently, and tough-looking men and women were pushing closer with serious expressions and *they had to get out of there.*

"GO!" she shouted over the music, still thudding around them like the dull roar of a rushing river. Eliza's pulse was so loud in her ears she could hardly hear it. "Go, go, go!"

Moose had managed to get Daisy to lower the spines that had burst from his hoodie and stabbed Joe. Clasping his brother's now-safe shoulder, he shoved him toward the door, jerking his head at Eliza. She nodded, grabbing Joe by his uninjured hand. And then they were running, weaving through the thin crowd and away from the screaming girl.

The music died.

The lights came on.

And then the crowd morphed from a passive grouping of half-drunk strangers to a living thing, writhing and panicked and unpredictable as a school of fish. Eliza lost sight of Daisy and Moose, yanking a stumbling Joe behind her.

Oh god, if something happens…

She could see the door, crowded with people trying to escape whatever was happening in the warehouse. With an aggressive shove, she managed to burst through a cluster of bodies, Joe stumbling behind her. They exploded into the clean night air, panting desperately. But there was no relief at finally being outside. Joe's hand was still bleeding and the two brothers were nowhere to be found.

"Where are they?" Eliza breathed.

"What the *hell* did he do to me?"

"Joe, we have to find them!"

Eliza spun in a circle, eyes raking through the parking lot. She could see Old Betty, Aquila looming behind it like a crouched gargoyle. She could see the army recruits snapping into mode, talking to the bouncers and pulling out weapons and glaring at the crowd with suspicious menace.

But where were Moose and Daisy?

"We can't lose them, we can't…" Eliza panted, terror clawing at her throat.

Joe straightened, taking a deep, steadying breath.

"Is that them?"

Eliza didn't even wait for her eyes to adjust, lunging toward where Joe pointed without a second thought. She crashed into the alley between the warehouse and a dilapidated apartment building, drawn forward by the rumble of a deep voice.

"Take off the goggles, kid. We need to see your face."

The words echoing out of the alley were tight, commanding. Eliza stumbled to a stop as her eyes adjusted. Moose was standing in front of Daisy, arms thrown wide, face jerking back and forth between two people in fatigues, holding guns on them.

"Hey now, no reason for that," he said with an attempt at a smile, goggles glinting in the bright fluorescent light now spilling from the club. "We were just, er, visiting."

"Hi there," Eliza said, stepping toward the two privates, a woman and a man, trying to gage their expressions. Duty made their faces cold and hard, but there was humanity there. Maybe she could still talk their way out of this. "What's going on?"

"Stay back, citizen, we're dealing with it," snapped the woman, her dirty blonde hair slicked back into a bun.

"Look, I think there's been some kind of misunderstanding, I—"

"What's on his *skin*." The man's face twisted with disgust and Eliza felt a moment of relief that Daisy couldn't hear.

But the boy could still see.

Hunching his shoulders, Daisy ducked and sprinted for the mouth of the alley where Eliza hovered, frozen, unsure what to do. There was a shout. A barked command. Eliza's mouth opened, a scream bubbling up from her stomach.

And then the night was split by the crack of a gunshot.

"NO!"

Moose moved so fast that Eliza's eyes couldn't track him. Daisy went sprawling as his taller brother slammed into him, knocking him aside, and then shuddering in a full-body tremor as the bullet threw him off his feet.

"Fuck," muttered the young private, staring down the barrel of his smoking gun and the teenager sprawled on the pavement.

"What did you do?!" Eliza shrieked.

Joe was the first to move, sliding to his knees, using his unbloodied hand to feel for the wound.

"It hit his arm," he said, eyes flying up to meet Eliza's. And then they widened.

Eliza turned.

A shadow passed over her as Aquila came out of nowhere, pounding the gun-wielding private against the wall with one hand.

"Aquila, no!" Eliza shouted, leaping forward and grabbing Aquila's other arm as he drew back to punch. "No, wait, stop!"

The woman was staring open-mouthed, her own gun held high, but Eliza was in her way, struggling to hold Aquila back.

"Don't, don't do this, don't make things worse. Aquila, *listen* to me!"

He was snarling like a rabid dog, face contorted with rage, wings curled around them like blue-black shadows. In the striped darkness he looked positively enormous. Wild and violent, like a demon pulled straight out of the most horrifying late-night stories. If Eliza hadn't already seen his smile, his honey-sweet eyes, his bashful shrug, she'd think he was a monster.

After a moment of struggle, Eliza felt his muscles soften under her hands.

His elbow drooped.

Finally, Aquila stepped back, letting the terrified soldier slump to the ground.

"Go," he spat.

The young private scrambled to his feet, grabbing the woman. Together, they sprinted around the back corner of the warehouse and out of sight.

Eliza met Aquila's eyes, frightened by the fury she saw in them. She touched his arm, but before she could say anything, Joe's voice rose behind her.

"Um, there's a lot of blood here."

CHAPTER TWENTY-FOUR
Ruined Seats

Aquila didn't hesitate. Sweeping over, he lifted Moose into his arms, ignoring the groan of pain.

"Damn, this hurts," Moose mumbled. "I sure hope everyone saw how heroic that was because I'm never doing it again, no way."

"We've got to get him home," Aquila said as Daisy hovered near Moose's feet, wringing his hands.

"Can you carry him?" Eliza asked.

"Not with Daisy." Aquila glanced at the other boy, hovering in the mouth of the alley with his shoulders bent in shame. "And not with all these people around. We'd be spotted."

Eliza caught Joe's eye, pursing her lips in question. Joe sighed.

"Alright, let's get to the truck. I've already aided and abetted one fugitive today."

Eliza yanked Joe to his feet and planted a kiss on his cheek. "You're the best."

"It's not like this night can get any weirder," Joe muttered as the three of them ran through the shadows, sprinting for Old Betty. Aquila hurried after them, Moose in his arms.

Daisy was the first in, crawling to the other side of the back seat and helping pull Moose inside. It wasn't easy. He kept twitching, legs spasming with pain as his brother tugged on his armpits.

"Watch it, *watch it*, ow, I think my arm's gonna fall off. Don't let Otto get my graphic novels, he doesn't know how to treat them."

"Just get in," Aquila grumbled, gingerly lifting Moose's knees.

Eliza bounced from foot to foot, casting nervous glances at Howl, which was now brightly lit and swarming with people.

"We've got to *go*," she said as sirens wailed toward them.

Joe was already in the driver's seat, Old Betty rumbling to life. Finally, Moose's long legs folded inside.

But there was a problem.

"I'll ride in the back," Aquila said, huge wings rustling.

"Can't you *fly*?" Joe called.

"I don't want to leave them." Aquila bent down to peer at Eliza. "I need to make sure everyone gets home safe."

Eliza nodded.

"Be careful," she said.

Aquila was already hopping into the truck bed, pressing himself against the cab. Eliza leapt into the passenger seat, throwing a look back at the bleeding, wincing Moose. Both of them glanced down at the red stain spreading over the hoodie Daisy had ripped off and pressed to the wound.

"Sorry about your car, man," Moose muttered.

"If I get pulled over right now..." Joe muttered.

"Just drive," Eliza said, not willing to think about the myriad of ways this could go wrong.

Joe drove them around the back side of the apartment complex, trundling out of the parking lot just as three police cruisers came screaming into it.

"That was close," he said, back to clutching the truck wheel as they swerved onto the main road.

"I think I'm dying," Moose groaned. "I didn't even get the chance to be famous. The world will be such a dark place without me. What a loss, what a tragedy."

"You're not dying," Eliza said, hoping it was true.

They all bounced as Joe crashed over a speed bump and Moose let out a surprised cough of pain.

"Holy mother of cheese!"

Daisy met Eliza's eyes and she saw in them such a humanity that she longed to reach out to comfort him, despite the blood staining the spines of his now bare shoulders and the mottled, armored skin.

"It's going to be okay," she said before remembering that he couldn't hear her anyway.

"You're awfully optimistic about all this," Joe inserted, swinging them onto the road that would take them to Ian Eckelson's estate.

"Has someone... called... to warn... Dad," Moose said between pants. "He's going to have... a heart attack... if we come in like this. Although I'd love to see... Otto's face."

Eliza pulled out her phone, but of course she only had Aquila's number. Rolling down the window as fast as she could, she leaned out into the night air as it whipped past them recklessly fast.

"Have you called—"

But before she could scream the question at Aquila, she saw a horrifying sight. There, on the crest of an upcoming hill, the unmistakable flash of spotlights cracked the darkness wide open.

"Joe, stop!"

The truck squealed as Joe slammed on the breaks, skidding them into the other lane.

"*What?*"

"Look."

Eliza pointed. In the distance she could just barely make out a brightly lit barricade right outside the Fitzgerald gates, blocking the road to keep it clear for the official vehicles spilling out of the base.

"Back up, back up," Eliza said breathlessly, tapping Joe's thigh in a staccato beat.

He was way ahead of her. Spinning the truck around with surprising dexterity, Joe veered Old Betty into the other lane and accelerated back towards Scottstown.

The back window slid open and Aquila's head poked in.

"Why did we turn around?"

"The road is blocked," Eliza said, eyes wild. "It looks like the army is responding to what happened at Howl. They must have been alerted by the privates who saw you."

Aquila's face paled. Moose howled in pain, arcing his back. Daisy looked ready to cry.

Eliza opened her mouth, but she had nothing to offer. Where could they go if not back to the Eckelson estate? They could hardly bring Moose to the hospital. Maybe Aquila could fly them over the barricade one by one, but that would take precious seconds that Moose didn't have, not to mention risk being seen by those spotlights currently slicing open the sky.

What were they going to do?

Joe sighed, drawing every eye in the truck.

"We could go to my parent's lake house." He winced as Eliza rounded on him. "Sorry, I never told you. It's kind of embarrassing. I mean, they bought it for me to, er, host parties and all that. But as you know, that was never really my... thing."

"How far away is it?"

"Ten minutes, if I drive fast."

Behind them, Moose groaned, eyes rolling back. He was going to pass out soon. Eliza glanced at Aquila, who looked ready to pass out himself. Everything had gone so wrong so quickly. It was dizzying, disorienting. Eliza felt like the world was tilting away beneath them.

But they had to do *something*.

Shifting around in her seat, she glared ahead at the small-town highway disappearing beneath Old Betty's wheels.

"Drive fast," she said.

CHAPTER TWENTY-FIVE
Getaway

For a long moment, no one moved, all of them frozen as they stared at the elegant lake house that seemed as much a part of the forest as the trees and ferns. It was beautiful, a thing of layered glass and wood with multiple tiers of decks and a gorgeous open front facing the water. Eliza gaped at it, watching the truck's high beams glitter on the enormous windows, wondering just how wealthy Joe's parents really were.

And then Moose moaned.

With a creak and a slam, Aquila leapt out of the truck bed and yanked open the door.

"I think he passed out when we pulled onto the driveway," Eliza said as Joe, Daisy, and Aquila struggled to extract the long-limbed boy from the back of Old Betty.

"He looks pale," Joe said, edging away from the exposed spines on Daisy's arms.

"He always looks like that." But Aquila's joke was weighed down by the worry creasing his brow and Moose's wordless shudders.

"Joe, where's the key?"

Joe ducked his head, shifting Moose's arm in his grip.

"Um, well, there's no key. There should be a fingerprint scanner by the door."

Eliza rolled her eyes but decided now wasn't the best time to comment. Instead she elbowed up to Joe, taking Moose's arm out of his hands and jerking her head toward the enormous lake house.

Joe nodded and scrambled up the front steps to unlock it.

"We need towels you don't care about," Aquila said, bending his knees to fit his massive wings through a door built for normal-sized people. "And bandages. Lots of bandages."

115

"Ok, right, yeah, I'll go look." Joe vanished into the shadows of the house as the lights flickered on, washing the interior with a warm, friendly glow.

"Jesus," Eliza breathed, almost dropping Moose's arm. The inside was even more spectacular, with sweeping arches of hardwood and at least three fireplaces in view.

"Moose, stay with us, ok man." Aquila's voice dragged Eliza back to the present. Meeting Daisy's terrified eyes, she helped them navigate Moose's twitching body to a stretch of hardwood floor. "C'mon dude, you're always saying you're the toughest of us."

"I... am... tough... you... jerk," Moose's words were jumbled and slurred, as if he was speaking around a mouthful of soft food.

Eliza and Aquila shared a worried look.

"Let's see the damage," she said, wracking her brain for the First Aid basics she'd learned that year Katie was a camp counselor. With hesitant fingers, she began to peel off the crusty, bloodstained sweater.

Moose screamed, head snapping up so fast that it almost hit Aquila's nose.

"Sorry, sorry," Eliza said, wincing as the sweater stuck. Blood began to ooze out of the reopened wound, pooling on the floor. "JOE!"

"Here," Joe said, dumping an armload of pristine white towels at Moose's feet. "I found these too."

Eliza took the tube of Bacitracin and the huge bottle of Vodka, crystal clear and shimmering ominously. She stared at them, weighing one in each hand, dreading the next part.

With a wince, she lifted her gaze.

"This is going to hurt," she said, staring at Aquila.

Moose muttered something unintelligible, but Aquila nodded, gently pressing Moose's shoulders to the ground.

Eliza opened the Vodka bottle, glanced back to Joe. He was lingering next to a rocking, silent Daisy, both of them wearing twin expressions of wide-eyed dread.

"Here goes nothing."

And then Eliza poured alcohol all over the wound.

Moose's body arced, every muscle tightening like violin strings. Aquila's shirt strained on his shoulders as he held his brother down, mumbling something that sounded suspiciously like a prayer. Moose's jaw clenched so tight that he couldn't even shout, but Eliza could see the pain in his limbs, his fists, the flashing glint of his goggles.

"I'm sorry," she muttered, using a towel to sponge off the Vodka. "I'm sorry, I'm sorry."

But she wasn't done. Squeezing out a gloppy handful of Bacitracin, she hesitated only a second before smearing it all over the carved-out hole in Moose's upper arm. The boy began to flop and shudder. His hands slapped the floor. But Aquila held him down and Eliza managed to coat the edges of the wound with antibacterial gel. She snatched a nearby towel, wrapped it tightly around Moose's bicep, pressed down.

Finally, everything went still.

Moose was panting, chest moving up and down so fast it blurred. Eliza would have been worried he was hyperventilating if she didn't know better.

"Hey, you okay?" she asked, leaning in close to Moose's face.

Moose lifted his head the tiniest bit, offering Eliza his best effort at a coy smile.

"Peachy," he said, thumping back down. "I knew... you wouldn't be able to keep... hands off me."

For the first time, Eliza glanced at her fingers, pressed against the stained towel. They were covered in blood and Bacitracin, congealing horribly in the webbing of her hands. She forced herself to swallow bile.

"I'm... definitely the most badass... one here," Moose muttered, head drifting to the side.

"We have to keep pressure on it," Eliza said, swallowing convulsively. "I think it's okay for him to sleep. We should take shifts though, to make sure he doesn't go into shock or something."

They all watched her, drinking in her every word, and Eliza felt the responsibility like an iron anchor. They were trusting her? *Eliza,* who was the reason they were all in this mess in the first place? Who had little to no idea what she was doing?

Her eyes met Daisy's and she saw in them the same guilt. The same terror.

"I'm sorry," Daisy said in that halting, unsure way of his. He folded over, wrapping his spiny arms around shaking knees.

Eliza burst to her feet.

"I need to wash up. Joe, would you please hold the towel on him?"

Before anyone could respond, she was sprinting for the telltale white ceramic of the nearest washroom, kicking the bamboo door shut behind her.

CHAPTER TWENTY-SIX
Blame Game

The tears came fast and torrential as she turned on the faucet, red and white blurring into a watercolor stain on the sink, a symbol of everything that had gone wrong. Eliza scrubbed at the gore on her hands, taking out her fury on the tender skin of her palms. She'd made a mess of things and worse, she'd dragged Joe into it. They were now a target, hunted by the army and that *woman*. Those privates had seen Aquila, *shot* Moose, and it was all her fault.

She turned off the sink and braced herself against its porcelain edge, trying to inhale past the sobs that threatened to crash over her like a wave. Adrenaline still pulsed through her, a rampaging stampede with nowhere to go.

We're safe, she said sternly to herself. *Calm down. We're safe now.*

But were they? How far would Amile Robillard go to find the Vagabonds?

What would Ian Eckelson think about her now?

She lifted her head only to see Aquila in the mirror, standing behind her.

"Don't," he said, holding out his hands as she opened her mouth to cry out in surprise. "I just... I wanted to see if you were okay."

Eliza swallowed, breathed. Snatching a hand towel, she scrubbed her face, furiously wiping at the tear-tracks on her cheeks.

"I'm fine." She turned to face him. "Totally fine."

"Daisy feels really bad about what happened."

"I bet he does," Eliza said with a wry smile. And then her smile faded. "But I don't think it's Daisy's fault. I have a feeling this wouldn't have happened if not for me."

Aquila shrugged, rustling the iridescent blue feathers and making them shimmer like seawater in the sun.

"Otto likes to push. If it wasn't you, it would have been something else."

"Has Daisy ever run away like this before?"

He ducked his head and Eliza knew the answer.

No.

"Aquila, there's nothing I can say to make this better. I feel like I've broken everything and I don't know how to make it right."

The tears were coming again, blurring Aquila around the edges. But then he stepped closer and she could see his features, open and warm and so damn *understanding* that she wanted to shove him away.

She didn't deserve his forgiveness.

"What are you talking about?" he said in a voice like velvet. You're the best thing that's happened to us in years. I mean, Ian's nice. He gets us everything we need. But it's not enough. You can't imagine how hard it is to live like that."

Oh, I think I can, Eliza thought. But when Aquila put a finger under her chin to lift her face, forcing her to look at him, her mind went as still as the lake outside.

"No matter what happens, we are *glad* to have met you. Remember that, okay?"

"Okay," Eliza said, barely able to get the word out as her thoughts became a wild tumble, as if someone had shoved them in the dryer. Aquila's mouth was so close, so perfect, his wings curving around her, making her feel safer than all the security features of the lake house combined.

He smelled like grass and pine needles and men's deodorant.

She leaned in.

"Sorry to interrupt," Joe said, making both of them jump. "But I think you should talk to Daisy."

Aquila and Eliza leapt apart, both blushing, both scrambling for something to grab.

"Of course," Aquila said, gaze flickering to Eliza. "I'll be right back."

He ducked out to where Moose lay in the middle of the living room, Daisy curled into a tight ball next to him. Joe folded his arms in the doorway, the wry, mocking smirk not quite hiding the ache in his eyes.

"I'm clean now," Eliza said, holding out her hands. She winced. *Really? That's the best you can do?*

"Look," Joe said, his smirk falling away. "I don't want to... I mean..."

Her heart fisted painfully as Joe's face flickered through a range of things she longed to wipe away. Anger. Hurt.

Betrayal.

She stepped forward and curled one dripping hand around his forearm, squeezing.

"It's been a long night. We're all confused."

Joe winced.

"I'm not so sure about that."

"Don't—"

"Look, I get it. He's tall and I guess he's kinda interesting with the wings and all that. That's not what... Well, I guess..." Joe sighed, tilting his head back to stare at the ceiling. "I thought we were friends."

Eliza reeled back, not understanding.

"Of course we are."

Joe dropped his gaze to her, holding her eyes with the vastness of his disappointment.

"Then why didn't you tell me what was going on before you had to?"

She opened her mouth but was saved having to respond as Aquila shouted from the other room.

"Eliza! Your phone!"

Meeting Joe's eyes one last time and praying she could fix the damage she'd done, Eliza crashed back into the main room. Aquila was holding out her Android, his other hand putting pressure on Moose's wound. She took the vibrating phone, glancing at the cracked screen.

It was Tori.

Eliza frowned, looking at each of the boys in turn. They were staring at her, waiting for her to decide, the air dense with worry.

She swiped to answer.

"Hi Tori, what's up?" Eliza cringed at the false cheer in her voice, but it didn't matter. Tori was sobbing on the other end of the line, her icy cool long forgotten.

"I-I... Eliza, I didn't know who else to call."

Eliza hunched over her phone, spinning away from the curious stares.

"Tori, what's wrong?"

"Look, I know you don't like me and I don't like you and this is probably a huge mistake, but no one else *knows*. And you went in the base and came out and I think you saw something and I don't know what else to do."

Wait, slow down, what's going on?"

Tori took a shuddering breath on the other end of the line and it crackled like static.

"It's my brother. He isn't answering his phone and no one at Fitzgerald will respond to my calls. Eliza, I think something happened to him."

CHAPTER TWENTY-SEVEN
Missing and Found

Despite the sun rising over the distant points of the evergreens and the cheerful, familiar rumble of Old Betty beneath her, Eliza felt dark. Cold. Worried. And Aquila wasn't helping.

"Tero's been watching Fitzgerald Base for months now," he was saying through the back window as Joe drove them over the sloping hillsides of Western Massachusetts.

"He's obsessed with our origin story, of course," Moose piped up, looking significantly better after a full night of sleep and lots of fluids, though still wincing every time he moved his left arm.

Aquila rolled his eyes but continued.

"We think they're doing some kind of genetic experimentation there. Sort of like whatever created us."

"Genetic experimentation?" Eliza breathed, twisting around in her seat to meet Aquila's eyes. It was hard to believe that those bright blue orbs were created in a lab.

"Tero managed to hack in once and found a file for something called the Superman Virus." Aquila held her gaze, his expression saturated with meaning. "It's a project led by a man named Dr. Oleander."

"The mad scientist who created *us*, in case you were wondering," Moose said, poking Daisy in the side and making the spines on his brother's shoulder twitch with irritation.

"That's it, I've lost my mind," Joe muttered, shaking his head as he watched the road pass, lit orange by the dawn. "I've *officially* lost my mind."

But Eliza wasn't listening. She was thinking about that night on Fitzgerald base, about the man who threw soldiers around like they were dolls.

The Superman Virus.

Had they *created* him? Somehow mucked around with his genetics and made him so strong and fast?

And monstrous?

"We've been watching the men and women who work on base," Aquila said, folding his arms on the edge of the open truck window as they bounced over a pothole. "There are a lot of faces who have gone in and never come out again."

Eliza swallowed. "So Tori's brother…"

"Could be their next test subject."

Tori might be Eliza's least favorite person in the world, but she couldn't help the sympathy that surged through her. She thought about that violent man, face ugly with rage and hate and animalistic violence. For Tori to lose her brother like *that*, twisted beyond recognition for some army experiment… it was horrible. Beyond horrible. It was wrong.

Eliza suppressed a groan.

She'd never been able to turn away from wrong.

"So what do we do?"

Joe's face snapped to the side, eyes wide.

"What do you mean *do*? You want to *help* her?"

Eliza ignored him, looking instead at Aquila.

"You said you've been watching the base for months. What should we do?"

Aquila pursed his lips, glancing first at Moose on one side, then at Daisy. He seemed to be gathering his courage, formulating the right answer.

Of course, Moose didn't give him the chance.

"Oooh, we should break in! You've been wanting to for ages, Aquila, you said so just the other night. This could be our chance! We could use this girl's brother as a way to finally figure out what happened to us. We could find our parents!"

Aquila sighed, giving Eliza the look of a long-suffering brother resigned to his fate.

"Something like that."

"Wait, wait, wait," Joe said from the front. "You want to *break in*? To a *military lab*? Guarded by literal *supermen*?"

"We haven't seen a successful version of the Superman Virus in action," Aquila said. "At least not one they can control. I think we'd be fairly safe."

Joe snorted.

"Besides," Moose said, almost bouncing in his seat. "Tero's been wanting to test his toys since *forever*. He's got all these doohikeys and thingamabobs for exactly this reason."

"What about Tori?"

"What about her?" Aquila asked. "We get her information and then use it to break in."

"But what should I tell her?"

Aquila winced and Eliza could imagine he was thinking about Tori's frantic call, about the worry of a sibling. But he shrugged.

"Nothing."

Joe began to laugh under his breath, the sound tinted with mania.

"This is insane. It's all insane. How can it keep getting *more insane*?"

Eliza put a hand on his arm, squeezing as her own mind wheeled into overdrive.

"Ok, so what do we need?"

They were pulling into Scottstown, heading toward the park where Eliza had agreed to meet Tori. Square homes and painted buildings flashed past. Eliza felt dizzy as their oddball party slipped into normal life without fanfare. Without screams. Just the gentle blooming of dawn light and the whisper of a city slowly waking up.

"We need Tori's brother's name and whatever she knows about him. An ID tag would be great, but I think Tero doesn't need one."

"That genius don't need *nothing*," Moose said, pumping one fist. Daisy eyed him nervously.

"And mostly, we need her to be quiet until we figure out what's going on."

Eliza nodded. Joe pulled over on the side of the road, hidden in the shadow of the trees. They couldn't get any closer without risking that Tori might spot Aquila's wings or Daisy's spines. Or, God forbid, that some innocent jogger or dog walker might see them and scream.

Eliza took a deep, calming breath, facing forward.

"Are you ok?" Aquila asked.

"I mean, she's been *living* with this girl," Joe said with irritation. "I think she can handle her for five minutes."

"Here," Eliza said, flipping her phone out of her sweatshirt pocket and dialing Joe. "So you all can listen."

She met Joe's eyes, wishing there was something else to say. Some comfort she could offer. But there wasn't. In the span of twenty-four hours, their lives had flipped on their heads in the most extreme way. She could sense the threats piling like mountains around her, but the only way to survive was to keep moving forward.

"I'll be back," Eliza said at last, shoving open the side door and jumping out of Old Betty.

Her heart was in her throat as she strode into the brightly lit park, passing a woman with a stroller and old man reading on a park bench. Her phone was loose in her hand, her head held high. She'd checked herself before leaving the lake house to make sure there was no blood or bacitracin smeared on her face. But she still felt vulnerable and prickly walking in full daylight in the middle of Scottstown. What if Amile was looking for her? What if the *police* were after them now?

How long until someone swept in to arrest her or question her or drag her back to Meru?

What if this was a trap?

She shook her head.

Eliza had made her decision. It was too late to turn back now.

Tori was standing in the shadow of the sycamore where only a few nights ago Eliza had abandoned her bike.

"Hey," Eliza said in greeting.

Tori spun around, eyes frantic and bloodshot.

"Where the *hell* have you been? Never mind, I don't care. Just help me find my brother."

"The brother you don't want anyone to know about?"

"Oh don't you start. Are you going to help me or not?"

Eliza pursed her lips, watching as Tori fought to stay calm.

"*Are you?*"

"Tell me what happened."

Tori took a deep, shuddering breath, closing her eyes.

"Martin texted me last week that he'd been promoted. Something about a new position. Whatever. He said he might be under the weather for a few days. And then he showed up to interrogate you and didn't say hi or anything. I haven't seen him since."

"Maybe he's sick," Eliza said.

Tori's head jerked back and forth, her blonde hair ragged and unbrushed as it fluttered around her face.

"No, that's not like him. He always texts me." Her voice broke. "Even if I don't text him back. He looks out for me. After our mom..." She stopped, face suddenly guarded.

"After your mom what?"

"Nevermind, I just need to find him."

"And you think I can help?"

Tori swallowed. Straightened.

"I think your boyfriend can."

Eliza didn't answer, heart thudding in her chest and drowning out the cheerful birdsong and rustle of the morning.

So that's why she wanted to talk to me. Tori didn't want *Eliza's* help.

She wanted Aquila's.

"I don't know what you're talking about."

Tori laughed, the sound half-crazed, bubbling with frenetic terror.

"Oh *please,* I saw that *thing* in our room. You think I'd miss it? He was like seven feet tall and had fucking *wings.*"

"Shhhhh," Eliza said, stepping closer and glancing around the park, terrified she was going to see Amile hiding behind the nearest tree.

"Look, that wasn't the first time I'd seen the freak." Eliza scowled at the word, but Tori didn't seem to notice. "He was at the army base too, wasn't he? That night you climbed the fence? I thought I'd gone crazy, but when I came back to our room and saw him there…" She trailed off, pursing her lips. "He's connected to Fitzgerald somehow and I want to know why. And I want *his* help getting inside."

"I don't know how to contact him. He hasn't come near me since that night in the dorm."

Tori snarled and lunged forward, grabbing the phone out of Eliza's hand. Eliza tried to snatch it back, but Tori danced out of her reach.

"Joe, huh?" she said with a sneer, holding the phone high. "Right. Whoever you are on the other side of this line, I want your help. If you don't meet with me and help me find my brother, I'm going straight to the police. And I'm sure they'll be *very* interested in what I have to say."

Tori sneered at Eliza, holding the phone between them with a victorious smirk. Eliza slapped her hand down, stealing back her cracked Android.

But it was too late.

She put the phone to her ear, glaring at Tori.

"Joe?" she asked, careful not to say more.

"Well, I guess she made a compelling case," Joe said, voices muttering in the background. "Aquila says yes. He'll help her. But only if she promises not to call any of them freaks again."

Eliza met Tori's eyes and wished desperately that she'd been placed with a different roommate.

CHAPTER TWENTY-EIGHT
An Old Man's Plea

"This is stupid."

Eliza rolled her eyes as she guided the blindfolded Tori up the stairs of the Eckelson Estate, following a limping Moose and fidgeting Daisy, Joe trailing close behind.

"You agreed to wear it."

"That doesn't mean I don't think it's stupid," Tori said, folding her arms and scowling at nothing. Joe glanced over with an expression that seemed to shout *this isn't going to go well*.

Eliza ignored him, glaring up at the roof and wondering where Aquila was. Had he already opened the window and crawled into the dusty attic? Would he have to deal with Mr. Eckelson? Or his brothers? Were Otto and Tero worried about them, maybe quizzing their brother on what happened? What were they going to say about Tori?

Eliza bit her lip.

"Look, you already took my phone." Tori said. "There's not much else I can do."

"That's for us to decide."

"Jeeze, have you always been this creepy?"

"Not. Helping."

Eliza could imagine Tori's blue eyes narrowing under the strip of Joe's shirt. But thankfully, despite her sneering skepticism, Tori didn't fight or struggle, letting Eliza lead her up the stairs like a newly trained puppy.

They just had to get her to the basement. Even Tori, who grew up in Scottstown, wouldn't recognize where she was down there.

But what will happen when she sees the rest of them?

130

With a thundering of footsteps and a creak of old metal, the door burst open. Aquila stood there, panting, feathers standing on end.

"Man, what's it like to be so *slow*?" Moose groaned, holding his injured arm against his chest to protect the stained bandage.

Aquila ignored him, glancing over his shoulder.

"Coast is clear. Come on."

Joe took charge of Tori, steering the girl into the massive entrance hall, dominated by the curling hardwood stairs and gently clinking chandelier. Eliza paused, lingering with Aquila as the others ducked pass. It was surreal to be beside him, guarding the house instead of trying to break into it.

How things had changed.

Together they watched Moose lead the others toward the back of the mansion and the creaky elevator, practically skipping despite his wound.

"He never slows down, does he?" Eliza said, shaking her head.

"What are you talking about? This *is* slow for him."

Eliza chuckled, but it trailed off as Tori stumbled over the kitchen threshold.

"Are you sure this is a good idea?" she muttered, leaning in close and swallowing the urge to tangle her fingers into his enormous hand and squeeze it for comfort. "Tori's not exactly a *nice* person. I'm not sure she's the best one to trust."

Aquila shrugged, eyebrows pulled together as he stared miserably after his brothers.

"She's seen me already. That's enough to get us all in trouble if she goes to the right people. Maybe we can make friends with her the way we did with you, convince her to stay silent."

Eliza winced, hating that Aquila was comparing her to *Tori*. But she didn't say anything. Aquila was bent over, his spine curved as if it held up the whole weight of the Eckelson mansion. Worry crashed over his features like waves, a distinct pulse for each new thought. Moose's wound. Daisy's shame. The secrecy of their mission. The army breathing down their necks.

Eliza ducked her head to catch his gaze, heart aching to see him so unhappy.

"Hey, it's gonna be okay. We'll figure this out."

Aquila sighed, offering her a wan smile.

"I think you're an optimist."

She grinned back.

"No, I'm a realist. Now c'mon, we don't want them getting into trouble without us." Jerking her head, Eliza led Aquila back toward the kitchen, stepping through a pair of swinging hardwood doors and into a part of the mansion she hadn't seen before.

Before she could take in the glittering white tile or pristine top-of-the-line kitchen equipment, Eliza froze.

Ian Eckelson was standing in front of the elevator grate, arms folded, flanked by Otto and a blinking, shivering Tero.

"*What* is the meaning of this?"

"Dad, I…"

But Eckelson didn't look at his son, his eyes riveted instead on Eliza. She moved to block Joe and Tori, holding her hands up.

"Mr. Eckelson, I'm sorry to—"

"You foolish girl. You thought I would let you sneak into my mansion *again*?"

"It was Aquila's—"

"My sons are restless. That I can forgive. But you, waltzing into this house and ruining the peace we've managed to keep for *sixteen years*." The old man's keen eyes flickered, lingering on Moose's arm, where the stain on the bandage looked like cranberries on snow. On Daisy's shoulder spines, still crusted with Joe's blood.

On Tori, swaying next to Joe, the intruders in his home multiplying like problems.

His expression darkened.

"You should be ashamed of yourself."

"Sir, I don't think—"

"Get out of my house at once, or else—"

"Dad, *stop*," Aquila said, stepping forward and snapping his wings out. All at once, he seemed to fill the kitchen, his feathered bulk making everyone take a step back. "None of this was Eliza's fault."

"What's going on?" Tori whispered, for once sounding nervous as the angry voices swirled around her.

Eliza put a hand on the girl's bony shoulder, pulling her away from Aquila and his adopted father.

"Son, you don't understand," Eckelson said.

"Then explain."

"It's not safe!"

"Neither are we!" Aquila shouted, voice swollen with rage. "We never have been! And unless we figure out what's going on, we never will be!" Aquila took a deep breath, folding his wings back in. His fists clenched at his sides, white staining the ridges of his knuckles. "That girl's brother has been recruited, father. He's their next victim. We have to do something."

"Victim? What does he mean victim?"

But no one seemed to hear Tori's frantic questions as Aquila continued, his menace like a thunderstorm.

"We're going to help her and we're going to find out who we are. What we are."

Mr. Eckelson shook his head.

"You're not ready—"

"And if you had a say, we'd never would be. We're going into that base, father. It's time we learned about our past. Unless you're willing to help us."

For a moment, the air between them felt electric, molten, like an ash cloud outside a bursting volcano. Eliza tried to swallow, tried to convince herself that this mess wasn't *all* her fault. Tori had something to do with it, and Moose got shot because Daisy ran away, and all the brothers wanted to discover the secrets hiding in Fitzgerald labs and it wasn't just *her*.

But even so, everything seemed to trace back to her single, stupid decision to jump the fence.

God damnit.

"I hope you know what you're doing," Mr. Eckelson said at last, stepping aside.

Aquila's face twisted, not in victory but in pain. And Eliza knew exactly how he felt. Despite the joyful rush she got from breaking the rules or knocking down a bully or doing something reckless, it always hurt to see the disappointment on her mother's face. The sadness on her father's. Katie had been the good kid. The one who was always so *easy*, so well-behaved.

And now all they had was Eliza.

Sometimes it was hard not to feel resentful about that.

Aquila jerked his head, leading the way to the back of the kitchen. Shifting nervously, Daisy and Otto followed, bending in to ask Moose what had happened. But even Moose was strained from the fight, his voice hesitant as he recounted his *brave sacrifice*.

Tero didn't move.

"Tero?" Aquila asked, standing at the elevator.

The white-eyed boy bit his lip, took a deep breath.

And followed.

Eliza wanted to cry. What had she done to this family? Would they ever forgive her?

Would Aquila?

She lingered, letting Joe lead the now-terrified Tori up to the elevator.

"I'm sorry, sir," Eliza said in a low voice, stepping up behind the old man, who was staring out the window at the perfectly manicured stretch of his lawn, bright green in the morning light.

He was silent for so long that Eliza wondered if he wasn't going to respond. She sighed, made to step around the enormous kitchen island. And then he spoke.

"I thought my life was over when my son died." Eliza froze. "My real son I mean, gone in a flash of high beams on a curvy back road. He lingered for months, holding onto a body that no longer wanted him back. Sam had always been so strong, like Aquila. A real fighter. But after a while, the doctors said there wasn't anything to bring back. They recommended we end things, told us we should move on with our lives." Mr. Eckelson's laugh was strangled, thick with unshed tears. "Like we had a life to move on to. Everything was gone and I... There was a man in the hospital who promised... he said..." Mr. Eckelson shook himself, turning to face Eliza with tears in his eyes but ferocity etched in his features. "These boys are my responsibility. They are my second chance."

"I'm not going to hurt them," Eliza said.

"You already have. How much worse does it have to get before you realize that you don't belong here."

Eliza pursed her lips. There was a cruel truth to what he was saying. She could see it reflected there, the cold knowledge that as much as Eliza wanted to believe she was here for them, she was here for herself too.

"I just want to help," Eliza whispered.

Ian Eckelson leaned in, his snarl strangely at odds with his white hair and weathered face.

"Then leave."

Eliza shook her head, temper snapping like a flag in the wind.

"Maybe I am selfish, but you're just as bad, aren't you?" she hissed, jerking her head back as the elevator grate crashed closed, bearing the first round of passengers downstairs. "They're not just pets that you can keep in your basement."

"How *dare* you—"

135

"They're *people*, Mr. Eckelson. They deserve freedom, same as everyone."

He shook his head.

"The world will not agree."

"Screw the world."

"That's a dangerous attitude, young lady."

"It's gotten me this far."

Mr. Eckelson sighed, staring after his sons and the newcomers who had brought it all crashing down.

"That's not comforting, child. Not comforting at all."

The silence between them stretched, tensile and fragile and filled with mutual dislike. The elevator trundled back, squealing as Otto opened the grate and swept a glistening hand to one side to lead the still-blindfolded Tori through. Eliza watched with a knot in her throat, suddenly thinking of something Joe had said.

I think the quiet life sounds pretty nice, don't you?

Well, she certainly wasn't going to get it anytime soon.

Sighing, Eliza made to follow the others into the elevator. But Eckelson spoke, holding her there for a single moment longer.

"Protect my sons, Eliza Mason. Please. I don't care what brought you here or why you insist on staying, but I beg you, keep them safe."

Eliza spun, ready to swear on her life, on her sister, on anything she could think of that she only had their best interest at heart.

But Mr. Eckelson was already gone, leaving the kitchen door swinging in his wake.

CHAPTER TWENTY-NINE
Lines Drawn

"What. The. Hell."

Tori's mouth fell open as Eliza stepped back, the blindfold now limp and useless in her hand. Sharing a grimace with Aquila, she moved forward to catch Tori's attention, drawing her gaze with a gentle wave of the ripped fabric.

"It's okay, I know things look weird, but everything's—"

"Weird? *Weird*? No, no, we've gone *way* past weird," Tori shook her head, eyes passing over Moose's coppery goggles, Daisy's spines, Aquila's wings, Tero's eyes.

Lingering on Otto.

"Hey pretty lady," said the glistening boy, grinning as if it were the most normal thing in the world for him to be standing there with a shock of snow-white hair and skin that shimmered like mother-of-pearl.

Tori folded her arms, the ghost of her old self flickering across her face.

"And what are you supposed to be?"

"Fucking dangerous."

"Oh yeah?"

"But not to you, of course." Otto winked. Tori sneered. Eliza took a step back, feeling distinctly like the world was crumbling away under her feet.

"Um, so what's next?" she asked in a sad attempt to regain control of a situation that had long ago careened out of her hands.

"W-w-well, it s-sounds like y-you guys have d-decided to break into F-Fitzgerald l-l-labs," Tero stammered, velvety wings rustling in disapproval.

"Her brother's disappeared in there," Aquila said, jerking his head at Tori. "We think he's our way to get inside."

"And figure out our super cool epic origin story," injected Moose, flexing his arms and wincing as his bandage pulled taut.

"Do you know how we can do that?" Eliza asked, looking to Tero before remembering that he couldn't see her anyway.

He ran a hand over his buzzed black hair, face twisting in thought.

"Whacha thinkin' there, Dracula?" Otto said, winking at Tori.

Tero cringed at the word but declined to comment, instead answering in Eliza's general direction. "O-one of the g-guards there has a r-rather distasteful a-anime habit."

"Gross," Moose said, sticking out his tongue.

"H-he has f-failed to realize that I-I've attached a v-virus to his latest d-d-download. I-it should a-allow us a-a-access to the m-mainframe."

"Nice one, batman" Moose said.

"D-don't c-c-call me t-that."

With hunched, thoughtful shoulders, Tero began to drift toward his vast array of monitors, fingers twitching as if they were already flying over the keys.

"H-however the virus will only g-get u-us inside. Then w-we'll have t-to f-find the l-lab, which w-won't be easy."

"No problem," Otto said, grinning at Tori and stepping aside to let her lead the way.

Eliza felt like driftwood floating in the back of the cavern, watching as her worlds collided. This was what she wanted, right? For Tori to be friends with them? For the blonde monster to maybe care enough to *not* go to the police and get them all arrested?

Then why did it feel so *wrong*?

"I hope my dad didn't upset you."

138

Eliza jumped as Aquila edged up next to her, smiling down in that adorably sheepish way that made her insides feel like they were on fire. She forced herself to return the smile.

"Of course not. I'm tougher than I look."

"Then you must be pretty darn tough."

"Hey," she said, shoving his arm. "Don't patronize shorter people."

"Everyone's shorter than me, I can't really help it."

Eliza laughed, the sound echoing around the cavern and offering a brief bubble of peace in a decidedly *un*-peaceful morning. Then it popped as reality slammed back in. They were planning to break into a top-secret facility with the help of a girl who only yesterday had been her enemy. One of them was injured, another was unsure, and they expected to go up against the US Army and *win?*

Her smile died.

"This is all pretty strange, isn't it?" Eliza asked, watching Otto wink at Tori.

"Strange is kind of our thing."

"No, not like that. I mean, I don't know what to do here. Your dad hates me. Moose is still *bleeding*." Eliza tilted her face up to Aquila's. "I feel so... confused."

Once again, they were close enough that Eliza only had to rock up onto her tiptoes to touch him, press her lips to his cheek or his mouth...

She looked away, mentally shaking herself.

Now was *not* the time.

"So, um, when all this is over." Aquila's voice was timid, incongruously small for such a big person. "I mean, when we've found Tori's brother and all, would you want to, er, hang out?"

Eliza lifted her eyebrows.

Apparently, it was *the time.*

"You mean like a date?"

"Not if you don't want to," Aquila said quickly. "I was just thinking, it's great that you get along with my brothers. I really appreciate that. But maybe we could do something just, you know... us?"

Eliza couldn't help the breath of laughter that burst out of her. It was so *odd* in this moment, with everything whirlpooling around them and danger circling like a predator, to be thinking about a future in which she and Aquila could spend a quiet moment together just talking. What would they do, fly to a drive-in theatre? Watch the sunset from the roof? Chase *seagulls?*

She chuckled again and immediately regretted it when she saw the flush of red curling up Aquila's neck.

"I'm sorry," Eliza said at once. "I didn't mean to laugh. It was just... I guess I'm kind of freaked out."

"Of course, I understand," Aquila said, straightening, stepping away, locking her out. She could see him forming those walls again, between the *normal* and the *freak*. Shutting down any hope for a life outside this mansion.

It broke her heart.

Eliza grabbed his arm.

"I'd love to go on a date with you," she said with as much sincerity as she could muster, pulling him back around to face her. "I'd love to get to know you better. I think that would be really nice."

Aquila's eyes were still guarded, distant in the way they'd been when she first met him. And she couldn't stand it. To have hurt him, shot him down in a vulnerable moment, that was worse than anything she'd done so far. She had to make things right.

So she did something stupid.

Grabbing the front of Aquila's shirt, she pulled him down to her level, yanked his face to hers, and kissed him.

Aquila was so surprised he didn't have time to react to the mouth suddenly jammed against his, the face pressing against his own. And Eliza couldn't help him because she felt wild and electric and light, as if she might lift off the ground and float away. The chattering voices and echoing cavern faded until Aquila was the only thing in her world, the center of gravity pulling her in, the strange and beautiful force that had eclipsed her life and changed *everything*. She'd wondered what it would feel like to kiss him since the moment they met, but the kinetic, breathless reality of it was better than anything she could have dreamed. He was warm and soft, his wings curved around her, cocooning the two of them against the violent outside world and Eliza felt, despite everything that had happened, safe. She would have stayed in that moment forever.

But she couldn't.

They couldn't afford to lose focus, not now when so much threatened to go wrong.

It took everything she had to pull away from the magnetism Aquila seemed to exude without even trying. She hated herself for ending such a perfect, crystalline, *wonderful* kiss, but her distraction had worked. The dejection on his face had been replaced with a shocked, blushing smile.

"I... what was...?"

"Let's get to work," Eliza answered, patting his cheek and grinning to herself. It hadn't been much—Aquila hadn't even had a chance to respond. Dizziness threatened to unsettle her as she thought about how much *more* could have happened. But it was enough. She was satisfied that his thoughts had been dragged into more cheerful territory as he led them back to the group.

And then she saw Joe.

"Wait, no!"

But Joe was already spinning toward the elevator, his shoulders a tense slash of a line.

"Joe, wait, stop."

Eliza ran up to him, grabbing his arm. It was taut with what he'd just seen. What Eliza had just done.

"I'm sorry. You weren't supposed to—"

"No, I get it," Joe said, turning just enough that she could see his effort at a smile. "I'm in the way, right? I don't have any part of this. What am I gonna do to help here, tell dumb jokes? Moose seems to have that covered."

"You're my *friend,* Joe! I want you here!"

He stared down at her, his eyes distant. Cold.

Foreign.

"Look, Eliza, I've gone along with everything. But this? Breaking into Fitzgerald?" He turned bodily to her now, leaning in so that she could feel his breath on her cheek. "This is too far. I know you, Eliza. I know you like to do dumb stuff. But a *federal crime*? I'm supposed to be your voice of reason, remember? And I'm here telling you this is a bad idea."

Eliza swallowed. He was too close, his voice too detached. It gave her chills to hear him like this.

"I have to help them," she said at last.

"Why? You just met them. A week ago, you didn't even know they were here."

"Well, I do now."

Joe straightened.

"Yeah, and that's it, right? They're all you can think about."

"It's not like that."

"Yes, it is. You're thrilled this happened."

"Of course I'm not *thrilled—*"

"You wanted this all along."

"No I didn't—"

"Then tell me you liked it. Our life at Meru, tell me you were happy."

Eliza opened her mouth, but the words wouldn't come. She couldn't lie, not to Joe's face, not now when it mattered so much.

For a single instant, his eyes swirled with anguish.

"Was it really that bad?" he whispered.

And then he spun away, jamming the button for the elevator. Eliza reached out, but the space between them was a canyon, a gulf of two lives so different that they'd never be compatible.

"Please, listen to me. I care about you."

Joe's shoulders hunched even tighter.

"Apparently not enough to listen."

"Joe wait—"

But he was already yanking open the elevator and disappearing inside. As the grate slammed shut behind him, Eliza couldn't look away from his face, shielded by the rusted bars, trundling out of sight.

"Come back," Eliza whispered.

What was she supposed to do? She couldn't run after him and leave Tori down here alone. And she wasn't even sure if she wanted to. If Eliza was being honest with herself, a small, logical part of her was glad Joe had left. They were about to do something rash and probably dangerous.

And danger didn't mesh well with her friend.

He might be leaving in a storm of hurt, but at least he would be safe.

"Hey, Eliza, you're missing out on all the scheming!" Moose called from the computer screens as Tero typed behind him.

Eliza stumbled over, ignoring the question in Aquila's eyes. Otto was listening to Tori, nodding sagely as she babbled about how her brother *always texted* and *wouldn't have done this unless they made him.* Moose was poking Daisy, trying to get a response. Tero's fingers were flying over his Braille keyboard.

And everything seemed like a dream.

It'll be worth it, Eliza told herself as she watched Tero work. *If I can help them, it'll be worth it. I'll fix it later. We can be friends again.*

But her mind kept going over and over that moment when Joe slammed the elevator door in her face, shutting Eliza out of his life.

She'd been waiting for him to do that for a long time.
That didn't make it any easier.

CHAPTER THIRTY
The Real Question

The base looked quiet. As a coppery sun dipped below the tree line and a gentle wind made the autumn leaves around them shiver, Eliza watched as a jeep bearing Amile Robillard and her posse pulled out onto the main road and headed toward Scottstown.

"T-t-there she g-goes," Tero said, head cocked as Moose's fingers flew over the tablet they'd brought with them. "R-right on s-schedule."

"Says here that the lab will be under lockdown." Moose looked up, goggles glinting. "Lockdown doesn't sound good."

"I-I can g-get us in, j-just g-get me to the d-door."

But still none of them moved. Eliza twisted her fingers into the chain-link fence, thinking of Joe. Wondering what he would say if here were here.

The thought was enough to make her feel like she'd eaten something rotten.

"What are we waiting for?" Tori said, folding her arms.

"Well fucking said," Otto piped in, grinning at Tori. The two of them were separated only by the bare minimum distance to keep Tori from touching Otto's venomous skin, glistening in the few places his hoodie and gloves didn't cover. Eliza had spent the last few hours at the mansion making whispered bets with Aquila. Apparently, Mr. Eckelson had anti-venom stocked up in the mansion in case of *emergencies*.

How long until Tori needed to use it?

"Alright, let's go," Aquila said, pushing off the tree he'd been leaning on. He held his arms out to her, but Eliza shook her head.

"Let's do this in one trip. I'll go in the old-fashioned way," she said with a wink, leaping up and grabbing the top of the fence.

Not to be outdone, Tori followed with a lofty sniff.

Eliza swung her leg around the spiny crest of the perimeter fence, pausing to watch Aquila swoop over them. He was so graceful. Even weighed down by Otto's bulk and Moose's twitching limbs, he rode the air with effortless elegance, wings curved as if flying were nothing. Something easy, natural even. Tero swept past with Daisy, smaller and lighter and silent without the rustle of feathers. But just as glorious.

"Where the hell did you *find* these guys?" Tori panted, clutching the top of the fence.

Eliza dropped herself to the other side, rolling her eyes.

"No, really, I mean I know like attracts like. But even *you're* not this weird."

Eliza glared at the sky, watching the sunset streak the low-hanging clouds crimson. Tori, oblivious to Eliza's frustration, continued.

"I always thought that getting paired with you would lead to some strange shit, but this is beyond—"

"Why do you have to do that?" Eliza hissed, rounding on Tori as her roommate dropped to the ground next to her. "You make everyone hate you and then seem surprised when no one's there to help. Where are your friends, huh? Where are Hector and the twins and all those kids from the woods? They're not *here*, are they?" Eliza leaned in, ignoring the surprised flicker of unease in Tori's eyes. "They're back at Meru and safe and have no idea that your brother is somewhere in *there*. Because you didn't want to tell them."

"Back off," Tori snarled, but Eliza didn't. She stepped closer, nose to nose, pulsing with that irresistible impulse to drag everything into the open.

"I'm here, Tori," Eliza spat. "Helping. Despite all the *shit* you said about me, I decided to do this stupid thing because it's the right thing to do. But if you're just going to bitch about it, maybe I'll go back and take my friends with me and leave you here to deal with it by *yourself*."

Eliza spun away, but Tori's voice stopped her.

"I'm sorry."

Eliza froze, hardly daring to believe.

"I…" Tori took a deep breath. "I'm not sure how to do all this. Asking for help?" She snorted. "Not exactly my thing."

"No kidding," Eliza muttered.

"I know what I'm like." She took a deep breath, the air hissing through her teeth. "I'm not that dense. But… well, I guess I could stop. Maybe."

The last word tilted up like a question. Eliza clenched her fists, spinning back. She was braced to see the joke, the sneer, the twist of words.

But all she found was a lost-looking girl who was scared for her brother.

Eliza released the breath she'd been holding.

"You could start by being nice."

Tori let out a half-laugh.

"How do I do that?"

"For one, stop making fun of them." Eliza jerked her head to where Aquila was setting down, nestled in the darkness beside the nearest barrack. "Maybe show a little gratitude."

Tori's lips twitched and Eliza wondered which Vagabond she was thinking about.

"Okay then." Tori stared at where the brothers were turning, Moose staring at them with his signature *why is everyone so slow* exasperation. She took a deep breath. "Thanks. I mean it. You had no reason to help me."

"I still don't."

"Well, maybe we can start over." Tori stuck out her hand. "Friends?"

147

Eliza stared at the hand for a long moment. A small, petty part of her longed to roll her eyes, turn away, take this offering and throw it back in the other girl's face. It's what *Tori* would have done, had their roles been reversed. But maybe the only way to help someone was to show them a better way.

It's what Katie would have told her to do.

Eliza slapped her palm into Tori's, squeezing perhaps a little harder than necessary.

"Friends."

Suddenly, Moose appeared next to them.

"What's going on, you guys are taking *forever*."

Chapter Thirty-One
Breaking Things

Eliza grinned.

"Sorry, we're coming." But before she could do anything, Moose was wrapping long, thin fingers around her wrist and dragging her toward the barrack. "Ow, ow, wait, too fast." But she couldn't help laughing when she saw Aquila's expression.

"Moose, we've talked about this," he said, folding his arms.

But the bespectacled boy was vibrating, bouncing between them like a ping-pong ball.

"They were *dillydallying*. We have the thingy to do!"

"Thingy," Aquila said, shaking his head. "How inspiring."

"W-we have exactly t-three minutes before my t-trojan takes h-hold," Tero said in a hushed voice, gesturing around the corner. "I j-just heard the g-guard patrol walk p-past."

Aquila rolled his shoulders. "Ok everyone, it's go time."

"Ooh, how original," Moose whispered, but no one laughed. The patrolling guards had reminded them all of the danger, the weight on their mission.

And the consequences if they failed.

Eliza swallowed and gestured forward.

"Lead the way," she said, smiling at Aquila.

He didn't smile back, his face as serious as if it were carved from stone. He stepped around the corner, tugging the group behind him like eddies of water. The seven intruders made their way silently to the only door they could see, a plain white rectangle embedded in the sleek wall, marked only by a simple plaque.

Fitzgerald Labs.

Eliza couldn't help the goosebumps that popped out along her arms. The last time she'd been here haunted her memories. She could still see the soldiers flying around, the dark-haired woman, that *man*.

Was he a victim of this Superman Virus? Had they tried to turn him into a super-solder?

Why hadn't it worked?

They slammed into the wall, Moose darting back and forth to check for anything Tero hadn't been prepared for.

"Looks clear," Moose said, returning with a salute.

"A-any minute n-now," Tero said, bent over a tiny security screen.

Suddenly, the screen flashed. The door hissed open, sliding noiselessly into the wall.

"Alright everyone," Aquila said, his voice as tight as his shoulders. "Stay together. And don't touch anything."

He led the way, closely followed by Tero, Moose, and a pale Tori. Eliza waited, letting Otto elbow Daisy to get him moving.

And then she was inside.

It looked exactly as she'd thought it would, like the pristine interior of a medical ward. Narrow halls and high-tech locks, cameras coating every surface.

She glanced up at the nearest one, but no red light blinked back at her.

Deactivated.

"Well done, batman," Moose said, returning from a length of the hall, having checked every single camera in the seconds it had taken the rest of them to file inside.

"D-don't c-call me—"

"Yeah, yeah, okay." Moose flapped a hand. "It looks like there's extra security down there, at the end. And stairs! Lots of stairs!"

"Don't get excited," Aquila muttered, but Moose was already disappearing down the corridor.

"I-I'll start hacking into the s-system," Tero said, fingers feeling over the nearest security keyboard.

"I'll help," Tori said, leaning over the monitor on the wall, muttering to Tero as she helped him find a port for his handheld tablet.

Eliza drifted down the hallway, leaving them behind. Why was it so empty? She'd been braced for a fight, had come in praying that no one else would get shot in whatever chaos bloomed out of their break-in. But Tero had managed to turn off the cameras without issue and they hadn't seen a single soldier beyond the patrol that had walked right past them.

Something was wrong.

Following a deep instinct that she couldn't explain, even to herself, Eliza ambled toward Moose, who was lingering at the mouth of a dark staircase that twisted into the ground. But she didn't quite reach him. Something compelled her to stop at a door, a simple swinging thing with a key-card lock, the panel dead from Tero's attack. It was probably a broom closet or bathroom or something equally innocuous.

But why would they lock a bathroom?

She curled her fingers around the handle. Waited a moment.

And opened it.

What the...?

As her eyes adjusted to the strange red glow of the room beyond and she saw the huge screens, the enormous tubes of gel-like liquid, the *beds,* she suddenly wished that Tero's hack-job hadn't worked so well.

"Holy shit," Eliza breathed, stepping inside.

There, spread out before her like the most surreal carpet, was row after row after row of empty cots, hooked up to blinking machinery. Around the edge of the room, pulsing scarlet, were pillars of fluid moving like eerie lava-lamps, sprouting tubes that snaked around the room like tree roots.

Or veins.

"Guys!"

Moose's call made her swing around in time to see the thin boy darting between cots and wires. His head seemed to blur as he cast around, absorbing the room orders of magnitude faster than she had.

Aquila swung around the door frame, stumbling as he took in what was inside.

"Woah," he whispered.

"Oh my god?" Tori breathed.

Tero was already at the nearest computer, plugging in his tablet as Otto read the screen over his shoulder.

"Says here this is for the secondary trials, after they complete mission *Labrador*, whatever that means," Otto said as Tori hovered behind him, biting her nails. "And that red shit on the wall... that's the virus. Apparently it's the strongest version they've made so far. Zeus line. But it's not... stabilized. Stabilized? What the fuck does that mean?"

Tero straightened, his hands dropping, stepping back from the monitor. He turned to face them, and his milky eyes yanked everyone's gaze in, holding their attention with an inescapable gravity that made Eliza's hair stand on end.

"T-that's w-why they're h-hunting us," Tero said, his words quiet but carrying, filling the red-tinted room. "T-they haven't m-managed to stabilize the m-mutation."

"What do you mean?" Aquila asked. They all hung on Tero's next words.

"T-they're trying to r-recreate what that scientist d-d-did to us," Tero said, gaping sightlessly at the beds, the tubes, the twisting IV lines. "O-our DNA h-held the mutation. F-f-for some reason, t-theirs d-doesn't."

"Why?" Eliza asked.

"Well asked, Ms. Mason," came a cold voice from the doorway. "We've been wondering the very same thing."

CHAPTER THIRTY-TWO
Busted

Amile Robillard stood in the door, backlit by the sterile lights of the hallway, wearing the coldest smile Eliza had ever seen. She was as pale as a corpse, lips the color of the liquid around them, black hair glittering and straight as a knife against the sharp line of her jaw.

Behind her, the corridor was thick with men and women in uniform.

They were trapped.

Eliza backed away, half aware of the Vagabonds as they scrambled to the other side of the room, congregating behind her.

Amile grinned.

"I suppose I should thank you. You've made it almost easy. A call from your roommate. A missing sibling pulling at the heartstrings." She tutted. "Family people are so *predictable*." Eliza's eyes narrowed and Amile feigned shock, laying three delicate fingers on her Kevlar chest plate. "You think we haven't been tapping your phone? How cute."

"What do you want?" Eliza snarled, watching from the corner of her eye as Aquila's wings snapped out.

"Not you, that's for sure," Amile said, striding between empty beds, coming closer. "You're nothing but trouble. Expelled five times, multiple counts of brawling. Always one to stand up for the poor and oppressed, hero of outcasts." She chuckled. "But you've been useful enough."

"Back. Off," Eliza said, throwing out her arms, but for what? Soldiers were filing into the room, training handheld pistols on them, pinning them there. The uniformed men and women shifted nervously as their eyes snagged on Eliza, on the figures behind her. She glanced back. Otto's fists were tight, his muscles bulging with rage. Daisy's

153

spines were all standing straight. Tero looked ready to pass out. And Aquila was shoving Tori behind him, stepping forward to grab Eliza.

But someone was missing.

Where did Moose go?

Eliza moved to meet Amile, stepping out of Aquila's reach.

"You won't get them," she said. "Not ever."

Amile was only feet away now, close enough for Eliza to see the yellow flecks in her eyes. They made the woman look feline, like a predator circling a meal.

"You don't seem to understand, Eliza," she said with a chuckle. "They aren't *boys*. They're *army property,* and therefore already mine."

"They're people, you sick bitch."

Amile folded her arms, cocking one hip.

"Not according to the government."

Eliza laughed, the sound half frantic as it echoed around the spooky tubes and encroaching soldiers.

"Really? Does the Senate know what's going on here? What about the President? Because I bet they'd be saying something different if they did."

Something flickered across Amile's expression, darkening her yellow-tinted eyes. Fear? Guilt?

Had Eliza struck a chord?

"Well I guess we'll never find out, will we—"

"Eliza, look out!"

Moose's shout broke the stillness, followed by a smash. Eliza threw a glance to the side, barely registering the fire axe as it swung, hit glass, shattered the nearest tube.

She gasped.

"You *cretin!*" Amile shrieked.

And then blood-like fluid was exploding out of the wall, splashing to the floor, surging toward them.

"Run!" Aquila shouted, grabbing Eliza's arms and dragging her away from Amile, who was now barking angry orders. They all knew she couldn't fire at the boys. The soldiers couldn't risk hurting the Vagabonds.

But the two perfectly normal girls were fair game.

Eliza ducked as a shot went over her head.

"Otto, grab Tori!" Aquila shouted sweeping Eliza into his arms as they all sprinted for the back of the long, narrow room. Air slammed out of Eliza's lungs as she was thrown into the air, pressed into Aquila's chest. She looked over his shoulder. The soldiers were swarming now, splashing through the swamp of red liquid with grim determination. They didn't seem concerned as the intruders sprinted for the back of the room.

Which meant there wasn't an exit back there.

"Aquila, we have go to back," Eliza said, struggling to get out of his grip.

"No," he snarled, eyes frantic as they hunted for another door.

"There's no other way."

"Tero!"

At Moose's shout, Eliza twisted in Aquila's grip to see Tero on the ceiling, hanging upside-down and ripping at the plaster.

"Stop them!" Amile barked.

"There's a vent!" Tero called down.

Before Eliza could do so much as gasp, Aquila used his significant strength to throw her into the air. She kicked, flailing as her body sailed up, up, up. The world spun. Soldiers shouted. A gun fired, crackling through the air by her head.

Tero grabbed her ankle and swung her into the piping.

"G-grab hold!"

She managed to lock her limbs around a thick water pipe, dangling like a sloth.

"Go, go, g-go," Tero breathed, hands shaking violently.

Eliza scrambled into the open vent, pulling her legs out of sight just as a bullet pinged against the pipe, too close to her thigh for comfort.

She heard Tori shriek as Aquila threw her up next. The others were following, surging for the exit Tero had created. But a problem was looming, huge and terrifying in Eliza's mind.

Aquila was never going to fit.

Perhaps Tero could squeeze himself inside, but there was no way that Aquila and his massive wings could follow. He was going to sacrifice himself to help the rest of them escape.

She couldn't let that happen.

Eliza ducked her head out, glimpsing Tori's tear-streaked face right by the opening. Tero was dangling next to her, waiting to grab Moose.

Otto was still on the ground.

"What's he doing?" Eliza gasped.

Tero didn't answer, swinging Moose up to the ceiling. Moose grinned manically.

"Just watch," he said, skittering along the nearest pipe.

They all looked down as Aquila snapped his wings open, lifting Daisy into the air. There was a moment of silence in which Eliza realized frantically, hysterically, that they were all now clear of the water-based fluid coating the floor. And, judging from Otto's grin, that was hardly a coincidence.

Then Aquila's voice rang out with a single, solid command.

"Now!"

CHAPTER THIRTY-THREE
Left Behind

Otto smirked, the skin of his face glistening. He was spreading his bare, shimmering fingers wide, gloves tossed aside, even as the soldiers moved to surround him.

"Freeze!" one ordered.

"Dumb fucks," Eliza heard Otto mutter before plunging his hands into the fluid lapping at his feet.

The very air seemed to crackle. There was a blinding flash and a sound like the loudest static Eliza had ever heard. She ducked back into the vent, but still she felt the *whoosh* of something fill the room, making her tightly curled hair rise like a cloud.

Soldiers screamed. Otto cackled.

And the ground sparkled like one big live wire.

"What the...?" Eliza breathed.

"He's shocking them," Tori said, mouth hanging open. "He's *electric*."

Eliza gaped at the scene.

Eagle. Housefly. Bat.

And...eel?

She shook her head. No time to think about that now. Otto might be delaying the attack, but he couldn't keep the soldiers at bay forever. She had to do *something*. Trying to swallow the oppressive claustrophobia, Eliza forced herself to turn herself around in the narrow vent and crawl toward the light of another grate. This one was over the hallway. She squinted down to see the soldiers crowded into the narrow space, all of them armed, all of them waiting.

There was no way out.

Unless...

Leaving the screams of electrocuted soldiers behind and ignoring Aquila's frantic shout for her to come back, Eliza edged her way down the vent until she was over the stairwell Moose had found, leading into the basement. Soldiers glanced up, their attention drawn by the warbling sound of her movements, but she passed them quickly, hunting, searching.

There.

A fire sprinkler right below the vent. Eliza squinted and could just make out the tiny glass tube in the middle of the sprinkler, the delicate signal waiting for heat.

If she could break that tube, soak *everyone*, maybe it would help Otto. Maybe he could fight more of them.

Maybe they could escape.

It was the only thing she could think to do. So, heart in her throat, Eliza kicked the grate open. Soldiers whirled toward her, but she was already leaning out of the grate as far as she could go, feet pressing into the sides of the vent to keep her steady. She reached, stretched, channeling all her best gymnastics lessons as her body shook with exhaustion and terror.

Almost…there…

Jamming her finger between the metal bars around the nozzle, she poked the glass tube once. Twice.

"Come *on*," she groaned as guns swung up toward her.

On the third jab, the glass shattered. Pain sizzled up her arm. Blood spurted from sliced fingers.

And a shrieking wail split the air.

There was a shout, a gunshot, an explosion of plaster by her head.

"AHH!" she screamed, toppling out of the vent. But she didn't make it to the floor. Arms locked around her, dragging her away from the wall just as water flooded from the line of sprinklers, filling the hall with rain.

Eliza looked up to find that horrible woman staring down at her, face twisted into a furious sneer.

"Kill her."

Amile's order was cold, emotionless, and final. Eliza struggled, kicking out, but thick hands were holding her there. Forcing her to her knees. Screams still reverberated from the testing room, Otto still protecting his brothers. But they felt so far away.

No one was there to save her this time.

Eliza watched as a new shadow approached, flexing his arms, grinning at her.

Tori's brother.

She wriggled like a fish, but it was no use. She was going to die. This man, the very person they'd come to save, was going to kill her.

She looked up to face him, chilled by the feral glint in his eyes.

We were too late, she realized. *He's already infected.*

This was all for nothing.

The man drew back to punch her, to destroy her with nothing more than brute force. It was almost offensive, the intimacy of it. The primal, ancient death rather than the clean end of a bullet.

She glared back at him, defiant to the end.

"*Martin?!*"

Suddenly, Tori dropped out of the ceiling. Martin Bent blinked at his sister, arm frozen midair. His mouth was pulled into that horrible, rictus grimace of a smile, but it faded as he gaped at the last person in the world he'd expected to see there.

"Tori?"

"Kill her, Private!"

But Amile's words fell on deaf ears.

Tori stepped between Eliza and her brother, mouth open, hands held out.

"Martin, what the hell are you doing?" she whispered.

And then Aquila crashed through the cluster of soldiers like a cannonball.

"NO!" Tori screamed as Aquila whipped Private Bent aside, shattering drywall. With a kick, Eliza burst out of the arms of her surprised captors.

And then everything descended into madness.

There were bodies all around her, crushed into the narrow space, fighting, punching, shoving. The flash of the fire alarm blended with the chaos of water, making the air blur, pulse, beat. Was this how Moose saw the world? As if drawn by the thought, Moose materialized at her elbow, linking his arms around Eliza and Tori and dragging them toward the door.

"Aquila!" Eliza shouted, but all she could see was a tangle of limbs and feathers and feet, Aquila roaring as he fought through the soldiers there to subdue him.

"Stop them!" Amile screamed. "Don't let them escape!"

Eliza tried to find the door, but she couldn't. Had it closed? Locked them in? What were they going to do? How long could they fight?

Amile was elbowing into the hallway, coming closer.

"No," Eliza moaned in desperation as even Moose paused, unable to find a way out. Daisy and Tero were with them, watching Otto crackle in the doorway. Even he looked nervous.

"What the fuck are we supposed—?"

But Otto's question was cut off by an earth-shattering, bone-jarring BOOM. The wall around the entrance cracked, curving toward them like a parallel universe reaching out. Moose hauled Tori and Eliza back just in time to miss the sliding door crumpling inward, folding like aluminum foil. Chunks of broken concrete snowed around them.

And there, over it all, she heard the whiny rumbling of an old-fashioned engine.

Eliza gasped, choking on drywall. She glimpsed a rusted grill through the bent doorframe, the glitter of a window as a truck door opened.

"Am I late?"

"*Joe*?!"

"GO!"

Aquila had appeared by her shoulder, grabbing her and Tori and throwing them bodily at the crack in the door. Tori slammed against the failing wall, scrambling through the opening. Joe passed her on his way inside, stumbling over a rockslide of concrete to grab Eliza's arm.

"That old girl's stronger than she looks," Joe said with a mad laugh, yanking her toward Old Betty.

"But... Aquila... Tero..."

Something black swept by her head with a high-pitched cry, vanishing into the night outside. Moose and Daisy were next, yanking a still sparking Otto into the darkness.

"Get out of here!" Aquila shouted.

"Not without you," Eliza screamed back, struggling against Joe's grip.

Joe's features twisted, but Eliza didn't have time to read them.

"You go," Joe shouted before releasing her. "I'll get him."

"No, wait—"

But Joe was already gone, sprinting into the mess of fluid and bodies and flying fists.

Aquila was fighting three soldiers at once, one of them Tori's brother. Eliza watched in horror as Amile strode up behind him, accepting a strange long-nosed rifle from a man in a lab coat.

She lifted the rifle, closed one eye, and aimed for Aquila.

"Watch out!"

Eliza made to scramble back, to stop that *woman*. But before she could, Joe picked up a hunk of concrete and threw it. Aquila ducked. It hit the private behind him, knocking them backwards.

There was a crunch of metal behind her as Tori backed Old Betty out of the hole the truck had made.

Amile leveled the rifle.

Joe grabbed Aquila's wing, hauling him backwards.

"Get. In. The. Truck!" Joe snarled, barely audible over the shriek of the alarm.

Eliza seemed to watch the whole scene unfold in slow-motion. Aquila, distracted by the strange sensation of someone pulling on his wing, winced, swung toward her with a resigned expression.

There was a near-silent *thump* from Amile as she squeezed the trigger.

A projectile went sailing into the air where Aquila had been a moment before.

Missing him.

Hitting Joe.

"NO!"

But Aquila's arm was already wrapping around her middle, grabbing her before she could lunge back into the hallway. Soldiers were descending on Joe, dragging him back, leaving only ripples in the red fluid to mark where he had fallen. Aquila hadn't seen, couldn't possibly know what he was carrying her away from.

She kicked out, desperate to get free.

"Joe! JOE!"

The last thing she saw was her friend's bleary eyes closing as Amile stepped in front of him, grinning at Eliza like a self-satisfied cat.

And then Aquila yanked her outside and leapt into the air, soaring over the fence and ignoring Eliza's screams as they followed a crumpled, wheezing truck into the darkness.

CHAPTER THIRTY-FOUR
The Guilty

"Go back! We have to go back! Turn around, we have to save him!"

Eliza squirmed in Aquila's arms, twisting to watch Fitzgerald Base disappearing to the slow, steady beat of Aquila's wings. She could see soldiers squeezing through the crack Joe's truck had created, congealing around shattered concrete like platelets around a wound. Jeeps swung into view, high beams slicing through the night, ready to chase Old Betty down. But she couldn't see her friend. That awful moment played in her mind again and again and again. Joe falling, Amile stepping in front of him, Aquila dragging her away.

Tears blurred her vision as they sailed into the rapidly darkening night, leaving the base behind.

"Please," she sobbed. "Please go back."

"It wouldn't do any good," Aquila said, his voice shaking even as he soared gracefully over the evergreen tips. "We need to regroup."

"Why would she want Joe? What's she going to do with him?"

"I think she was aiming for me."

Eliza wasn't sure it was that simple. Amile had wanted Aquila, there was no doubt about that. But she'd seemed just as pleased to get the tall redheaded boy instead. Eliza blinked and that chilling serpentine smile appeared on the back of her eyelids.

What was Amile thinking as her men dragged Joe away?

The question was enough to make Eliza shiver.

Hanging limp in Aquila's arms, her mind vortexed with panic. It was her fault, all her fault. She'd been the one to drag Joe into the woods, ask for his help in escaping Amile's men. She'd used him at every turn, taken his friendship for granted, and now...

Now he was gone.

Through blurry eyes, Eliza saw something approaching them, a dark shape against the clouds.

Tero.

He waved at Aquila with one hand, the glitter of a cellphone light illuminating the underside of his face.

"T-t-the others w-will meet us in t-t-the woods. D-d-don't want to lead them h-h-home."

The dark-skinned boy looked almost pale in the moonlight, his white eyes wide, his stutter worse than ever. Tero's leathery wings might be silent, but Eliza could almost hear his thudding worry. Only last week, this Vagabond had been reading, playing video games, safe in his adopted father's basement.

And now he was running for his life.

Another thing for Eliza to take blame for.

Aquila nodded and tilted his wings, sweeping them away from the distant spires of the Eckelson estate and deeper into the forest. Eliza didn't react. She watched her feet pass over the carpet of greenery, a detached numbness spreading through her. She'd failed, utterly and completely, and it was impossible to face. Instead, she found her mind shutting down, blocking out the night like a TV screen going dark.

A memory popped into her emptying mind: Katie coming home from her freshman year of college, right before she was diagnosed. Thin and pale, the beginnings of the illness making her hair look like tattered thread, she'd come up to Eliza and opened her arms. And Eliza had turned away. At twelve, Eliza was already struggling with anger and the strange tides of puberty. Some of her nameless rage had settled on her sister. After all, Katie had left. Katie had abandoned her. Katie had *moved on*. To a younger Eliza, it had seemed like the most unforgivable of sins.

Until Katie left for good.

What would you have done? Eliza thought, lifting the question like a lantern. *What would you do now?*

Aquila folded his wings and they began to drop, but this time Eliza didn't scream. The two of them plummeted through tree branches and leaves, a few whacking Eliza beneath the chin. She barely noticed. The moment they landed, Eliza's knees gave out. She sagged into Aquila's arms. The other Vagabonds and Tori clustered around, voices swirling, beating against the numb edges of Eliza's mind.

But she couldn't think through the tears.

"What in the *fucking* hell was that?"

"We have to save my brother!"

"Did you see what I did in there? They were like *woah* and I was like *oh no*, but that Joe guy, Eliza's friend, his truck must be made of *steel* to break through that door. I guess it might literally be made of steel..."

Aquila wasn't listening, turning his back on the cluster of bodies and crouching down to catch Eliza's eye.

"You okay?"

Slowly, as if she was drugged, Eliza raised her gaze.

"No," she said, not sure what else to offer. What else to give. She was broken, finally brought down by the very thing her mother had always warned her about.

One of these days you're going to land yourself in real trouble, and then what will you do?

But the problem was that she hadn't landed *herself* in real trouble.

She'd landed Joe in it.

Suddenly, Aquila was shoved aside. Tori's face appeared, blocking out the moon with a halo of blonde hair.

"We need to make a plan, Eliza. My brother's still in there, and now your friend, whatever his name is. We need to act fast."

I suppose I should thank you, Amile had said. *You've made it almost easy. A call from your roommate. A missing sibling pulling at the heartstrings.*

Something stirred in Eliza's chest.

A missing sibling pulling at the heartstrings.

"You knew," Eliza whispered.

"Pull yourself together, Eliza," Tori went on. "You need to—
"

"You *knew*."

That time, her words broke through. Tori fell silent, mouth falling open.

"What are you talking about?"

Eliza clenched her fists.

"You called me when your brother went missing. You helped her lure us in." She spat on the ground between them. "You planned this."

"Don't be ridiculous."

"Why should we trust you? Why did I *ever* trust you? You've been nothing but cruel and petty and stupid—"

Without warning, Tori's hand came out of nowhere, slapping Eliza, snapping her head to the side. Her teeth clicked together, cheek burning in the perfect imprint of Tori's palm. Eliza gasped, clutched her face, but Tori was leaning in like all the challenges Eliza had never been able to turn down.

"I'm not *stupid*," Tori growled, voice red-hot and violent.

Maybe it was the numbness, or maybe it was just years of cultivated impulsiveness, but Eliza was powerless to stop the wave of pure, unfiltered *rage* that washed through her. Fists clenched. Muscles pulled taut. Her stomach roiled with the nauseated hunger for *blood*.

Without pausing to think, Eliza lunged at Tori.

CHAPTER THIRTY-FIVE
Territorial

They fell.

The autumn leaves crunched like radio static beneath them as they rolled, shrieking, punching, grabbing.

"Catfight!" Moose crowed.

"Pull them apart!" Aquila snapped, shoving his brother aside.

But the two girls couldn't hear them, each consumed by their own passions. Eliza wrapped her dark fingers into Tori's light hair. Tori responded by elbowing Eliza in the gut. A branch jammed into the tender skin behind Eliza's knee and she jerked, giving Tori the opportunity to wrap an arm around her neck. Eliza shifted, bit down. Tori shrieked and threw out a wild punch that collided with Eliza's hip.

Someone grabbed Eliza's feet, yanking her away. She tried to roll back, claw her way closer, but Aquila was too strong. Like the unforgiving pull of a tow truck, he hauled her to safety, ignoring her spitting and cursing. On the other side of the clearing, close to where Old Betty sat crumpled and silent, Otto lifted Tori from the ground, careful to keep his hands from touching her bare skin.

"Calm down!" Aquila barked, breaking through Eliza's fury. "Everyone calm down!"

Eliza would have ignored him and kept on fighting if not for Tero's expression. The boy was curled into the shadow of his own wings, mouth open, sightless eyes huge and terrified.

So she forced herself to stop, taking a deep breath.

"I'm done," she spat, not yet able to mean it.

Aquila grip relaxed. Across from her, Tori swayed, a glistening handprint on her sweater.

"Sorry," Otto said, ducking his head.

Tori ignored him, nostrils still flared as she met Eliza's gaze.

"I didn't plan this," Tori said again, breathing deeply.

"Bullshit," Eliza snapped.

"Look, you don't know the first thing about me. So I'll tell you. My mom left when I was five. My dad raised the two of us with what he earned in his hardware store, but there was no way he could afford Meru. So I studied my *ass* off for the scholarship that lets me go there. So no, I'm not stupid. I wanna go to law school. But I can't do that if I get kicked out or involved in some weird *shit* that ends up on my record. So no, I did not *plan* any of this."

Eliza shook her head, ready to turn away and leave Tori to her lies. But then the other girl spoke again and Eliza was rooted to the spot.

"And with Martin, I… I didn't want you to know about him because…" Tori swallowed. Eliza watched her pale throat pulse. "He doesn't like me. Meru me I mean. He says I've changed. So I keep him separate from that life and that life separate from him."

"Are you sure it's not because you're embarrassed that your brother's in the army?"

Tori straightened, lifting her chin with the most imperious expression Eliza had ever seen.

"My brother is a goddamned hero."

Eliza stepped forward, extracting herself from Aquila's arms.

"If it weren't for you, we wouldn't have gone into that lab," Eliza said.

"If it weren't for you, Joe wouldn't have either," Tori shot back.

"Um, ladies…." Moose said, head whipping back and forth between them.

They both ignored him, stepping closer like predators about to strike. Tori spoke first.

"I'm not giving up on them. You can accuse me all you like, but I'm going back in there and finding my brother. You owe it to Joe to do the same."

"Don't you tell me—"

"We need to work *together*. So are you with me or not?"

Eliza clenched her fists, but Tori was right. She couldn't dissolve into her own self-pity and anger, not now when someone she cared about was in trouble. Her eyes drifted around the clearing, to jittering Moose, petrified Tero, Daisy in the shadows, Otto in the light. And Aquila, who looked ready to collapse.

She swallowed. Forced herself to relax.

"Fine," she said at last. "I'm with you. So what do *you* want to do?"

Tori glanced back at Otto.

"We need to get back to the dorm."

"Excuse me?" Eliza said.

"We need weapons."

"What are you going to fight them with, *pencils?*"

When Tori swung back around to Eliza, there was a ferocity in her gaze that Eliza had never seen before. But now that she saw it, she realized it had been there all along and she'd just never wanted to admit it. Flinty, crackling, *terrifying*, there was something about Tori that made Eliza think of tigers and wildfires.

"There's a lockbox under my bunk."

"I remember," Eliza said, suddenly cautious.

"I have three handguns in there, plus ammo. Should be enough to get us started."

"Woah, I did *not* see that coming," Moose said, bouncing from foot to foot.

Eliza gaped at her roommate, this creature she'd lived with for two months and suddenly realized she didn't know at all.

"My dad's into guns," Tori continued with a shrug. "I've had one of my own since I was seven."

Eliza had thought that after meeting the boys and seeing the test-subjects in Fitzgerald Labs, her world couldn't possibly get any weirder. But here it was, sliding out of control again. Tori was a *gun person*? A girl who'd grown up *shooting* things and then somehow clawed her way to the top of a prep school?

"That's... new," Eliza said, hating that she sounded impressed.

"Whatever. It's not important. What's important is that we get back there before that woman does something weird to Joe or weird*er* to my brother."

"Alright then," Eliza said, rolling her stiff shoulders. "I guess it's high time I learned to hold a weapon."

The expression on Tori's face, despite everything that had happened, was enough to make Eliza laugh.

CHAPTER THIRTY-SIX
Waiting Up

"So you could have shot me anytime you wanted?"

Even in the dim illumination of the streetlights as they crept toward Meru's main green, Eliza could see Tori rolling her eyes.

"I mean, that's insane, isn't it?" Eliza went on. "You could have killed me whenever we had a fight."

"Jesus, Eliza, get *over* it," Tori muttered, dragging Eliza behind a tree to wait for a blue Subaru to drift past them. Eliza flexed her bandaged hand as she watched the car disappear around the corner, wincing as the padding pulled tight over her palm.

It was the dark, dead period past midnight and before dawn when the world seemed like a different universe. Things moved slower. Shadows shifted lazily as the moon peeked through the clouds, making the dim park look like it was underwater. This close to Halloween, there were enough pumpkins on front lawns and bats hanging from false spiderwebs to give Eliza the creeps.

Luckily, she was too distracted to let herself get scared.

"I'd never seen a gun in my life," Eliza said, shaking her head. "And then I come here and have to clean a gunshot, almost get shot myself, *and* find out that my roommate has been hiding weapons under her bed."

"I wasn't *hiding* them."

"I'm seeing my whole year differently."

"It's only been three months."

"Yeah, but three months where I didn't understand what was going on *at all*."

"Drop it, Eliza," Tori growled, leading the way through the hedge that separated Scottstown from Meru's campus.

"Did the other girls know?"

"I'm warning you…"

"I mean, if Yuri and Marta found out—"

Tori stopped walking, her whole body tightening like a violin string. Eliza took a step back, bracing for the explosion, but after a prolonged moment of tense silence, Tori's shoulders slumped. She tilted her head back to stare at the sky and Eliza felt a moment of guilt for pushing so hard.

"Why didn't you just tell people?" Eliza asked in a quiet voice. "It would have been so much easier."

Tori snorted.

"Easier to be labeled a weirdo and never talked to again?"

A laugh burst out of Eliza. "You mean like me?"

Tori winced. "I don't care what they think," she said in a would-be certain voice. But Eliza chuckled again

"Yeah, and I'm a possum. Come on, I know you say you're proud of your brother and your dad. But maybe you're embarrassed of them too. Just a bit."

Tori rounded on Eliza, eyes blazing.

"I am *not* embarrassed of my family."

"Then why hide them? And don't give me that *they don't like the Meru you* crap."

For a moment, Tori didn't respond. She stood like a statue in the stretching shadows close to the home they had shared for the better part of a semester, her face angry, cold, inhuman.

Then her mask cracked.

Tori spun away.

"We should hurry," she muttered in a strangled voice.

Eliza grabbed her shoulder to stop her. Leaning in, Eliza squeezed the sharp line of Tori's delicate collarbone with the hand not covered in bandages.

"It's okay. We all have thoughts we're not proud of. I'm certainly not one to judge."

172

Things welled up in Eliza's mind, enough examples to make her flush with shame. The anger she still sometimes found buried in her brain that Katie had to die and leave her alone. The selfish yearning for the Vagabonds to include her, no matter how much danger it put them in. The even more selfish desire for Joe to abandon them and stay safe.

And now, her horrible guilt that she'd been the one to drive Joe to do what he did.

Tori yanked her shoulder out of Eliza's grip.

"I'm fine."

"I didn't say you weren't."

"Then what are you waiting for?"

Now it was Eliza's turn to roll her eyes, but Tori was already trotting up the walkway, drawn by the familiar sight of their squat dorm hemmed in by manicured flower gardens and a pristine lawn.

Eliza caught up, peering around the bushes at the front door.

"It really is as boring as it looks," she whispered.

"There are no lights on," Tori replied, still not quite looking at Eliza.

"Doesn't mean someone's not reading under their covers."

They both watched for a moment, breaths held, hearts hammering, waiting for their dorm mom to come bursting out and find them there or police sirens to shatter the silence. How much had the school rallied around their absence? Tori had only been missing for a night, but Eliza? She cringed to think about what the headmaster was thinking about her now. What her *parents* would be thinking. They'd probably been called, told their daughter had *run off*. It wouldn't be long until they came here in person to drag her home. Eliza had turned off her phone after they fled the base and had refused to turn it back on ever since, knowing Amile could track them. So she could only imagine the flood of increasingly furious voicemails from her mother.

But Eliza had bigger things to worry about at the moment. She'd deal with that later.

"I guess there's no use waiting out here all night." Eliza straightened with a rustle of autumn leaves and dry branches. Tori followed, flinching at every sound. "I hope you have your key," Eliza added. "I have zero idea where mine is."

Tori reached into her skirt pocket and produced the glimmering silver object and her student ID card, which would get them through the front door.

On the way back into Scottstown, Eliza had thought that it would feel risky, even dangerous, sneaking into their dorm as wanted fugitives. But really, it was pretty mundane. Following Tori through the entrance and into their corridor reverberated with so much *deja vu* that Eliza had a wild moment where she wondered if the events of the past few days had been nothing more than a dream.

Then she saw their door and knew it was all too real.

"Oh god," Tori breathed.

The lock was shattered, the door bent in at an odd angle. Bits of wood peppered the ground and a piece of the lock rested innocently in the shadow of the half-open room.

Tori and Eliza exchanged a look.

"That must have happened recently," Eliza whispered. "Or the janitors would have cleaned up the mess."

"Wouldn't someone have heard it?"

Eliza didn't have an answer, but she suspected that a bang in the middle of the night might not be all that unusual in a dorm full of teenage girls. Doors slam and fists connect to walls and perhaps there was the odd boyfriend who snuck in. She couldn't speak for Tori, but Eliza certainly wouldn't have stirred from a dead sleep if she'd heard the singular crash of a door being broken open.

Not that the thought made her feel any better.

"Well?" Eliza whispered. "Should we check it out?"

Neither of them moved. Their pulses hammered in tandem. Two pairs of eyes remained fixed on that little piece of broken lock, inviting them inside.

"Fuck it," Eliza muttered, stepping around Tori and edging up to the door.

Eliza put her hip against it, glancing back at the other girl. Tori nodded, fingers twitching, as if she longed for the weapons hiding inside.

They both braced themselves.

And then Eliza slid into their room on silent feet, flicking on the light and bumping open the door with a single smooth movement.

"*Joe?*"

"Shhhh," Tori hissed from behind her, but Eliza barely noticed. Joe was sitting on her bed, hair disheveled, face streaked in blood. She ran up to him, crashing to her knees to grab his face, peering into his eyes.

They were lost. Vacant.

Terrifying.

"Joe, what happened? How did you escape?"

He met her gaze and the dimness in his expression made Eliza's blood turn to ice.

"Escape?" He shook his head once, violently, as if trying to scare away insects. Then he looked at her again, frowning, puzzling something out. "Eliza, is that you?"

"What's wrong with him?" Tori asked, but Eliza didn't answer. She didn't have one. All she could do was cup Joe's face, try to yank some of her friend back into it.

"Joe, you were at Fitzgerald Base," she said, forcing her voice to be steady and calm. "Remember? You drove Old Betty into a wall to save us."

He was frowning, his eyebrows furrowing in that way that made him look boyish and innocent. But there was nothing cute about this. Eliza shook him, hating how slack his mouth looked, how dead his eyes were.

"Joe, listen to me, you have to remember. You saved us. You were the hero. And then that woman, Amile Robillard, she took you. Come *on*, Joe, give me something."

"Eliza, keep your voice down."

But Tori's words barely registered as Eliza grabbed Joe by the shoulders, pulling him close.

"Joe, *say something*.

He blinked and for a moment Eliza could almost see the old Joe in there, swirling like a storm. But there was something else too, a black shadow clouding out the blue that made her hair stand on end. It was Joe, but different. Joe, but colder and harder and *wrong*.

Suddenly, he shoved her away.

"Don't touch me," Joe snarled, the tone as foreign as another language.

Eliza sat back on her heels, panic rising treacherously up her spine. As Joe's eyes widened in horror at what he'd just done, realization struck Eliza like a slap.

"Eliza, I'm sorry, I didn't mean—"

"She injected you with the Superman Virus," Eliza whispered.

Joe fell silent, pursing his lips, his arms wrapping around his torso like a frightened child.

"She gave you the Virus, didn't she?"

"The one they hadn't stabilized yet?" Tori asked, leaning around Eliza to look at him.

Joe didn't answer, but Eliza didn't need him to. What else could explain this different person who had come back to her, this fractured version of her best friend?

Tori spoke up again.

"What's gonna happen to him? Is he… safe?"

Eliza met Joe's eyes and saw reflected in them all the terror she now shared.

"I don't know," she said.

At that moment, the silence was broken by a loud ringing. Eliza leapt up, scrambling to find the source of the noise.

"Mine's turned off," Tori said, fumbling for her own phone.

And Eliza hadn't even brought hers. No, it had to be in the room somewhere. She fumbled over the sheets, the shoes, the floor.

Tori tapped her on the shoulder.

Eliza froze, looked up, turned to see what Tori was pointing at.

Joe was holding his cellphone out as if he'd never seen it before. It was buzzing in his hand, the light throwing long shadows over its owner's face. Eliza grabbed it, glanced at the screen. It was an unknown local number. She looked to Tori, who shrugged. And then, finally, she swept the bar to answer, holding it to her face without speaking, hardly daring to breathe.

"Eliza?"

The air abandoned Eliza's lungs as that clinical, *horrible* voice reverberated in her ear, chilling even as the bad reception of their dorm made it fritz with static. Eliza couldn't have responded even if she wanted to. It didn't matter. The person at the other end of the line didn't wait for a reply.

"This is Amile Robillard. I believe we have something to discuss."

CHAPTER THIRTY-SEVEN
Offers and Promises

Eliza turned away from Joe and Tori, curling in closer to the window as she focused everything she had on that voice, knowing that with a creature like Amile Robillard, one wrong step could mean disaster.

"You tried to hurt my friends," Eliza said in a low, threatening tone, ignoring Tori's waving attempts to catch her attention. "You ordered Martin Bent to kill me. We have nothing to discuss."

Amile chuckled and to Eliza it sounded like wind howling over arctic ice.

"There seems to be a misunderstanding, my dear girl. I have no intention of hurting those boys."

"You called them *property*," Eliza snarled, her injured hand pulsing against the phone. "You said they had no rights."

"All true things, but not the reasons I'm after them. You see, Eliza, I only want a tiny part of them. The tiniest part of all, if you will." There was a pause in which all Eliza could hear was the grinding of her own teeth. "I want their DNA."

"To stabilize your virus?" Eliza turned to glare at Joe, her heart hammering loud enough that she began to fear she might miss whatever Amile said next. Tori was leaning in close, breath hot against Eliza's neck as she tried to listen in.

"I'm impressed," Amile said. "It looks like your break-in wasn't so pointless after all."

"I'm not helping you. Not for anything."

"Not even for Joe Fagan's life?"

Eliza froze, exchanging a wide-eyed look with Tori. Tori mouthed *ask her what she wants*.

Instead, Eliza said, "You don't have a cure. That's why your soldier was so out of control when I was there. You don't know what you're doing, but you keep infecting people anyway."

"We don't know what we're doing *yet*," Amile said, and Eliza could imagine those dark eyes glittering. "It's embarrassing to admit, but you're right, Eliza. We've been fumbling in the dark ever since those boys escaped and took all of our research with them. It's taken us years to catch up after the lab fire, but we're almost there."

Lab fire? Tori mouthed, but Eliza shook her head as Amile continued.

"All we need is a bit of DNA from each of the boys. That's it, just a hair follicle, a sample of saliva. You bring me that and we'll share our... cure. You help me in this small way and Joe lives."

Eliza stared at her friend. His arms were wrapped around his torso as if he could hold himself together with nothing more than will. She frowned, swallowing hard.

"What will happen to him if we don't?"

"He'll go mad," Amile said, the words so short, so brutal, that they punched right through Eliza's defenses. "First he'll attack his enemies. Then he'll attack his friends. Then he'll attack himself. There's nothing to be done. Unless you help me."

Tori was shaking her head, her blonde hair tickling Eliza's cheek. But Eliza stepped away, closer to the window.

"If I bring you these samples," she said, hating herself for even entertaining the idea but hating the way Joe looked more, "You'll leave them alone? Forever?"

"You have my word," Amile said. "I have no interest in your friends beyond the secrets contained in their genetic material. Once we've perfected our virus, they'll be free to do as they will."

"And what do you plan to do? With the virus?"

Amile chuckled.

"Army secrets, dear, but I'm sure you can imagine what kind of use these... enhancements could provide."

Eliza could, and the thought was terrifying. Perhaps super-strength would be useful in war against the country's enemies, but she could also imagine how wrong it could go. Her mind drifted to that man with the dragon tattoo who had grabbed her. What if he had been stronger, faster, more aggressive?

That night could have ended very differently.

What would the world look like if more people had the kind of powers that the Vagabonds had? Or even simple things like elevated smell or speed? Would people use those newfound powers for good?

Would the Government?

Tori's head was still jerking back and forth, her lips mouthing *no* over and over. But Eliza only had eyes for Joe. Her friend, her loyal partner who had endured so much already. She thought about the pain in his eyes when he'd seen her with Aquila, the crash of Old Betty hitting the lab.

His choice to dive back into the fight and help Aquila.

Eliza owed him the world, even if she had to burn it down to give it to him.

"Okay," Eliza said, revulsion rising in her throat like bile.

"Wonderful. I'll give you however long you need to gather the samples. But remember, Joe is running out of time. You have a few days, maybe a week, but soon the neurological effects of the virus will be irreversible."

Eliza's blood felt like sludge in her veins as she thought of trying to trick the Vagabonds, or worse, convince them to help Amile. But she had to try. For Joe.

"I'll get them to you by tomorrow," Eliza said.

"I await your call."

And then the line went dead.

"Are you crazy?" Tori whisper-shouted the moment Eliza dropped the phone from her ear. "You think she can be *trusted*?"

"I'm not trusting her," Eliza snapped, moving over to put an arm around Joe.

"She's got something up her sleeve, Eliza, and you're a fucking idiot if you think she doesn't."

Eliza's eyes snapped up, but she was distracted by Joe lifting his head with a murmur.

"Hey, you okay?" she asked, detesting her soft, sickbed voice, unable to help it.

Joe's eyes were haunted, layered in shadows, as if he was fighting through hell just to look at her.

"I'm scared," he whispered. "Can't you hear it? All those things, all the lights." He squinted. "It's like the world got turned up."

"It's okay, Joe, it's gonna be okay."

"I think I should go to the hospital," Joe said, putting his head back on his knees.

"Ok, we'll go to the hospital," Eliza said, ignoring Tori's incredulous expression. "We'll get you some help."

But of course, she wasn't going to take him to Scottstown Medical, because what could they do? The Joe she knew and loved would be long gone by the time they figured out what was wrong with him. No, she was going to take him to the forest and meet with Aquila. And she was going to figure out a way to deal with this, even if it meant convincing the Vagabonds to help.

Or tricking them.

Pulling Joe's arm over her shoulder, Eliza tugged him off the bed.

"Come on, let's go," she said in a soothing voice. And then to Tori, "Are you gonna help or what?"

Tori groaned before stepping forward to take Joe's other arm.

"I just want to go on record that I don't think *he'd* want you to do this."

"If he doesn't get cured, neither does your brother."

That was enough to make Tori shut up.

~~~

Amile hung up the phone with a slide of her finger, quietly longing for the days when cellphones snapped shut. There used to be a satisfying *snick* to shutting down a call that made her feel powerful.

Well, she supposed there were other reasons for her to feel powerful nowadays.

"She'll cooperate," Amile said, moving around to watch Dr. Oleander fiddle with his instruments.

"I can do it myself; I don't need that *girl's* help."

Amile rolled her eyes. It was so *odious* working with the tufted, gray-haired old misogynist. Sometimes she marveled at how much his brain had decayed after the blaze that had destroyed all his research, including the test subjects, or so they'd thought until recently. Some of the older privates shared stories of Dr. Oleander in his prime, when he was powerful and decisive and angry and brilliant. But that man was gone, diluted by the weight of failure and loss. Amile had once thought that Fitzgerald Base was as dry and dusty as the doctor's mind, a stifling place to suffocate what should have been a bright and dangerous career. Until she'd stumbled upon a YouTube video outside Howl, posted by a drunk teenager who hadn't even noticed the wingspan silhouetted against the clouds.

Even now, Dr. Oleander refused to admit that she'd done well.

Well, this woman *is going to solve your mess, Doctor,* Amile thought with vitriol, but she didn't say it aloud. Instead, she peered over Oleander's shoulder at the enormous monitor, upon which rotated a twisting, globular shape.

"That's the latest model?" she asked.

"This one will work, I'm sure of it," Dr. Oleander muttered. "We don't need those samples."

"Think of them as my insurance policy," Amile said, straightening.

"I don't know why you're wasting your time." There was a petulance in his voice that made Amile grit her teeth.

You're almost done with him. Almost done with all this. And then you'll move on to bigger and better things.

Amile plastered a smile on her face as she responded.

"I'm *wasting my time*, Doctor, because we can't have your failed experiments running amok. I'm *wasting my time* because if the public found out about this, we'd be shut down before you could say gene splicer." She leaned closer, gratified when he took a nervous step back. "I'm *wasting my time* because those five boys need to be destroyed, or else everything we're doing now will be for nothing."

"They're harmless," Dr. Oleander whined, his white hair quivering.

Amile snorted, shaking her head.

"They are quite the opposite. And I intend to make sure they stay... contained."

Dr. Oleander mumbled something unintelligible, but Amile chose not to hear it. Instead she checked her watch.

"If you'll excuse me, I have an important phone call. Carry on, Doctor, although I doubt it will do you much good."

Smirking as Dr. Oleander's eyes widened in impotent rage, Amile turned on her heel and marched out of the lab, back to her office.

In truth, she had no important call, but she dreamed of the day she would. It was easy, intoxicating even, to imagine herself on the phone with generals and media personalities, maybe even the President himself. It had been an embarrassment to be sent to Scottstown. A snub, to oversee a lab long gone derelict after the tragedy that had struck it down in its prime.

Well, look how she'd risen from the ashes.

However, no matter how big Amile's dreams were, they would never work if the boys who called themselves the Vagabonds were allowed to roam free. It was true she needed their DNA to speed up Dr. Oleander's meandering process.

But really, she needed them gone.

Clarity of mission, as her business school advisor had once said, and Amile planned to take that to heart. No mistakes. No imperfections.

And no complications.

Amile's heels clicked as she marched down the hall, accompanied by the cheerful sound of her whistling.

CHAPTER THIRTY-EIGHT
Unraveling

"This is a terrible idea."

"Shut up, Tori."

But Eliza's instincts whined louder with every step as they neared the clearing where Old Betty was parked. She had Joe's arm over her shoulder, half-dragging him forward as Tori pulled branches aside with the hand not lugging the enormous safe box she'd dragged out from beneath her bed. Every so often, Joe would freeze, his eyes widening or his head tilting as he heard something they couldn't, saw something they didn't. Through the taut muscle of his underarm, Eliza could feel her friend's heart hammering, thudding frantically against her shoulder.

"Almost there," she said as Joe froze again, head swiveling.

"What's that noise?"

"It's just the woods," Eliza said, trying to ignore the look Tori was giving her as they stepped over a thick root. "Nothing to worry about."

She'd texted Aquila, telling him only that Joe was infected and they needed help. It had taken their combined effort—and more luck than Eliza cared to think about—to sneak into the quiet safety of the woods without being spotted by pre-dawn drivers or the night-shift cops patrolling Scottstown. Joe had pulled himself together after the initial shock of appearing in their room and seemed to understand the severity of the situation, but every so often his eyes would drift, darken, swirl with the kinds of shadows that made Eliza's hair stand on end.

They had to hurry.

"She said we have a week?" Tori asked for the thousandth time, the handle of her lockbox rattling with every step.

Eliza didn't respond as Joe froze again, tilting his head back to stare at the stars.

"That means my brother has even less time."

"We've been over this," Eliza said.

"Yeah, and I don't think you're taking it seriously. Martin was infected with this virus thing at *least* two days ago."

"We need to figure out what we're doing first."

"No, *you* need to get your head on straight. Screw this whole *samples* idea. We need to break back into the labs *now*."

Eliza sighed, leaning Joe against a tree and rounding on Tori.

"And what? Shoot our way inside? Ask them politely for the cure? Make it *ourselves?*" She snorted. "I think we need a better plan than that."

Tori glared at her, eyes narrow and bitter and scared. But she had no answer, so Eliza spun back to lead Joe deeper into the forest.

"Where are we going?" Joe asked in a surprisingly lucid voice.

"To meet Aquila."

Eliza watched his reaction, but Joe nodded, the only sign of what had happened in the mansion's basement a slight furrowing between his eyebrows.

He seems almost like himself, Eliza thought as they made the final trek into the clearing where they'd hidden the crumpled, dented, miserable-looking truck. Joe winced when branches hit him. Curled his shoulders in that self-protective way he always did when he was nervous. He hadn't made a joke yet and he seemed overstimulated by everything and anything, but if Eliza didn't know better, she would just think he'd just had too much coffee.

How long until he loses it? How long until he hurts one of us, or himself? How long until it's too late for Tori's brother? What is Aquila going to say when I ask him about the samples?

Am I going to ask at all?

The questions made quick, frantic laps around her mind, interrupted by nothing but the sleepy chitter of squirrels and the hooting of owls and the forest around them. They reached Old Betty and Eliza paused, taking a deep breath of crisp autumn air. The sky above was clear and open, the stars glittering like distant invitations.

I could almost believe everything's fine on a night like this.

She sighed, patting the truck's hood before leading Joe to a fallen tree.

"Fine. *You* might have lost your shit, but *I'm* gonna get ready," Tori said, hauling her lockbox to the other side of the clearing and setting it down with a crash. Eliza rolled her eyes, plopping beside Joe on the crooked trunk and bumping his arm with her bandaged fist.

"You in there?" she asked, forcing a smile.

Joe blinked at her, eyes reflective in the silver moonlight. It took a long moment, but eventually his own lips twitched up in an answering grin.

"It isn't so bad, once you get used to it," he said, his elbows draped over his knees, head hanging low. "I kinda feel like the volume's been turned up on the world. You know when you're sneaking into the dorm kitchen at night and the motion-sensor lights come on and everything hurts for a second?"

Eliza nodded.

"It's like that, but all the time." Joe flexed his hands and Eliza watched the tendons of his lanky arm ripple, wondering how strong they were now. How fast the virus was acting. "It's kinda cool, you know, minus the going crazy part."

"You're not gonna go crazy," Eliza said. "We'll find a way to stop it."

Joe snorted.

"I heard what she said." He grimaced. "I know I wasn't exactly at my best, back in your room. I don't even remember how I got there. But I heard everything." He slanted his gaze, peering at Eliza from beneath long auburn lashes. "I think you should leave."

"*What?*"

"Eliza, if what she said was true, I'm going to hurt someone, right? What if it's you? I... I could never live with myself if I..."

Eliza swallowed, pulled in by the pools of his eyes. She wanted to deny it, but hadn't she been wondering the same thing? As much as she hated to acknowledge her fear, Joe was a ticking bomb. A looming storm-cloud threatening to break.

And she was bringing him closer to the Vagabonds. To her friends.

Was he right? She hated herself for even thinking it, but...

There was a heavy *click* from the other end of the clearing. They both jumped.

"Sorry," Tori said without remorse, snapping shut the barrel of a small revolver and aiming it into the trees.

Eliza shook her head, exchanging an amused look with Joe.

"That might be the weirdest thing I've seen all week," he said.

They both burst out laughing. It was a glorious, blissful moment of calm that Eliza wanted to savor forever.

Unfortunately, Aquila chose that moment to touch down in front of them.

"Eliza, are you okay? How is he?"

Aquila rushed toward her, but she put up a hand. He froze, feathers rustling. His gaze flicked between Eliza and Joe, who was still sitting on the fallen tree.

"What's going on?"

There was a crunching noise as Tero landed behind his brother, next to the rusty truck.

"Where's Otto?" Tori asked.

"T-t-the others a-a-are back at h-home," he said, his unseeing eyes roving around the clearing. "I s-said we'd b-be right b-behind them. T-they went through the t-t-tunnel, to a-a-avoid attention."

"Moose needed new bandages," Aquila interjected, eyes never leaving Joe. "His wound reopened during the fight."

Eliza nodded, but Aquila didn't nod back. Nerves tingling, Eliza looked between the two boys, one seated, one standing. Joe's head was tilted, his eyebrows pulled together. He was staring at Aquila as if the Vagabond was a puzzle, a math problem he was on the verge of solving.

And he wasn't blinking.

"Eliza, what's going on?" Aquila asked again.

Tori was watching the exchange, the revolver still in her hand, the lockbox open at her knees and bursting with guns and ammo. Slowly, she rose to her feet, as if she, like Eliza, could sense that the air had suddenly become tainted. Dangerous.

She stepped in front of her lockbox.

"Hey, Joe," Eliza said, holding her hands out. "Whatcha thinking there?"

Joe didn't answer.

"Eliza, get away from him."

She ignored Aquila, stepping in closer to try and snag Joe's attention.

"Daydreaming about comic books again?" she said with a tense smile.

"Eliza, I really think you should—"

Joe shoved to his feet, impossibly fast. One second he was slumped on the fallen tree, the next he was standing. It took all of Eliza's courage not to step back in surprise. Instead, she forced herself to reach out to put a hand on his taut forearm.

"Joe?"

"I think I need to...." But his voice trailed off, his eyes lost. Distant.

Terrifying.

Tori was moving in now, revolver pointed at the ground, and Eliza hated her. In that moment she hated Aquila and Tero and everyone for thinking that her friend was anything but the sweet, loyal boy she'd spent so much time with. Most of all, she hated that they might be right. Even Eliza felt the prickle of fear, of unease as Joe's cheek twitched and his muscle flexed. He was like a caged animal, docile for the moment but unpredictable and full of violent potential.

Tori's words rang in her head again.

This is a bad idea.

"Look, we should get him somewhere—"

Everything happened at once. Joe, moving so quickly that Eliza hardly saw it, made to grab her hand. Perhaps to steady himself, perhaps to pull her in. She would never know, because Aquila's instinctive response was to lunge in and whip her away.

Eliza stumbled to the other side of the clearing, spinning around so fast she almost lost her footing.

For a single, stretching heartbeat, everything went still. Aquila's wings were out, his knees bent, his stance ready. But Joe only stood there, swaying, lips tugging into a tiny, almost joking smile. As if he'd just thought of something funny. His gaze drifted over the treetops, down the nearest trunk.

To Eliza.

His lips twisted higher, humorless now.

And then Joe bared his teeth and lunged.

CHAPTER THIRTY-NINE
Bystander

"No," Eliza shrieked, leaping forward, but she was too slow. Joe hit Aquila squarely in the middle of his torso, launching them both halfway across the clearing.

"Woah!" Tori shouted, throwing herself out of the way as the two bodies crashed into the tree beside her, splintering the trunk.

"G-g-guys," Tero said.

But Aquila and Joe weren't listening. Eliza watched with open-mouthed shock as her gangly, pale friend matched Aquila's strength with barely a grimace. Aquila threw Joe to the side, but Joe grabbed his arm and dragged him along. They hit Old Betty with a clang, rolling along the truck's rusty cab, the thuds of fists hitting metal accompanied by guttural snarls. Aquila's wings snapped open, engulfing them for a moment before Joe swept his leg out, making Aquila stumble.

"Stop!" Eliza screamed, finding her voice. "Stop, stop, stop!"

But they didn't listen. Aquila beat his wings, thumping Joe's head. Joe immediately spun on him, yanking on a fistful of feathers and making Aquila shout with pain. Tero shifted from foot to foot, his blind eyes wide, his hands twitching as if with the urge to help.

But the two figures were such a tumble of arms and legs and wings that even if Tero *could* see, he wouldn't have been able to intervene.

Tori stepped up beside Eliza, her revolver pointed at the ground.

"Is this what you had in mind?"

Eliza ignored the hissed remark. Her heart was like a drum in her chest as she watched two people she cared about contort and growl and snarl. Where were the boys who had smiled at her? Laughed with her? Comforted her?

With astonishing power, Joe propelled the two of them into a sapling as big around as Eliza's thigh, snapping it in half. Aquila threw a punch that dented Old Betty's bed.

Finally, one of Joe's hits landed.

Aquila's head snapped to the side.

Blood sprayed.

That's it, Eliza thought.

Gathering the fraying edges of her courage, Eliza strode forward.

"STOP!" she shouted, putting a hand on the nearest shoulder to drag it away. Aquila's muscles tensed beneath her hand, rippling with power.

It was instinct. It must have been. Instinct or raw nerves or the pain of the hit. Whatever the reason, Aquila swung around, fist clenched, arm driving with all the supernatural power of his modified genes.

The punch hit Eliza right in the sternum.

For a moment, the world went dark. She flew backward, sailing through the air with no concept of where she was or what was around her. It was almost... pleasant. Floating. Drifting. An endless note of soft darkness.

And then she hit a tree and the world crashed back in with enough pain to make her gasp.

She heard another snarl, felt the distant reverberations of the fight through the fog in her brain.

"How dare you, you goddamn *animal*," came Joe's voice, accompanied by the pulpy sound of fists hitting flesh. It seemed so far away, the echo of an unpleasant world spearing through the miasma of her agony.

Eliza only rallied when she heard the gunshot.

She blinked as the clearing finally went silent, struggling to breathe through lungs that felt like they'd shrunk. The crack of the pistol still reverberated around her like a ghostly threat.

"That's enough," Tori said, her gun still pointed at the sky, glaring at each of the three boys in turn. Tero looked positively petrified, hovering in the shadows of the nearest oak and wringing his dark hands. Joe was glaring at Aquila with all the pent-up hatred Eliza had never acknowledged, lips curled back in a feral snarl.

Aquila was staring at her, his features twisted in horror.

"Eliza, I'm so sorry—"

"This is insane," Tori interrupted, pointing the smoking nozzle at the ground again. "We're wasting time."

Eliza tried to say something, but her voice only came out as a croak. She fought to swallow.

Tori looked at Joe and then back at Aquila. "You two need to get a handle on it, or else we're all fucked."

"He hit her," Joe said in a voice like a rumbling engine.

"And you hit him," Tori answered, tucking the gun into the waistband of her skirt.

A massive shadow fell over Eliza.

"Are you okay? I'm so sorry, I didn't mean to..."

But she couldn't respond, not even to comfort Aquila. She was still struggling to breathe and beginning to hyperventilate as her brain screamed for oxygen. Rolling onto her hands and knees, Eliza gulped for air.

"We need to get her home," Aquila said. "I'll fly her—"

"No you won't," Joe spat.

"We can drive her to the mansion," Tori said, kicking Old Betty's hubcap. "If this crumpled up rust bucket still works."

"The r-r-road is s-shut d-d-down," Tero said, his stutter worse than ever.

Eliza was blinking, trying to see straight as her body roiled with the shock of the punch. But she managed to focus on the deep, resonant sound of Aquila's voice.

"There's a back entrance," he said quietly. "A tunnel that goes right into the cave. You can follow me down the logging road that will take us there."

When Eliza looked up, the first thing she saw was Tero looking at his brother as if he'd just shared something personal, private. Dangerous.

A back entrance.

A secret way into the mansion.

What would Amile do if she knew?

Eliza swallowed, shoving onto her knees.

"Joe..." she gulped, coughing as her voice caught on the jagged epicenter of pain in her rib cage. "He's..."

"We'll blindfold him," Tori said, taking command. "And I'll take his phone."

If she'd had any breath left in her body, Eliza would have laughed at the irony.

CHAPTER FORTY
Secret Lair

The back entrance was enormous, carved out of a small cliff deep in the woods. It looked like a gaping mouth, complete with jagged toothy edges and a moustache of hanging greenery. But the overgrown, rugged appearance was deceptive, because when Old Betty passed into the shadow of the overhang, the truck went from trundling over a rocky, uneven logging road onto smoothly paved ground. They slowed for a moment, losing momentum as Tori took in the dense underground stillness. Eliza leaned her head against the cool window and struggled to make sense of it through the ache in her ribcage.

And then the glitter of Aquila's feathers appeared over them, swooping into the darkness.

She chuckled as Tori accelerated the truck into the cold, clammy tunnel, following Aquila.

"What?" Tori snapped, glancing back to where Joe and Tero sat uneasily in the truck bed, as far from each other as possible.

"It's just kinda... I dunno, cliché, isn't it?" Eliza said, still not quite able to take deep breaths.

"Cliché?"

"Didn't you ever watch superhero movies?"

Tori rolled her eyes.

"Jesus, Eliza, you're such a weirdo."

"Hey, I'm not the one... with the gun in her belt." Eliza panted.

"It's not in my belt." But Tori's hand twitched to her waistband and the molded handle.

Eliza glanced back to see Joe and Tero silhouetted against the bright opening of the cave. Joe had allowed Eliza to put on the blindfold without complaint, although he wouldn't let Aquila get near him. And when Tori had snatched his phone, he hadn't said a single word against it. After the fight, he'd settled into a tenuous calm, his teeth gritted and his muscles tight but otherwise peaceful.

For now.

How long do we have? Eliza thought to herself as the light behind them grew further away, the pinpoint of the world outside almost drowned out by Old Betty's high-beams. *How long does* he *have?*

She swallowed.

Finally, Tori pulled them into the cavern. Eliza blinked, eyes adjusting just in time to see Otto, Moose, Daisy, and Ian Eckelson spin to face them wearing matching expressions of shock. Moose was beside the truck in a flash, darting from the window Eliza was slumped against, to Tero, to the blindfolded Joe.

"What happened, what happened you guys, Aquila why is there a bruise on your face and what happened to Eliza and wow, this guy looks different—"

"It's okay," Aquila rumbled, landing surprisingly lightly for all his bulk. "Everyone's fine."

But Eliza caught him glancing in her direction, his face still flushed red with shame. Even though she hadn't known him long, Eliza could imagine what was going through his mind. He was the leader, the protector, the one who made the right call. He wasn't supposed to hurt those smaller and weaker than himself. But not only had he failed to protect her; he'd failed to protect her *from himself*. Eliza wanted to go to him, comfort him, tell him she'd be fine.

Unfortunately, he wasn't the one who needed her most right now.

Inhaling as deeply as she could, Eliza gathered her energy to sit upright and kick open the passenger door, ignoring Eckelson's glower as she limped her way to the truck bed and helped Joe out. She took off the blindfold.

"He's infected," she said without preamble, her fingers tangling into Joe's and praying that it would be enough to keep him calm. "They gave him the virus. The one that's not stable yet."

There was a collective intake of breath from behind her. Eliza curled her shoulders in before turning to face them.

The first eyes she found were Ian Eckelson's.

"Why did you bring him here?"

Eliza forced herself to meet the old man's gaze, viciously suppressing the bone-deep desire to curl up and cry.

"I didn't know what else to do."

"That seems to be a theme."

"Dad don't—" Aquila said.

Eckelson shook his head, stepping back from the circle of teenagers.

"I gave so much to keep you all safe and then you share our most precious secrets with the first stranger you meet. I'm disappointed in you, Aquila. I thought I'd taught you better."

"Wait, Dad…"

But he was already walking away, striding back to the computer monitors he'd been working on moments before.

Silence fell in his wake.

Eliza tried to catch Aquila's eye, but the winged boy was staring at his adopted father's back as if it might speak to him, offer words of wisdom. Daisy was peering around, his eyes wide and questioning, but even Moose had gone silent. Eliza wondered if the others had the same question circling endlessly in their minds.

What do we do now?

It was the burden they all shared, the problem they all faced. And Eliza hadn't even told them the worst of it.

I'll give you however long you need to get the samples. But remember, Joe is running out of time.

How could she possibly ask for what she needed?

Tori was eyeing her, waiting for her to admit why she'd brought Joe here. What Amile had said on the phone. But Eliza found that she couldn't do it. Instead, she put a tender hand on Joe's back.

"Come on, let's find a place for you to sit."

And keep you from getting into any more trouble.

"Quite some goddamn armaments you've got here," Otto said, tugging Tori's attention to the bed of the truck and her green lockbox.

Before Tori went to join Otto in admiring her weapons, she threw a look at Eliza as if to say *this is only going to get worse.*

Unfortunately, Eliza couldn't quite convince herself that Tori was wrong.

CHAPTER FORTY-ONE
The Best of Intentions

Everyone had a different idea about what to do next.

"I think we should shoot the fuckers," Otto said, punching a fist in the air.

"That's *not* what the guns are for," Tori said, folding her arms. Otto ducked his head at her baleful glare.

"W-w-we should t-t-think this through."

"Naw, man," Moose injected, "We gotta be *spontaneous.*"

"T-t-that's a t-terrible idea."

Aquila hadn't said a word since Eliza settled Joe on the couch in the far corner. There had been a harrowing moment when Joe stumbled sideways into Tori, bumping her into the wall. Luckily, it had passed without incident, but the others had been shooting looks into the corner ever since. Even though Joe seemed quietly settled, Eliza had caught Aquila staring at her, throwing her sidelong glances every time he thought she was turned away. The guilt was as obvious as the bruise blooming on his face, making him clench and unclench his fists. But she didn't have the wherewithal to comfort him.

"We need to know more about this Superman Virus," Eckelson said, spinning away from the monitor and pacing in front of the screens, stroking his jaw in thought. "If it really is as dangerous as you say—"

"It is," Eliza said.

Eckelson ignored her.

"We can't just let them continue with it."

"Yeah, we don't want them to stabilize it and make *more* of us," Moose said, goggles glittering excitedly. "Then we wouldn't be special anymore."

199

"More importantly, you wouldn't be safe," Eckelson said as Daisy edged closer to the circle like a moth drawn to the flame of people. "Imagine if news of this got out. It would be infinitely harder to remain hidden."

"What about my brother?" Tori asked.

"What about Joe?" Eliza added.

The way Ian looked at her could have lit a wet log on fire, but she met his gaze with the steel spine she'd cultivated from years of staring down angry adults. She hadn't told any of them about Amile's offer. The words kept rising, drifting to the tip of her tongue, but every time the old man glared at her, her request for DNA samples withered. She knew how he'd look at her when she asked. How they'd all look at her. Conspiring with the enemy, agreeing to help the woman who had tried to *kill* them? It sounded bad even in her head.

But Joe was rocking on the other side of the cavern, his arms wrapped around his middle as he closed his eyes against the flood of information his brain was struggling to process. As he fought the urge to attack everything that moved.

Eliza gritted her teeth, stepping up to Ian Eckelson.

"We need to do something soon. Martin, Joe, they don't have much time."

"I'm afraid *they* aren't my main concern. My *sons* need to stay safe, and now that you know the ins and outs of my home..." His voice trailed off, the threat obvious.

"Dad, we talked about this," Aquila said in a tired voice. Eliza jumped at the sound of his voice, but he wouldn't meet her gaze. "If you want to be involved, you have to be nice."

Eckelson sniffed but didn't answer. Tero moved around him, dark fingers flying over the Braille keyboard.

"F-from the information I g-gathered during our b-break-in, I've d-deduced that it's a m-modified r-retrovirus. It a-attacks all the c-cells in the human body, c-changing them all at once."

"Is that how we were made?" Otto asked.

"N-no," Tero said, his milky eyes reflecting the screen in front of him. "W-we were b-born with m-modified DNA. This is an a-attempt to c-change pre-existing g-genetic m-m-material."

"Can it be done?" Eckelson asked, folding his arms.

"T-theoretically." Tero paused, straightening and cocking his head. "It's a-already working in J-Joe's body. B-but his cells are r-rejecting it."

"Why?" Eliza asked.

"Because the v-virus is not c-complete."

All we need is a tiny bit of DNA from each of the boys. That's it, just a hair follicle or a sample of saliva.

Eliza was so close to them. She could reach out now, pluck a hair here, a flake of dead skin there. Maybe swab some of Otto's slime or yank a spine from Daisy's shoulder. She could feel Tori watching her, waiting for her to speak, but what could she say?

Just give me a bit of your DNA and let me bring it to Amile. Then she'll leave us all alone.

She'd be lucky if they thought it was a joke.

But what else could she do?

Frustrated, head spinning, Eliza stepped back from the circle, watching from a distance as Tero talked about what was going on in Joe's body, breaking down how every cell was changing, how his brain was sagging under the weight of the new information coming from every neuron, every follicle, every bit of himself.

How does a mind respond when the body no longer looks like itself?

She turned away, ignoring the heat of eyes on her back as she made her way over to where Joe was sitting, head in his hands.

"Hey," she said, settling down beside him and letting the murmur of voices wash over her. "How you holding up?"

Joe tilted his head to the side and offered her a wan smile.

"Peachy."

Eliza couldn't quite smile back.

"What does it feel like?"

Joe straightened, his hands clenched between his knees hard enough that Eliza wouldn't have been surprised to hear the crack of breaking fingers.

"Like I'm in a dream," he said. Then chuckled. "Even that doesn't sound quite right. I keep getting all these weird... shocks? Just these pieces of things and thoughts and impulses." He shuddered. "I understand why that soldier you saw went bonkers."

"It's gonna be okay," Eliza said, feeling like a broken record. "We'll figure it out."

Joe's lips curved and Eliza felt the flutter of protective instinct at that familiar expression. He almost looked like himself again, bashful and embarrassed and eager to please.

"I wanted to show you something," he said.

"What is it?"

"Well, it doesn't really...." His eyes unfocused for a moment before he shook himself, dragging his attention back to the moment. "It doesn't matter now. I mean, everything's changed. But I really wanted... I guess I wanted you to know."

"Joe, what are you talking about?"

His hands unclenched and in the bed of his palms was his iPhone, screen glowing and waiting to be unlocked.

Panic zinged up Eliza's spine.

"Wait, where did you get that?" she demanded, leaping to her feet.

"I..." Joe cocked his head. "I don't remember. I think I grabbed it out of Tori's pocket."

"Give it back, we need to turn it off or—"

"Look," he said in a voice so small, so childlike, that Eliza froze.

Joe unlocked the phone, turned it on.

Even from there, Eliza could see the little network sign pulsing with three out of five bars, hovering ominously over two digital tickets for skydiving in western Massachusetts.

"I thought you'd want to—"

Eliza grabbed the phone, jamming on the top button.

"Turn off, turn off, turn off," she chanted, but that sliding bar didn't show up.

Why do they make iPhones so difficult to deactivate? Eliza thought frantically.

"Eliza, what—?"

Finally, she managed to turn off the phone.

"I'm sorry, I thought you'd like—"

"Joe, shut up," Eliza snapped, hating herself for how abrupt and harsh she sounded. But now wasn't the time for tact. Her senses were on high alert, her instincts humming desperately. The others hadn't noticed anything, were still grouped around the monitor as Tero spoke. Aquila threw another glance over his shoulder at them. Eliza ignored him too, her ears pricked, her heart hammering.

"What did I do?" Joe whispered from behind her.

Eliza swallowed, keeping her voice steady as she answered.

"Amile could be tracking your phone. Didn't you think of that before you turned it on?"

"I... Oh." he said.

She looked at him, hating that vagueness, that stain of disconnectedness. His mouth fell open, his eyes widening in horror.

"Joe," Eliza said, leaning in close, planting her hands on either side of his face and pulling him in as if in a kiss. "How long has your phone been on?"

"I mean, I turned it on after you put me here. I...I just wanted to feel normal for a second."

"Shit," Eliza said, releasing him, spinning away.

"What's going on?"

Suddenly, Aquila was there, looming over the two of them with his wings rustling in agitation. And Eliza didn't even know where to start. She opened her mouth but the words wouldn't come.

She was spared having to answer when Daisy's voice shattered the low murmur of planning.

"Intruders!"

Everyone turned to face the strange, armored Vagabond who so rarely spoke. Daisy's spines were standing on end as he pointed frantically at the security monitors Eckelson had been studying when they'd come in. They were arrayed to show every inch of the mansion and the hidden exit in the woods. But they were no longer empty and peaceful, filled with swaying branches or manicured gardens.

Now all the screens were swarming with soldiers.

Amile's forces had come.

CHAPTER FORTY-TWO
End of the Line

"Move!"

Aquila's voice broke through everyone's shock and suddenly all the Vagabonds were in motion. Tero spinning back to the screen. Ian bent over his shoulder. Moose disappearing into the cavern. Otto putting a hand on Tori's sweater.

"What do we do?" Eliza asked as Aquila grabbed her hand.

"We need to get out of here."

"How—?"

But her question was cut off by a deep, bone-chilling rumble. She twisted to look over her shoulder, watching two pairs of headlights slice through the inky darkness of the tunnel, announcing the arrival of military-grade jeeps.

"The elevator!" Aquila bellowed as soldiers spilled into the cavern, all of them armed and wearing helmets that made them look coldly inhuman.

Aquila tugged her away, but Eliza ripped free, lunging for Joe. He hadn't moved since she'd taken his phone, his mouth still open in that frozen realization of what he'd done.

"Come on!"

Her scream seemed to break through whatever the virus was doing to his mind. Joe shook himself and popped to his feet, following as Aquila yanked her toward the elevator shaft.

"W-w-we'll be t-trapped," Tero said in panic, but his voice was lost beneath the growl of more cars coming in, more soldiers shouting.

And then they started firing.

"DUCK!"

Eckelson's voice boomed through the tunnel as the hail of bullets rained down on them.

But no, they weren't bullets.

They were darts.

Eliza shoved Joe behind a plushy upturned couch before Aquila spun her out of range, curling them both into the protection of a bookshelf. She leaned out just in time to see Moose darting through the nearest cluster of soldiers, knocking aside the dart rifles and tearing off helmets with gleeful, cackling laughter.

"I gotcha there, haha, oh now you see me now you don't. I wouldn't do that, but I don't expect you to—"

He was silenced by a dart hitting him squarely in the neck.

"NO!" Eliza screamed.

"Feels… like a bee sting…" Moose muttered, stumbling into the no-man's-land between them and the soldiers.

And then he collapsed.

"Go," Aquila said, shoving her toward the elevator, but she grabbed his arm.

"You can't go out there alone. They'll get you."

"I can't let them take Moose."

But it was too late for that. Moose was already being dragged behind enemy lines, his long limbs dangling limply as two thick shadows bundled him into the back of a jeep.

"We have to save him," Aquila said, pushing against Eliza's arm.

"You can't help him if you're unconscious," she growled back. "We have to get to that elevator shaft."

But even as she spoke, the elevator's grate burst open. Six new uniformed figures came spilling into the cavern, draped in climbing gear.

Tero was right.

They were trapped.

Casting about for a way to help, Eliza spotted Tori crouched behind an upended table, Otto peering out from the other side.

Tori had the revolver clenched tightly between her knees.

"Do it!" Eliza screamed, but Tori's eyebrows were drawn together, her eyes haunted. Eliza could imagine the debate raging in her mind. Maybe Tori had used guns before, perhaps even killed animals, but of course she'd never shot at a *person*. And those soldiers were just following orders, just men and women like her brother who had to do whatever their commanding officer instructed.

"DO IT!" Eliza screamed again, but they were both distracted by a dark flash.

Tero swooped overhead, dumping a bucket of water over the soldiers.

"O-Otto!" he called before one of them darted him in the thigh. His wings flinched in, his body careening to the side.

"Fuckers aren't getting away with that," Otto growled beside Tori.

"No, wait—"

But he didn't listen. Instead, Otto lunged out and barreled towards the soldiers, hands crackling with static.

"God damnit," Aquila muttered, ripping out of Eliza's grip and leaping over the bookshelf to catch Tero before he crashed blindly into the wall.

Eliza didn't hesitate, didn't even stop to think before running out after them, scampering through the battlefield to the rhythm of her terrified pulse. She cartwheeled out of the way of a dart that brushed her calf before springing into the thicket of soldiers. Fists swung at her head, rifle butts altogether too close for comfort, and everywhere was the haze of Otto's electricity making her muscles spasm without warning. Pain arced through her, but she ignored it, focusing all her energy on causing as much of a distraction as physically possible. She couldn't fight them off, but maybe she could keep them busy. Offer the Vagabonds an extra moment to pull together, plan an escape. Something. *Anything.*

A rough arm grabbed her by the neck, pulling her in close.

"Remember me?" growled a familiar voice in her ear, hot breath nauseating against her cheek.

A dragon tattoo curled around the bicep choking off her air supply.

And then the arm was ripped away with a howl of rage.

Joe had joined the fight.

The tattooed soldier went flying as Joe swung wide, clearing a circle as he punched, kicked, lunged. Eliza took the opportunity to glance behind her.

Otto was unconscious on the ground between her and Tori, a terrified Daisy tugging at his arms. The darts were glancing off the armored boy's skin, falling in a useless ring. But soldiers were curling toward them like smoke and even Daisy couldn't stand up against their raw numbers.

"Come on, we have to help them!" Eliza screamed, tugging on the back of Joe's shirt as he kept the soldiers at bay.

A truck engine roared as one of the jeeps retreated, no doubt bearing Moose away, but Eliza couldn't think about that, not with Daisy and Otto being slowly surrounded and Aquila helping Tero land. Ian Eckelson had come forward to help, settling Tero gently against the wall as his milky eyes fluttered shut. Aquila spread his wings, slamming down in front of his adopted father and brother with his teeth bared.

Eliza was trying to catch Aquila's eye, desperate to formulate some kind of plan.

So she was looking right at him when three darts sank into his chest.

"NO!"

But no one heard her, because at that moment a different kind of sound filled the cave, reverberating with chilling finality.

A gunshot.

Tori was marching out from behind her table to stand in front of Otto and Daisy, legs wide, arms braced.

"Don't. Touch. Them." Tori's voice was a growl, her expression steely as she trained her revolver on the nearest soldier.

"Quite the little warrior clan we have here."

The sound of that voice was enough to make Eliza's hair stand on end. Amile Robillard stepped out from behind the nearest jeep, covered the same beetle-like armor. But unlike her soldiers, she wasn't wearing a helmet, leaving her free to sneer at the world.

She had her own handgun pointed right at Tori's chest.

Joe shoved Eliza behind him.

"Step aside, dear," Amile said in a light voice as Aquila fought to remain upright over an already unconscious Tero, his movements sluggish and clumsy.

"No," Tori said.

I have to do something, Eliza thought frantically, breathing fast. *I can't just let this happen.*

And then she saw the grate on the nearest jeep, at the perfect height to swing her feet into Amile Robillard's head.

Perfect.

Eliza slipped away from Joe, sliding along the back edge of an armored vehicle. If she could just get that gun away from Amile, maybe unnerve her long enough for Tori to act. Surely Amile wouldn't keep fighting if her own life was in danger.

"I don't want to kill you," Amile said with no sincerity.

"Too bad."

Notyetnotyetnotyet, Eliza thought hysterically as she inched toward the grate. *Don't shoot yet.*

A clicking footstep echoed as Ian Eckelson stepped away from the wall, drawing every eye — and rifle — to himself.

"Amile, that's quite enough."

"What a surprise," Amile grinned, shaking her head. "I should have known you were the mysterious benefactor of the original trials."

"You've crossed the line this time. Trespassing on private property? Threatening assault? *Kidnapping*? I can't imagine this is good for those lofty ambitions of yours."

Amile's smile widened.

"What those old plugs in D.C. don't know won't hurt them."

There was a thud as Aquila finally collapsed. Eliza was getting closer, almost to the rim of the truck where two dark shapes stood guard.

She'd have to leap over them.

"This is madness. You must see that."

Amile laughed, the sound echoing eerily around the cavernous home that had once been a peaceful haven for five teenage misfits.

Eliza bent her knees, braced to launch herself over the two soldiers.

"Oh Ian, you just don't seem to understand the *scope* of what I'm doing here. If I succeed, then none of this will matter."

"And if you fail?"

Amile swung her revolver around in answer.

"Well I guess you'll never know."

Eliza bounced once, twice…

And then Amile fired.

Eliza gasped, making the two men spin toward her. But she scarcely noticed, because Ian Eckelson was stumbling back, clutching at a bloodstain rapidly growing on his perfectly pressed linen shirt.

Daisy screamed wordlessly.

Soldiers darted forward and Eliza lost track of everything in the sudden chaos. Joe was fighting, Tori shrieking, firing. Eliza squirmed between thickly muscled shoulders, desperate to reach Eckelson or Aquila or Amile or *someone*. She had to act. She had to help.

Finally, she broke through with a stumble.

The old man was alone on the floor, lying in a rapidly growing puddle of his own blood.

A laugh made Eliza spin.

"Thank you for your help, Ms. Mason," Amile said as six burly figures wrestled a struggling Daisy into the nearest car. "It was much appreciated."

Eliza lunged at the woman with a deep, feral snarl, but something hit her in the chest, kicking her sideways. It was Tori, thrown bodily into her by a sneering soldier. The revolver skittered away from them with a metallic clang. Both girls scrambled to their feet, but Amile and her soldiers were already retreating, leaving only the rumble of engines in their wake. Eliza tried to sprint after them, but they accelerated away, too fast, too powerful, disappearing like sharks into dark water.

"No, no, no," Eliza chanted, yanking her fingers through her thick hair as she stumbled to a stop. Joe was swaying behind her, a handful of darts sticking out of his sweater. The cavern was a mess, and worst of all, the Vagabonds were gone.

What were they going to do?

Joe slumped against the wall at the same time Tori's scream reached her.

"Eliza! Come quick! I think he's dying!"

Swallowing air, Eliza forced down her panic. She had to pull herself together, because maybe she'd lost Aquila and his brothers and ruined absolutely everything, but she'd be damned if she was going to let their father die.

CHAPTER FORTY-THREE
Blood and Guts

"Help me get him in the truck!"

"Jesus, Eliza, there's blood everywhere."

"Pull yourself together and *help me!*"

Eliza didn't wait for Tori to stop gaping as she lifted Ian Eckelson's shoulders, trying to ignore how much the carpet was stained an inky, sticky red.

Oh God, can someone even survive losing that much?

Eliza shook herself. She couldn't afford to give up yet.

"Tori, *move!*"

The blonde girl looked paler than ever, making even her straw-colored hair stand out. Finally, she bit her lip and nodded. Darting forward, Tori grabbed Eckelson's legs and together they managed to haul him into the open passenger side of Old Betty.

"What about Joe?"

"I'll get him," Eliza snapped. "You start the car."

Tori jerked her head in a nod as Eliza carefully folded Eckelson's legs in. She took a moment to check his pulse.

Still there, tremulous and quiet but beating steadily. Stubbornly.

"Hold on, sir," Eliza murmured before slamming the door and throwing herself around the bed.

"Joe! Joe, get up!"

The roar of the truck drowned out Joe's confused, half-conscious groan, but Eliza didn't wait for him to gather himself. Grabbing his armpits, she heaved with all her might and somehow managed to shove him to his feet.

"Can you walk?"

"Nnnn...."

Joe's lips could hardly form words, so Eliza slipped under his arm and dragged him to where Tori was spinning the truck around. They stumbled, almost going down, but Eliza just managed to keep her feet. She couldn't fall now. If Joe slumped, if he hit the ground again, she wasn't sure she had the strength to get him back up.

And who knew what would happen if they left him here.

The truck hadn't even stopped moving when Eliza popped open the back, hopped into the bed, and yanked Joe's limp, swaying body onto the metal floor.

"GO!" she screamed, Joe's legs still dangling out the back.

Tori slammed the gas and Eliza was almost launched from the truck as it accelerated wildly out of the tunnel, swerving into the forest with all the growling horsepower it could muster.

Every bump and hole in the dilapidated logging road felt like an apocalypse. Eliza shoved Joe against the truck cab and fought to keep them both from being ejected into the bushes with every bounce and tumble. She kept wondering what this kamikaze swerving would do to Eckelson's injury. What if they were too late? What if this was only making things worse? What if they were just drawing out his last few moments, making his end even more painful and agonizing than it needed to be?

No.

She couldn't think like that.

"Whathappened...?"

Joe's head was tilting from side to side as he mumbled, trying to blink through the drugs they'd pumped into him. Eliza ignored him, tossing the darts she'd pulled from his chest over her shoulder and carefully checking him for more as Tori swung them onto the paved road.

Eliza breathed a sigh of relief as they rocketed onto the smoother surface.

"Eliza...?"

"It's okay, we're okay."

She wasn't convincing anyone.

Dawn was breaking, light forking through the clouds above them in aggressive, piercing talons. It was overcast, the sky heavy with unshed rain, and as Eliza tilted her head back she almost wished that a storm would break on her. Everything was so wrong, so horribly, terribly, abysmally wrong. The soldiers had taken Aquila and his brothers and now Amile had access to all the samples she wanted. What would she do with them? Would she keep them alive the way she'd promised?

A small voice whispered from the back of Eliza's brain with all the logic she didn't want to face.

Of course Amile won't. And even if she does, it won't be a life worth living.

Sobs were building in Eliza's chest, pushing against the cracked dam of her defenses, but she swallowed them ruthlessly. She couldn't lose it, not with the old man bleeding out in Joe's car and Joe himself slowly unraveling beside her.

Old Betty's tires squealed as Tori skidded around a corner, making a crazed U-turn and freewheeling onto the highway.

"You're gonna kill us!" Eliza screamed, slapping the cab hood.

But Tori didn't seem to hear. If anything, the truck sped up, whining in protest as Tori pushed it to its limits and beyond. Eliza had never seen the old girl go this fast, hadn't even thought it could.

Desperate times…

"Hold on, Mr. Eckelson," Eliza muttered, keeping Joe upright as they screamed towards Scottstown.

Tori took the exit like a madwoman, the back two wheels sliding off the pavement's edge as she bumped onto the main road.

We're gonna get pulled over, we're gonna get arrested, we're gonna die.

But no one stopped them as Tori careened into the center of the city and up the narrow side-road of the biggest hospital for a hundred miles. Scottstown Medical. Faces whipped past, eyes barely able to track the rogue vehicle and two people struggling to stay in the back as Old Betty sailed over speed bumps and mounted curbs with wild abandon.

Finally, Tori slammed the breaks. Eliza and Joe folded over, their feet scrambling for traction as the truck shrieked, spinning in a full circle before thunking to a stop. The ground behind them was still smoking when Eliza leapt out of the bed, running to meet the security guards sprinting out to them. Their faces were etched in anger, hands on their weapons.

"He's been shot!" Eliza shouted, waving her arms. "He's been shot!"

To their credit, the guards hesitated only a moment before pulling out their radios. In less time than Eliza would have believed possible, the truck was surrounded by EMTs, security personnel, technicians hooking Mr. Eckelson up to IVs and machines and lifting him onto a gurney. Eliza backed away, bumping against the bed of the truck.

She almost screamed when a hand fell on her shoulder. But it was only Joe, struggling against the drugs in his system to squeeze her arm in comfort.

"Is he gonna be okay?" Tori asked, coming around the front of the truck and twisting her hands with uncharacteristic nervousness, her eyes wide and frantic from the drive.

"We have to get him in surgery *now*," said a woman, not really answering so much as barking orders to her team. "Take him inside, prep OR 5. Alert the trauma team…"

And with that, the men and women of the hospital were wheeling Ian Eckelson away from the three teenagers hovering by the bloodstained truck. Only a beefy security guard was left, folding his arms as he made his way toward them.

"Tori did you leave…?" Eliza whispered.

"Of course I didn't bring it," Tori hissed back. "What kind of idiot do you think I am?"

Eliza only nodded, not even sure what she was agreeing to. It was too late to talk anyway, because the guard was there, two more approaching fast.

"You kids are gonna tell us what happened," he said, his frown an ominous warning.

"We don't know," Eliza said numbly. "We don't know, we just found him."

The guard softened an almost imperceptible amount, taking in their pale faces, shocked eyes, slack shoulders.

"Come inside," he said in a would-be comforting voice. "We can talk more comfortably there."

Horror crawled up Eliza's spine as she realized what was happening. These guards were going to take them to a room, question them, *detain* them. All the while Aquila and his brothers would be at Amile's mercy. No one was going to help the Vagabonds. No one even knew they were *there*. But what could Eliza do? There was no escape. They were surrounded, not to mention caged in by the sirens whistling toward them. In seconds, the police would be there. Joe was half-asleep. Tori was unarmed.

And Eliza was out of ideas.

No, she thought. *No, no, no.*

"Come along," the guard was saying, planting a hand on Eliza's shoulder.

"We need to see our uncle," she said on impulse. "Please, we just want to know if he's okay."

The guards exchanged a look, luckily missing Tori's eyes widening in surprise.

Please, fall for it. Please.

"Your... uncle?"

"Yes, of course, we're really worried about him."

"Ian Eckelson is your *uncle*?" the guard repeated with disbelief.

"He's kind of our adopted father," Tori said, catching on. "Please, let us see him. We're terrified."

"He just went into surgery. Who knows when he'll be out."

"We'll wait," Eliza said.

The guard's eyebrows rose, but after a long moment his shoulders slumped. He glanced at Joe in the truck bed.

"What's wrong with him?"

"Nothing," Eliza said quickly, praying Joe could rally enough to look normal. "Just squeamish. Please, sir, we won't be able to deal with anything until we know he's alright."

The guard sighed.

"Fine then, you three can come inside. But nothing funny, ok. We'll talk when your... uncle is out of surgery."

Eliza took a moment to offer a silent prayer of thanks for small-town security. These men had probably never dealt with a gunshot in their lives. They wouldn't believe, even for a moment, that a couple of Meru runaways could have anything to do with the shooting of an old millionaire. Which would buy them a bit of time.

But not enough.

They had to get out of there and *fast*. They were no doubt wanted by the police at this point. Eliza could imagine the panic at Meru with three students missing, two from a dorm room with a shattered door. Her, at least, they could explain away as bad behavior, but Joe? Tori?

No, she had to find a way out of the hospital and back to that lab. Because Aquila needed her. Joe needed her. Tori's brother needed her.

The Vagabonds were in trouble, and it was up to Eliza to get them out.

So as she let the guards steer them through the hospital entrance and towards the quiet waiting room, barely staffed this early

217

in the morning except by the EMTs who had leapt into action, Eliza began to string together the wildest, most reckless escape plan she could think of.

Finally, something she was good at.

CHAPTER FORTY-FOUR
The Whole Story

Eliza felt like a caged animal as she paced back and forth in the waiting room, her eyes occasionally flickering to the armed guards standing at the door.

"Would you sit down?" Tori hissed as Eliza made yet another loop around the molded plastic chairs designed for anything but comfort.

But Eliza couldn't. She felt electrified with worry, terror gnawing at her stomach as if she'd eaten something rotten. What was Amile doing to the Vagabonds right now? Was Ian Eckelson already dead? How soon until the police dragged them in for questioning? How long did Joe have left?

Eliza glanced over her shoulder. Joe met her gaze with his own dazed, heavy-lidded eyes, his face still limp from whatever drugs were in the darts he'd pulled out of his chest. Every time a gurney crashed through the main doors of the emergency room or the receptionist lifted her voice beyond a whisper, Joe winced. He looked like a drowning man, struggling to breathe through the flood of information cramming into his brain.

Eliza wanted to throw something. She wanted to punch, scream, *fight*.

She wanted to curl up and cry.

How the hell was she going to make this right?

Suddenly, the massive double doors leading into the main corridor of the hospital swung open and a young doctor strode through them, her surgical mask pulled down around her neck, her scrubs a pristine baby blue.

"He's ready to see you," she said, jerking her head impatiently.

Eliza was at Joe's side in a flash, helping him rise onto unsteady feet as Tori scrambled upright on her other side. With one last glance at the guards—watching the three teenagers with expressions of sympathetic suspicion—Eliza, Tori, and Joe followed the doctor into the intestines of Scottstown Medical.

It was a chaos of white light, sterile walls, shouting voices, beeping machines. Eliza felt like she didn't have enough eyes to take it all in. There were nurses rushing by, arms overflowing with things Eliza couldn't name. Doctors with charts disappearing behind curtains. Techs and receptionists trotting from room to room, wheeling computers and portable tables full of needles and bandages and frightening tools. And over it all, the steady thrum of frenetic energy fueled by all the urgent needs of humanity swirling around them.

If Eliza was overwhelmed, she couldn't even begin to imagine how Joe felt.

"Come on," she whispered, tugging on his elbow as he stumbled to a halt, his half-conscious eyes as big as eggs.

Even Tori looked uncomfortable as the young doctor led them through another set of double doors and into a quieter corridor lined with frosted windows.

"He's in here," she said, jerking her thumb into a dimly lit room. "I'm sorry, I have to get back to the OR, but if you need anything, press the button for nurse assistance."

"Got it," Eliza said, but the doctor was already gone, shoving through another set of doors and plunging deeper into the strange hospital maze they'd all stumbled into.

The three of them hesitated at the room's entrance for a moment, squinting into the murky darkness where Ian Eckelson lay tucked into a high bed, IV lines and wires sprouting around him like roots. The man who had only hours ago been looming, intimidating, strong, now looked tiny. Shriveled in the big white bed, sunken and weak and desperately pale.

It took Eliza a minute to realize she was holding her breath as she watched his chest rise and fall, as if she could lend her oxygen to him.

Suddenly, the old man opened one eye.

"Are you planning to stand there and stare all day?"

Eliza jumped, freezing like a startled animal before Tori shoved them inside with her signature eye-roll.

"How are you feeling?" Eliza asked in a quiet voice, settling Joe against the sill of the only window in the room, the curtain beside him hiding all but one narrow band of parking lot.

"Like a million bucks," Eckelson said, coughing out a laugh and laying spindly fingers across his chest.

Eliza stepped closer to the bed. "I see where Moose gets his humor."

"I'm glad you find the amount of gun injuries that have happened since you came along amusing."

Eliza pursed her lips and folded her arms, but Eckelson only sighed.

"Don't be petulant, child, I don't have enough energy for a war. I just want to know what happened to my sons."

The air rushed out of her. She glanced back at Tori. They shared a wince.

"They're... gone." Eliza swallowed. "Amile took them."

Eckelson lifted his tufted eyebrows.

"And you're still here?"

"We couldn't get away. We tried..."

But Eliza swallowed the end of her sentence. How exactly had they tried? What had they done while waiting for news on the old man's health? She'd been so paralyzed, so frozen by the terror of him dying that she had only considered their escape obliquely, and then only to discard the more ludicrous options.

Ian Eckelson exhaled again and the sound wasn't filled with the disappointment Eliza was expecting.

No, this sigh was strangely... forgiving.

"I'm sorry," Eckelson wheezed, the two small words enough to make Eliza freeze. "I've been... most unfair to you. I forget what it's like to come upon something like this when you're young." He grimaced. "And I should know better than anyone what it means to be rash. After all, I was the one who paid to create them."

"*What?*"

He wouldn't meet her gaze, his exhausted eyes drifting to that narrow band of light filtering through the window, to the ugly view of the hospital parking lot.

"I told you my son died. What I didn't tell you is that I tried to save him. There was a local man—a scientist—who told me about an experiment that could change human genetics in real-time. He made so many promises about rebuilding my boy's neurons with specific animal DNA, helping him recover the pieces of himself that were lost. I would have done anything he asked of me. I was so desperate for hope." Eckelson offered Eliza a wan, self-deprecating smile. "It's impossible to explain that kind of yearning."

"No," Eliza whispered. "It's not."

Eckelson continued as if he hadn't heard her.

"He asked only for money, something I had in abundance and no longer cared for. So I gave it to him, everything he wanted. My son died anyway."

"I'm so sorry."

Eckelson coughed again and a spot of red appeared at the corner of his mouth. He swallowed, gathering himself before continuing.

"I had all but forgotten about the project until the man contacted me again three years later. He called me to his lab to show me the product of his research. I almost didn't go. It was too much of a reminder. I didn't want to reckon with how badly I'd failed my only child." Eckelson took a deep, shuddering breath. "I'm still haunted by how close I came to ignoring his summons. Because it was in that lab that I found them."

Eliza didn't have to ask who Eckelson meant by *them*.

"The boys were still small, barely out of infancy, but already suffering from neglect. The scientist who'd requested my aid wanted to show me the *brilliance of his research*, convince me how *far* he could go, given more funding." Eckelson shook his head. "But all I saw were five motherless boys desperate for a home. I shut down the project at once and convinced the doctor to give the children to me and my wife."

"He just… let you take them?" Eliza asked.

Eckelson chuckled and then cringed from the pain.

"It took some convincing, but I managed to uncover the guilt that had already been festering in him. No matter how hard he tried, he couldn't silence the shame of what he'd done. He was the one to cover our tracks, at least until recently."

"Wait, wait, wait," Tori said, stepping forward. "You're saying that someone knew the, er, Vagabonds were with you this whole time?"

Eckelson smiled.

"Indeed. Doesn't it speak to the incongruous goodness of human beings?"

"Or the blind trust of old people," Tori muttered.

Eliza ignored her, focusing on Eckelson.

"So you took them home? Raised them in secret?"

"My wife wasn't pleased; God rest her soul."

"What happened to her?"

Eckelson looked, if possible, even more exhausted. His eyes drilled into Eliza's, filled with all the secret burdens of a long life.

"She was killed. In an accident."

Eliza knew she shouldn't push; knew she should leave it alone. But she couldn't. Not now, when so much depended on her knowing as much as possible.

"What kind of accident?"

Eckelson didn't respond for so long that Eliza was worried he wasn't going to. Finally he spoke.

"An accident in our basement. Involving Daisy."

Eliza fought the urge to step back, but Eckelson continued, holding her there.

"You've been around my sons long enough to understand that they're dangerous. Their powers have not always been in control, and even to this day there are... incidents. Strength, speed, electrical energy. Spines. These things are not always compatible with fragile human bodies."

Eliza was surprised to find her mouth hanging open. She shut it with a snap, straightening her spine.

"Unfortunately," Eckelson said. "I don't believe Daisy has ever forgiven himself for what happened."

Eliza shook her head, remembering the night Daisy had run off. Remembering his expression when they found him in the club. He'd looked so hopelessly lonely.

Or guilty.

"Does this change anything?" Eckelson asked after a moment of silence, eyes glinting.

"Of course not," Eliza snapped.

Eckelson's eyes shifted to Tori.

"And you?"

Tori snorted.

"I've lived around hunters my whole life. Your boys don't scare me."

Eckelson nodded, wincing again. He splayed his fingers on his chest, over the already-bloody bandage Eliza could see through the thin hospital gown.

"Sir," she said in a hesitant voice. "Why... why did you tell us all this?"

"When you first came, you saw them as a novelty. I don't blame you." His lips twitched. "They are that. But I want you to understand what they've been through, what they continue to go through. And I want you to fight for them as people. Not lab experiments. Not victims. Just teenage boys who deserve the same rights as anyone else." Eckelson's eyes found Eliza's again, holding her there with a power as undeniable as gravity. "Will you?"

"I never saw them as lab experiments. You didn't change anything."

But he had. Eckelson's story had made Eliza think about the doctor, the scientist behind the research.

Our research, Amile had said.

Was the man responsible still alive? Still working at Fitzgerald Labs? Did they have someone on the inside who had once been sympathetic to the Vagabonds' humanity?

Could he be trusted to help them again?

"We have to go," Eliza said, swinging around. "We've wasted enough time already."

"I agree," Eckelson said from behind.

"Yeah, but how do you suggest getting back out there?" Tori was standing with her feet apart, arms folded, her posture etched with skepticism. "We can hardly go out flashing our weapons, even if we had any."

Flashing our weapons.

Flashing.

"That's it!" Eliza said, leaping over to the window and yanking aside the curtain.

"What, now you want to crawl out the window?"

"Shut up and look," Eliza said, pointing.

Tori was silent for a single heartbeat.

"Oh no, no way, are you *crazy*?"

"What is it?" Eckelson said, but Eliza was already sliding open the window as quietly as she could and peering over the ledge. It was only an eight-foot drop to the ground, an easy jump after her gymnastics days. She only prayed that Joe and Tori could manage it.

"Eliza, you've lost your mind!" Tori snapped.

"Please explain—"

"Mr. Eckelson," Eliza interrupted. "Do you have any idea how to hotwire an ambulance?"

CHAPTER FORTY-FIVE
Lab Rats

Examining herself in the mirror, Amile thought of her mother. Pricilla Robillard was a woman of elegance who was never seen without pearls and a pressed dress. She'd always told her daughter that beauty was important, that it was one of the best tools at a woman's disposal. It could grant her a rich husband, preferential treatment, social power, the luxury of respect.

Amile tilted her head, tucking a single strand of hair back into place.

Her beauty wasn't the soft, inviting sort that her mother had tried to cultivate. Amile's sharp features and piercing eyes were *weapons*. Double-edged knives that asked for nothing, played at nothing. No, her countenance *demanded* respect. Even as a child being lectured about all the ways she might secure a good *match*, Amile had failed to understand the necessity of pleasing the men in her life. Why did she even *want* a husband? Why did she need men to ogle her, desire her, treat her like a doll that might break at any moment?

She only needed them to fear her.

And the higher she climbed, the less she needed them at all.

There was a distant crash from the other room, followed by an angry shout. Amile rolled her eyes.

These boys were proving to be more trouble than they were worth.

Blinking one last time at her reflection, Amile swirled away from her small vanity—the only feminine object in her austere cell of a room—and marched into the hall. The noises escalated as she grew closer to the lab: guttural snarls matching the shouts of her soldiers,

Dr. Oleander's whiney voice struggling to give orders, and the insistent clanking of chains.

Amile swung into the lab without hesitation.

"What's going on?" she demanded.

A flush of pleasure spread through her as the lab fell quiet, subdued by her very presence.

Who's powerful now, Mother? Amile thought, holding back a smile as her cold eyes passed over Dr. Oleander, the handful of privates assigned to help him.

And the test subjects.

It had taken months to design and ship the five special-order tables that would secure them. Two with ruts large enough for huge bony wings. One padded with electrical-retardant plastic. One with reinforced, spine-proof straps.

Mercifully, the skinny one only needed an extra-long frame.

The eagle-boy—Aquila—glared at Amile as she clicked her way across the room, his eyes narrow, trying to mask his fear with rage. But it was no use. She could almost smell the terror wafting off them, even as the one with bleached-white hair snarled obscenities.

She inhaled the power like a fine perfume, scanning the damage.

There was an overturned table near one of the subjects, shattered beakers leaking clear fluid on the floor. An antiseptic scent of rubbing alcohol made her nose twitch.

She smiled. "Have you been giving my soldiers trouble?"

"Fuck off lady," spat the foul-mouthed brother. *Gymnotiformes.* Electric eel. Amile barely spared him a glance.

"Let us go," Aquila rumbled, his voice a strange blend of pleading and threat.

"I'm afraid that's not possible," Amile said, side-stepping the growing pool of alcohol to get closer to the winged boy. "You five are quite essential to our research. But I promise, our procedures won't hurt. Much."

She tilted her head to examine the boy's feathers. They were iridescent, shimmering in a thousand shades of blue and green. Quite beautiful, actually. Perhaps she'd keep one for herself.

"What do you want from us?" he asked. "Maybe we can make an arrangement."

Amile returned her attention to his face, trying to ignore the depth of those blue eyes.

They're just test subjects, she reminded herself sternly as she straightened.

"I'm afraid no human in the history of the world would volunteer for what I plan to do."

Aquila lunged, exploding against the chain that bound him to the table. But Amile didn't even flinch. She'd tested those chains herself, gone over every inch of the restraints that would eventually hold her prizes. So she let him lean toward her until their noses were almost touching.

"You're a monster," Aquila said, his breath hot against her cheeks.

"I'm afraid the public would see quite the reverse."

Dr. Oleander's voice rose from one corner. "Amile!" Her teeth clicked together at the sound of the old man's voice, but he continued, as oblivious as ever to her irritation. "This is hardly necessary. These boys—"

"We've been through this, doctor."

"But—"

Amile's temper snapped. She swung around, eyes blazing, crashing down on the infantile scientist like a wave.

"I don't care. I don't care if they're your precious experiments, I don't care if you used your own genetics, I don't care if they're your goddamn *babies*. I will. Not. Allow. Complications."

Her words fell on the boys, the privates, and the withered old doctor like a volley of arrows. The room fell so silent that she could have heard a ghost speak.

And then another voice broke the silence, this one new.

"H-he used his o-own g-g-genetics?"

Amile's eyebrows lifted in surprise as she turned to the boy with the leathery wings. *Pteropus*. Fruit bat, also known as flying foxes. He'd been silent ever since the soldiers had wheeled them in here, almost holding his breath with fear.

And yet *this* was what made him speak?

Interesting.

Amile allowed her lips to spread in an inviting, taunting grin.

"Oh, didn't you know?" she chuckled. "This old bag of dust is your father."

Shock colored every single face. Even Aquila's anger broke for a moment, letting surprise shine through.

The slime-covered subject spoke first. "Well... shit."

"How did he have the *energy*?" Asked the skinny one. *Musca*. One of the privates had ripped off the boy's goggles. Out of all of them, he looked the most inhuman with his enormous, multifaceted eyes.

Amile met them anyway.

"He didn't need *energy*," she said, folding her arms and smirking at Dr. Oleander. "He just needed a few test tubes and enough stolen egg cells to cook you up."

"It was more complicated than that," Dr. Oleander muttered, but everyone ignored him.

He had no power here.

"A-and our....m-mothers?"

Amile turned to those milky white eyes and when she did, that strange sensation tugged at her spine again. Pity? Guilt?

She shook herself to clear it.

"Who knows? The eggs were taken from a donation center in Boston. Military subpoena. We never bothered to collect their information."

Dr. Oleander was shifting at the lie, but what was the point of telling these boys about the women who didn't, and never would, know they existed? Amile tightened her arms, wondering if she was going soft by showing such a mercy. But no, she wasn't cruel. She was efficient. Effective. And would be rewarded for it.

There was no need to cause any more suffering than she already planned to.

"What are you going to do with us?" Aquila said, his words low and desperate.

"First, we're going to use your genes to stabilize our virus," Amile said, stepping around the broken beakers and toward the row of monitors. "When we're sure we've accomplished that, we'll catalogue every part of your system. Recover all the research that was lost in the fire." Dr. Oleander flinched, but she pretended not to see it. "And then, when we're done, we'll terminate this experiment."

"But... why?"

Amile looked at him then, looked at all five of them. They were strange and different and vital to their research.

But they were also teenage boys.

She shook her head violently. Now wasn't the time for such thoughts. These *creatures* were collateral to her ambitious dreams. She had to remember that. There would be other, worse challenges ahead if she wanted to rise to the kinds of heights she'd been dreaming about since she was fifteen.

Amile would have to get used to leaving graves in her wake.

She straightened.

"Your freedom is a risk I can't afford to take."

"But—"

"Enough," Amile said, jerking her head at the waiting privates and pointing at the largest subject. "Take the other four to the secondary lab. We'll start with him."

She turned away so that she didn't have to watch, but she still heard the struggle. The clatter of chains, the growls, the shouts, the kicks. The fleshy sound of a punch was accompanied by a gasp. A wheel shrieked as one of the tables tilted too far. Her soldiers weren't operating at their best efficiency, not with two of their number infected by the unstable virus. Perhaps it had been unwise to use an agent she knew wasn't 100% ready, but the human immune system is such a malleable thing. She'd hoped their bodies would compensate, perhaps adapt into what she needed them to be. But they hadn't and now she had to deal with the ticking clock of six men and three women who needed boosters fast.

Listening to the scuffle behind her, she thought of Private Bent and the others she'd sent home to wait out their infection. They'd passed into the less useful stage, fainting and muscle spasms and hallucinations. There was no use for them here. Perhaps she'd call them back if they found a cure, but Amile suspected it might be too late for those unlucky early volunteers.

Amile held her breath, but at long last the sounds faded, echoing down the hallway toward the elevator. The others would be secure downstairs by the gene splicer, waiting their turn.

When she was sure the rest of her test subjects were gone, she swung back around to face Aquila.

"Now," she said, ignoring the strain of his muscles as he yanked stubbornly on unforgiving chains. "Let's get started."

CHAPTER FORTY-SIX
Brave Enough to Try

It turned out that no hot-wiring was necessary, because the keys were already in the ambulance.

"Why the hell did they just *leave* them here?" Tori asked, supporting Joe as Eliza leapt into the driver's seat.

"Who cares? Get in!"

"Eliza—"

"What?" Eliza said, nerves too tight to bother moderating her voice into some semblance of patience. "Are you gonna tell me this is a bad idea? Tell me we should go back? Leave everything alone? Let the authorities take care of it?"

Tori pursed her lips, Joe leaning away from her as if he was fighting the urge to be sick.

Finally, she spoke.

"Put on your fucking seatbelt, dumbass."

Eliza clenched her jaw so tight it hurt. But she yanked the seatbelt around her as Tori and Joe tottered to the other side of the strange vehicle.

The inside was like something out of a science fiction movie. There were buttons everywhere, switches lining the panel in front of her, things hanging down from the roof. Even though the little door to the back was closed, Eliza could smell the tang of blood. This one had been used recently, perhaps just swung into the parking lot carrying some unfortunate soul.

Maybe that's why the keys were still in it.

Whatever the reason, Eliza wasn't about to question their stroke of good fortune.

"Ready?" Eliza asked as Tori and Joe squeezed into the passenger seat.

"We're going to be in so much trouble," Tori muttered as Joe jerked his head in some semblance of a nod.

"Here goes nothing." Eliza turned the key. For a heart-stopping moment, she thought the ambulance wasn't going to start, that maybe there was a switch or button she needed to press to turn it on.

And then it roared to life.

"Go, go, go," Tori moaned, twisting to look out the other window as Eliza accelerated out of the parking lot. They swung onto the hospital drive just as the guards spilled out of the emergency room.

And then they were sailing through Scottstown.

"Are we going to Fitzgerald Base?" Joe asked, his forehead pressed into the cluttered dashboard as if he could shield his overstimulated senses.

"We can't go there, not like this," Tori said, glaring at the side-view mirror.

Eliza gritted her teeth even tighter as she swerved to avoid a dog-walker who came out of nowhere. Angry shouts echoed in their wake.

"Someone find the goddamn lights!"

Tori began to fumble with the various switches and dials, leaning over Joe to reach Eliza's side.

"There are so many!"

"Hurry up!"

Suddenly the air was split by the shriek of a siren, too close for comfort. Eliza couldn't tell if their lights were on in the waning afternoon, but the sound was enough to make the Scottstown pedestrians skitter out of their way. Eliza swung through stop signs, ignoring traffic signals, swerving around corners like a maniac.

But she was a maniac with nowhere to go.

"What do we do?" she snapped, her eyes wide, her heart hammering frantically.

Joe only groaned in response, holding his hands over his ears.

"I've got it!" Tori's words cut off in a shriek as Eliza barreled through a busy intersection, leaving the whine of skidding tires behind them. "My brother's apartment!"

"*What?*"

Tori clutched the dashboard as Eliza took a turn so hard their back wheels spun out for a second.

"I have a key. He has guns. We'll go there and… figure things out."

"Where does he live?"

"Greenwald Street."

They gasped as Eliza took a speed bump hard enough to make them lift off their seats. The metal frame of the ambulance creaked in protest.

"That's in the middle of town!" Eliza snarled.

"Do you have a better idea?"

Suddenly, Joe's voice broke in, quiet but surprising enough to make the two girls shut up.

"Does he have a spare uniform?"

Eliza held her breath, waiting for Tori to respond.

"Yeah. Why?"

"Because I can wear it," Joe said, arms wrapped around his middle. "Maybe get us inside."

"Joe, you're in no condition—"

But he straightened, using the dashboard to shove himself upright.

"I want to help. I *need* to. Or else I'm toast, right?"

Eliza exchanged a frantic look with Tori before taking a hard U-turn around a divider to turn back towards Martin Bent's apartment.

"Fine," she said, electric with adrenaline as they accelerated down the quiet residential road. "Fine, but we have to be fast."

Tori was already shifting through her keychain.

"Got it," she said, holding up the jagged metal.

"Where am I going?" Eliza snapped.

"There. The one with the porch swing."

"*Porch swing?*"

"What can I say? My brother's a country boy at heart. Pull up on the curb and leave it running."

Eliza would have growled at Tori for giving her orders if she wasn't so tense. For a moment, she considered having someone stay with the ambulance. But who? They needed Joe inside to try on uniforms, Tori had the key.

And Eliza would lose her mind if she didn't know what was happening in there.

"Ok everyone, as quick as possible."

Tori was already out of the ambulance and sprinting up the walkway. Eliza climbed down from the high cab, shaking all over but somehow able to meet Joe on the steps leading up to the two-unit house. As Tori struggled with the lock, Eliza shifted from foot to foot, casting panicked glances up the quiet road, waiting for the police to come screaming in after them. What time was it? Would people be getting home from work? How long until someone called in the three teenagers driving the stolen ambulance?

The questions felt like they were wrapping around her throat and choking off her air supply and everything around them seemed hostile and leering and bracing for attack...

After what felt like an eternity, the door swung open.

"Let's go," Tori said, leading them inside.

CHAPTER FORTY-SEVEN
Horror Movie

The first thing Eliza noticed was the smell. The air inside the first-floor apartment was rotten, thick and pungent with unwashed dishes, food going bad, sweaty clothes. She lifted a hand to cover her nose as she climbed over a pile of overturned things in the middle of what used to be a living room. The table was on its side, DVD's were everywhere, and the flat-screen television had a wide slice down the middle, as if someone had taken a knife to it.

"What the hell...?" Eliza whispered.

"Oh my god, *Martin!*"

Before anyone could stop her, Tori had lunged across the room. Eliza surged after her, ready for anything.

Except what she found lying by the couch.

Martin Bent looked terrifying. He was pale, sweating, shivering on the ground where he'd toppled off the plushy cushions. His eyes were wide and wild as they darted between his sister and the two shadows looming behind her.

"Martin? Martin, are you okay?"

"He's clearly not okay," Eliza said, putting out an arm to keep Joe back. But she couldn't keep Joe from seeing.

Is this what the virus leads to? Eliza thought hopelessly.

Tori was sobbing, her hands on her brother's face.

"Martin, please, tell me what to do?"

"Go away, Mom. Go away, you're not real."

The words were muttered so low that Tori didn't hear them over her desperate sobs. But Eliza did.

"Tori..."

"Come on, Eliza, we have to get him to the hospital—"

Suddenly, Martin shouted, *"Go away!"*

And then Tori was airborne, flying across the room and smashing into a bookshelf. Heavy instruction manuals and encyclopedias rained down on her as she curled into a ball, but Eliza was powerless to help because Martin Bent was on his feet, advancing on them with barred teeth.

"You're not real," he growled, his eyes both sharp and unseeing, his fingers curved into claws. Eliza shoved Joe behind her, mind whirring into overdrive as she tried to think of a way out of this. Maybe Joe could counter this man's strength, but not without getting hurt. And they couldn't afford another injury, not now when they had to—

Without warning, Martin's eyes rolled back in his head. He collapsed to the floor with a muffled *thump*.

"What happened?" Joe asked, his voice taut with the unspoken knowledge that his body was swarming with the same agent that had turned Martin Bent into *this*.

Eliza was already moving, flipping the limp soldier over near the coffee table.

"Joe, find me some rope."

"Eliza..."

"Not now, Tori."

But glancing up, Eliza couldn't help the flush of shame and pity. A massive bruise was already spreading over Tori's cheek where a book had hit her. Worse were her eyes, bloodshot and puffy and frantic. Tori wrapped pale arms around her torso, rocking back and forth as Joe handed Eliza a game controller with a long wire.

"Best I could find," he said.

Eliza began to tie Martin's hands to the coffee table, wrapping the wire around his hot wrists as many times as she could, trying not to think about how feverish he felt.

"It's for his own good," Eliza said as she worked. "This way he won't hurt himself while we're gone."

Tori hiccupped. Panic swarmed Eliza's brain as she thought about how much had already gone wrong. But they had to focus. They had to get to Fitzgerald Base.

They had to save the Vagabonds.

"Tori," Eliza said, trying to keep her voice calm. "Can you find Joe a uniform?"

It took the other girl so long to respond that Eliza had to swallow the urge to shout. With every second that passed, Eliza could imagine the police cars shrieking towards them and the handcuffs snapping around their wrists.

Finally, Tori shook herself.

"They're in here," she said, stepping over the pile of books and to a side-closet.

Eliza kept her attention on Martin as Tori yanked out pants and jackets, throwing them haphazardly at Joe. Thankfully, he didn't need to be told twice, quickly stripping down to his boxers and pulling on the various pieces of uniform. Everything was too large on his lean frame, but it would be enough.

It had to be.

"I feel ridiculous," Joe said, tugging at the ID tag Tori had found on a side-table.

Eliza's grin was strained but sincere.

"You don't look ridiculous."

It was true. Even ill-fitting, the khaki made Joe look intimidating. Official. Handsome even.

"Here," Tori said, interrupting Eliza's thoughts as she emerged from the closet. Something glinted in her hand as she offered it to Joe.

A gun.

"Oh no," Joe said, backing away. "No, no, no."

"You have to, it's part of the uniform."

"I'm too dangerous. I might hurt someone."

239

Tori lifted one eyebrow, looking almost like herself. "That's kind of the point."

"It's okay," Eliza said, putting a hand on Joe's forearm and accepting the gun herself. She slid it into the holster on her friend's belt. "I trust you."

It took everything Eliza had not to glance at the figure on the floor, the young man who'd become so dangerous that they had to leave him tied to his own coffee table. But when Joe met her eyes, she knew he was thinking about it too.

How long did he have before he was like that?

There was a metallic crash and a curse as Tori continued to rummage through the closet, toppling back out with her arms overflowing with weapons. Revolvers and pistols threatened to spill all over the floor. A hysterical half-laugh burst out of Eliza.

"Tori?" she said in a choked voice.

"No way am I going in there unarmed," Tori said as she began to tuck the guns into her skirt's waistband.

Eliza swallowed. Nodded. And then held out her hand.

"Me neither," she said, accepting a pistol and praying she wouldn't have to use it.

"Hey," Joe said, making them both swing around. "Isn't that a Fitzgerald Jeep?"

All three of them clustered by the back window, peering into Martin Bent's driveway. Sure enough, a green-painted vehicle was pulled haphazardly up beside the neighbor's begonias.

Eliza, still gripping the pistol, cast around the apartment, stepping over Tori's brother.

She found the keys on the coffee table.

"Well guys, guess it's time for an upgrade," she said, baring her teeth in what might almost be called a smile, jingling the keys with her free hand.

CHAPTER FORTY-EIGHT
Stowaways

Nestled in the open back of the Jeep, covered by a thick army blanket they'd found in a metal crate and listening to the gentle rumble of the pristine, top-of-the-line vehicle, Eliza and Tori crouched in tense silence as Joe drove them into Fitzgerald Base. Their waistbands were full of weapons, hearts hammering in tandem, both daunted for their own reasons by the impossible task ahead. Not quite able to ignore Tori's hitched breathing and shaking hands, Eliza tried not to wonder if they were too late. Would Amile be ready for them, suspect a counterattack after leaving them alive? Whatever her agenda, that woman would be rushing things along just in case the three teenagers decided to make a ruckus.

Which was, of course, exactly what they planned to do.

Eliza felt the Jeep drop off the main highway, swinging onto the gravel side-road that would lead them into the base. She wondered how Joe was doing. He'd insisted that he was sane enough to drive, but Eliza had seen the way his fingers twitched, his eyes shifted, how he winced at every noise and flash of light. She knew her friend well enough to see that he was walking that razor-blade edge of panic, struggling to hold onto rationality as his mind was slowly crushed beneath the weight of the Superman Virus.

Would he be able to hold it together long enough for them to get inside?

Eliza swallowed, wrapping her arms around her knees.

It had been more than twelve hours since Amile took the Vagabonds. Almost a whole day. How much damage could that horrible woman have already done?

"He's doing surprisingly well," Tori said, her whisper breaking their silence like a gunshot. Eliza jerked and Tori flinched, both of them listening to the gentle crunch of gravel beneath the wheels as the Jeep decelerated.

"What?"

"Joe. He's doing well. You know, for a nerd."

Eliza slanted her eyes at the other girl, unnerved by how much Tori was shaking, how her eyes were red-rimmed and puffy.

"And what about you?"

Tori sniffed. "I'm fine."

"I know what it feels like to worry about a sibling. You don't have to be fine."

"Yes I do," Tori said. Eliza shrugged, forced herself to take a deep, calming breath as she clenched and unclenched her fists. Her thoughts turned, as they so often did, to Katie. Was she watching? Guarding the baby sister still trapped in the real world without her?

Eliza liked to think so.

They both froze at the sound of voices, deep and male. The slap of a palm on the Jeep's hood.

They'd reached the front gate. Their first hurdle.

Come on, Joe. Come on.

Would the soldiers immediately recognize an imposter? Would they know Martin Bent personally, look at the ID tag and realize that they were dealing with a fraud?

Eliza pursed her lips. Tori leaned into her shoulder.

Finally, impossibly, Eliza heard the sound of a chain-link gate rattling over gravel.

The Jeep started moving again.

They both took a shaky breath, exchanging a wide-eyed look of partial relief as they moved blindly into the hornet's nest.

"What happened to your sister?" Tori's voice, though quiet, made them both wince. "You never told me."

Eliza swallowed a chuckle. *What a weird way to ease tension.* But maybe her pain threw such an enormous shadow that it was unavoidable even in this dire of a situation.

"Leukemia," Eliza answered without emotion. "Katie had it for almost a year before it was diagnosed. When they did it was too late."

For a long, stretching moment, Tori didn't respond. The only sound between them was the growl of the engine and their pounding hearts.

"I'm so sorry," Tori said at last.

"I'm sorry about Martin."

Tori's chuckle was so surprising that Eliza twisted around to face her. But there was no malice in the other girl's shadowed face, just a grim acceptance of how weird their lives had become.

"You know, I hated you when you showed up. You were loud and brave and didn't seem to give a shit what anyone thought about you. I thought you didn't care about anything." Tori shook her head as the Jeep slowed. "I guess I was jealous or something. But turns out you have baggage just like the rest of us."

In a different world, Eliza would have been insulted at Tori's distillation of her awful history into the word *baggage*. But she didn't say anything, because here, in this moment, it seemed right. Katie was the burden she carried, the weight on her shoulders. Just like Ian Eckelson's son. Just like Tori's family. Just like the Vagabonds themselves.

Everyone had a history.

Outside the fabric cover of the Jeep and their stifling blanket, Eliza listened to the distant murmur of voices, the men and women standing guard around Fitzgerald, joking, shouting, commanding.

Here we go, Eliza thought.

"Well, let's see if a couple of fucked up teenagers can face down the U.S. Army..."

But Eliza's joke was choked into silence as she heard the creak of a garage door opening, accompanied by a stern female voice.

"Pull in there for inspection! You know the drill, private. Hurry up!"

"Oh shit," Tori whispered. They both curled tighter, but Eliza could see the next few minutes playing out like a movie in her head. The soldiers would climb in, whip off the blanket.

Find them.

What were they going to do?

She heard Joe's voice, light and joking, too muffled to make out words. The vehicle trundled forward, jerked to a halt. Heavy footsteps circled toward them, accompanied by the whine of gears and the slam of a metal door.

The garage had closed.

They were locked inside.

Someone was grumbling under her breath beside the Jeep, that same stern voice Eliza had heard ordering Joe into the garage.

"Idiot recruits don't know shit about security protocols."

Velcro tore and light spilled over the thin weave of their blanket. Eliza fought the urge to shudder.

No, no, no, she chanted silently.

Tori's fingers were curling painfully over Eliza's wrist, but Eliza ignored them, her mind whirring as she cascaded through options.

Their rescue was about to be over before it had even begun.

Suddenly, Tori's hand disappeared. Eliza tilted her head infinitesimally, squinting through the sudden brightness, trying not to think about the woman climbing in.

Tori was gripping the handle of her gun, her expression set and stubborn.

Bile climbed up Eliza's throat.

Had it really come to this?

Wrapping her shaking fingers around the handle of her borrowed gun, Eliza wondered if it was cocked. *Do you have to cock a pistol? Is there a safety? How do I know if it's ready?*

Tori really should have offered lessons.

Eliza braced herself, ready to leap from the shadows and shoot at the poor woman just doing her job.

Suddenly, Joe spoke.

"Hey lady, is there a restroom—"

His question ended in an abrupt grunt. Eliza burst out from beneath the blanket just in time to see Joe whip a blurred figure to the side, into the wall. The woman in uniform hit with bruising force, coughing, scrambling for the gun on her belt. But Joe was there, knocking her hand away, slamming her in the solar plexus.

"Joe, stop!" Eliza hissed, but the woman's eyes were already rolling up. She collapsed to the floor in a heap.

Joe stumbled back into the Jeep's bumper, staring around the narrow garage hung with heavy military-grade equipment, as if looking for comfort among the tools of violence.

"Did I... Did I...?"

Eliza darted forward, her fingers crawling along the woman's collar.

There was a pulse.

"It looks like she's—"

Suddenly, the wail of an alarm split the silence of the garage.

"What *now*?" Tori moaned.

On a whim, Eliza yanked the woman's other hand out from under her hip.

There, nestled in one palm, was an alarm button.

Blinking red.

"Uh oh," Joe said, peering over Eliza's shoulder.

A door crashed open on the other side of the Jeep.

"Come on!" Eliza said, grabbing Joe's arm and yanking him behind the Jeep. The alarm wail was painful, sharp and blaring, but she had to focus. With Joe and Tori behind her, Eliza fell to her knees. Watched the boots crash past them.

She could see the door, watched the feet pound through it.

And then it was empty.

Soldiers were coming around the jeep.

"Let's go!" Eliza hissed, shoving her friends forward.

But Tori was ahead of her, sliding over the hood of the Jeep and running through the entrance in a dead sprint. Eliza followed, dragging Joe.

"Lock the door!" Eliza panted, pointing frantically at the panel on the inside of the garage entrance.

With fumbling hands, Joe pressed the stolen tag to the small black square.

Please work, oh please work.

The panel light turned green just as the soldiers turned to face them, just as Eliza swung the door shut and jammed her finger into the bright red button beside the panel.

The door locked them in with an ominous *click*.

"Well, we're committed now," Joe said.

"Run!" Eliza shouted as the hall to their right began to echo with the sound of pounding feet.

It was frenetic and dizzying to sprint through the endless maze of sterile hallways. Eliza led the way, barreling around corners, skidding through open doors. Where were they going? What would they do now? How long would their luck hold out?

Not long enough.

Eliza took a corner too fast and slid right into the wide chest of a man in uniform.

"I found them!"

Windmilling her arms, Eliza stumbled back, hitting Tori and Joe. There was a mad scramble. Soldiers rushed forward. Joe shoved one back, threw another into a wall. Tori grabbed him by the back of his borrowed uniform, yanking him into a dark stairwell. They half-fell down a floor before crashing through another entrance. Tori leaned back, bracing her body against the stairwell door, holding her breath.

From the other side came the unmistakable sound of heavy combat boots thundering past.

"Don't let them reach the basement!"

"Protect the Splicer!"

"Stop them!"

The voices echoed, receding down the stairwell and into the ground.

"I think we lost them," Tori panted at last, peeking through the door, quivering all over.

"Hey," Joe said from behind her, voice high and worried. "Where's Eliza?"

CHAPTER FORTY-NINE
Eye of the Storm

"We have to go back."

"Don't be an idiot, Joe, we have no idea where she is."

"Tori—"

But Tori just yanked out one of the three guns sprouting from her waistband, cutting off Joe's protests.

"Look, there's nothing we can do for her except find the others and hope she's with them. Unless you have a better suggestion?"

Joe looked like he very much wished he did. But he remained silent. Satisfied, Tori nodded and bounced her knees, peering through the tiny window in the stairwell door.

"I guess we'll start with this floor," she said with as much authority as she could muster. Then, turning back to Joe, she lifted her eyebrows. "You know, your gun isn't going to do any good on your hip."

Gingerly, as if it was something that might bite him, Joe wiggled his weapon out of the holster on Martin's belt. Tori's eyes took in his nervousness, the way his fingers didn't quite curl around the handle, and she sighed.

"Here, let me show you."

Trying to hide the instinctual fear of how dangerous Joe had become and what he could do to her if he wanted, Tori stepped in closer, tapping under Joe's elbows.

"Straight arms, but careful not to lock your elbows, or else the kick will hurt. Squeeze the trigger, don't pull it. And don't hold it like a baby bird or it won't stay in your hands. Got it?"

"No," Joe said, but his hands tightened around the molded grip.

"Not here!" Tori snapped, shoving the barrel down. Joe swallowed, but Tori was already moving to the door, muttering beneath her breath. "Of all the people to have my back in here..."

But her voice withered as she poked her head around a corner and peered down a long, empty hallway. She was braced for anything. Her breathing tightened as she thought of her brother, tied to his own coffee table. Martin would help them, if he was able. Martin would have seen through Amile's plan if he'd been of sound mind, would have fought by their side for the rights of the Vagabonds.

Wouldn't he?

She would just have to cure him and find out.

Tori braced herself to plunge out of the relative safety of the stairwell doorway.

"Let's go," Tori said, not allowing her fear any more time to grow. Carefully, slowly, she slid along the wall to the nearest door. Peered inside.

An empty office.

Her instincts were tuned so tight that even Joe's steps behind her made her jump. She jerked her head, leading him further down the hall, trying to ignore the glimmer of cameras over their heads, still active. Was someone watching them, or had the chaos in the garage been enough to distract the guards?

Either way, they had to hurry.

The next room was a pristine lab, a few people in white coats clustered near a fume hood in the back.

She ducked to the other side of the open entrance before one of the scientists could see her, grabbing Joe's arm and dragging him further away from the stairwell and their exit and any scrap of the familiar.

After another few peeks into empty or near-empty rooms, they came upon a door with no window.

What is it? Joe mouthed.

Tori could only shrug, clutching her revolver with white-knuckled hands.

One way to find out.

She tried the handle. Locked. Joe fumbled with Martin's ID, holding up as if in question. Tori shrugged again.

Maybe they'd get lucky.

Joe pressed the key card against the square side-panel. They both held their breaths, watching the blinking light.

After a tense, stretching moment, it turned green.

"Watch the hall," Tori hissed to Joe, opening the door just wide enough to duck her head inside.

It was the strangest thing she'd ever seen.

An enormous machine filled the middle of the room. It stretched two stories, bracketed by a walkway on their floor and disappearing into the deep-sea darkness below. *The basement?* Whirring and clicking and surrounded by monitors, Tori couldn't even begin to make sense of it. She took a hesitant step onto the metal walkway, only to see movement on the other side of the strange mechanical pillar. Two voices were echoing toward her, accompanied by the soft sound of rubber shoes on tile.

"...shouldn't take much time to splice in those mutations."

"You think, what, forty minutes?"

"With this baby? Ten."

"No way."

"I'd put my money on it. But of course, she wants duplicates of everything."

"Well, let's hurry up and get more samples. After what she did to..."

Tori yanked her head back and pulled the door closed as quietly as she could. Her heart was hammering, her face flushed. She glanced around frantically as Joe's eyes widened in question. But there was no time.

Let's hurry up and get more samples.

Were these scientists on their way to the Vagabonds?

Tori grabbed Joe's hand and hauled him down the hall, ignoring the doors and windows. Finally, about thirty feet from the door, Tori found a side-table, laden with beakers and chemicals, file boxes crammed underneath. She shoved Joe behind it.

"What's—?"

"Shhh," Tori hissed, sliding in next to him and leaning out from behind a shelf of test tubes. They rattled at her touch, making her flinch. She squinted down the corridor, watched two people in white coats emerge where they'd just been standing. The scientists moved down the hall, toward Tori and Joe's hiding place, one of them carrying a tray of vials and needles.

Please be right, Tori thought, refusing to blink as the pair of voices echoed toward her, too jumbled to make out words. *Oh please let me be right.*

They stopped by a black door on the opposite wall. One of them unlocked it.

They both disappeared inside.

"Come on," Tori whispered, launching herself from behind the table like a sprinter down a track. She pumped her arms, her sneakers squeaking on the linoleum. She could hear Joe panting behind her, their breathing equally panicked. Equally raw.

The door was drifting shut.

She slid the last few feet, stuck her foot into the door, shoved it back open.

"Hey—!"

Tori had only a single breathless moment to take in the room. Two scientists, three soldiers, arranged around a cluster of misshapen cots. And there, watching her with wide eyes, were four of the five Vagabonds, their faces white with terror.

CHAPTER FIFTY
Peekaboo

"Watch out!" Otto shouted.

Tori was already on it, training a revolver on the nearest upright body with one hand while the other whipped out her brother's Glock.

"Don't move!"

Joe skidded in behind her, panting.

"Tori, what—?"

"Untie them."

She didn't have to tell him twice. Joe stepped around the two scientists, moving to the table where Otto struggled against his plastic-padded restraints.

But the shock was wearing off. The soldiers were gathering. One of them reached for their belt.

"Don't. Move." Tori repeated, trying to keep her eyes on everyone at the same time. But the soldiers were splitting, moving apart with well-trained, tactical steps.

Damnit.

"Joe..."

"It's locked!"

"That one has a key on his belt," Moose piped up, jerking his head at the largest soldier, a burly man with a sour expression. "I saw it when he wheeled us in."

"Put down the gun, little girl," the man said. "You don't want to do this."

She curled one lip. "Don't test me."

Terror was a living, breathing thing in Tori's chest as everything slowed, as her mind whirred, desperate to find a way out of this. Her eyes raked over the lab benches lining the room, the tubes of blood, the IV lines protruding from the boys' arms.

There.

A scalpel.

Tori took a deep breath. She'd only have a second.

Pointing the gun at the ceiling, Tori fired. Everyone jumped. Hands flew to weapons and the soldiers shouted and plaster rained down on the scene like volcanic ash. But Tori was already throwing herself to the side, grabbing the scalpel.

"Joe!"

He looked up right as she threw it. For a terrifying moment she wondered if the gangly nerd who had always been infamously bad at sports would be able to grab it before it hit him in the face. She needn't have worried. Joe snatched the scalpel out of the air with Moose-quick reflexes, bringing it down on the plastic padding.

A normal person might have taken precious seconds to saw through the reinforced straps, but Joe's arm came down in a powerful swipe.

And right away, Otto's arms were free.

"Hell yeah," Otto said, flexing his fingers as Joe sliced through the other restraints, releasing knees, feet, neck. Otto leapt off the table just as one of the soldiers took aim at Tori's head. "Not today, fucknut."

The soldier went down in a sparking tangle of limbs, screaming as Otto slammed a crackling hand into his chest.

Tori was backing away, but someone grabbed her arm. One of the scientists, face hidden by a fabric mask.

"What do you think you're — ?"

But the hand disappeared as Joe flung the woman into her partner. Both bodies crashed into a table full of equipment. Vials of blood shattered, staining the white tiles.

"Get that one!" Tori shouted, pointing at the guard with the keychain hanging from his belt.

"I wanna help, I wanna help," Moose was chanting even as Tero and Daisy looked ready to faint. But Otto paid no attention as he circled the man with the keys, followed by Joe. Tori watched, hesitating, wondering what to do.

But then, with a chill, she realized something.

Where was the third guard?

She turned, eyes raking across the room, just in time to see the woman speaking into a radio attached to the wall.

"Don't!" Tori shouted, leveling one of her guns.

But it was no use. The message had already been sent. Tori leapt forward, cracking the handle of her Glock on the back of the woman's skull. The soldier staggered to the side.

Right then, the air was split by the wail of an alarm.

"Shit," Tori breathed, rounding on the others who were wrestling the keychain away from the now weaponless guard. "Guys, hurry!"

"You... asshole..." Otto snarled, smearing his hand over the man's face.

"You're not going to—"

But the snarl was cut off as Otto rabbit-punched the guard, knocking his head into the floor. The white-haired boy straightened, standing over the unconscious body with fresh slime glistening on harsh stubble.

"Fucker should hope he doesn't wake up anytime soon."

"Otto, hurry!" Tori shrieked in horror as the scientists stirred and two of the three guards shoved to their feet.

"Right."

"Me first!" Moose said, wriggling against his restraints.

Otto leapt over to his brother's table, unlocking the heavy chains. It took three endless seconds to throw off the final restraint, enough time for Tori to finally register the enormous, glittering, faceted eyes that took up half of Moose's face. She tried to swallow the natural revulsion, reminding herself that, goggles or not, he was still the same person who had cracked dumb jokes in the mansion basement.

And then Moose was airborne, eyes sparkling eerily in the light.

"Give me *that*," he said, snatching the keys from Otto.

He became a blur, darting between Tero and Daisy like a distortion of light. Otto took the opportunity to shock one of the scientists into unconsciousness while Tori braced herself against the door.

How long until the reinforcements arrived?

And more importantly, how would they escape now?

"Hurry up," Otto snarled.

"Who do you think you're talking to?" Moose said, throwing his arms wide as Daisy and Tero swung their legs free.

"T-thanks," Tero stuttered, rubbing his arms, his chalky eyes huge and eerie in the flashing red lights.

"What do we do now?" Otto asked, looking at Tori even as his foot pressed down on one of the scientists, the only one still conscious.

"We have to find Aquila," Moose said. "That crazy lady kept him in the other place, the one upstairs, and I can't imagine it's for anything good."

Tori threw a glance at Joe, who was leaning against the wall with his arms tight around his torso, gulping deep, shuddering breaths. She swallowed. Straightened.

Sorry Eliza.

"We'll find Aquila later," Tori said, making a snap decision. "First, we need to figure out that cure." She strode over to where the shorter scientist was struggling to get out from beneath Otto's boot. "And you're going to help us."

255

CHAPTER FIFTY-ONE
A First Time for Everything

Eliza tried to make herself as small as possible in the tiny space between the vending machine and the wall as shapes trotted past her, wavering in the flashing red alarm like deep-sea creatures.

Please don't look in here, just keep going, don't look right.

They didn't. The men and women in uniform made a beeline for the stairs, swarming down where Tori and Joe had disappeared.

She'd been staring at that door for the past ten minutes as the cluster of guards who had stumbled upon them flashed in and out of her line of vision, calling for backup, shouting orders, locking down the base. They might have managed the seemingly impossible task of sneaking inside, but their cover was officially blown. The army knew they were there.

The real game was on.

Eliza could only pray that Joe and Tori were safe, because there was no way she was getting through that door without being seen.

Finally, as the last of the swarm disappeared into the stairwell, Eliza stuck her head out. She looked left, right, squinting through the emergency lights. There was no hope of escaping at this point. Not that Eliza planned to go anywhere without her friends, but she wondered how deep the lockdown would go. What would she do if all the rooms were shut? What if even the soldiers couldn't get through in the case of such an emergency?

How would she find Aquila and his brothers?

Feeling overwhelmed by the task at hand, Eliza forced herself to swallow.

One step at a time, she thought.

And the first step was emerging from her hiding place.

Taking a deep, calming breath, Eliza curled herself around the vending machine. When no one shot at her, she stepped out of the shadows, into the flashing red hallway. Picking a direction at random, she began to side-step along the wall.

She came upon the corner closest to the stairwell and peeked around it, careful not to let too much of her hair show.

There were two men standing by a door, arms folded, looking angry and ominous.

It was the only guarded door in the hallway.

Something must be in there.

But Eliza was alone and armed only with a gun she had no idea how to use. She raked her eyes along the ceiling, but there were no vent openings anywhere near the guards. The alarms were already going off, so she couldn't distract them that way.

Gritting her teeth, Eliza glanced around for something, anything, to help.

Her eyes fell on a wheeling cart, stacked high with paperwork.

It was a terrible plan, really, with an endless number of things that could go wrong. But she couldn't think of a better one.

If you're there, Katie, I could really use some supernatural protection right about now.

Grabbing the handle of the cart, Eliza tested it. Rolled it once, twice. With a sweep of her arm, she cleared out the bottom shelf. The folders rustled to the ground, falling open, spilling pictures all over the white floor.

Eliza froze.

The photos were of her. Of Joe and Tori and all the faces that made up her life at Meru. Greta, Marta, Yuri, Hector. Snapshots of Eliza's homeroom teacher, Mrs. Henderson, and the headmaster who had scolded her for being rude to Amile. All of it mixed in with blurry Polaroids of hulking wings and glinting goggles.

Crouching down, Eliza flicked open the nearest file. And the next one. There were hundreds, if not *thousands* of pictures, notes, records. All obsessively catalogued, all labeled with the mysterious stamp of MISSION LABRADOR.

In the third file she opened, Eliza found her parents staring back at her. There was a sticky note on the bottom of the page that read *potential leverage?* Underlined twice.

Eliza's fear was replaced by a crashing wave of rage.

How *dare* Amile drag Eliza's parents into this? It was bad enough to target Joe and Tori, but *this*?

Emboldened by the knowledge of what Amile was capable of, Eliza straightened. Leaned into the cart. Swallowed.

And launched herself down the hallway.

"Hey!"

"Freeze!"

Eliza barely glimpsed the two men drawing their weapons as she dove into the cleared-out middle of the cart. The files on top took off like frightened birds as she swerved down the slick hallway. Papers fell around the kamikaze little vehicle in a rustling chaos, shielding the vulnerable human body inside. Eliza heard a gunshot, another surprised shout.

And then the cart's wheel caught.

She tumbled into a roll.

Eliza tried to jump out, but her leg got stuck. She swung, tangled into the sharp metal legs, bit back a scream.

"Get her!"

Forcing herself to think through the pain, Eliza managed to find her feet and launch upright. An arm was already swinging at her face. She ducked, toppling into a backbend. Her muscles protested, long out of the habit of contorting into unnatural shapes. But she kicked off the ground and wheeled backwards, snapping the nearest guard's mouth shut with the toe of her shoe. He reeled back, clutching his jaw.

"You little..."

But she was springing backwards, out of danger.

There was a metallic clatter as the gun fell out of Eliza's waistband.

"No!" she cried, twisting, lunging for it. A boot was already kicking the weapon aside. Two guns were trained on her face now, holding her against the wall, coming closer.

"Hands up!" snapped one of the guards.

Eliza's heart was a thundering stampede in her chest, frantically counting down the moments it had left.

Suddenly, the lights flashed bright, blinding.

And died.

Eliza blinked, but she couldn't see anything. The corridor became thick with the kind of darkness that makes time warp and space feel endless. She took a step to the side, padding silently along the wall as she listened to the soldiers in front of her.

"What happened?"

"I dunno, but take out your flashlight, dumbass."

"The backup generator should come on any second."

But it didn't. Eliza fought the urge to pant, trying to stay as silent as possible as she edged away. She could picture where the soldiers had just been, could imagine where they might be now.

There was the sound of bodies shifting, fingers fumbling.

"Must have been that loud, slimy one."

"But the backup generators—"

"If he shorted the whole system, it would need a hard reboot. God damnit, where the hell is my flashlight?"

In the act of shifting to the opposite side of the hall, Eliza's toe hit something heavy.

Tori's gun.

Metal scraped softly over tile.

"Hey!" called a deep voice

Eliza froze, holding her breath. Slowly, deliberately, she bent over to pick up the weapon.

"Stop moving, kid. We don't want to hurt you."

You might not, she thought silently. *But I bet Amile does*.

Eliza's fingers were shaking as they curled around the molded handle. Could she do it? Could she shoot the two men point blank like this? What if they were like Martin, just following orders? What if they were already under the influence of the virus like Joe?

She hefted the gun, swallowed. Footsteps echoed in the infinite darkness, growing closer.

And then, with a stuttering blink, one of the guards switched on a flashlight.

Eliza reacted without thinking, raw terror taking full control of her body as she swung the gun up, wrapping both hands around it, pointing it at the nearest thigh. The sudden brightness was sharp, almost painful. Instinctually, the panicked animal part of her brain registered the beam of light swinging toward her, the black noses of twin barrels roving her way.

It was her or them.

Aquila or them.

Eliza fired.

Pain exploded up her arm as the gun kicked back, ripping the skin off the top of her right hand. But her cry was nothing compared to the scream of the soldier. He fell to one knee, clutching the wound now pulsing blood down his leg. The flashlight spun dizzyingly away from him. Eliza planted a foot on its handle to stop the frenetic roll, too terrified to reach down and grab it.

"FREEZE!" the other soldier shouted, rounding on Eliza. But she swallowed the agony in her hand, pointed at his shoulder.

Fired again.

Her whole body was shaking as the second guard went down, weapon flying out of his hand. Everything danced like shadows, unreal in the half-light. A bullet cracked by her head. She dove out of the way. The kneeling soldier took aim, but Eliza darted in and swung her foot around, kicking his hand.

His gun flew away.

Eliza scrambled back, snatched the flashlight off the ground, quivering like the autumn leaves outside. The two men glared at her, radiating hate. Bile climbed Eliza's throat, threatening to join the blood now pooling around their knees.

"I'm sorry," Eliza whispered, taking a shaky step back.

"We'll get you for this," snarled the one still standing, shoving off the wall to lumber toward her.

Eliza's fingers fumbled. She dropped the flashlight, lunged for the door, throwing herself against it even as her eyes blurred with tears.

It popped open.

With a grateful sob, Eliza tumbled inside, shoving it closed behind her, leaning against the handle. She gulped air, swallowed frantically, tried to steady her trembling limbs.

I just shot two people. I just wounded two human beings. What I hit an artery or something? What if I just killed them? What if—

But her horrified thoughts were interrupted by the sardonic sound of someone clapping.

"Well done, Miss Mason," Amile said. "I must say, I never expected you to get this far."

CHAPTER FIFTY-TWO
Fun and Games

"Well that was a great idea, *Otto*."

"Fuck you, Moose. It stopped them getting in, didn't it?"

"Hey," Tori snapped, squinting in the impenetrable darkness. "Everyone keep your head, we have to think."

"There are approximately one million soldiers out there," Moose said, his voice echoing weirdly around the room he darted from the door to the back wall. "And no other exits. But hey, at least we have some *beakers*."

"We have *guns*, dumbass."

"Wait, wait, wait," Tori cut in, taking an unsteady step forward. "Guys, if we want to find the cure—"

"I'd really like to find Aquila and get the heck out of here," Moose said.

"W-we need p-power," Tero piped in. "If we w-w-want to g-get out. A-all the d-d-doors will be a-auto l-locked."

"Otto?"

"What? You think I can jumpstart the whole goddamn building?" He snorted, the sound accompanied by the meaty thud of a kick. "What about this smarty-pants?"

"I'm not helping *you*," spat the scientist.

A bright light flared in the darkness as Otto's skin crackled. Tori blinked, eyes adjusting enough to see the boy leaning over the prone body, grin terrifying in the spasmodic light.

"You wanna rethink that?"

"Wait, ok, fine. You have to reboot the system." The man swallowed. "The fact that the emergency lights haven't come on yet means you shorted everything when you electrified the lock."

"So how do we reboot the system?" Tori asked, edging closer.

"The utilities room. It's at the end of the hall."

"Well… shit," Otto said.

It's what they were all thinking. Otto had fried the door in an attempt to keep the swarming soldiers from breaking in. But the swarm was still out there, probably swelling ranks even in the oppressive darkness. They'd have to fight through the armed men and women of the U.S. Army in the dark without enough weapons to go around.

And that was just to turn the electricity back on.

"H-hold o-on."

Tori twisted to see Tero moving, stepping among the empty cots like a wraith, demonic and strange in the shadows thrown by Otto.

"What are you doing?"

"I c-can still n-navigate just f-f-fine."

Tori looked to Otto, his face lit from below by the static running over the skin of his hand.

"Echolocation," Otto said in explanation.

"What do you see, brother?" Moose interjected. "The mysterious shadows of beyond? The messages in the dark?"

Tero interrupted by flicking on a flashlight and pointing it at his brother's face.

"T-they have them o-on their b-belts."

With Tero's help, Joe, Tori, Daisy, and Moose gathered the flashlights. One of the guards fought to keep his, but Joe knocked him out with a punch to the side of the head.

A new problem became immediately apparent

There were only three.

Tori stared at the flashlight in her palm, her brain whirring into action.

"I think Tero and I should go to the splicer… room… thing," she said when no one spoke. "We'll take that one—" she pointed at the scientist still under Otto's foot, "— and find a cure so we can leave right away."

"What about us?" Moose asked, eyes glittering.

Otto met Tori's gaze with a feral grin. "We'll clear the fucking road."

"H-how?"

"The utilities room." Otto's skin crackled with renewed fervor. "We'll bring the power back, but on *our* terms."

"And be heroes in the process," Moose said, flexing his arms.

A small voice piped up from the far wall.

"I'll help."

Joe stepped into the dim circle of light, looking pale and stretched but determined. Tori knew that if Eliza were here, she'd argue that Joe should stay behind. That he wasn't safe, wasn't a part of this fight. Eliza would want to keep Joe out of it.

Tori didn't give a shit.

"Alright," she said, nodding. "Let's do it."

Otto kicked the scientist, sliding the man along the floor until he was at Tori's feet. She trained her gun on him, shining the stolen flashlight right into his eyes.

"Don't get any ideas."

Tero was at her shoulder, his wings rustling nervously. But the plan was in motion. At this point, all they could do was play it out.

Otto grabbed the door handle, pressing his palm against the dead panel.

"Wakey wakey."

~~~

"Shoot the lock."

"We have men in there."

"Who knows what they're doing, we need to act fast."

"Will someone get the goddamn power back on?"

The basement corridor looked like a scene from a horror movie, flashlights slicing through the darkness, dim shapes crowding close to the door, weapons glinting in the shifting illumination. There was a nervousness to the crowd, a tension thickened by the lack of proper visibility and the bulk of a few key figures that the rest of them seemed to be avoiding.

"Hey, maybe we should get Terry to just punch through the—"

Suddenly, the door exploded outward with a blast of white light. There was a shout of surprise. A gunshot.

And then four new figures burst into the crowd.

"Playtime, motherfuckers!"

Otto struck the closest soldier's chest. Another burst of light sent the body flying. Joe surged into the crowd after him, lunging, kicking, swinging bodies out of his way.

"This way, guys," Moose said, darting between shadows to the end of the hall.

But the soldiers were rallying. Weapons were being cocked, aimed.

"Don't kill them!" someone barked from the middle.

Joe's fist swung. But something stopped it. He looked down to find his hand locked in place by smaller, narrower fingers.

"Not so fast," snarled a minuscule Asian woman.

And then she whipped Joe around like he weighed nothing at all.

"Oh snap!" Moose said as Daisy dragged him to the door labeled *Utilities*.

People were swirling around the sparking, crackling center of energy that was Otto. He laughed madly as he fought with unpredictable efficiency. A swipe here. A punch there. All around him bodies fell, still convulsing, bare skin coated in slime.

A few of them began to scream.

"Otto!" Moose shouted. "We need you!"

Joe and the Asian woman were wrestling, knocking people aside like bowling pins as their brawl escalated. Otto darted past them, grabbing Joe by the back of his sweatshirt.

"This way," he growled, yanking Joe away.

They were cornered at the end of the hallway now, Moose bent over the Utilities door handle. Otto ducked into their group, Daisy and Joe guarding the rear.

Soldiers circled closer, too distracted to notice the blonde girl and short man in a lab coat duck out behind them, followed by the Tero's winged silhouette.

"Hurry, hurry, hurry," Moose chanted.

"Shut the fuck up!"

There was a crackle and a flash and then the pop of a door opening.

"Get in!"

But Otto's shout was interrupted by the ludicrous sound of a phone ringing.

Joe exchanged a look with the silent Daisy, whose spines were all standing on end.

"Dude, it's coming from your pocket," Moose said as he and Otto ducked through the door.

Spinning into the protection of the now-open room, Joe flipped out his phone. In all the chaos, he'd forgotten that he'd turned it on in the cave beneath Eckelson's mansion.

He squinted at the bright screen.

It was his parents.

If he'd been in his right mind, Joe wouldn't have answered. He would have let it go straight to voicemail, focused on the fight. But in the delirium of Joe's failing brain, he longed to hear his mother's voice or listen to his father call him *son*. The swirling, violent, awful darkness down here in the bowels of Fitzgerald base faded until all he could see was that bar on his iPhone that read *slide to answer*.

He slid.

"*Dude*, what are you doing?" Moose said. "Look out!"

The Asian woman lunged into the room after them, right as Joe put the phone to his face.

"Mom?"

And then the woman slammed into his chest.

Small knuckles landed on Joe's shoulder with astonishing power. He cried out in pain as the bones of his socket protested.

The phone went flying.

"Come on!" Moose shouted as Otto ran to the back, fumbling for the electrical panel. "Come on, come on, come *on*!"

Joe and the woman were on the floor now, leaving fist-sized dents in the tile. Joe tried to roll on top of her, but she wrapped her legs around him, flipped him onto his back.

"Get off!"

But she ignored Joe's snarl, bringing her elbow down hard on his stomach. He groaned. She straightened, ready to finish him off.

Out of nowhere, a spiny fist connected with her head.

She shrieked, blood spurting from a hundred tiny holes.

"Help me!" Daisy's voice was hoarse with fear and disuse, but Joe didn't need to be told twice. Scrambling upright, he and Daisy grabbed the reeling woman and threw her bodily out of the Utilities room.

"Close it!" Joe shouted uselessly.

But when Daisy grabbed the handle, it all but swung off its frame.

Otto had snapped the hinges when he'd blasted it open.

Daisy leapt back with Joe, away from the soldiers swirling inside, guns drawn, flashlights making them squint.

"Otto!" Moose cried.

"I'm fucking working here," Otto answered from near the electrical panels.

A wall of bodies now blocked their exit, led by the short woman, face bleeding from an array of puncture wounds. She cracked her knuckles.

Joe took a step back, bumping into Daisy. Spines poked into his arm, but it was almost a relief to feel them, to ground himself in the moment and focus on the danger advancing toward them, the guns trained on his face.

There was a crackle, a rustle, a resounding snap.

The lights surged on, filling the basement, shining down on the crowd of armed men and women training guns on the four teenage boys.

"Well," Moose said, eyes glittering in the sudden illumination, leaning out from behind Joe. "This doesn't look much better."

CHAPTER FIFTY-THREE
Already in Motion

"Holy hell...."

Tori's exhaled words echoed through the cavernous space. The room was two stories tall at least, broken in the middle by a stretching pillar of machinery, even more impressive upon closer inspection. Encased in giant screens filled with scrolling numbers, it was a monstrosity of wires and blinking lights, broken by rows of test tubes sticking out of wide panels that looked like airplane controls. Tori took a stumbling step inside, only to realize that she was nauseatingly close to the edge of the gangplank, nothing but air standing between her and a long, lethal drop to the tile floor below.

She felt the scientist shift next to her.

"Don't move," Tori said, pointing the gun at him without turning.

"Don't be stupid, you're stuck here," the man said. "You don't even know how to use this machine. What are you going to do?"

Now Tori faced him, lifting her eyebrows as she advanced on the short, balding man.

"*I* don't plan to do anything." She pressed the Glock to his forehead. "*You're* going to help *him* get inside the system."

"I-I d-don't know if I-I—"

"Just do it, Tero."

Standing behind them, Tori watched as the scientist grudgingly unlocked the nearest monitor, Tero hovering by his shoulder. Looking at the two bodies felt like an encapsulation of the whole night. Worlds colliding. Human and....

What was Tero?

What was Otto?

Tori shook her head. She could hear gunshots echoing from the hall outside, hear the crackle of Otto's electricity, the shrieks of men and women waking up to the effects of his slime.

It had been like pulling teeth, getting Otto to admit what his shimmering skin did. Tori had pushed, cajoled, prodded. It had become a joke between them in the quiet moments in the cavern, watching Aquila lead and Tero plan and Eliza worry. Tori had wanted to know more about him. She'd never thought of her herself as particularly interested in people—in fact, she sort of preferred not to deal with them at all. But Otto was different. Otto was *fascinating*. Beneath the bravado and profanities was a young man unlike any Tori had ever met. He was rabidly defensive and vulgar, yet soft. Polite in his own strange way. Happy to curse around her, but also the first to pull out a chair or offer his help. And where the others saw simple aggression, Tori, who had grown up around brusque, gruff men, saw hidden depths.

Otto was more than he appeared.

She'd wanted to know everything about him.

But when he'd finally told her the truth, she'd gone pale.

The iridescent layer on Otto's skin was a venom. From a platypus, Otto said. Tori had almost laughed. Almost. Until he described what it did. Whenever his venom touched someone else's skin, his victim would become paralyzed. Their muscles would go slack. And then every pain receptor in the afflicted area would be activated, jacked up to the most intolerable degree. Otto had ducked his head, white-blonde hair quivering, as he described the first time he'd accidentally poisoned one of his brothers with it. He'd been thirteen, already accustomed to the strange coating of opalescence that he'd been born with. But something changed. The chemical component of the substance altered abruptly, almost overnight. And then one day, when Moose pushed too far and Otto tackled him to the floor, their fight was broken by Moose going terrifyingly still. Limbs freezing. Muscles twitching.

And then, Otto had been forced to watch his brother scream.

After that, the Vagabonds had figured out the hard way that you don't wrestle with Otto unless there's antivenom nearby.

Tori tightened her fingers on the gun, watching Tero and the scientist talk, thinking about Otto. About the sparks—sometimes literally—that would fly between his skin and hers. The infinite, crackling, impassable space between them. She'd had boyfriends before. Tori was no stranger to the risk of sneaking an unwelcome boy into her childhood home, of the breathless terror that accompanied making out with her father sleeping in the next room, a shotgun under his bed. She was accustomed to the heady intoxication of falling in love with the kinds of guys the men in her family wouldn't approve of.

But she couldn't even *touch* this one.

What did that mean for their future?

It was enough to make her snort. Here she was thinking about a future with someone she'd just met when it wasn't even clear they'd survive the night.

"S-s-so it's already b-been *made*?"

Tori jerked back to the moment.

"I'm not saying anything."

The scientist was hunched, glaring at Tero, whose wings were rustling in that nervous way that made him seem enormous.

"But y-y-you said—"

"Fine, yeah, we made the booster. But it's already been sent upstairs. I can't make any more, at least not without more samples. Besides, the system is still rebooting—"

Tori stepped forward, holding her weapon steady as she leaned over the monitors. "Tero, what's going on?"

"H-he says that the c-c-cure h-has already b-been m-made."

"So where is it?"

271

Tori rounded on the scientist, distantly aware of Tero typing behind her and the computer speaking to him in a soft, vaguely British voice.

"It's not a cure," the scientist said, folding his arms, his chin jutting out.

"But it fixes the damage?"

"It updates the virus."

"So if it were given to someone... afflicted?" Tori's throat tightened as she thought of Martin. Of Joe. "They would get better, right?"

The man shrugged, uncaring. Tori had never hated anyone so much in her life.

"I mean, maybe. We don't know."

Tori took a threatening step forward. "Then *guess*."

"Sure, yeah." The scientist lifted his hands, eying Tori's gun nervously. "I suppose it might reverse the cascade of damage. Accelerated healing is part of the virus's profile."

"And you didn't think to use it on your *friends,* you useless piece of shit*?*"

He bristled, but Tori didn't care. She inhaled, fighting the urge to hurt more than just his ego. How could this man, this awful, tiny, small-eyed man have the *gall* to withhold something that could bring his own comrades back from the brink of destruction? How could he stand there coldly and shrug when Martin was tied to his own coffee table, burning up as the virus ate his body alive?

Tori could have cheerfully shot the man in the head, but she swallowed. Held herself together as she let the silence stretch and the man squirm.

At last, he spoke.

"Our first priority was to make a stable version of the virus."

"Oh yeah, for what?"

But he didn't need to answer. Tori could think of a thousand reasons to use the booster on healthy men and women first. Amile

272

wouldn't have to worry about defending the base if she had a cadre of super-soldiers. She could fight them off without even breaking a sweat. Kill them all with a snap of her fingers.

A snap of her fingers.

No…

Tori froze, brain wheeling into overdrive.

What if…?

"W-where's my b-b-brother," Tero was saying, his voice edging into a snarl as he loomed over the scientist like an old-world monster. The scientist balked, paled, but Tori barely noticed. She was thinking about what she would do, if she were in charge here.

"Aquila's with Amile, isn't he?" Tori asked in a daze. She turned to the scientist. "She's going to infect herself."

And kill him.

The scientist didn't say anything, but Tori could see the knowledge in his eyes. It was awful, perhaps, that Tori could understand Amile's insane grab for power. But she could. Because Tori also knew that selfish desire to see fear in an enemy's eyes. The yearning to show people that she wasn't any less strong because she was girl. The thirst to *prove* herself.

Tori shoved the man aside in disgust, stepping up to Tero's elbow.

"Can we reverse it?"

"W-what?"

Tori waved at the column, her hands shaky with frustration.

"Can you bring it back or something? Stop the samples from being sent to Amile?"

"I d-don't k-know how a-any of this—"

"*Try.*"

Tori shifted from foot to foot, thinking of Otto and Joe and Daisy and Moose out in the hall. Of Aquila somewhere in the building, probably still tied to a table. Of Eliza, God knew where. How much time did they have? How many new infected soldiers were already marching down? How would they survive Amile Robillard's wrath?

Tori leaned closer to read for Tero as his fingers flew across the closest keyboard.

"It says the update has already been claimed on the first floor. *Shit*, we have to get up there."

"M-maybe Aquila w-w-will—"

"Tero... It says the update is stronger." Tori squinted. "There's a note here, that it's even more potent than—"

But Tori's words were abruptly cut off by a kick to the ribs. She gasped. Tilted. The gun went flying from her hand as an arm locked around her throat, dragging her backwards. Something cold pressed to her temple—another gun, stolen from her cluttered waistband.

Maybe I shouldn't have brought so many, she thought with blinding panic.

The scientist's breathing in her ear was quick, restless, nervous. But when he spoke, his words were black with malice.

"Alright now, it's time for you to do what I want for a change."

CHAPTER FIFTY-FOUR
The Butterfly and the Wasp

Eliza pressed her body against the door, watching with wide-eyed horror as Amile Robillard pulled a needle out of her arm with a delicate shudder.

"How... strange," Amile said, cracking her neck, black hair glistening like oil in the fluorescent lights that had just surged back on.

"Run, Eliza!" Aquila shouted, strapped to a misshapen table beside Amile, tugging against the metal restraints. "Get out of here! She's dangerous, run!"

But Eliza was frozen, unable to move as Amile bounced the syringe in one hand. Even if Eliza wanted to escape, there was nowhere to go. She could hardly run back into the bloodstained hallway with the two men she'd wounded. Or into the base that was now crawling with soldiers.

And no matter how terrified she was, Eliza had no intention of leaving Aquila behind.

Amile's head was cocked, her frown curious. Like a child examining something astonishing. Her dark eyes flicked up, drilling into Eliza, threatening and malevolent and filled with the crackling fire of a woman possessed.

Then she cocked her elbow and threw the syringe at the side of the lab.

The flat end of the plunger embedded itself into the drywall.

"Amazing," Amile purred, staring at her hands. "I never expected it to work so quickly."

Eliza's gaze slid over Amile to Aquila and then to the man hovering behind Aquila's table. Old and gray with wild white hair and hunched, protective shoulders.

There was a local man—a scientist—who told me about an experiment that could change human genetics in real-time.

That must be him.

Could Eliza convince him to help?

But then Amile was stepping forward and Eliza's attention caught on her like clothing on a barbed-wire fence.

"How marvelous," Amile said, circling around Aquila's table and ignoring the jangling of his struggle to escape. "I was hoping I'd have a chance to test out the virus for myself. For months I've been watching my men and women go through the transformation, only to see them fall apart." Amile stretched her arms wide, like a ballerina about to pirouette. "Well, now it's my turn to feel the power of what science is capable of. Fitting, don't you think, that I get to be the first functional beneficiary of the Superman Virus."

"That's stretching the word functional," Eliza said, her eyes flashing around the room, looking for a weapon. A shield.

Anything.

Amile took another step toward her, grinning like a bobcat.

"Time to teach you some manners, Miss Mason."

And then Amile launched herself at Eliza's face.

~~~

Aquila's muscles bulged and his neck strained, but it was no use. He could only watch helplessly as that awful woman scratched her nails along the wall, narrowly missing Eliza as she backflipped out of the way. The urge to help, to fight, to *protect* welled up in him like a tidal wave, but he was trapped.

He twisted his head around.

His eyes met Dr. Oleander's.

The old man was watching Amile leap onto a table, fly at Eliza. The two women crashed into an array of monitors with a snarl. Aquila tried to ignore the cascade of equipment, focusing on the old man, whose face was papery and pale, gaze distant and weirdly detached.

"Sir," Aquila said.

Dr. Oleander swiveled to face him, expression unreadable.

"Sir, please," Aquila continued. "I know you don't want this." He shifted his body to one side, suppressing a wince as the grooves dug into the tender bones of his wings. "You cared about my brothers once, didn't you? When you made us?"

The doctor's eyes never left Aquila's. They were like pools, deep and reflective and eerily vacant. Gone was the old man who had mumbled in Amile's shadow, ducked his head every time she raised her voice. Something else was there, a distant fire reignited in his mind.

Aquila pressed on.

"Do you really want to let that woman destroy your creations?" Aquila leaned in as far as the chains would allow. "Your sons?"

At that word, Dr. Oleander clenched his fists.

"Do the right thing, Sir," Aquila said, forcing himself to keep his attention steady as the fight echoed catastrophically around the lab. "Make the right choice."

Suddenly, Dr. Oleander's lips curled up in a smile.

~~~

Eliza tumbled under a table, sliding to the other side and scrambling upright as Amile slammed her fist down, denting the solid metal surface. Sharp tools flew in all directions.

"Let it go, Eliza," Amile said with a laugh, missing Eliza and punching into the frosted glass of a fume hood. It shattered. Blood dripped from Amile's knuckles. She hardly seemed to notice. "If I don't catch you, my soldiers will. You've lost. But then again, you were lost a long time ago."

Eliza somersaulted over a research table, crying out as her shoulder hit the sharp edge of a faucet, as the bandages on her hand caught on something and pulled tight. But there was no time to process the pain. She threw herself to the side. Amile's fist whistled by her head, shifting air, threatening broken bones.

"I read your file. No one cares about you." Amile swung around the bench, advancing on Eliza with white-knuckled fists. "Your parents wrote a letter to Meru Academy. Apparently, they only wanted to hear about any trouble you might get into. They didn't care about report cards or faculty letters because Mr. And Mrs. Mason just wanted a break from their troublesome, reckless, *lesser* daughter."

Eliza grabbed a beaker and hurled it at Amile's head. The black-haired woman swatted it away as if it was just a mosquito.

"Do you think they would change things, if they could?" Amile laughed and the sound made Eliza's nerves feel like they were on fire. She clenched her fingers, ducked behind a lab bench.

She couldn't let Amile needle her, couldn't let the pain of Katie's memory distract her now.

Eliza had to *focus*.

But Amile continued, words weighted with cruelty.

"Do you think, if they had the choice, they would have chosen Katie instead of you?"

That's it.

The thin leash around Eliza's temper snapped. She exploded from behind the bench, planted both feet on the marble top of the research table, threw herself at Amile. They went down together, rolling, crashing into a stool. Eliza's knuckles hit flesh, her other hand landing hard on a bony protrusion. Her vision was awash with furious red as she bent over, every piece of her wanting to pulp Amile's face into the ground.

But Eliza's victory was short-lived because it didn't take long for Amile's fingers to find Eliza's throat.

"So predictable," Amile said, straightening, dragging Eliza with her. Eliza's feet scrabbled against the ground as she gulped, wheezed, frantically trying to breathe through Amile's crushing grip. "So foolish. I liked you, you know. That's why I didn't finish things back in the cavern. I'd hoped that you might give up when we took the subjects, back away from trouble that wasn't yours. But teenage stubbornness knows no bounds. I see now that my own sentimentality got in the way. You are a complication as much as they are." Eliza couldn't breathe, couldn't see. Darkness was encroaching on her vision. Her windpipe felt like glass about to shatter. "I'm afraid I can't leave any loose ends, no matter how much I've enjoyed your spunk."

Eliza's eyes ached with the pressure. She was about to faint. Her mind drifted to Joe and Tori in the basement, to the other Vagabonds somewhere in the base. All the faces of the people she'd failed.

She thought of Aquila.

When we've found Tori's brother and all, would you want to, er, hang out?

Eliza struggled harder against Amile's iron hold as she thought about the promise of a date with Aquila, the promise of a *future*. After watching Katie's life end so tragically before its time, Eliza had always vowed to make the most of hers. Had understood that time was precious.

She wasn't ready to die.

"N...no," she choked, scratching at Amile's forearm.

The woman didn't even wince.

"Apologies, Miss Mason," Amile said as if she were discussing the protocol of some new experiment, not the end of a young person's existence. "I'm afraid it can't be avoided."

"That's what you think," growled a deep voice.

Suddenly, Eliza was flying to the side, yanked along by the sharp fingers wrapped around her neck. Then the hand disappeared. She crashed headfirst into the marble top of the nearest lab bench. Stars popped in the darkness that had overtaken her, sparkling, dancing around her head. She groped along the floor, listening to the crash and tumble of something huge nearby.

Blinking frantically, Eliza looked up.

The old scientist was standing there, grinning, his hair shifting in the ventilation from the broken fume hood. In his hand was a glittering key.

And beside him was an empty table with two huge grooves down the middle.

There was another crash and a rumbling growl. A growl Eliza knew all too well.

Grabbing the edge of the marble table, Eliza lifted herself upright.

And froze.

Aquila and Amile were rolling over a mess of broken glass, askew chairs, toppled computer monitors, sparking wires. They tumbled and flipped, neither managing to gain the advantage, both snarling through bared teeth. Eliza took a stumbling step forward, ready to help, but stopped when Amile's fist slammed into the floor, leaving a crater in the hard tiles.

Aquila snarled, pinning Amile to the floor.

"You deserve this," he spat, cocking his arm to hit her.

Amile grinned.

"Yes I do," she said, before bucking her hips and knocking Aquila aside.

And then she was on him again.

CHAPTER FIFTY-FIVE
Limits

"Otto…"

"Not now, Moose!"

Joe hovered beside Daisy, trying to focus. The suddenly bright lights seemed to warp and shift the air, making him feel like he'd been plunged underwater. In front of him, soldiers prowled, their eyes red, their mouths glowing like blown embers. The shortest among them seemed to beat with some evil luminescence, pulsing like a heart.

He shook his head, swaying in place.

It's not real. It's not real. It's not real.

"Hands up," snapped the nearest soldier, who had suddenly sprouted horns. The voice echoed, as if from the other end of a cave.

Joe barred his teeth.

The short woman stepped forward, grinning back at him through the blood dribbling down one side of her face.

"I'm not done with you yet," she spat.

Joe blinked.

Was he imagining the fangs?

"Otto….," Moose said, backing into his brother.

"One fucking second! I have an idea."

The ground seemed to tilt beneath Joe's feet as two soldiers advanced, flanking the short woman. There were more behind them. Always more. The soldiers were like a flood come to wash them away, pull them into darkness.

Joe shook his head again.

The visions were getting worse.

"There's nowhere to go," purred the short woman, holding her hands out like claws. They stretched long and sharp, ten glinting daggers. Ten lethal icicles. "May as well give up now. Our boss might even let you live."

"I think I've got it…," Otto snarled.

Suddenly, the air itself seemed to crackle. There was a flash, a jolt, a sudden swing from night to day as all the lights all surged at once.

"Look out!"

A ripping sound made Joe turn, but Daisy's arm hit his stomach, spines biting, shoving him out of the way as Otto plunged toward the soldiers with two wrist-thick wires crackling in his hands, the sparks playing up his arms like fairy lights.

"Time to play, donkey-fuckers."

The short woman's eyes flew wide. She scrambled back, barking orders.

"Shoot him! Knock him down!"

But it was too late. Otto charged at them like a bull, roaring obscenities, diving into the crowd with a blinding, horrible flash.

Joe closed his eyes, curled into the wall to shield himself from the screams, the wails, the crackling, the groan of the strained generators around them, sleeping giants waking up. It was a storm of strobing light, a wildfire of pain. Spines needled Joe's right arm as he hunched himself into the corner, holding his ears, waiting for the noise to tear him apart.

"Come on, morons!"

A hand grabbed Joe's elbow, yanking him away from the wall. Joe blinked, blinded by the sheer maelstrom of sensation, but it didn't matter. Daisy pulled him back through the door and into the now-bright hallway, dragged forward in Otto's violent, flashing wake.

Bodies twitched around them, bowled over. The tiny woman spasmed in one corner, all the muscles in her body straining, a fish on a line. Moose was darting between them, little more than a blur in the beating fluorescent lights.

"Alive. This one too. Alive, alive, alive. Hum, alive but not so lucky. Otto, you touched this dude here."

"Shut it, Moose," Otto snarled weakly, stumbling sideways into the wall. The two huge cables dropped from his hands, still sparking gently. Joe watched in fascinated horror as Otto shivered, eyes rolling back in his head.

Finally, the Vagabond with the glossy skin collapsed.

The wires went dead.

Moose was next to Otto in a flash, followed by Daisy and Joe. They were fifteen feet from the door Tori and Tero had disappeared into. A little more than two body-lengths to reunite with the rest of their team.

But the remaining soldiers were lifting their guns, no longer hesitant now that Otto was down. As they advanced, Joe thought the distance might as well have been a mile.

~~~

"W-w-wait a s-second. Y-you don't w-want—"

"Shut up, freak," the scientist said, breath hot against Tori's neck as he dragged her backwards. "We're doing this my way now."

Tori gulped air, trying not to think about the cold press of the barrel against her forehead. She'd shot too many guns in her life not to know exactly how close she was to her own death. A squeeze of the trigger, a flash of light, a tiny bit of pressure from the terrified man panting in her ear and she'd be gone. Wiped off the Earth.

Not today, Tori said, clenching her fists.

Tero was gaping at her, his hands spread wide, helpless as he blinked sightlessly in their vague direction. Maybe he couldn't see them.

But Otto had told her that he could *hear*.

Please let this work.

"Now, you're both going to come upstairs with me," the scientist was saying, dragging Tori toward the door. "Amile will want to know what's going on down here."

Tori cleared her throat, as quietly as she could. She watched unblinkingly, eyes drinking in Tero's face.

He twitched at the sound.

Perfect, Tori thought, fighting to swallow against the cruel press of the man's hairy arm on her throat.

"Tero," Tori whispered, barely audible even to herself. "I'm going to fall backwards."

He cocked his head. The scientist had almost reached the door, edging along the fatal rim of the railing-free catwalk.

"Come on, you," the scientist snapped at Tero. "Don't just stand there, hurry up!"

"Can you catch me?" Tori breathed.

Tero jerked his head in a nod, stepping back, rustling his wings.

Tori swallowed again.

She already had death pressed against her forehead. What was a little fall?

Yeah right, she thought.

"One," she exhaled.

"What are you saying?" snapped the scientist, squeezing tighter. "What are you whispering?!"

"Two."

"Shut *up*!"

Tero's heels dangled off the catwalk, hovering over a whole story of air. Tori's muscles bunched, her knees bending, her fists clenching.

She closed her eyes.

Here goes nothing.

"Three!"

Tori dug her feet in and *pushed*, catching the scientist off-guard as she threw them both over the edge and into the oblivion of empty space.

The man shrieked. Tori screamed. Her eyes flew wide, her limbs flailing with the deep-seated instinct to stop her fall. But it was too late. Gravity had claimed them. The gun went off, a blossom of heat by Tori's right cheek, but the bullet missed her, pinging off the roof, echoing through the room. She was falling, spinning, distantly aware of Tero hurling himself around the edge of the catwalk. Tori's body peeled away from the scientist's chest. Air whistled between them, around them, swallowing their panicked yells. Another sound joined the cacophony, a distant shriek, bone-deep and resonant.

Tero, Tori thought

And then he slammed into her. She folded over his shoulder. Thin, bony wings hit her face, whipping her head to the side.

"S-sorry!" Tero said, rolling in the air and adjusting her at the same time so that she was curled in his arms, pressed into his chest. Tori felt the ludicrous urge to laugh.

Tero was *apologizing* for saving her life?

And then she looked down.

The laugh curdled.

Tero's wings were almost silent, their gentle beat announced only by the *whomping* of air as they hovered over the scientist's body. The man below them was broken, limbs angled awkwardly, face jerked to the side. He looked both unnatural and peaceful, jagged in a broken-glass way. Eyes closed and face slack, the fear of his last moments wiped away in the oblivion of death.

Time seemed to slow as the two teenagers stared down at the corpse they had created.

We killed him, Tori thought.

No.

I killed him.

Bile crawled up her throat. Or was it a sob? Either way, she swallowed.

"I'm sorry," Tori whispered, not sure who she was apologizing to but filled with the need to say something.

"H-he tried to k-kill you."

Tero might have meant the words to be comforting, but they came out doubtful. A question. As if he wasn't quite certain if it was right that they were alive and the man below them was dead.

Tori wanted to cry.

A memory drifted into her head, unwelcome but sticky. The first time she'd ever killed. For *years*, Tori had begged and pleaded to be taken out to her father's hunting platform in the middle of the woods. When he'd finally relented, Tori had been so excited, overjoyed at the opportunity to use the rifle she'd been given for Christmas. Martin had been the one to point out the wide-eyed doe with the limp, the perfect target for a beginner.

But then, in the moment before the shot, Tori had been unable to look away from the creature's wide and innocent eyes.

She'd hesitated.

Her hands had shaken.

Her father had whispered encouragements, adjusted her scope, told her to breathe.

When Tori finally pulled the trigger and watched the deer fall, she'd immediately dropped the rifle and vomited over the side of the high platform.

That memory haunted her, followed her despite all the things she'd shot since that day. So Tori knew deep in her soul that, no matter how justified or necessary it had been, the image of the man's broken body on the floor below would be with her for the rest of her life.

Just like that doe.

Suddenly, shouts echoed from the door by the catwalk, accompanied by the chaotic patter of gunshots and a roared curse.

Otto.

Tori and Tero shared a wide-eyed look, glancing up at the door, now bright in the cheerful fluorescent illumination.

"Let's go," Tori said.

Throwing one last look at the corpse they had created and wishing things had gone a different way, Tori let Tero carry her away from one danger.

And toward another.

CHAPTER FIFTY-SIX
The Merciful

Watching Amile and Aquila fight was like watching a clash of titans, a battle of gods. Their knuckles left craters in the floor, knocked cabinet doors askew, destroyed beakers and petri dishes and monitors and keyboards. Eliza had to lunge to one side to avoid their swinging mass, stumbling back to join Dr. Oleander and trace the violent dance, Eliza with dumbfounded awe, Dr. Oleander with a sly, self-satisfied grin.

But Eliza had never been good at just watching.

Twisting away from the man in the lab coat, she began to scour through this undisturbed corner of the research room. She had to help Aquila. He might be bigger than Amile, but she was faster. More vicious.

And Eliza had to help.

"You hurt... my... family," Aquila snarled, each word punctuated by a crash as Eliza rummaged through the contents of a drawer. "You shot... my... father!"

"Ah, but I told you. Old Ian Eckelson isn't your father."

There was a meaty thud accompanied by a pained gasp.

Aquila's.

Eliza began to throw things over her shoulder as she looked, casting a frantic look at Dr. Oleander.

"Help me!" she said, not bothering to pause in her search as the old man dropped his key and stepped back into the relative safety of the computer stand. He folded his arms, as if to say *I'm just here for the show*. Eliza snarled in frustration, glancing over her shoulder in time to see Aquila roar and launch himself over a lab table, hitting Amile's chest. They both disappeared between the neat rows of marble-top benches.

Eliza returned to her hunt.

"They're not... your family," Amile panted. There was a metallic crash. "Because you're not... people. You're. Just. Test. Subjects."

"*No we're not.*" Eliza had never heard Aquila sound so dangerous, so deranged. Her heartbeat was almost loud enough to drown out the noise, the chaos roiling behind her.

"This is a military base!" Eliza snapped, heaving a box of empty text tubes over one shoulder. "Where the fuck are all the weapons?!"

Suddenly, a hand appeared. Old, withered, veined.

Holding a rope.

Dr. Oleander looked at Eliza, eyes glittering with mischief.

Eliza slapped her palm down across his, accepting the long piece of twine. It wasn't much, but she was done hanging back.

Swinging around, Eliza found Amile on Aquila's chest, her knees on his wings, her fist colliding with his face over and over and over. Blood spouted from Aquila's nose, leaked from a split lip. Amile herself had a swelling bruise that was beginning to close her left eye, but she grinned maniacally as she pounded down on Aquila, drunk on her own strength.

Eliza pulled the rope taut between her two hands, dug her toes into the shattered tile floor.

And lunged back into the fight.

The rope wrapped around Amile's neck, making her choke in surprise. As Eliza's weight shifted the woman's light body, Aquila managed to roll upright. His wings snapped, slapping Amile's face. She sputtered, rolled away, but Amile was now outnumbered. Eliza ducked in close, twisting the rope tighter. An arm came out of nowhere, hitting her in the head. Eliza saw stars, toppled to the side, but managed to keep hold of the twine.

Amile was choking, her limbs jerking in erratic, frantic bursts. But she wasn't done yet. Amile punched Aquila in the ribs, kicked out at Eliza, foot hitting knee. Eliza screamed as her leg protested the abuse, but leaned further away, tautening the rope. Aquila loomed over them, holding down Amile's jerking feet, and Eliza felt the world slow. Time became as thick as molasses, holding them there, sticking to her skin.

She watched her enemy's face turn blue.

Amile's eyes brimmed with tears.

"No..." Amile wheezed, suddenly panicked. Suddenly frightened. "Not again... Not again...."

Not again.

Tori's words flashed bright across Eliza's subconscious, somehow ignited by Amile's pleading, terrified expression.

You have baggage, just like the rest of us.

Just like the rest of us.

Almost against her will, Eliza's fingers went slack. She felt the rope catch on the raw skin of her palms, on her bandages, but she couldn't stop it. Couldn't help it. Amile jerked out of her grip, lunged at a shocked Aquila. Aquila's wings snapped out, but too slow. Amile was already past him, clawing her way toward the door.

But the woman who'd risen from the ground wasn't the coiffed, confident leader of Fitzgerald Base. No, when Amile twisted back to face them, her face was blotchy and red, her eyes haunted. Her hand—knuckles bloodstained and raw—lifted to her throat, fish-belly white and convulsing.

"This isn't the end," she rasped.

And then she was through the door, disappearing into the dark hallway.

Aquila leapt after her, throwing himself over the nearest lab table and crashing through the door. But Eliza couldn't move. Couldn't breathe.

She'd let Amile go.

Why?

Maybe because, in that cresting moment right before death, Eliza had seen a ghost in Amile's face as potent and heavy as her own. Maybe because she understood the kinds of things that made people do stupid, selfish, *horrible* things.

Maybe because she couldn't kill someone while looking into their eyes.

Eliza leaned against the nearest table, dimly aware of Dr. Olander watching her with his rheumy eyes, of the wounded soldiers shouting as Aquila tried to go after Amile. There was a gunshot, a rising cry, and then Aquila was back, slamming the door behind him.

"Those assholes are covering her retreat," he said, lip curled, voice thick with frustration. "She's gone."

Eliza's world telescoped to Aquila's face as she thought of how badly she'd let him down. Again. If Amile was a monster, then Eliza was the monster who had released her back into the world.

"I'm sorry." Her voice was so quiet, so tender and small, that it didn't even sound like her own anymore. "Aquila, I'm so sorry."

He froze, looking at her as if seeing Eliza for the first time. For a single, awful moment, the anger swirled in his expression like a hurricane. And Eliza knew that his forgiveness wouldn't come easily, if ever.

And then he melted.

He came over to her, lifting Eliza into his arms and wrapping himself around her.

"It's okay. We're alive. That's what matters."

Is it? Eliza wondered, thinking about the vengeful wrath she'd just witnessed in him. But Aquila was stroking her back, squeezing her tight, and she imagined he was thinking about the punch to her chest, the knee-jerk reaction that had hurt her. Maybe there was no getting around the pain they'd caused each other, would continue to cause each other as long as they were flawed and restless human beings.

The exhausting realization made Eliza want to sink to the floor and stay there forever.

But Aquila was looking over her head, glaring at the white-haired old man who had saved him. Eliza turned, following his gaze.

Dr. Oleander hovered at the end of the lab table, looking strangely tall, his shadow thrown long by the flickering lights.

"You let me go," Aquila said. It wasn't a question, but Dr. Oleander shrugged in answer. "Why?"

"Why do any of us do things? To see what happens."

"Is that it? That's why you made us?"

The old man's mouth curled up and Eliza was reminded of Ian Eckelson's rueful smile, that classic, tolerant exasperation the old have for the young.

"I've learned a great deal through this experiment."

Eliza wanted to scream at him. *They're not an experiment! They're teenage boys and they deserve your fucking compassion!*

But Aquila spoke first.

"And now?"

Dr. Oleander took a deep breath, peering around the lab.

"Well, I suppose that's the question, isn't it?"

Aquila stared at him, but Dr. Oleander didn't meet his gaze. Instead, the old man touched the monitor behind him like a college-bound student touching their childhood home for the last time.

And then he chuckled.

"What a curiosity, life. Wouldn't you say?"

Dr. Oleander began to drift toward the door, a dust mote on a gentle breeze. He seemed at once lost and purposeful, strong and shambling. He was still the stuttering scientist Amile had cowed, but also a brave explorer lost in the landscape of his own mind. Walking his own path.

Eliza had never met anyone so strange.

"Should we—?"

"Let him go," Aquila said, voice low enough to rumble through Eliza's chest.

So they did. Together, Eliza and Aquila watched as Dr. Oleander reached the door, threw it open, and without so much as a backwards glance, stepped through it. There were no voices, no gunshots, no sounds to add to the surreal reality lit by the guttering bulbs over their heads.

"Why?" Eliza asked.

Aquila released her, stepping back, staring at his hands.

"Why did you let Amile escape?" He shrugged, not waiting for an answer. "I might have been made by the army, but I'm not a soldier. And I'm certainly not a killer." His lips twitched. "Looks like you aren't either." Then a cold sadness stole into his eyes, chilling his expression. "I'm sorry, Eliza. I'm sorry for everything. For hitting you, for dragging you into this, for being angry before..." His fingers moved, as if he could find the right words in the sterile air of the lab. "This, all this, it's my fault." Aquila hung his head. "You deserve better."

A surge of emotion filled Eliza, burning away her fear and shame and rage. She leapt forward, throwing her arms around Aquila's neck, pulling his face to hers.

"I don't want better," she whispered ferociously, pressing her forehead to his. "I want you."

She tilted her face to the side, her breathing tangling with his, their exquisite inadequacies a perfect puzzle fit. They were both reckless and protective, sensitive and strong, and Eliza hadn't felt so much affection for another person since Katie died. She wanted to breathe Aquila in, to wipe away his fear and guilt and hold their souls together with the strength of her will.

But she never got the chance, because at that moment all the lights surged, blindingly bright. Both their heads snapped up.

Eliza saw the same realization reflected in Aquila's eyes.

"Otto."

CHAPTER FIFTY-SEVEN
Convergence

Eliza and Aquila exploded out of the stairwell just as Tori and Tero burst into the hallway. And Eliza had to bite her tongue to stop the manic laughter that threatened to bubble out of her. The hallway was utter chaos, flashing with unstable lights, echoing with the clatter of gunfire. Bodies were scattered everywhere, twitching, sparking. Otto was slumped against one wall, defended by Joe and Daisy who were barely holding their own against a swarm of armed guards.

Tori's eyes found Eliza's face, flashed to the handful of vials in Eliza's hand, then to the syringe in the other. The booster, stolen from Amile's lab.

Tori's lips twitched up, the dawn of a smile breaking over her terror.

And then she went down, tackled by a woman in uniform.

"Come on!" Eliza shouted, dragging Aquila into the fray.

It was like wading through a raging river, like being a rock in a tumbler. Heavy bodies crashed into her. The flash of the lights made her dizzy. Even more disorienting was the peppering sound of weapons. The punches. The cries of pain and fear and rage.

"JOE!" Eliza screamed, elbowing bodies aside. Her fingers were ripped out of Aquila's hand and she swung around, trying to find him. Instead, she saw Joe. Met his gaze.

Joe exhaled.

And fainted.

"NO!"

Eliza plunged through the thicket of legs, ducking the fists and heavy gun handles as they flew at her head. She slid up next to her friend, shaking his shoulder as Daisy threw spiny fists above them, defending an unconscious Otto.

"Joe, Joe wake up," Eliza said, slapping his face with one hand as the other fumbled with vials. Her shaking fingers weren't enough to hold them and they slipped, rolling around her, their clinking almost inaudible over the cacophony. *"Shit!"* One crunched beneath a heavy boot, another disappeared into the corner, glittering distantly. But Eliza managed to grab one, jam the syringe into the soft tip.

"Eliza, look out!"

But she hardly heard Tori's scream, hardly noticed as Daisy was thrown aside by a strong hand. All her attention was on the syringe, on the tiny bit of fluid that could stop the damage burning through Joe's body.

She slammed the needle into his thigh and pressed down the plunger at the exact same moment that a hand came down on her shoulder.

"Remember me?"

The voice from the bridge was enough to make nausea roll through her, but she didn't have time to react as a supernaturally strong hand dragged her upright by the back of her neck. She glimpsed a dragon tattoo curling up one bare forearm. Eliza snarled and kicked, but it was no use. She couldn't find purchase, couldn't get her feet under her.

Something cold and hard dug into her belly.

"EVERYONE FREEZE OR I SHOOT!"

The deep voice boomed through the hall, echoing louder than any gunshot.

All eyes fell on Eliza and the tattooed solder and the black gun burrowing into her side.

"Let me go," Eliza spat, struggling to swing free. But the man had everyone's attention now. He pulled her in tight, wrapping a hard forearm around her neck. And Eliza felt like she was back on that bridge, back under the stars on that fateful night when she'd met Aquila. Only this time, the man was ready for her, pinning her arms by her sides, holding her aloft so that only her toes could scrape the broken floor.

Aquila looked ready to kill him, but everyone had stopped moving.

To Eliza, it felt like the world was holding its breath.

"I was hoping we might meet again," the man purred, half-growling, half-laughing as he dragged Eliza back, away from help. Then he lifted his voice. "Surrender now or I shoot your pretty friend in the belly and you get to watch her die."

Aquila's rage had returned, murderous and raw, but he couldn't do anything. He was too far away. Moose lingered in the nearest doorway, fidgeting, fast enough to help but not strong enough to counter the man's power. Otto was unconscious, Joe was beginning to spasm on the floor. Tero and Tori blinked from a thicket of soldiers, guns trained on their faces.

But where was Daisy?

"Alright now, line up along the wall. Come on, hurry up now."

Aquila began to comply, his eyes never leaving Eliza. But Eliza wasn't watching, because she was staring at the nearest soldier. A woman, fresh-faced and redheaded, expression filled with doubts.

"Help," Eliza breathed, meeting the young woman's eyes. "Amile's gone, she's already left the base. Help us."

"Shut up," snapped the man, jerking Eliza's body.

"Help us!" Eliza said, voice gaining strength as she lunged against the man's arm.

The woman took a step forward, glancing from side to side as if expecting someone to stop her.

"Hey... Marcus, that kid isn't one of the, um, subjects. We can't just kill her."

"She attacked our base," the man—Marcus—spat. "She's an enemy of the state."

Someone else spoke, a man with Latino-dark hair and wide brown eyes.

"Is Amile really gone?"

Aquila twisted, pulling his wings tight to his body, as if to look less imposing as he met the man's gaze.

"Yes."

"Maybe we should wait, bro," said the Hispanic soldier, the nose of his gun dropping to the ground. "Killing local kids, that might be going too far."

"Stop it," snarled Marcus, yanking Eliza back another step. "All of you, focus! We have our orders!"

"I'm sure as shit not taking the fall if Amile's gone," said the woman.

"I never approved of this mission anyway," piped in another voice.

Eliza could feel the soldier's heartbeat against her spine, rising, frantic. Violence throbbed from his body like a bad smell. She could imagine panic blending in, poisoning his intentions as the tide turned against him. She tried to breathe against the iron press of his arm.

Marcus was cornered and Eliza didn't need to be a hunter to know that cornered animals were the most violent.

At the edge of her vision, Eliza saw two soldiers shake their heads, back away, and then disappear into the stairwell.

The creak of the door opening rippled through the gathered men and women.

"I think we should go," one said.

"This has gone far enough," said another.

"Cowards!" Marcus's voice was rough with fear. "Get back here!"

But it was as if a spell had broken. The soldiers were in full retreat now. A few dropped their weapons entirely as they joined the crush of people struggling to escape through the narrow stairwell. They were like balloons whose strings had been cut, no longer held together by Amile's strong hand. No longer following orders but following their conscience. Waking up.

Marcus took another step back, growling in Eliza's ear.

"You think you can get away with this. You're not getting away, none of you are. I'll shoot you all if I have to."

The gun in Eliza's side was painful, digging deeper, a threatening force that pulled at her attention like a black hole. She tried to breathe, tried to think of something to say.

Her eyes met Aquila's, Tori's, Moose's.

Where was Daisy?

And then, as if summoned by her thoughts, spiny fingers came out of nowhere and wrapped around the hand pressing the gun to her ribs.

It went off, but the bullet skittered harmlessly down the hallway.

Eliza acted on instinct, going limp, sliding down the man's muscled chest. He didn't bother to grab her as Daisy flew at him, spines digging into flesh, fists hitting tattooed neck. Eliza rolled to the side, scrambled to grab the gun out of his hands. She couldn't let him hurt Daisy, couldn't let this man's vendetta against her turn fatal.

The gun slid out of her grasp.

Daisy cocked his bristled forearm back, slammed it into the man's open eyes, just as the crack of a shot filled the hall.

Marcus shrieked as spines punctured his tender eyeballs, but it was Daisy's silent expression that made everything slow down. Eliza stumbled back, still propelled by her own momentum, unable to do anything but watch as the bullet entered Daisy's chest at point-blank range. A red stain spread over his Green Arrow T-shirt, blood bursting from his ribcage like a starburst. Marcus staggered away, clutching his face, but Daisy only swayed. Stared down at his torso, mouth open in surprise.

When he looked up, his gaze found Aquila's.

"I… helped…" he said, the words clumsy. Fumbled. Heartbreaking.

To his credit, I don't believe Daisy has ever forgiven himself for the event.

Eliza watched helplessly as the armored Vagabond hit the wall and slid to the floor. She felt something within her click into place, a kind of horrified understanding that provided no comfort. Because meeting Daisy's dimming eyes, she knew that the boy had just saved her to make up for someone else that his brothers had loved, someone he'd killed so many years ago.

And now he could die in peace.

CHAPTER FIFTY-EIGHT
Not So Bulletproof

"*Daisy!*"

"O-oh no, oh n-n-no."

"Isn't he supposed to be *invincible*?!"

"Shut up and help me, Moose!"

Eliza's mouth hung open as the three conscious brothers descended on the bleeding, slumping body. Aquila was there in a flash, his strong arm wrapping around Daisy's back, lowering him gently, slowly. Moose darted around them, wringing his hands.

Tero looked ready to cry.

Eliza took a step back, only distantly aware of the blinded man now careening from wall to wall, clutching his face and howling. The cluster of soldiers fleeing through the stairwell had thinned and the basement of Fitzgerald Base was now eerily empty and echoing with the lingering shadow of violence.

"Eliza....?"

She swung around to see Joe waking up, supported by a sheet-white Tori.

"Joe...?" Eliza's lips were numb, her mind reeling. Joe opened his mouth to answer, but before he could say anything, Daisy's body began to jerk.

"What's going on?" Moose whined as Daisy's eyes rolled up in his head.

"I think he's going into shock." Aquila looked up and met Eliza's gaze, his expression pleading and lost and horribly frightened.

For a single heartbeat, Eliza faltered. She could feel that familiar drowning sensation threatening to crash over her head again, the weight of the bodies around them ready to drag her into panic. Otto was still unconscious. Joe was only just awake, and who knew how much of his old self had come back from the brink of whatever the virus had done to him. She didn't want to be responsible anymore.

But Daisy needed her.

He needed all of them.

With a deep, furious breath, Eliza pulled herself together.

"Pick him up," Eliza snapped. "We'll take him to the hospital."

"*What?*" Moose's question was a whip-crack, breaking through the groans of waking soldiers and the howls of one blinded man. "You're joking, right? We can't take Daisy to a hospital—"

"He's bleeding out," Eliza said, ripping off her polo shirt and pressing it to Daisy's chest as Aquila hefted him up. The cold air of the basement made goosebumps rise on her bare back, prickling against the straps of her bra. She ignored all of it, focusing on the limp body in front of her. "If he doesn't get professional help, he'll die. Tori, you help Joe. Moose, Tero, get Otto. We all go together."

No one moved. No one breathed. Everyone stared at her as if she'd lost her mind.

"Come *on*," Eliza said, glaring at them in frustration.

Aquila ducked his head.

"If we go to the hospital… then we're…"

Eliza straightened.

"Out in the open," she said, finishing his sentence. "It's our only option."

Finally, Aquila nodded.

"Let's go, guys."

Almost half their party was unconscious or wounded in some way, and all of them were so tired that their knees could barely hold their weight. But somehow, they managed to carry Joe, Otto, and Daisy up the stairs. Tori paused briefly to grab the last remaining vial of booster, wedged safely beneath a door. She tucked it into her skirt pocket. Eliza squinted, trying to remember how to reach the garage.

"This way," she said, leading them down a side-hall.

A few stragglers wandered through the flashing corridors, soldiers running or scientists wandering in a daze, quick to avoid the strange, lopsided party of bleeding teenagers. Otherwise the lab building was empty. No one bothered them.

"This is not normal," Tori said, hefting Joe onto her shoulder as Eliza supported his other side.

"Urg, man, why did Otto have to be the one to pass out," Moose complained, struggling to keep Otto's slime from smearing over his bare neck.

"W-w-watch it!" Tero said as Moose's jittery shifting almost made Otto topple over.

"Stay with us, Daisy," Aquila said, ignoring the rest, voice breaking on his brother's name. Daisy's eyes were rolling, his armored skin bleaching pale.

They were close to the garage. Eliza leaned Joe into Tori and darted ahead to check the door. The panel blinked innocently, waiting for a command.

Here goes nothing.

She grabbed Martin's ID tag from Joe's belt, pressed it against the door.

It clicked.

She kicked it open.

And froze.

The garage was empty, door open, vehicles gone.

And the lawn beyond it was a scene of utter pandemonium.

Jeeps revved to life, accelerating out of Fitzgerald as a hail of trucks and ambulances came screaming in. Eliza watched in dumbfounded shock as spotlights roved over the lawn, accompanied by the persistent *thwack thwack thwack* of helicopter blades. Sirens wailed, cameras flashed, soldiers shouted orders as they piled into their vehicles and escaped down the main road.

"What the…?" Eliza breathed.

"Ohno," Joe slurred from behind her.

And then Eliza saw it. Emblazoned across the nearest van were three bold letters.

HNN.

Hermes News Network.

"They called me," said Joe, his voice distant, astonished. "In the middle of the fight, they called. And I answered..."

Eliza's brain ached as she put the pieces together. Two overbearing parents calling their only son, worried, perhaps, about his disappearance from school. When he picks up the phone, they hear him dazed. Lost. And then what? Shouting? Screaming? Gunfire?

Eliza shook her head to clear it.

Whatever the reason, the reporters were here, swarming the base.

And they needed a new plan.

"How are we going to reach the hospital without making a scene?" Eliza asked, almost to herself, scanning the grass.

"Here. Take him," Tori said, shoving Joe at Eliza. She grabbed him around the waist just in time to stop him from toppling over. Tori strode forward into the flashing chaos, pulling the final gun from her waistband.

It was like magnetism.

Every spotlight and camera and eyeball swiveled to the girl with blood streaked on her face, caked in her blonde hair, and the weapon trained on the nearest paramedic lingering by his flashing ambulance.

"You there," Tori snapped, her voice carrying. "We need medical assistance. Back that truck up to this garage, *now*."

The man stared at her for a long moment, mouth open in shock.

Tori took a threatening step toward him.

The paramedic jerked, leapt into his ambulance.

Eliza held her breath. The man could leave right now, drive away and abandon them. Cops were already swarming around Tori, their own guns drawn. What would happen if they were stopped?

How long did Daisy have left?

And then the white and red vehicle was backing into the garage, throwing them into shadow.

"Come on!" Eliza shouted, lunging forward with Joe and trying not to think about Tori disappearing in a cluster of police officers.

The back doors of the ambulance burst open. The paramedic leaned out.

And almost fell over in shock.

Eliza could only imagine the strangeness of what the poor man was seeing. Two hulking shapes with wings. Another with armored skin, bleeding out. Otto, limp between his brothers, shimmering like mother-of-pearl. Moose, whose goggles were long gone. And her, a dark-skinned, black-haired girl, bare torso covered in goosebumps.

Eliza waved, snagging man's attention.

"We need your help," she said, struggling to instill calm in a very *un*-calm situation. "That boy has been shot and needs medical attention. Please." Eliza's voice was shaking now, quivering with panic. "Please, we have to reach the hospital."

It was a mark of EMT professionalism that the man snapped his jaw shut and leapt out of the ambulance to approach Daisy. He recoiled at the feel of Daisy's hard, mottled skin and glanced nervously at Aquila, looming over him. But the paramedic nodded.

"Let's get him inside."

In moments, Daisy was being strapped to a gurney.

"I need to call my team back, they're inside checking—"

"No," Eliza said as the others leapt in. "Just drive."

"But—"

Aquila growled in threat. The man raised his hands.

"Fine, fine, but I can't fit all of you inside."

They exchanged a nervous glance. Aquila looked out at the sloping lawn as if in resignation.

He sighed.

"Tero and I will fly," he said, watching as Moose dragged a groaning Otto into the ambulance. "We'll make sure the road is clear."

"But..." Eliza swallowed. "They'll see you."

Aquila's lips twitched. He rolled his shoulders.

"Maybe it's time they did."

Eliza wanted to say more, but the paramedic was revving the engine.

"Eliza, get the fuck out of here!" Tori screamed from the lawn, struggling as the police wrestled her into a pair of handcuffs. "GO!"

Glancing back one last time at Aquila, Eliza stepped into the ambulance and shut the door.

As soon as the lock clicked shut, they were flying down the driveway of Fitzgerald Base, sirens blaring.

Eliza picked her way around Daisy, over Otto and Joe and a shaking, frantic Moose to join the paramedic in the front. The scene unfolding before them was like something out of a video game, trucks and news vans shifting in and out of their vision, people sprinting, spotlights dancing. And swooping around them like guardian angels, Tero and Aquila flew in plain view of everyone, their wings bright and bold in the unforgiving helicopter lights.

"Jesus almighty," the paramedic breathed as Aquila swept in front of them, whipping a reporter out of the ambulance's way.

"You get used to it," Eliza said with a halfhearted smile, even though she wasn't sure she ever would.

They came up to the main road in no time, skidding onto it with practiced dexterity.

Eliza glanced back. Moose was hovering over Daisy, fingers fluttering. But there was nothing they could do. There was nothing anyone could do.

Except reach Scottstown Medical as fast as possible.

"Thank you," Eliza said to the paramedic. He was glaring at the road, as if he could ignore the sweeping shadows of the teenage boys flying around him.

He chuckled weakly.

"Don't thank me yet," he said, jerking his head to the side-view mirror.

Eliza's skin prickled as she leaned out the window.

An entire army of news vans and police cars were on their tail, cluttering the road, stampeding after their story. What seemed like every single HNN employee was leaning out of their cars, desperate to snag the perfect picture of the ambulance's winged guard.

"Shit," Eliza breathed.

"That's one word for it."

Eliza pulled back inside, too shocked to say anything else.

"Oh man, we're going to be in so much trouble," Moose was saying as he peered through the back windows. "Dad's going to *kill* us. He's going to see us on the news and he's going to be so mad..."

Eliza wondered if Ian Eckelson got the news in his hospital room.

Either way, we're bringing the show to him...

With a squeal of tires, the paramedic threw them off the highway, careening down the exit ramp. Eliza leaned closer to Daisy, stroking the boy's spiny head.

"Hold on," she said, meeting Joe's eyes. Guilt curled in Eliza's chest like burnt paper as she thought of the one they'd left behind. The it-girl she was just beginning to like.

Tori will be fine, she told herself sternly. *She'll understand. It'll be worth it.*

It had to be.

The ambulance bounced over the hospital's speed bump.

"Get ready!" the paramedic called back.

And then they were screeching to a stop.

Before Eliza could gather herself, the back doors were swinging open. A crowd of people in scrubs appeared, ready to accept their newest patient. But upon seeing what was inside, every single one of them stopped, mouths agape.

One of the doctors took a shaky step back, clutching his chest.

Twin thumps on the roof announced Aquila and Tero's arrival. Eliza grabbed the door, tilted herself out just in time to see Aquila crouch down, his body like a gargoyle, his face like a frightened child.

"Please," he said.

Finally, one of the nurses snapped out of it. She grabbed the gurney, yanked it toward her. The sudden movement jarred the others into motion and then, in a swirl of blue scrubs and tense faces, Daisy disappeared.

"Come on, let's get inside," Eliza said, pulling Joe upright.

As she leapt out of the ambulance to the flash of high-powered cameras, Eliza couldn't help but feel like they'd just stepped into a whole new kind of mess.

CHAPTER FIFTY-NINE
Next Steps

Eliza lingered by the window in the top-story corridor they had been moved to after Daisy's surgery, watching restless flocks of news crews spool and curl in the morning light. Her arms tightened around the fresh blue top that a kindly nurse had given her, shivering despite the warmth inside the hospital.

It had been almost six hours since they'd come screaming into the parking lot, but already news of their arrival had spread to every corner of the country, attracting reporters and journalists like moths to a candelabra. Of course, HNN had the advantage of being first. Between a sheepish statement from Joe and a breathless interview with Joe's relieved and excited parents, the news station's viewership had been steadily gaining momentum all morning.

Watching the cops glower from the front of the barricade they'd erected around the emergency entrance, Eliza swallowed a sad laugh.

It was only going to get worse.

"Hey."

She turned to see Joe standing in the middle of the hall, hands in his pockets, shoulders bunched like fists.

"Hey," Eliza said in response, stepping aside to invite him to join her. "How are your folks?"

Joe chuckled.

"Well, they can't exactly claim I'm an easy kid anymore." He sighed. "But apparently it's the biggest news story they've ever covered. The President himself has called six times. Their stocks are through the roof." His lips curled into a wry smile. "I guess this is a pretty big deal."

"And I'm sure the fact that it all happened in a government research facility makes it even juicier, huh?" Eliza tried to smile back, but the joke didn't quite land. She was still picturing the bodies, the flashlights, the darkness. Still feeling the frayed twine scrape across her palms as Amile fought to escape.

Eliza shuddered, but Joe didn't notice, too busy leaning out to watch the reporters jostle against the barricade, only to wilt when they realized that the person leaving was just a local who'd come in with stomach pain the night before.

"And to think," Joe said with a grin. "Scottstown used to be one of those *quiet* places."

"Not anymore. How long until the FBI shows up?"

"Oh, ten minutes?" Joe's smile faded as he faced Eliza, met her eyes. "How's everyone else?"

Eliza glanced over her shoulder at the two dark doors, beyond which Daisy, Ian Eckelson, and Martin Bent lay in matching beds, all under sedation as their bodies recovered.

"The docs say everyone will be fine. But what do they know? They've never dealt with anyone like Daisy before."

In fact, the surgeons—after they'd gotten over their open-mouthed shock—had been *fascinated* by Daisy. Eliza had watched the residents and medical students file into the operating room, excitedly elbowing one another to be first inside. When a tall man who introduced himself as head of general surgery came out to share the good news that Daisy would recover, he'd peppered Eliza with questions about who the Vagabonds were, where she'd found them, did they speak English, were they *from Earth?*

Eliza would have laughed if she hadn't been so close to tears, adrenaline still pumping through her veins like a ferocious drug.

Now the boys were with their father in one room, Tori with her freshly cured brother in the one across the hall. Both doors were guarded by sleepy hospital guards, eying Joe and Eliza surreptitiously as they pretended not to be eavesdropping. The police were busy keeping the curious spectators out of Scottstown Medical, but had checked in every half hour to make sure they didn't go *anywhere.*

"You know, maybe everyone will write it off as a wacky Halloween prank," Joe said thoughtfully, squinting against the sun as it drifted slowly through the clear October sky.

"Yeah, and maybe Meru will open a bar," Eliza said with a laugh, spinning away from the window and leaning against it with her arms folded. "Tell me, what happens in those comic books you have stacked under your bed? How do people respond to things like this?"

Joe sniffed indignantly.

"They're graphic novels, thank you very much. And to be honest, I have no idea. The weird things always stay quiet in those stories. Who knows how the public will react?"

Who knows indeed, Eliza thought, tilting her head to watch the milling reporters from the corner of her eye.

Joe bumped her arm.

"Don't worry. You've got Aquila, right?"

Eliza turned back, her mouth open, ready to say… what?

But when she met Joe's eyes, her voice wouldn't come.

He took a deep breath, letting it out in a long, slow whistle.

"I really like you, Eliza." He was blushing, a furious red creeping up between his freckles, but Joe's voice didn't shake. He didn't stammer. This was a different boy than the one Eliza had dragged into the parking lot only a few days ago. He was stronger in more than just the physical sense. "I have since the first day you came to Meru." His eyes flicked up, meeting hers beneath those thick red lashes. "But I think you've always seen me as a friend."

"Joe…"

He took a step back, hunching his shoulders in a wry shrug.

"Maybe there's another super-soldier I can date." He grimaced. "I mean, I already met one, right? Hopefully there are more out there."

Eliza's lips pinched. What could she say to soothe the agony swirling in his eyes? What could she do?

She stretched out one hand, but he was already out of reach.

"I'd better go tend our garden of chaos down there. My parents will be wanting another *statement*."

"Joe…" Eliza swallowed, wishing she had more to offer this wonderful person who deserved better. Who would always mean so much to her. Just not in the way he wanted. "I'm sorry."

One side of his mouth twitched up.

"Me too."

And then he was gone, striding down the hall, his flaming hair glittering like copper in the fluorescent lights.

Aquila stepped out of Eckelson's dark room just as Joe passed it, frowning at Eliza.

"Something going on with the news station?"

"Stations," Eliza corrected him, shoving away from the glass. "And tons, I'm sure. But he's keeping it at bay."

Aquila shook his head, his smile rueful.

"Moose is so excited. It's been a nightmare trying to keep him from sprinting downstairs and giving an interview to the first person he finds. Otto's about to kill him."

Eliza snorted.

"Well, he'll have his pick. I think you guys just became the most famous people in the United States overnight. Maybe the world."

Aquila ducked his head, bracing one arm against the door frame as if to hold himself up against the onslaught of unwanted attention.

"I never wanted to be famous," he said, staring at his feet. "Moose always has, but I didn't understand it. I just wanted to be normal."

The longing in his voice was enough to break Eliza's heart.

Maybe she couldn't solve the shifting, messy puzzle between her and Joe, but at least she could help Aquila.

Stepping in, she wrapped her arms around his middle, relishing the way his thick feathers dusted the tops of her arms, inhaling the perfume of his chest. His heartbeat beat against her cheek.

311

"We'll get through this," she said, staring at the window and the press of the unforgiving world beyond. "Together."

"Yeah, about that..." Aquila took a deep breath and his lungs rasped against her ear. "Listen to me, Eliza, you don't have to be a part of this."

She straightened, shoving off his ribs, tilting her head back to face him.

"What are you talking about?"

His feathers rustled uncomfortably.

"I just mean that this is... a lot, right? All the attention? Ian's warned us about this for years. We know what's coming. People will try to control us, blackmail us, even kill us. The response is going to be intense, maybe dangerous, and I don't think you need to be... involved."

Aquila wouldn't meet her gaze, as if he was afraid of her answer.

As if, once again, he was bracing for her to leave.

"Don't be ridiculous," Eliza said gently, touching his arm. "I have no intention of going anywhere."

"Eliza…"

"I warned you, didn't I? You're not getting rid of me that easy." Eliza's voice edged into a laugh as she ducked her head, trying to get him to look at her. "And I strongly suspect Tori and Joe feel the same way. Aquila, we're a part of this now, as much as you are. We're staying."

It took a long moment for him to lift his head. When he finally did, it took her breath away.

She'd forgotten how beautiful his eyes were.

"I thought you'd be scared of me. After what happened in the woods."

"I don't scare that easy."

His lips tugged up in that bashful smile she loved with all her heart.

"I've noticed."

"Besides," Eliza added conversationally. "You're going to need me. I'm terrific at public relations."

"I think you're terrific at keeping the public *away*."

"Same thing."

"I'm not so sure."

She smirked. "What do you know? You grew up in a cave."

Aquila's grin was growing now, spreading like a sunrise. He shook his head.

"Low blow."

Eliza leaned in closer, lifting one eyebrow.

"I recommend you get used to it. I can picture the headlines now. *Alien invaders strike Massachusetts.*"

"Oh, shut up," Aquila chuckled, shoving her arm. She stumbled back, laughing.

"*Hell hath come to Earth,*" Eliza crowed. "*It's the end of days. Gather your rosaries and holy water!*"

Aquila was smiling wide, his ruffled feathers settling.

"I love you," he said suddenly, thoughtlessly, throwing it between them like a handful of seeds.

Eliza froze.

"What... what did you say?"

Aquila didn't answer. He only stared at her, smile gone, eyes molten. Eliza felt like she was floating in a sea of light as she melted into his gaze, as his face obscured everything else. Her ripped hand pulsed, the knee Amile had kicked ached, the guards watching them shifted. Her hair was a mess, face streaked with dirt, body still quivering from the panic of their escape.

Suddenly, all of that faded away.

With exquisite tenderness, Aquila reached out. Wrapped one huge hand around her face and drew her in. He stopped right before his lips touched hers, leaving only infinite, crackling space between them. And in that moment, Eliza wouldn't have noticed if a bomb had gone off next to them. She didn't care about the vast and ravenous public out there, already churning with news of the Vagabonds'

313

existence. She didn't care about her parents flying to Scottstown, or Meru's headmaster on his way to the hospital, or Amile loose in the world. She didn't care about the spotlight she'd just been thrust into or the mountain range of problems they would have to face in the coming days.

Because right then, the only thing that mattered were Aquila's fingers pressing into the back of her neck, his lips millimeters from her own. The air around them was electric and inviting, thick with the potential energy of their two bodies. Their matching souls. His warm breath washed over her cheeks and, after so many years chasing all the wrong things, Eliza Mason felt her heart unfold. Release. *Forgive.* At long, long last, the pain and guilt she'd diligently carried blew away like dandelion seeds.

She was safe. She was *home*.

When Aquila finally kissed her, Eliza could have taken on the world.

To be continued...

Thank you for reading!

As an author, it's my highest joy in life to entertain and inspire. Having grown up on a steady diet of science fiction and fantasy, I understand the value of escapism all the way to my marrow. I love the process of creating characters, falling in love with them, tracking them through difficult, life-changing situations. It's the best kind of work.

And my favorite part is sharing that finished product with readers like you!

If you enjoyed this book, I would absolutely love to hear about it. I read all my reviews and check email often, so please let me know what you thought on Amazon, Goodreads, or at aawoodsbooks.com.

Reviews are also a fantastic way to help budding writers grow and keep working, so if you have time to leave one, I would appreciate it so, so much.

If you want to further support me—and keep the Scottstown Heroes Series going strong—then please consider sharing Vagabonds with a friend who might enjoy it. The ebook will remain free for foreseeable future, so there's no investment required. ☺

Most importantly, I hope that Eliza's story was able to bring some fun and adventure into your life.

Stay tuned by subscribing at aawoodsbooks.com, because there's lots more coming!

Keep reading for a teaser of RUNAWAYS, available now...

A. A. WOODS

RENEGADES

BOOK 2 *OF THE* SCOTTSTOWN HEROES SERIES

CHAPTER ONE

Stormclouds

Daniel Keys knew he was walking a dangerous line. As he signed off his daily livestream with a jaunty "See ya tomorrow, suckers," he felt the certainty, the thrill in his chest.

He lived for that thrill.

Layla turned off the camera with the sultry grin that always made him wild.

"That was pretty ballsy," she said.

"My middle name."

She set the tripod aside, trailing her fingers along the back of the couch as she drifted toward him. "And after Hans sent out specific instructions not to mention those self-proclaimed Vagabonds. Your video is certainly gonna ruffle some feathers."

Daniel shrugged, his breath catching as she stepped around the couch, toward him. "My viewers deserve the truth, just like I promised them last week. Besides, people are talking about the latest sighting all over Reddit. Hans doesn't have the control he thinks he has, not anymore."

Layla only smiled, settling beside him with a lithe folding of her long limbs.

Daniel wasn't sure what he'd done to earn Layla's attention. She was eerily beautiful, strangely graceful, and utterly fascinating. She could sneak up on a cat if she wanted to. Sometimes, when she disappeared in the middle of the night to go to the bathroom or get a glass of water, he wondered. Now, with the appearance of real-live superheroes in that small Massachusetts town, he wondered even more.

But her fingernails on his arm was, as always, enough to distract him.

"I'm proud of you," she said.

"You should be," he joked. "It was your idea."

"But your face on the platform," she whispered, trailing kisses on his neck. "You're the one taking a stand."

"People deserve to know," he said in a dazed voice.

"And Hans deserves a reckoning," she answered, but he wasn't listening anymore. He was thinking only of her, of the hip shifting to straddle him, of their shared bed only a few feet away.

Without warning, the door crashed open.

"What the—?"

"Hold them," said a man backlit by the assaultingly bright lights of the apartment complex hallway.

Daniel surged to his feet, shoving Layla behind him. But new figures were swirling in like smoke, too fast, too strong. A small, thin young man grabbed Layla's arm and pulled her away. A short, rounded figure stepped out of the shadows.

"Pan," Daniel said as the young woman flicked a butterfly knife open, slicing her hand in the process. Blood sprayed on the carpet.

She cocked her head, unconcerned. "Nice to see you, Daniel."

He curled his lip in a snarl, but the big man spoke next.

"I'm troubled, young Mr. Keys" Hans Schneider said, shaking his head and closing the apartment door behind him with a funerial *click*. "Very troubled. It seems my instructions weren't clear enough, although I thought the order was quite simple. Don't speak about the Vagabonds. Don't post about them. Don't acknowledge their existence, except to make it clear what a farce it is." Those ice-blue eyes turned on Daniel and he felt a whole new set of chills shiver through his body. "Tell me, what about that was not specific enough for you?"

Daniel lifted his chin, fighting to subdue the wild terror crawling up his spine. He tried to look strong, secure. But he felt like the teenage kid Hans had pulled out of rural nowhere.

It had been Daniel's personal dream-come-true when the big blonde man had knocked on his door, impressed by his little YouTube channel. He'd offered funding, fame, connections. *Too good to be true*, his mom had warned, shaking her head.

Turns out, she'd been right.

As Daniel's channel blew up, he began to learn that certain restrictions came with Hans, rules he hadn't signed up for. Things he was allowed to cover... and not.

Daniel lifted his chin, facing Hans with all the boldness that had attracted his attention in the first place. "This is the biggest news story of the century. I can't just keep ignoring it."

Hans's eyes flashed. "You can't? Or you won't?"

"I have a duty to my subscribers. I'm not about this cover-up conspiracy shit!"

Hans didn't respond to that, and Daniel felt like he was walking on ice, like the ground was about to fall out beneath him. Something was wrong here. He'd always wondered if Hans was dangerous, what kind of force lay behind the subtle threats and promises.

He had an ominous feeling he was about to find out.

Hans nodded, as if to himself. "Very well, it appears you have outlived your usefulness." He reached into the inside pocket of his tailored jacket.

Layla surged against the small man holding her. "No!"

Daniel took a nervous step back, away from Pan, away from Hans. He wasn't sure what was in that pocket, but he was suddenly very certain he didn't want to know.

"I'll deal with you later," Hans said, not looking at her.

Layla snarled, an otherworldly sound. To Daniel's surprise, she swung around and scratched her captor across the face, leaving four long bloody slices.

How had she done that?

Daniel watched, helpless, as she leapt sideways, twisting around with feline grace to face the invading trio. She crouched in front of him.

"Babe, stay—"

"Head for the window," Layla growled, arms thrown out. "Get out of here, I'll follow."

"But—"

"*Now.*"

What the hell was happening? he thought as he cast around, looking for an exit. The door was blocked. The window was six stories up.

What was he supposed to do?

Hans interrupted his frantic search with a longsuffering sigh. "Don't make this worse for yourself, Ghost."

Layla only growled.

Ghost?

Daniel blinked.

Ghost...

Vagabonds.

"You're... one of them," he whispered.

No one responded, but they didn't need to. Daniel looked at Pan, whose hand had already healed. Then at the slender man who had kicked open his door. Then at Layla, who suddenly made too much sense.

"Tut tut, look what you've done now," Pan said in a singsong voice, flipping the knife again and streaking more blood on the carpet

"Remember, you'll have to clean that up," Hans said sharply.

Pan's smile didn't shift.

Daniel felt like he'd suddenly fallen down a rabbit hole. Not only were superheroes real, they were in his life, in his fucking apartment. He'd been surrounded by them all along. *Dating* one of them.

No wonder Hans wanted to cover up those Vagabonds.

They were everywhere!

"This is insane…" he said, looking from Layla to Pan to Hans. "People will find out about this. You can't keep this quiet."

"We'll see about that," Hans said, withdrawing a small canister. It looked like a perfume bottle, with a locking cap. The liquid inside shimmered like the sun on fresh snow. "Such a pity."

Daniel took another step back, but his knees hit the couch. He swayed, fighting to stay on his feet. "What's that?"

"Don't you dare," spat Layla in a desperate voice.

Hans shook his head again. "It appears your training was far from sufficient. We'll have to work on that." From another pocket, he withdrew a black face covering with twin fittings on either side.

A gas mask.

Layla's voice was frantic now. "You can't!"

Daniel cut in on top of her. "Hey, stop it!"

But Hans ignored them both, holding the mask in place with one hand and spraying the bottle with the other.

For a moment, nothing happened. Daniel stood, staring at Layla, wondering why her expression was contorted in rage and horror. He held his breath on instinct, not even sure why he was doing it.

But when the slender boy stepped forward to grab Layla again, he burst out, "Don't you—"

And then he felt it.

A tightness in his chest.

A sudden flooding of his senses, everything electric, everything on fire.

He staggered back and fell onto the couch, struggling for air, fighting a haze of pain and panic.

"Daniel!" Layla screamed as she was pulled away, but all Daniel saw was Hans's cold, blue eyes. The eyes of the devil, he thought frantically. The devil he'd sold his soul to.

As Daniel's body began to fail, between the spasms of suffocating pain, all he felt was regret.

~~~

Layla was crying, but Hans ignored her. These teenage hormones were so terribly *troublesome*. It was an odious downside of working with live specimens, but he supposed it was just the cost of his business. Pan, at least, watched the scene with the dispassionate detachment he'd trained into her.

She was one of his greatest successes.

"Take her away, Tiny," Hans said through the mask, gesturing at the small man. Boy, really. At twenty-two, Tiny was one of the first generation, loyal and obedient to a fault. His attributes were a triumph, although Hans wished he had more personal directive.

Layla—or Ghost as she was called in Hans's inner circle—shrieked and clawed as Tiny dragged her away. It was no use, of course. With a proper grip and undistracted focus, he overpowered her easily. The hall would be empty, courtesy of a generous bribe to the building manager. No one would see Layla bundled into the unmarked van waiting for them in the parking lot, or notice the clean-up team that Pan would lead over the next few hours.

Everything according to plan.

Well, almost everything.

"The video already went out, sir," Pan said, checking the laptop on the kitchen table, still unlocked. "It's been watched almost a thousand times already."

"Delete it," Hans said, voice still muffled by the gas mask. "Delete the whole channel."

"People will notice."

"They will, for a day. But by tomorrow morning there will be something new to talk about. I'll make sure of it."

Pan nodded, her fingers clacking on the keyboard.

Standing over the jerking, dying body of the young man, Hans gave himself a moment to feel the loss of yet another valuable resource. Daniel had showed tremendous promise; poor, hungry, desperate for glory. And Hans could have given it to him. He could have made something out of the boy, beyond his wildest dreams.

But those truthful, seditious instincts were a stubborn disease, one so common among the young.

Such a pity.

Hans sighed, careful to keep the mask in place. It wouldn't hurt his team, but he wasn't like them. He was quite ordinary, or at least as ordinary as any billionaire ever was. The agent he was now sliding back into his jacket would kill him too if he wasn't careful.

Of course, Hans was very, very careful.

"Clean this place up," he said to Pan. "And meet us back at the heliport. The plane is already prepping, so don't take too long."

Pan offered a respectful nod as he left. But Hans was already planning his next move, already lost in a sea of schemes and plots. He still had to figure out how he was going to deal with those Vagabonds, not to mention reassert his dominance during the week of media dinners coming up. The industry had to be *reminded*, or else Daniel might not be the last young star to lose his life in the coming weeks. There was so much at stake, with him in the middle carefully juggling the balls.

Lots to think about, but he had time. Things weren't dire yet.

Closing the door behind him, Hans drifted down the hall, the YouTuber and his folly already forgotten.

Keep reading at:
https://www.amazon.com/gp/product/B08PC8PQ59

A. A. Woods is a Boston-based writer of science fiction and fantasy. She's lived in Montana, Costa Rica, Vermont, and Scotland, which has given her a soul-deep wanderlust that she treats by exploring her own imagination. Her deepest ambition is to make people think.

Find out more at aawoodsbooks.com.

www.ingramcontent.com/pod-product-compliance
Lightning Source LLC
Chambersburg PA
CBHW031657170626
46808CB00005B/1486